Also by Hilary Spiers
Hester & Harriet

HILARY SPIERS

Hester
&
HARRIET

Love, Lies and Linguine

ALLEN&UNWIN

First published in Great Britain in 2017 by Allen & Unwin

First published in Australia in 2017 by Allen & Unwin

Allen & Unwin
c/o Atlantic Books
Ormond House
26–27 Boswell Street
London WC1N 3JZ
Phone: 020 7269 1610
Fax: 020 7430 0916
Email: UK@allenandunwin.com
Web: www.allenandunwin.com/uk

A CIP catalogue record for this book is available from the British Library.

Paperback ISBN 978 1 76029 466 3
E-Book ISBN 978 1 95253 529 1

Set in 12/17 pt Minion Pro by Midland Typesetters, Australia
Printed and bound by CPI Group (UK) Ltd, Croydon, CR0 4YY

10 9 8 7 6 5 4 3 2 1

For ACS especially and all those friends and readers
who wanted to know what happened next . . .

SUNDAY

CHAPTER 1

'I *hate* airports.'

Hester, fingering the edge of the letter in her pocket, feels the cold of the metal seat seep through the layers of clothing. A greasy all-day breakfast—or at least as much of it as she had been able to swallow—solidifies in her stomach. 'Fourteen pounds ninety-nine!' she had hissed at Harriet as the waitress apologetically slid the bill under the ketchup and sprinted away, presumably anticipating the incredulous reaction. 'I could feed a family of four for a week on that!'

Harriet, deep in her Kindle, does not reply. Either she is lost in her thriller or she wants Hester to believe that she is. Hester, who has long and vociferously resisted the lure of an e-reader, now throws covetous glances at the slim device, only too conscious of the weight of paperbacks clogging her case. Too thrifty ('mean,' said Harriet) to pay for excess baggage, she had jettisoned four tops, a spare pair of shoes and three pairs of knickers to accommodate the books. 'For heaven's sake,' she had replied when her sister remonstrated, 'I can rinse out my smalls! Or don't they have washing facilities in Italy?'

Italy. Land of sunshine, pasta and Chianti. Birthplace of Donatello, Giotto, Caravaggio. Holiday destination of Hester and Harriet, who had discussed endlessly a change from their customary Scilly Isles sojourn until, exasperated, Harriet had suggested they toss a coin to break the stalemate. She had won, and now they are bound for Italy, to an hotel of Harriet's choice, while Moldova, Hester's somewhat outré first suggestion, had been comprehensively rejected.

'Moldova?' Harriet had snorted. '*Moldova*? Do you even know where Moldova is?'

Hester, stung, had retorted haughtily, 'It's sandwiched between Romania and the Ukraine, actually. I understand it's supposed to be very beautiful and well worth visiting.'

'Wasn't there a *Guardian* article about it a month or so back? Appalling human rights record, as I recall. Anyway, Eastern bloc—the food will be atrocious.'

Hester had sniffed. 'I know that, but the wine is supposed to be—'

'The wine! Typical! Never mind murderous totalitarian states, people locked up without trial or worse, as long as the wine is good. Anyway, what's wrong with Italian wine?'

Hester, who has absolutely no quarrel with Italian wine, save the unspeakable Asti Spumante, and was only (as she had secretly and shamefacedly admitted to herself later) resisting Italy because Harriet had suggested it, had bitten her tongue. She and her sister seemed increasingly at odds these days, each quick to take offence, if not actually pick a quarrel, over the most petty matters. Still, she had—hating herself—resolutely refused to show any interest in their destination, ignoring Harriet's hints about the hotel, the cuisine, the local attractions.

Hester catches the baleful eye of a toddler sitting opposite. Trussed up in a violent orange anorak, he is methodically picking his nose and wiping the spoils on his mother's coat as she, oblivious, thumb-texts at astounding speed. Hester flexes her arthritic fingers irritably in her lap; the envelope crackles in her pocket. 'I hate airports,' she repeats. Only this time a little louder.

What on earth is wrong with Hester these days? thinks Harriet, trying to re-immerse herself in her novel. She had managed to block out the incomprehensible announcements, delivered by someone apparently broadcasting from a mineshaft, the sudden irruptions of excited football fans en route to Hamburg, fortifying themselves against the horrors of air travel and tribal warfare with copious quantities of overpriced lager, and the fractious children milling around the concourse under the eyes of their exhausted parents. But Hester's complaint has punctured her bubble and the airport's cacophony now crowds in on her again. She knows she ought at least to acknowledge her sister's remark. Hester has been snappy for weeks, complaining about everything: their nephew Ben's inability to wash up after his frequent culinary experiments, the price of local vegetables, the postman's refusal to snick the front gate shut, the cost of their impending holiday . . . even Milo, now of an age where he is able to sit up and grab whatever is within reach, ecstatically thrusting anything he finds—cups, biros, pieces of fluff (of which there is no shortage in their cottage) and once, gruesomely, a very large, very dead spider—either into his mouth or eager adult hands. Hester had been the unfortunate recipient of the desiccated spider.

Harriet shoots a glance at her sister beside her, arms crossed, glaring at a small boy who is wiping his fingers on the coat of the woman beside him. Were it not for Hester's advanced years, Harriet might almost imagine her to be going through a midlife crisis. Still, presumably some hormones, however sluggish and enervated, continue to chug their disruptive way around her system. What could be better than a week under a warm sun to ease tensions?

'Not long now,' she murmurs.

'You said that an hour ago,' snaps Hester, thinking of the leisurely ferry crossing from Penzance to St Mary's, the sun sparkling on the water, the salty tang of the sea air. She banishes memories of numerous crossings in near-gale conditions, the vessel rolling sickeningly, rain driving against the windows, the Scilly Isles blanketed in fog.

'Read your book,' suggests Harriet, adopting the head-down posture booklovers employ to repel interruption.

'I've *read* my book.'

No point suggesting unpacking another as their suitcases have already been checked in and are even now probably being loaded onto a plane for Thailand or Abu Dhabi. As for foraging in WH Smith's while they wait ... she can imagine all too easily the derisive set of Hester's face when confronted with row after row of gaudy covers promising sadomasochistic thrills, foul-mouthed detectives with complicated private lives or the ghosted autobiographies of airbrushed minor celebrities. Her phone trills in her bag. As she rootles for it through the depths of mints and tissues and crumpled receipts (what on earth is a piece of Lego doing in there?), she registers Hester's tut: she knows, *she knows*, but try as she might, she cannot find a way to change the dreadful ringtone. Another thing she had intended to ask their nephew before they left. Perhaps this is him calling now.

But it isn't.

'Daria!'

Beside her, Hester tenses. Months on from the chance encounter at a bus stop on Christmas Day that led to their unofficial adoption of the young woman from Belarus and her infant son Milo, they remain on permanent alert about their two foundlings.

'Everything all right?'

'Yes! Yes!' Daria, as ever, is shouting as though she doubts the technology's ability to carry her voice all that distance. 'I have to tell! Today there is a letter! From the immigration peoples.'

'On a Sunday?'

'Postman, he take to wrong house. So nice neighbour just come—'

'What does it say?!'

Harriet sits up straighter, her heart doing an irregular and faintly alarming dance. 'She's heard from the authorities,' she mouths at Hester. Her sister's eyes widen.

'What? What!'

Harriet flaps her hand at Hester and presses the phone closer to her ear as though this will deliver the news all the quicker. There is the crackle of paper down the line.

'For heaven's sake, tell us! What does it say, Daria?'

'It say I have—what is this?—leave to ...'

'Leave to remain?'

'Yes! Leave to remain. Yes! I can stay. In England. With Milo! Oh,

Harriet! My heart is full, so full. I am crying. No, no, Milo, Mummy is happy! Happy! Thank you. Thank you. Thank God for Milo!'

Thank God for Milo's English father, thinks Harriet.

'Oh, Daria, this is wonderful. I wish we were there.'

'I also. I think, as I am ringing, perhaps they are already on plane. And I have such news!'

'The plane is late, I'm afraid. Three hours so far. We're a bit fed up. Well, we were!'

'Yes, but see! The plane is late but that mean I can tell you this.'

'Ah, well, every cloud has a—'

'You have cloud? Here is sunny. Like my heart.'

Harriet laughs. 'Hang on, I'll let you speak to Hester.' She passes the phone over and sits, overwhelmed with relief and joy, as Daria yells at her sister, who is similarly wreathed in smiles, trying—and failing—to get a word in.

A thought cuts through her happiness. She grabs Hester's arm.

'Ask if there's any news about Artem.'

Hester somehow manages to interrupt the torrent of words to ask Daria about the status of her brother, who is seeking political asylum in Britain. From her sister's frown, Harriet deduces that the news is at best disappointing.

'Well, tell him not to worry,' Hester is saying. 'Asylum applications take time. They did warn us.'

Harriet glances up at the departures board to see—at last—their gate displayed. She leans towards the phone. 'Daria.'

The girl's excited narrative rolls on.

'Daria! We have to go! Our flight is called. 'Bye. We'll text you when we arrive. Love to Milo and Artem.'

Hester closes the conversation and returns the mobile. They hurriedly gather their things and make their way towards the distant departure gate, gathering pace as their stiff limbs loosen, buoyed and rejuvenated by the happy news and, for the present, in harmony. *Let it last*, thinks Harriet. *Please let it last.*

CHAPTER 2

'Wotcha,' says Ben, poking his head around the kitchen door of Daria and Artem's little cottage in Pellington.

'Ben! Hello!' Daria beams. She is busy spooning some indeterminate mush into Milo's mouth. Or, rather, trying to: most of it seems to be smeared across his cheeks. Some clings stalactite-like to his wispy fringe. The baby's face lights up with delight at the sound of Ben's voice and, restrained in his highchair, he begins vigorously kicking his feet (and his mother). Frantic hands send the spoon and its contents flying across the kitchen floor, the clatter prompting a cry of triumph, followed almost instantaneously by a wail.

'Hey! Hey, mate! No need for all that racket.' Ben holds an admonitory finger in front of Milo's face; in short order, it is grabbed and inserted into the baby's mouth, where he gums it enthusiastically. Ben rolls his eyes at Daria. 'A rusk, d'you reckon?'

Seconds later Milo is sucking away on a Farley's while Ben fills the kettle. 'Got your text. 'S why I rode over. Needed a break.'

'Oh, Ben! Is dream come true.'

'Serious? I don't get it. What's the big deal about England? Being allowed to live in this poxy sh—'

'No,' says Daria sternly, 'do not insult your country. You are wicked boy who knows nothing.'

Ben, suddenly reminded of all she has endured, has the grace to look ashamed. 'Yeah. Fair comment. Sorry.'

'Yes.' Daria's eyes glitter. 'Here is freedom, kindness. I can speak the words I want to speak. No police knocking at the door.'

'Oh, I dunno,' says Ben, remembering the interminable interviews and visits from the police his aunts and Daria had endured after the events at Parson's Farm last Christmas. 'Seen enough of the rozzers to last me a lifetime.'

'Rozzers?'

'The Old Bill.'

Daria looks even more bemused. Ben explains.

'Is hard, this language. Poor Milo.'

'Nah,' says Ben, ruffling the baby's hair, 'he'll be fine. He'll be brought up with it. It's only difficult for you 'cos you had to learn it as an adult. Anyway, look at Artem: his English is brilliant. 'Sides, Milo's got his two grannies to keep him on the straight and narrow. Did you get hold of them, by the way?'

'The *babulki*? I did. I am crying. They crying, I think. Was cloudy at the airport.'

'Cloudy?' says Ben, peering out the window at the sunshine. The tiny garden is planted in neat rows with vegetables, all Artem's handiwork. He is still earning their keep with odd jobs around the village while he waits for his asylum application to be processed, with his customers paying in kind so as not to jeopardise his chances. 'What's Artem up to today?'

'Putting up a . . . like a . . . what is it . . .?' Daria mimes a barrier.

'A fence?'

'A fence, yes. It break in wind. For Hester and Harriet's friend, Mrs Wilson.' She glances up at the clock. 'Soon he will be here. He is watching Milo while I clean.'

'I thought you took Milo with you?'

'Not to Mrs Wilson. He make her cry.'

'Milo does?'

'Yes. Tears all the time. She say, "Oh, such a beautiful baby. I had beautiful baby, but no more. My boy is never here. Always he is out."'

Ben, who knows Molly Wilson by reputation and Josh only slightly, since he is away at boarding school for most of the year, is not surprised that her son keeps his distance. With his father on bail awaiting trial and his mother, as has long been her custom, taking refuge in the contents of the drinks cupboard, Josh is understandably eager to put as much distance between himself and the village as possible. There had been rumours of divorce proceedings when the full extent of Teddy's dalliance with the vicar's wife had come to light—in the aftermath of the police raid on the farm he owned and on which the tenant was discovered to be growing industrial quantities of cannabis—and he's now holed up in a poky flat in nearby Stote, Molly having refused to let him stay in the matrimonial home.

Now Daria is saying severely, 'This is a cruel boy. Children should honour their parents. Mrs Wilson is sad lady. Her boy should be with her.'

Ben, whose primary aim in life is to spend as little time as possible in the company of his own parents, reddens. 'Yeah, well . . .'

Daria glances up at the clock. 'Where is Artem? He promise me he will be here to watch Milo. I will be late!'

'I'll stay, if you like,' says Ben, helping himself to one of Daria's biscuits. He savours it. 'Mmm . . . vanilla?'

'Almond. You like?'

'Prefer the chocolate ones you made last week.' He takes another, all the same. 'You want me to babysit or what?'

Daria moves the tray of biscuits out of reach. She reaches for a roll of foil and tears off a square, then wraps up half a dozen of the biscuits. Ben knows without asking for whom they are bound: Finbar, the village tramp, whom his aunts, and now Daria, keep regularly provisioned.

'No school today?' She is wise to Ben's little tricks.

'Half-term, innit? I gotta revise for my exams.'

8

'You have books with you?'

'God, you're beginning to sound like the rents. Give us a break, will you?'

Daria frowns. 'Education is important. If you want to be cook—'

'*Chef.* I know, I know: I have to put the work in. Jesus!'

Daria tuts, gathers her things and unhooks her coat from behind the door.

'Okay. But one day—'

'I'll thank you, yeah.'

'Not me. Hester and Harriet. And your parents.' She looks over at Milo, who is inspecting the stump of his rusk intently. 'You sure you will be okay with him?'

'Oh, thanks,' says Ben indignantly. 'I've only looked after him, like, a million times. Haven't I, mate?'

Milo crows in assent.

'We might go for a walk. Bit of fresh air. If that's all right.'

'Yes, yes, okay.' Daria, late, flustered, swoops in to give Milo a kiss. 'Be good, little one.'

The door slams behind her.

Milo's face crinkles crossly and he bangs his fist on the tray in front of him.

'Temper, temper,' says Ben, thrusting his own half-eaten biscuit in Milo's hand. 'There you go. Get your gums wrapped around that.'

Grabbing a cloth, he wipes the food out of the baby's hair and gives his hands and mouth a quick swipe, then lifts him out. 'You're getting to be a right tubby guts, you little monster. Now, where's the buggy?'

⌣⌣⌣

They've fed the ducks, had a rather unsatisfactory one-sided go on the seesaw and a much more successful swing in the special baby seats. Ben straps a sleepy Milo back into the buggy and starts to push him home. His phone rings.

'Hi, Daria.'

'Is Milo okay?'

'No, he's just been kidnapped by pirates and sold into slavery. Of course he's okay. We've just been to the park. He loved the swing.'

'Good. That is good. Fresh air for babies—good. Ben, do you have key to aunts' house?'

'Yeah.'

'On way home, could you check heating? Hester say if it gets warmer to turn it right down to twelve. Can you do this?'

''Course.'

'Did you see Artem?'

'Nah. Left him a note, though.'

'Thank you, Ben. You are kind boy, thoughtful. Well, sometimes you are. But I think your poor mother—'

'Got to go, Daria. See ya.'

⌣⌣⌣

Ben wheels the buggy up the path to The Laurels and parks it by the front door. Milo is fast asleep.

'Oi, Ben, bro. What you up to?'

He turns to find his best bud Jez Nairstrom peering over the top of the hedge. Six months ago he would have been mortified to be caught in possession of a buggy and a baby, but since all the publicity following the furore at the farm, Ben's standing has risen considerably and his newfound confidence has not only endowed him with a certain coolness among his peers but has also made him far less anxious about other people's opinions. So he says with considerable sangfroid, 'Just looking after Milo for a bit, aren't I? Helping Daria out.'

'Oh yeah,' jeers Jez. 'Helping Daria out, are you?' Jez, like most of Ben's circle, thinks Daria is both exotic and hot.

Ben ignores the jibe. 'Anyway, what you doing over here?'

Jez pulls a face and raises aloft a pile of flyers. 'Old man's only got me delivering these shitty things.'

'What are they for?' Ben retraces his steps down the path.

'Some crappy barn dance thing him and my mum are organising for our village. Or trying to. God only knows why. 'Cept they've hardly sold any tickets. He thinks people over here might be interested. As if! I told them no-one's gonna be interested. But they won't listen, will they?'

Jez thrusts a flyer at him. 'Here, give this to your aunts, will ya.'

Ben thinks it highly unlikely either of his relatives would set foot at a barn dance, but he supposes taking one helps reduce the huge pile Jez still has to get through. 'All right, only they're away until next Monday or something.'

'Shove it in the bin, then—it's on Friday. What you doing here anyway?'

'Gotta turn the heating down for 'em. Daria was supposed to do it, 'cept she was late for work so—'

'You said you'd help her out. Quite the knight in shining armour, aren'tcha?'

'Piss off, Jez,' says Ben good-humouredly. 'Catch you later.'

'I'll wait. Walk up to the main road with you.'

'You sure? Someone might see you.' Ben nods at the sleeping baby slumped in the buggy.

'Yeah, well, I'm not the knob pushing the pram, am I?'

'Buggy, not pram.'

'Whatevs. Get a move on, I've still got hundreds of these fuckers to get rid of.'

Ben slips into the house and heads for the boiler. Returning to the front door a few minutes later, he's surprised to find Jez in the hallway, peering into the sitting room.

'Your shoes better be clean. The aunts'll go apeshit if you get mud on the carpet.'

This is a slight overstatement because even Ben, young and unobservant, is aware that his aunts are not what you'd call houseproud.

'Bigger than I remember,' says Jez.

'Yeah?'

'I mean, if there wasn't all this crap in here, chairs and that, and all them books and old newspapers, it'd be quite roomy.'

'So?'

'Just saying.'

'Gonna be an estate agent, are you, when you grow up?'

'Ha bleedin' ha. Come on, I need to get going.'

Jez is in a markedly more cheerful mood as they make their way towards the main road, running up the paths to the few other houses along the lane and shoving several flyers at a time through letterboxes.

'Why you so pleased with yourself all of a sudden?' says Ben.

Jez smirks. 'No reason. Anyway, there's my bus. You just carry on babysitting, saddo.' And sprinting up the road as the bus trickles to a halt at the stop, he just has time to shove the remaining flyers in the rubbish bin before leaping aboard.

CHAPTER 3

Hester has been trying to find a handle for her ill-humour ever since the plane took off but the flight has been uneventful, the cabin crew pleasant, the other passengers inoffensive. They touch down at Ancona in a textbook landing, the wheels smoothly skimming the runway and the pilot bringing the aircraft to a jerk-free halt. No delay with disembarkation, the stewardesses waving them off with a smile. The warm breeze as they emerge from the plane, carrying with it, under the inescapable smell of aviation fuel, that curious pine-scented, lemony Mediterranean perfume, hasn't made her job any easier either. Nor the miraculously swift passage through the arrivals hall, to find their cases waiting by the carousel, or the ease with which Harriet identifies their courier (helpfully holding up a large, well-written sign bearing their names), who solicitously installs them in a comfortable people-carrier and hands them each a chilled bottle of water with a wide, engaging grin.

Finally, she gives up trying to find fault and relaxes into the seat. Beside her, Harriet sighs happily and fishes in her handbag for her sunglasses. '*Bellissima!*' she calls gaily to their driver, Cosimo, waving a hand over the landscape as they leave the airport and city far behind them. He looks up into the rear-view mirror and nods approvingly.

'You speak Italian?'

'No,' Hester cuts in. 'She watches *Montalbano*.'

'Ah! *Il commissario!* You like this?'

'She likes Luca Zingaretti,' says Hester drily.

Cosimo laughs. 'All the ladies, they like Zingaretti. He is very *bello*, no?'

Harriet laughs; Hester snorts.

'You have been here before, *signore*? Italy?'

Harriet has a sudden memory of herself and Jim on the balcony of a dilapidated hotel near St Mark's Square over forty years before. They had been married the previous year and had saved religiously month after month, scraping together just enough money for the cheapest *albergo*, a strict food budget and stout shoes in which to weave their marvelling way through the secret alleys and over countless bridges. Tears spring unexpectedly to her eyes; she turns away to look out of the window. Ridiculous how these old memories can ambush you at the most unexpected moments.

'I haven't,' says Hester, with a glance at her sister. 'But you went to Venice once, didn't you, Harry?'

Harriet can only nod.

Cosimo is scornful. 'Tcha, Venezia! That is for tourists. *This* is Italy!' He takes both hands off the steering wheel to gesture expansively at the countryside through which they are now travelling. To one side, carefully cultivated fields stretch away in neat rows to a distant farmhouse; to the other, a precipitous drop through swaying trees to a fast-running river. In the far distance, a line of mountains, wreathed in cloud, frames the horizon. Cosimo retakes the wheel to ease around a sharp bend, shaving past a vast lorry hurtling down the hill towards them. Hester, inured though she is to Harriet's erratic driving, can barely suppress a gasp. Harriet is still staring fixedly out of the window.

Cosimo mutters a curse under his breath.

'You know why is so special? Le Marche?' he asks, catching Hester's eye in the rear-view mirror. He doesn't wait for her reply. 'Because is secret! Nobody come. Nobody except special people! Like you! You will love. And soon,' a faintly wolfish smile in the mirror reveals a large gold tooth, 'soon we are at Il Santuario. You will like ver' much. Marco and Alfonso, they are so . . . *attento*, yes?'

Hester scrabbles through her rusty Latin. 'Ah! Thoughtful?'

'*Sì*. Nothing is trouble to them. You want something, they get. What are you doing at Il Santuario?'

'Doing?' says Hester. 'I'm not doing anything. We're on holiday.'

Beside her, Harriet stiffens.

Cosimo frowns. 'Of course, but—'

'Oh, look!' cries Harriet, 'what a wonderful view!'

And Cosimo swings the car suddenly off the road and between crumbling stone pillars.

∽∽∽

Marco, squat, toothy, with extravagant pepper-and-salt eyebrows and suspiciously dark hair, guides the women into the cool of the foyer, ushering them with some ceremony to a small cream sofa. The walls are roughly but artfully painted; discreet lamps illuminate the abstract artwork. A snap of his fingers and a lanky youth is conjured to wheel their cases away. Then Marco is thrusting glasses of wine—a rich ruby red—into their hands, accompanied by a little plate of biscuits.

Hester sips. Marco raises an enquiring eyebrow as she rolls the liquid around her mouth. She swallows.

'Is it . . . cherries?'

'Of course! You know this, *signora*?'

'I don't think so—but it's chilled!'

'*Sì*. Is our very own dessert wine from Le Marche—Visciolata del Cardinale.'

'And these—' she takes a biscuit '—these are cantuccini?'

'Tozzetti, we say. Almond. Traditional.'

Hester dips the biscuit in her wine and takes a bite. 'Oh! They are perfect together! Harriet, do try one.'

Marco beams. He turns to Harriet. 'You are enjoying the wine also, *signora*? As you said in your email, your sister is a true lover of the grape. I hope she will—'

'Yes, yes,' says Harriet quickly. 'We are both very fond of wine. But Hester knows much more about it than me. I wonder: might we see our rooms now? The journey, you know . . .'

There is a brief flicker of surprise in his eyes at her response, then he recovers.

'But of course. You must be tired.'

'Tired? I'm not tired,' says Hester with asperity, sensitive to any suggestion that the advancing years might be taking their toll. 'For heaven's sake, Harry, it was hardly a long-haul flight.' She takes another mouthful. 'This really is superb. Local?'

Marco smiles modestly. 'Our own vineyards.'

'Your own?'

'Of course. We have been making wine here for over one hundred years. Well, not Alfonso and me, obviously! But you will learn all about this when you—'

Harriet is on her feet, wineglass in hand. She picks up her bag and says hurriedly, 'Once we've settled in and relaxed a little, perhaps you or one of the staff would be good enough to show us around the grounds? I know my sister would love to see the vineyard.'

This time there is a definite coolness in the smile he turns on her. 'It will be my pleasure, Signora Pearson. You must forgive my enthusiasm. Alfonso and I, we are very proud of our little kingdom—we like to show it off to our guests.'

'Quite understandably,' says Hester, glaring at her sister. What has got into her?

Marco indicates a stone corridor running off the foyer. 'Please.'

In silence, he leads them to their rooms.

⌣⌣⌣

Harriet takes in the thick cream cotton bedspread, the crisp bed linen, the simple but elegantly appointed bathroom with its basket of luxury toiletries: surely Hester can't fail to be anything but charmed? She has spent so long studying Il Santuario's website, she feels she knows it already, but the reality is even better than she had dared hope. From the window, there is a spectacular view across a patchwork valley dotted with ridge-tiled farm buildings and houses stretching away to the foothills of the Apennines. The air is still, sweet with the scent of herbs, the silence broken only by the murmur of voices from unseen guests in the garden. She knocks back the last of her wine and turns to lift her case onto the bed to begin unpacking. Her eye falls on a brochure on the dressing table, adorned with pictures of the hotel and assorted shots of various guests smiling beatifically. She opens it. Blenches. Tears open the door and hares down the corridor to the next room. Raps on the wood. 'Hester?'

Silence.

⌣⌣⌣

Alfonso is handsome, with the smoothly polished skin, hair and clothes that sophisticated Italian men seem to possess as a birthright. His teeth—straight and even as an American's—dazzle like his shirt, his aftershave is subtle, while the linen trousers are creased to perfection. As for his shoes . . .

He had spotted Hester the minute she emerged onto the steps leading down into the garden, squinting against the sun reflected off the bleached stonework, and bounded over gracefully to introduce himself. Now he leads her to a shady loggia and installs her at a wrought-iron table.

'Signora Greene, may I welcome you to Il Santuario. I am Alfonso. Your room is comfortable?'

'Very.'

'Your sister is unpacking, perhaps. May I get you something to drink? To eat?'

'I'll wait for Harriet, I think.' Hester remembers her manners and softens her tone.

'Of course. Food and drink is available throughout the day. And the night, also, should you be—what do you say?' An enchanting smile. 'Peckish? We hope not, after our magnificent meals! But I see you have our brochure.' Hester is clutching a copy firmly. 'You have already seen what wonderful things are on offer here.'

'Indeed I have.'

'Marco and I, we like to think Il Santuario is a very special place. You have perhaps seen us on TripAdvisor? One of the top hotels in Le Marche. Certificate of Excellence!'

'Regrettably, no,' says Hester through a tight smile, berating herself for so stupidly resisting all Harriet's invitations to inspect the website. *Hoist with my own petard*, she thinks grimly, as Alfonso's eyes sweep around the garden. 'Please, don't let me keep you. I'm sure you have other guests to look after.'

Alfonso checks his discreet but very expensive watch. 'Not for another half an hour, happily. But, forgive me, I see a guest in the topiary garden. The gentleman left his spectacles in the lobby when he was filling in his details this morning and I must return them to him. If you will excuse me, I will bid you *arrivederci*, *signora*, for the moment. Oh, look! I think this is Signora Pearson, no?'

It is indeed Harriet, looking around the gardens anxiously. Alfonso waves, runs lightly up the steps and leads her down to join her sister in the shade, introducing himself as he does so. He excuses himself smoothly, promises to send over some chilled water—Hester having declined anything else and Harriet too apprehensive to disagree—and makes for a corner of the garden where the myopic guest is presumably cloistered.

The sisters sit for a moment or two in uncomfortable silence.

'So!' says Hester, unable to contain herself any longer.

'Nice room?' enquires Harriet simultaneously.

Hester sniffs. 'I have no complaints about my room.'

Well, that's a start, thinks Harriet. 'Good,' she says. 'That's good. He seems nice, Alfonso.' No response. 'So does Marco. Although, perhaps a little . . . unctuous? Do you suppose they're—'

'What exactly is this place?' hisses Hester, trying—unsuccessfully— to maintain a veneer of calm.

Harriet, nonplussed, looks around at the buildings and the beautifully tended gardens. A gentle breeze begins to ruffle the leaves of the twisted olive trees in the nearby planters. 'A hotel?'

Hester narrows her eyes. 'An hotel?' she corrects.

'If you must. *An* hotel.'

The balmy air crackles with ill-temper. Harriet feels her blood pressure on the march. Was ever a sister so *ungrateful*? She has made every arrangement, sent every single email, checked and rechecked their departure times, looked after all the tickets and reservation forms, put up with Hester's unaccountable grumpiness for weeks in the hope that a change of scene might restore her equilibrium or whatever it was that was making her such an unbearable curmudgeon. And they've been here less than an hour!

'You've seen the brochure, I see,' she says coldly.

'Oh, yes, I've seen the brochure, thank you very much. It all looks the most marvellous *fun*.'

Fun, thinks Harriet bitterly, is not something one associates with Hester, however many other worthy qualities she may possess. Loyal, steadfast, dependable, practical, dry, acerbic: no-one who knows her will quarrel with these characteristics. But fun—in the mindless, mass-market meaning of the word—no, that is anathema to her, smacking of game shows, sitcoms, TV adverts and the host of other activities she scorns. Her sister is such a *snob*. And a killjoy. And an ingrate.

'Painting, embroidery, ceramics, archaeology, cultural tours . . .' Hester is flicking through the brochure, face wrinkled with distaste as though it were some trashy flyer shoved through the front door. 'Unbelievable! You've brought me to a *holiday camp*.'

There are occasions in life when people so wilfully misconstrue one's good intentions that it is impossible to respond rationally. This is such a one. Harriet finds herself breathless, almost speechless with outrage. All the planning, the delay at the airport, the journey itself, that unexpected reminder of her early married life, all these now culminate in feelings so strong it might be best to remove herself from the source of her fury. Hester. At this very moment, she could cheerfully see her sister plunge over a thousand-foot cliff; indeed, were one to hand, she might—in her view quite justifiably—shove her over herself.

Harriet wrenches her handbag open, extracts a thick envelope and slams it down on the table in front of Hester.

'And a very happy birthday to you.'

CHAPTER 4

'Be a laugh.' Jez ambushes his friend outside the local sweet shop, where Ben has just replenished his revision provisions: a Twix, a Crunchie, two Flakes and a bag of wine gums.

'Piss off.'

'C'mon, Benji-baby, it will. Who's gonna know?'

'Fuck's sake, Jez, it's my *aunts*' house.'

'So?'

'I can't just use the place 'cos they're out the country.'

'Why not?'

Ben throws up his hands in disbelief and stomps off towards home. Jez follows, walking backwards in front of him.

'Listen. We put everything out in those sheds in the garden, roll up the carpets, clean it all after. Be like it never happened.'

'Oh yeah? Can just see you with a hoover and a duster.' There's a lamppost looming. Should he warn Jez? 'Look what happened when your lot went on holiday that time.'

Some sixth sense alerts Jez to the imminent collision and he swerves around the obstruction just in time. 'That was Hedge, not me. I wasn't even there, worse luck.'

Henry, Jez's older and even more wayward brother, for some unaccountable reason known to all and sundry as Hedge, is a legend locally among anyone under twenty. A prolific shoplifter, he had fathered a child at fifteen with a neighbour twice his age, written off his father's car the day he passed his test and at one time or another been barred from every pub within a ten-mile radius of his home. Famously, a party he had hosted when his parents unwisely went to Florida for some winter sun a few years previously had culminated in the fire brigade being summoned at three am when one guest decided to deep-fry some Creme Eggs and then passed out. Hedge is now mercifully many hundreds of miles away at university studying, rather alarmingly in many people's opinion, automotive design technology. Jez hero-worships him.

'Awesome, that was.'

'You said you weren't there.'

'No, but I seen the pictures on Instagram.'

So has Ben. 'That's what I'm saying. No way.' He runs up the path and slams his front door before Jez can follow him in.

This conversation has been repeated several times, with minor variations, all afternoon via various social media before this latest encounter, but Ben remains adamant. Not only does he not trust Jez to make a cup of tea, let alone organise a trouble-free party, he does not even want to contemplate his aunts' reactions to the presence of any of his peers in their home. Besides, his parents have woken kraken-like from their torpor—he guesses it's partially due to the aunts' absence and the lack of their stalwart support for his ambitions—and they are once again raising objections to his choice of career, with ever-increasing force. The last thing he needs right now is Jez badgering him with his half-arsed ideas when he needs to keep focused on outwitting his parents.

He's just reached the sanctuary of his bedroom when his phone rings.

'Ben!'

'Yeah?' A girl's voice. A *girl's* voice?

'How's it going?'

'Yeah. Good?' He can't suppress a slight upward intonation that indicates uncertainty, even apprehension.

A little giggle.

'Oh, God, like, you have no idea who this is!'

Ben is racking his brains, trying to identify the caller. The voice sounds familiar, but not that familiar. He decides laughter is the best response. It comes out extremely lamely.

'God, I am such an idiot!' the voice says. Another giggle. 'It's Louisa, yeah?'

'Louisa?' Of course! What a numpty. The name emerges as no more than a croak. Louisa? Louisa *Jellinek*? Is it possible? What is she, the hottest babe in Year 12, doing phoning him? Deigning to speak to someone whom she customarily swans past, unseeing, wreathed in clouds of Miss Dior.

'Hello? You still there? Ben?'

She said his name. She actually said his name. Again.

'Yeah. Yeah?' Wow! Wait till he tells Jez!

'So, like, I was wondering? How's it going?'

How's *what* going? Has he missed a page? He opts for nonchalance. 'Good, yeah.'

'Wanna a hand?'

'Sorry?'

'With this party you're having?'

'Sorry?' His throat suddenly feels very thick. 'Party?'

'Yeah, like everyone's talking about it.'

Who? *Who?*

'And I was wondering if, like, anyone could come?'

'Well, actually . . .'

'I mean, like, could I come?'

'You?!' The word only just makes it out; Ben fears his airways are about to close permanently.

'I was only asking!' There's a change of tone, a steely note in her voice now. ''Course, if you don't want me to . . .'

'No! No, I do!'

There is an agonising silence. Ben's heart thumps.

When Louisa finally speaks, she sounds distant, hurt. 'I'm really, like, disappointed. I thought you were different, Ben.'

'Me? How? Why?' He's gabbling; he must stop gabbling . . .

'Oh . . . you know . . .' Her voice is so faint, she is almost whispering.

'No, please. I'm sorry.' He's not sure what he's apologising for. 'Tell me.' His stomach is in knots, the phone slippery in his clammy hand.

The pause is so long he fears she has rung off, until she murmurs, 'See, the thing is, I always had you down as . . . well, not like the others. I mean, sensitive, caring . . .'

'Oh, I am! Yeah, dead sensitive.' Is that a *good* thing?

'Like, the way you are with that girl's baby and all that.' Everyone in the area knows about Milo after all the coverage in the papers. 'Like, most guys wouldn't be seen dead with a kid. But you, well, you just don't care. I like that in a guy. That's pretty rad.'

'Oh yeah . . . right. Thanks.'

'And I just thought it might be nice to hang out together . . .'

'It would! Oh, God, yeah. It would be—' The words don't exist that would do justice to the wonder of such a prospect.

Louisa's voice recovers, swooping down to its habitual seductive purr. 'Oh, babes, that is awesome!' Babes! 'Can I, like, bring a few friends as well? You know, Kat and Els?'

Oh my God. Ben can hardly process this information. Not just the unbelievably cool Louisa but also her two best friends, almost as goddess-like as she is . . .

'Kat and Els?'

'Yeah, like, they really like a good time. They are soooo up for it.'

'They are? Well, great!' Ben feels he's floating in a dream. Is this for real?

'We are gonna have a seriously good night, I'm telling you. Can't wait!'

'Nor me.'

'Okay. Laters!'

She's gone. And only as he stares, gobsmacked, at his now-silent phone, that magical piece of technology that has somehow enabled him to have a conversation—an actual conversation!—with Louisa Jellinek, does reality rear its extremely ugly head. What was he thinking?

⁓⁓⁓

'You total and utter twat! You can't start organising a party at my aunts' without asking me!'

'I did ask you.' Jez sounds smug.

'Yeah and I said no! Like, a million times!'

'Chill, will you? Only gonna be small. I just sent out a closed invite on Facebook—from me and you.'

'You did what?'

'Yeah, just the usual suspects: Luke and Liam and Dom and—'

'Luke? You invited Luke?' Ben hates Luke: the feeling's mutual. 'How many altogether?'

'Eighteen. Well, plus girlfriends.'

'Right. Listen. That's it, okay?'

Ben reckons twenty, twenty-five is manageable. Just.

'You tell Louisa?' he asks. 'About numbers?'

'No.'

'Fuck's sake! She's already talking about bringing friends. Do it—like, now!'

'You do it. It wasn't me that invited Louisa Jellinek to my party.' Jez sniggers.

'You gave her my number!' Amid the panic, reason prevails. 'No. No! This is mad. Forget it, we're cancelling. There's not gonna be a party!'

'That's not what Louisa and her mates think. They think they're invited to yours on Friday. We're talking Louisa Jellinek here, dickhead. At your crib. Imagine!'

'It's not my crib!'

'Well, it is sort of is, temporarily. Your aunties need never know. What the eye doesn't, et cetera.'

Ben's blood runs cold. A vision of the two aunts swims into his mind. Aunt Harriet might, if she understood the stakes here and was the right side of several large glasses of wine, have a smidgeon of compassion for his dilemma, but Aunt Hester . . . Sweat trickles from his armpits.

'Who else have you . . . ? No, I can't. Jez, I mean it. They'll kill me.'

'I promise you, mate, nothing they can do will come close to what lovely Lou-Lou and her gang will do to you if you let them down. Remember Nathan Nyland?'

'Oh, Jesus . . .' Ben shudders. What happened to Nathan Nyland is the stuff of nightmares.

'Yeah. 'Nuff said. Wanna come round to mine tonight and start planning?'

CHAPTER 5

'It was meant to be a surprise.'

Hester is still staring thunderstruck at the card in her hand. Mount Rushmore has nothing on her face.

'A nice surprise. For your birthday.'

Why, thinks Harriet, *am I sounding so apologetic? If anyone should be apologising, it's the ingrate opposite, sitting there as though I had given her a season ticket to the pantomime.*

A silence does not so much fall as totally flatten them.

'Forgive me for disturbing you, but might I try to persuade you ladies to take a glass of wine?' Where has he materialised from? And how did he know an intervention was needed at this precise moment? Alfonso, dapper, solicitous, charming of smile, proffering the wine list as the sisters exclaim simultaneously, 'Thank you!' He is a true hotelier: nothing escapes his watchful eye. Oil is urgently required for these clearly troubled waters.

'May I perhaps suggest the Barolo?' Before Hester can ask, he adds with some satisfaction, 'It's a 2008 Mirafiore Lazzarito.'

Hester's face softens, almost manages a smile. 'That would be most acceptable.'

Harriet, still smarting, says, 'I don't suppose you have a Barbaresco?' She knows Hester will have shot her a withering, if not accusatory, glance that says, *Don't overreach yourself,* but she refuses to catch her sister's eye. Nor does she wither.

Alfonso positively beams. 'My favourite also!' He leans towards her confidentially. 'An acquired taste, no? A little more—shall we say—subtle than the Barolo?'

'Precisely,' says Harriet. 'Subtle, that's the word.' She exchanges a complicit smile with him.

'And some olives?'

'Thank you. My sister is particularly fond of olives,' says Harriet, turning her sweetest smile on her sibling.

Alfonso sketches the subtlest of bows and disappears.

Birds flit gaily in and out of the bushes. The slightest of breezes takes the edge off the sun and rustles the leaves in a riot of greens and russets. The air is scented with rosemary. Faint voices drift up from the lower terrace, where couples engrossed in paperbacks look up from time to time to pass comment. Someone snaps the pages of a broadsheet; the report is like a pistol shot in the peace of the late afternoon. Harriet tips back her head, drinking in the warmth, lets her eyelids droop, and waits. She can hear Hester unfolding the papers she had enclosed with the card. There is a sniff from across the table. Behind her, a chair scrapes on the gravel; a male voice murmurs, 'Good afternoon.' Hester returns the greeting, as does Harriet without opening her eyes. The clink of a wineglass on the marble table behind her; the crack of a hardback spine.

'A cookery course,' says Hester finally, through, her sister imagines, clenched teeth.

Harriet does not reply.

Hester's hissing increases fractionally in volume. 'You have spent God alone knows how much sending me on a cookery course!'

Harriet's eyes remain resolutely closed. 'An *Italian* cookery course,' she murmurs, brushing a fly from her cheek.

'Well, given the location I hardly thought it would be French!'

The crunch of feet on the gravel signals Alfonso's return. '*Signor,*' he murmurs as he passes their neighbour, fetching up at their table with a tray bearing two large glasses and a rustic earthenware bowl of fat green olives. He spies the papers in Hester's lap.

'Ah! Signora Greene, I see the secret is out!' He places a glass in front of each of them. 'So, the surprise was wonderful, no? You are excited about tomorrow?'

Hester's hand, halfway towards her glass, hesitates. 'Excited?'

Harriet takes a tentative sip of her wine, scrutinising with great interest a bee on a nearby flower.

'Of course! Signora Pearson has been so anxious that you will like it. I assure her, who would not like to learn at the feet of the great Franco? The best of teachers! Everybody loves him!'

Harriet takes another, longer, sip. The bee really is most fascinating.

'Franco?' repeats Hester.

Alfonso laughs, gesturing at the course literature. 'You did not see? Franco Riccardi is your tutor. You know the magnificent Franco, surely?'

Harriet permits herself a brief squint across the table. Were she not in such a bate with her sister, she might have laughed at the look of incredulity on Hester's face. 'Franco *Riccardi*?' Hester stammers.

'*Sì, sì* . . . the same. The master. He is here this week. A great honour for us. For all the students.'

Hester gulps a great slug of her wine. 'Good Lord.'

'Ladies . . . excuse me, please.' He runs swiftly down the steps to attend to a guest. Harriet transfers her gaze from her bee to his departing back.

'Harriet . . .' begins Hester, her fingers fretting the edge of the papers. 'I had no idea . . . for heaven's sake, it's not a special birthday, is it?' Then, with a frisson of alarm, 'It isn't, is it?'

'No, no, not really. Sixty-six, that's all.'

Hester gives a huge sigh of relief. 'I thought for one minute . . .'

Harriet regards her benignly. 'It's all right, you're not losing your marbles. I simply thought you could do with a treat. And when I saw it was—'

'Franco Riccardi, yes.' Hester breathes his name with all the reverence an acolyte might afford the Pope. She avidly watches any cookery programmes featuring the great man, rare as they are, since he is generally immured in his Tuscan restaurant concocting undreamt-of delights from local ingredients. A thought strikes. 'Yes, but, Harry, how much—'

Harriet waves away the question with a decisive, 'Money and fair words.' *Harry.* Not *Harriet.* The thaw has started. It pleases her inordinately that she has managed to discombobulate Hester so comprehensively. She takes a mouthful of her delicious wine.

'I don't know what to say.' Hester gulps her wine unthinkingly. Then, as it hits her tastebuds, 'Golly, this is superb!'

'Thank you would be sufficient.'

Hester wriggles uncomfortably on her chair and rearranges her face.

'Thank you, Harry—really,' she says gruffly. 'It's the most marvellous birthday present.' And to Harriet's considerable surprise, she gets up to give her sister a peck on the cheek. 'I am sorry I've been so . . .' She leaves the unspoken word hanging. Impossible? Infuriating? Diabolical?

Harriet grasps the olive branch with both hands. 'It's okay,' she says, erasing in an instant the irritations and anxieties of the past few months. She grins happily. 'I think we're in for a treat.' But she can't fail to notice that as Hester resumes her seat and picks up her glass, her face still bears a faint look of strain.

'You know what an old grump I am,' says Hester by way of apology, or as close to an apology as Harriet is likely to get. 'I don't like it when you keep things from me.'

Harriet smiles. 'I like that! You're the one who plays things close to your chest. Getting anything out of you requires the patience of a saint, not to mention a crowbar.' But if she's expecting a light-hearted reaction from Hester, she's disappointed. All she gets is a perfunctory tightening of the lips, before Hester turns away to look out over the valley. *One day at a time*, thinks Harriet, as the little flame of worry reignites in her stomach.

Across the table, hand grasping the stem of her glass just a little too tightly, Hester's thoughts are in turmoil. Their brief rapprochement feels such a relief after the days, the weeks, of apprehension. Harriet's wonderfully generous birthday present has deeply unsettled her. If only she could simply enjoy it. If only she could unknow what she knows! If only, if only . . . the possibilities whirl around her brain with sickening familiarity. She is aware of Harriet's scrutiny, aware also that they know each other too well to keep secrets concealed. Or she had thought they did . . .

'I do hope I'm not intruding,' says a deep, slightly husky voice behind them, with a regretful cough. Both women turn, squinting up through the sunlight at the figure looming over them. 'I couldn't help but overhear . . .' The man realises their disadvantage and moves around the table to face them. Tallish, thin, slightly stooping. A good head of grey hair, perhaps a little long on the collar, brushed back vigorously from a broad forehead. Startling blue eyes, reassuringly crinkled, presumably from much smiling. And he is smiling now, extending a hand first to Hester, then Harriet, as though instinctively aware of the pecking order. 'Lionel Parchment,' he says, 'From Greenwich.'

'An unusual name,' says Harriet, introducing herself. 'And this is my sister, Hester Greene.'

'So I gathered,' says Lionel warmly. 'I believe we are to be fellow students, Mrs Greene.'

'Hester, please.'

'Hester. Both worshipping at the Riccardi shrine. Isn't it too wonderful for words? I don't know if you've had a chance to study the programme yet—'

'No, not really,' says Hester. 'I've only just—'

'—but one of the things he'll be doing is *abbacchio alla cacciatora*. Apologies for my pronunciation.' He laughs self-deprecatingly. In truth, his accent is pretty good. 'Well, his version. You know, with the *balsamico bianco*? I mean, that's inspired, don't you think?' He sounds boyishly excited. His hand flies to his forehead. 'Oh, I am so sorry—I really must learn to curb my enthusiasm. Forgive me.' He holds both hands up in apology and backs away.

'Not at all,' says Harriet, sensitive to the fact that his remarks were directed primarily at Hester, who seems disinclined to respond. 'It's refreshing to find someone so passionate about something.'

Lionel laughs again, now patently embarrassed. 'You are too kind, Harriet. Sorry, may I call you that?' Harriet nods her permission. 'These days, I find myself ridiculously excited by the least thing.'

Hester reaches for her glass. An uncomfortable hiatus, through which Harriet grins maniacally.

'Well . . . I will retire and leave you to your wine.' He inclines his head. 'I shall see you both later, no doubt.'

'We look forward to it,' says Harriet, ignoring her sister's averted head. Lionel retreats to his table. Hester raises an eyebrow at her sister that needs no interpretation; given the delicate state of relations, Harriet decides not to address Hester's rudeness right now. As they finish their drinks, they somewhat self-consciously discuss a recent U3A lecture they had attended on therapeutic eurythmy, which Hester had considered a load of codswallop and Harriet had been persuaded might have its merits. It is with some relief that, ten minutes or so later, they hear Lionel tramp across the gravel back towards the hotel. Hester rolls her eyes.

'Do you think he's going to behave like Tigger for the entire five days?'

'I thought he was rather . . .' Harriet is about to say *charming*, then instantly thinks better of it. Teddy Wilson had been charming, and look where that got them. 'Friendly,' she finishes lamely. 'Lovely voice.' She's a sucker for rich, round voices with a hint of gravel.

'Friendly!' sniffs Hester, well aware of the adjective her sister had rejected and bridling at her misplaced sensitivity. Ever since the calamitous events culminating in Teddy's arrest, she has berated herself daily for her naivety and and her susceptibility to his legendary charisma, a charisma that she is chagrined to admit never impressed Harriet. Anyone with the faintest hint of charm is now anathema to her, provoking the most violent antipathy. Her reaction affords her blameless sister frequent mortification.

'He may just be very shy,' says Harriet. 'You know how people over-compensate.'

'Or he may just be a crashing bore who latches on to people.'

'Well, I think he's highly unlikely to try latching on to you,' says Harriet tartly. *Honestly, sometimes Hester is the absolute limit!*

Hester ignores the barb and gets to her feet. 'I think I'll just take a shower before dinner. Do you suppose it's posh?'

Posh to Hester means pretentious. It means sparkly tops, heels and costume jewellery.

'According to the brochure the ambience is relaxed,' says Harriet, adding quickly, 'Your black skirt and top will be fine.' She's praying Hetty hadn't jettisoned those two ancient but serviceable standbys in favour of a couple more paperbacks. She cringes at the thought of her sister sitting down in the restaurant in her customary holiday garb—indeed, the outfit she is currently sporting is a prime example: a pair of elderly polyester slacks rather short in the leg (bought in the era when such garments were still called slacks) and a shapeless T-shirt purchased a decade or so ago from a market stall. All she can hope is that Hester has packed at least a couple of her hand-knitted tops, which, in contrast to most of the rest of her wardrobe (her old work suits and winter cashmere excepted), both fit her well and are beautifully made.

'Okey-dokey,' says Hester, making for the steps. 'I'll knock for you about seven thirty, shall I?'

'Perfect,' says Harriet, rejoicing that she'll have plenty of time for a long soak in the bath and a snooze on her very comfortable-looking bed, not necessarily in that order. 'I'll just enjoy the sun for another few minutes. It's such a novelty.'

Hester hurries down the corridor to her room, ferreting in her bag for her phone to check for messages. Nothing. Shoving it back into the depths of her handbag, her hand encounters the creased envelope whose contents have preoccupied her for weeks. She unlocks the door and shuts it thankfully behind her.

MONDAY

CHAPTER 6

'Mind the paintwork!'

'Fucking hell!'

Jez has dropped his end of the sofa, leaving Ben trapped between the doorway and the hall stairs, the weight of the furniture borne mainly by his left knee. It is not a light sofa. He grapples to keep hold of the frame as it starts to slide to the floor. Unable to take the burden any longer, he too lets go and it thumps down with an alarming crack.

'Now look what you done! Only gone and broken the friggin' thing!' Ben drops to his knees to peer underneath. He reaches through the skein of cobwebs clinging to the base to run his hand over the stubby wooden legs, finding an ominous split running up from one of the tiny brass castors. 'I think it's cracked. You twat!'

Jez moodily punches the sofa with the back of his hand. A puff of dust dances in the sunlight. 'Get out of my face, will you! Weighs a fucking ton. Pile of old crap. Was probably already fucked.'

'No it wasn't!' shouts Ben. 'It was perfectly okay.'

Perfectly okay is perhaps a bit of a stretch. The shabby Victorian drop-arm Chesterfield is badly in need not only of reupholstering (particularly in the middle, which canny guests avoid in view of its protuberant springs) but also of what Ben knows his mother would refer to as a 'damn good clean'. The legs, however, as far as Ben knows, had until today been sound.

Their morning of preparation, a full five days in advance due to Jez's inescapable commitments to his father over the four days running up to the party, has swiftly degenerated into rancour. Partly on account of some of the people Jez has invited (many of whom Ben loathes or who loathe him) and partly because neither of them is accustomed to such hard physical work, not having properly assessed the amount of *stuff* in the cottage. Any piece of furniture that might conceivably house papers or books is full to overflowing, drawers and cupboards spilling their contents at the slightest provocation; every surface is piled high with old magazines, more books, holiday brochures (when would the aunts ever go on a Mediterranean cruise or trek through Vietnam?), printouts from websites (surely neither Hester nor Harriet would ever purchase a firepit? Or laser-guided scissors?) and numerous catalogues of assorted vintages from The Wine Society and other vintners. Ben has taken the wise precaution of photographing each room they are clearing from every angle so that after the party they can replace everything in exactly the right position.

'That's well sensible,' Jez grudgingly acknowledges.

'Website,' mutters Ben. 'Secretparty dot com or something.' The meticulous planning required is making the whole escapade seem even more treacherous.

'Yeah?' Jez pulls out a packet of cigarettes.

'You can't smoke in here!' cries Ben.

'Dickhead, you're having, like, a *party*,' says Jez, lighting up. 'What you gonna do? Make everyone go outside? Like that's gonna happen.'

Ben's blood, already running cold, now turns to ice. This is insanity. The aunts can smell smoke a mile away and Aunt Hester is notorious for commenting loudly and critically on any pedestrians puffing away in her vicinity; she would be incandescent if anyone actually dared to smoke in her home. An incandescent Aunt Hester. Suddenly, even the wrath of a thwarted Louisa seems insignificant by comparison.

'Forget it,' says Ben. 'I'm cancelling.'

'You what?'

'You heard. It's off. You better help me put everything back.'

Jez stares at Ben in disbelief for several seconds and then he cackles. 'You can't cancel! It's too late, you loser. It's out there. Everyone knows. You call it off, they'll just break in.'

'Break in?' Ben snorts incredulously. 'What, our mates?'

'They're not all our mates, though, are they?' says Jez slyly.

'What?'

'I mean, we don't know everyone that's accepted, do we? Or the maybes.'

'Yeah, we—' Ben stops, as realisation strikes. Jez smirks. 'You bastard! You've been going behind my back, haven't you?'

Jez's face tightens; he refuses to look his friend in the eye, instead cagily drawing on his cigarette. 'What's a few more matter?'

'I told you. I told you!' Ben waves the smoke away. 'Twenty-five, thirty max. We *agreed*. What, so every time I've said no to extras, they've gone back to you and you've said yes?' Ben's been fending off numerous messages from their invitees 'just checking' it's okay to bring some mates; every time, he's firmly refused permission. From the shifty look on Jez's face, their subsequent appeals to him have met with success. 'How many?' he says, cold with dread.

Jez hesitates.

'*How many?*'

''Bout forty.' Jez's voice sounds slightly strangled; he's lying. Ben skewers him with a malevolent glare and he crumbles. 'Forty-four. So far.'

For a few seconds, Ben is unable to find the words. He conjures a room full of loud, drunk idiots, spilling drinks, stubbing out fags . . . His heart is leapfrogging around his chest.

'Right. Get onto Facebook or whatever and send out a cancellation. Now!'

Jez grimaces. 'No point. They'll come anyway.'

'I'll call the police!' says Ben desperately.

'Oh yeah? How you gonna explain that to your rellies? "Oooh, Auntie, I don't know how these naughty people got in or why all your furniture is piled up in the shed." Yeah, that'll work.'

Ben, despairing, collapses onto the arm of the wedged sofa. It groans. He leaps up. 'God, Jez, you gotta stop this. We gotta call it off. Please. I'm begging you.' He thinks he might be about to cry.

Jez shrugs. 'Ben, mate, I would if I could, but I'm telling you, you got totally no idea how these things take off. 'Specially once people start tweeting and that . . .'

'It's on Twitter?' The blood drains from Ben's face, leaving only pinpricks of red as his pimples flare. 'You put it on Twitter?'

'Not me. Lou-Lou tweeted straight after she spoke to you and—'

Ben's legs give way. This time he ignores the sofa's complaints. 'I'm dead. I might as well kill myself now.'

'Who's killing themselves?' Louisa Jellinek, as if conjured, appears in the doorway. She peers into the hall. 'Oh, how cute is this? A real live cottage, like, buried in the woods. This is so cool!' And she totters over the threshold in ridiculously high heels and a skirt surely fashioned from a scarf—an extremely narrow scarf at that—displaying in all its glory a delicate rose tattoo, complete with thorns, on her right thigh. Her ensemble is topped with a tight, tight T-shirt in shocking pink. She trails a flirty finger down Ben's face as she blows a kiss across the sofa at Jez.

Oh my God, thinks Ben, almost swooning, *she touched me!*

'How did you . . .?' he stammers.

'What? Know you were here? Jez texted me.'

Did he? Oh yes, of course he did!

'And look how hard you're both working! Wow! Why'd you say you were doing all this today?'

Jez explains with a mulish expression about his tyrannical father while Ben gazes transfixed at the vision before him. He is so lost in his worship that he fails to spot the ambush. 'Bastard'd skin me alive if he knew about all this,' whines Jez, then adds treacherously, 'Thing is, though, Lou, Ben's getting cold feet.'

'Cold feet?' purrs Louisa, turning her smoky eyes on Ben.

'Yeah,' the viper continues. 'Like, he's chickening out.'

Louisa pouts, her bottom lip protruding deliciously. 'No way! What's up, Ben babes?'

He tries to marshal his arguments, pleading the decrepitude of his aunts, the (wholly fictitious) parlous state of their finances should anything get damaged, to no avail.

Louisa hears him out, then leans towards him. For one blissful minute, he thinks she is about to kiss him. She smells of flowers, of Juicy Fruit, and faintly, and surprisingly erotically, of sweat. 'Babes,' she breathes, 'it's going to be fine. I've had, like, loads of parties at mine and, trust me, the duffers never knew a thing about any of them. You seriously think I'd let anyone do anything out of order?'

'Er . . .'

'Do you?' she presses, seemingly genuinely astonished that anyone, least of all someone like Ben, would entertain any doubts as to her authority.

'No . . .' exhales Ben, lost. Of course she wouldn't! Who on earth would have the balls to argue with Louisa Jellinek? If she says it's going to be fine, then fine it's going to be. His legs turn once more to jelly, only this time from relief. 'It's just . . . please don't invite anyone else, will you?'

'Babes, we got anyone who's anyone. Who else am I gonna ask?'

'Good. Great. That's . . . thanks,' says Ben faintly.

Louisa smiles triumphantly; behind her, unseen by Ben, Jez pumps his fist.

'C'mon, fellas,' says Louisa, whipping off her pelmet to reveal even tinier shorts underneath, 'let's get this place ready to *party*!' She kicks off her shoes and, with a strength that belies her willowy physique, seizes the end of the sofa, upends it with one astonishing upward thrust and tugs it through the doorway and into the hall, sandwiching Ben momentarily between her heavenly haunches and the stairs. Had his number been called at that precise juncture, he would have died a very happy boy.

Three hours later the two downstairs rooms in the cottage are empty; pictures removed from the walls ('Can't be too careful,' says Louisa); the carpets rolled against one wall, enveloped in bin bags ('Best way, trust me,' says Louisa); an ancient key has been discovered in the dresser drawer and the larder (that also houses the wine fridge) locked ('Don't want anyone getting the munchies,' says Louisa); further keys have been identified that fit all the bedrooms and have been put to their intended use ('You don't want people shagging in your beds,' says Louisa); and all shelves have been cleared and their contents packed away. Louisa has taken the preparations out of Ben's hands in light of her vast experience, directing her far less able lieutenants and even, after close inspection, getting Ben to patch a hole in the roof of one of the sheds to prevent the ingress of water in the event of rain.

Ben and Jez are shattered; never mind partying, all they want to do is collapse into bed and sleep for a fortnight. Louisa, however, who has done as much if not more lifting and shifting than either boy, looks as fresh as when she arrived, but for her hair, which has got steadily more bedraggled but also inexplicably more sexy, the wispy tendrils floating around her face.

'Doesn't it look great!' she exclaims, surveying the denuded rooms. 'All this space! It's like a fairy story: rinky-dinky cottage buried in the trees. I *love* all this shit getting ready for a party. Use iPods for music, yeah? I just got some fab travel speakers; I'll bring them. Oooh, Jez, nice iPhone, you poser.' Ben's hand, fingering his old Nokia, stays firmly in his pocket. 'Wanna Facebook everyone who's coming about music?'

'No,' says Ben quickly. 'We choose the music.' There's already far too much noise on Facebook as it is.

'Cool. We doing food or what?'

Food? He hasn't given it the slightest thought. Suddenly a chance to assert himself. 'No sweat. Leave that to me.'

'Serious?' She frowns prettily, then her brow clears. 'Oh, 'course! You the man! Love the blog, babes. Get rattlin' those pans! I can't wait!' She grabs both Ben's hands to steady herself as she climbs back into her shoes while Jez looks on jealously. 'You know what? You are pretty fucking badass, Ben babes. Awesome!'

And as she presses her luscious lips to his, the little porcelain shepherdess forgotten at the back of the top shelf in the sitting room simpers down on them.

TUESDAY

CHAPTER 7

Hester is having a wonderful time. She is enjoying herself far more than she would ever have dreamt possible, particularly in light of the strain she has been living under recently. The cooking course is run from a huge converted barn from whose weathered beams hang bunches of drying herbs and a plethora of sausages and hams. The kitchens are a cook's dream, all stainless steel, with razor-sharp knives (she thought she knew how to sharpen knives until shown how to do it properly by her terrifying teacher), huge gas ranges ('Induction hobs, pah!' Franco had spat in response to a timid enquiry from Melanie, one of the other students, a nervous slip of a girl in her twenties who had won the week's course in a competition), and the most beautiful copper saucepans Hester has ever seen. It is her not-so-secret secret that she adores cookware and is physically incapable of walking past an unfamiliar kitchenware shop. She rarely parts with any cash; what delights her is the opportunity to weigh a saucepan or utensil in her hand and fantasise about the uses she might put it to. So this kitchen, with its superb equipment, is like a dream made flesh—especially as, at the end of each long but glorious day, unseen hands work overnight washing everything up and returning all the surfaces to a pristine shine.

Hester has tried to explain to Harriet the depths of her pleasure, in part as an indirect way of saying thank you. Harriet recognises the ruse and is glad of it; it is indescribably heartening to see the old

Hester emerging once more. And yet ... and yet ... every so often Harriet will catch a look in Hester's eye, a shadow of something she cannot quite name but that, against all reason, seems in some way to pertain to her. Once or twice she has been tempted to probe, but under the glorious Italian sun, cosseted and pampered by the attentive staff, replete with fine food and even finer wines, it seems safer not to poke the suspected hornet's nest. If that shadow still lurks when they return home, she'll tackle it then.

Hester, wondering how Harriet was going to entertain herself for the week of her course, had been astonished to discover that she was going to try her hand at watercolours.

'Painting? You?'

'Well, thanks a bunch! Don't you remember that picture of lilies of the valley in a brown jug that I did at school? Pa hung it in his study for years.'

'Indeed he did,' Hester had replied, thinking that no-one but their father and the cleaner had thus ever needed to look at it once it had been fulsomely praised however insincerely by both parents. She and her sister may be possessed of many talents but she does not fool herself that artistic ability ranks among them.

'I am perfectly well aware that I am hopeless,' Harriet had continued with a twinkle in her eye, 'but it says "no experience required" and someone has to be the class dunce, so it might just as well be me. Anyway, apparently on one or two days we go tramping in the hills in pursuit of flowers and butterflies and suchlike to paint. I thought that would please you: I might shift a bit of this weight.' And she had slapped her ample backside to emphasise the point, her weight being a perennial concern of Hester, who is forever adjusting recipes to reduce their fat or sugar content for her sister's supposed benefit. Harriet, however, remains resolutely rotund (and, she would be the first to attest, perfectly happy about it), while Hester, an archetypal ectomorph, is as bony in her mid-sixties as she had been at fifteen.

'And dare I ask how *il Franco fantastico* is shaping up?' asks Harriet at the end of the second day, as she and Hester enjoy another of Alfonso's recommendations under the pergola before dinner. She thinks how nice Hester looks in one of her knitted tops, a pale mauve mohair, complemented by the amethyst earrings their parents had given her on her twenty-first birthday, which rarely see the light of day.

Hester frowns. 'Well, there's no doubting his innate genius. He has such a vivid imagination and is never afraid to experiment. You wouldn't believe the things he can do with the most ordinary of ingredients.'

'Bit like Ben, then,' says Harriet, recalling the times their nephew had eschewed Hester's advice and still managed to produce something delicious. The competitiveness between them affords Harriet endless amusement.

Hester harrumphs. 'I think the boy has many years ahead of him before he approaches the maestro. He needs to learn the basics first. He's not even in the foothills yet.' Despite her public scepticism, Hester is inordinately proud that she, however reluctantly at the time, had kindled in Ben that first flicker of interest in cooking. The surly teenager is transformed in the kitchen into another being altogether: eager to learn, even more eager to experiment.

'I sense a "but" coming, though,' says Harriet, draining her glass. Alfonso is an excellent sommelier; he has fathomed her particular palate and every wine he has suggested to date has been sublime. 'About Signor Riccardi?'

Hester nods vigorously and sits forward on her wicker chair, a certain precursor to a good old moan. 'I have no problem with his cooking—far from it. I've already learnt so much. I have no quarrel either with his short temper: God knows there are one or two idiots in the group and that must be incredibly frustrating for a man of his talents. Do you know that girl Melanie had no idea how to prepare an aubergine? Can you blame the man for being so dismissive?' Harriet, who has no idea how to handle an aubergine either, feels a sneaking sympathy for the unfortunate Melanie, whom in one brief encounter at the bar she had found to be perfectly inoffensive. 'But my major beef is his arrogance. Don't you dare question his instructions! Good heavens, you'd think you were gainsaying Moses on the Mount!'

Aha, thinks Harriet, seeing where this is going, *so you had the temerity to challenge the great Riccardi, did you?*

'He practically spat at me!' Hester's indignation swelling with every remembered word. 'All I said was that Giorgio Bassanelli uses red not black pepper in his *panforte*. I thought he was going to explode! He slammed his fist down on the counter and swore—at least I assume he was swearing. Lionel, who speaks a fair bit of Italian, told me afterwards it was pretty salty. "That man," he yelled—Franco, not Lionel—"he is an idiot!" I said, "That's as may be, but he does have two Michelin stars." Well! You should have seen his face!'

'I thought he had two stars as well.'

'Exactly. That's why he was so furious. He obviously doesn't rate Bassanelli at all. Or anyone else come to that. Riccardi thinks that just because he's on television from time to time and runs a restaurant you have to book years in advance, he's the bee's knees.'

'You don't suppose it's all part of his shtick? You know, volatile Italian with a short fuse? They all play up to the cameras, after all, these TV chefs.'

'Mary Berry doesn't play up to the cameras,' says Hester frostily.

'Ah, but she's a woman. She doesn't need to prove anything.'

Hester, who does not share her sister's feminism to such a marked degree, gives Harriet a beady look and, noting her smugly raised eyebrow, is suddenly assailed by the recollection of the letter in her handbag.

Harriet, who has been buoyed by their badinage, sees Hester's face harden. 'What is it?' She's not at all sure she wants to know.

'Nothing.' Hester gives a tight smile. 'Oh, I meant to say, I asked

Lionel if he'd like to join us at dinner. Seems a bit mean to leave him sitting all alone.'

'Oh,' says Harriet, slightly taken aback. 'Okay.'

'You don't mind, do you?'

'No, no . . . it's just . . .'

'What?'

'I thought you felt . . .'

'Oh, that! I think I was a bit hasty.'

Oh yes? thinks Harriet. *And does the dinner invitation explain the earrings?*

There is a faint blush mottling Hester's cheeks. 'In point of fact, he's rather good company. He finds Franco as ridiculous as I do. OTT, you know.'

'Yes. You said.'

'But if you'd rather . . .'

'Not at all,' says Harriet quickly. She would hate to be thought mean-spirited. And why not get to know Lionel a little better? She had found him perfectly decent, if a little excitable, that first day. It will be a novelty: they are usually fairly antisocial on their holidays.

Hester's phone rings. She digs in her bag and flips her glasses up to read the screen. Her face changes. 'Oh . . .' She jumps up. 'Stretch my legs,' she says to Harriet, and hurries down the steps towards the lower terrace, waiting until she's some way away before answering. Even then, she keeps moving until she disappears into the shrubbery. Harriet watches her go, hand shielding her eyes against the late-afternoon sun. Since when has Hester taken calls in private? She can just about make out her sister slowly wandering down the path, visible from time to time between the bushes, hunched over the phone. Harriet looks away, a sudden rush of self-pity overwhelming her, extinguishing her happiness in an instant. The fragile harmony between them has been destroyed. She feels both angry and bereft, a displaced foreigner. Right now, she would like nothing more than to be back at The Laurels. She finds her phone. Dials.

'Oh! What's wrong?'

'Nothing's wrong. Have you been running, Ben?'

'No!'

Harriet holds the phone away from her ear, temporarily deafened.

Then Ben says more quietly, 'Sorry. I mean, no. Surprised me, that's all.'

'What have you been up to then?'

'Me? Why?'

The boy sounds awfully jumpy.

'I just wondered. First exam on Monday, isn't it?'

'Yeah. Revising. Yeah. That's what I been doing, revising.'

'Good.' The line is silent. 'Mum and Dad all right?'

'Yeah.'

Is texting to blame for young people's inability to hold a normal conversation? Harriet wonders.

'And you've heard Daria's wonderful news, of course?'

This time Ben seems genuinely animated. 'Yeah. Awesome, innit? She's well pleased.'

'We're both so happy for her. Give her a hug from us when you see her, will you?' Harriet regrets this as soon as she says it. They both fear Ben might be a little too fond of Daria, the age difference notwithstanding.

'Yeah, 'course.' Another pause. 'You having a good time?'

'Yes, yes, we are, thanks. It's a fabulous hotel.'

'Aunt Hester like her present?' Harriet had consulted Ben and Daria about the course when she was havering over whether or not to book it. 'You're kidding, right?' Ben had said. 'He's, like, the main man. Go for it.' So she had.

'Yes, I think so. Riccardi seems to be a bit full of himself, though.'

'If I could cook like that, I'd be full of myself.'

'I suppose. She says she's learning lots.'

'Yeah? Cool. She can teach me when you get back.'

'She'd like that, I'm sure.' Harriet knows she will. 'So, anything exciting on the horizon?'

Silence.

'Ben?'

'Oh, yeah . . . sorry. What d'you mean?'

'Well, you don't want to spend every waking minute revising. You need to pace yourself. Take breaks. A bit of relaxation from time to time. Perhaps get together with your friends.'

'Yeah . . . Yeah, I will.'

'Good. Well, I'd better let you get on, then . . .'

'Yeah . . . ta.' As Ben goes to terminate the call, a thought strikes.

'Oh, Ben, if you're seeing Daria, could you double-check she turned down the heating?'

'Yeah, she did. Well, I did.'

'Oh, you are a good lad! Well, don't work too hard. Bye!'

Harriet's good temper is restored. He may be a moody little tyke sometimes—what teenager isn't?—but his heart is in the right place. She is confident that once he's negotiated the rocky shallows of adolescence, he's set fair for a promising adulthood.

She drops her mobile back in her bag as Hester emerges from the shrubbery, her conversation over but phone still in hand, and strides up the steps towards her. With the sun behind her, her face is in shadow, but even so Harriet notes the rigid set of her mouth. There is a brief but definite hiatus when Harriet waits expectantly for Hester to make some reference to her mystery call. She doesn't. Instead she checks her watch.

'Must be about time to go in to dinner.' Hester drains her glass and reaches for her bag.

'Everything all right?' says Harriet, unable to help herself.

'What? This?' says Hester, just a little too gaily, waggling her phone comically before thrusting it into her bag without meeting her eyes. 'Oh, you know, just wanted to pick my brains about a recipe.'

'A recipe?'

'Yes . . . boeuf bourguignon. I said, that'll cost you.'

'Who?'

'Who do you think? Ben, of course.'

CHAPTER 8

'Ben? Are you there?'

Isabelle taps nervously on her son's bedroom door. 'Darling?'

Ben lies on his back staring up at the ceiling, thoughts racing, stomach churning. Why would Aunt Harriet interrupt her holiday to ring him just now out of the blue? It's not as if she had anything important to say.

'Benjamin?' croons his mother.

No-one calls him Benjamin! Except his lamebrain mother when she's trying to get him to do something he doesn't want to do. As now.

'Do come down, darling. Ralph is waiting.'

Ben grunts noncommittally. At least she knows better than to open the door and violate his sanctum. Not after the last time. 'Coupla minutes,' he growls and listens to her pad apologetically down the hallway to the top of the stairs.

'He'll just be a little while,' he hears her say as she descends. Below, from the sitting room, comes the low rumble of male voices—his father's and Ralph's—punctuated by his mother's occasional interjection, invariably accompanied by a nervous giggle. Anyone would think they had royalty in the house instead of just Ralph Pickerlees, eldest son and Great White Hope of George's boss, Victor.

Ben returns to his review of the conversation with his aunt. Does she suspect something? He answers his own question with a metaphorical snort: of course not! How can she? Why would she? Chances are she was simply being an attentive aunt, reassuring herself that her favourite nephew was pursuing his studies with sufficient rigour to achieve his dreams. She, more than anyone, has always had faith in him, defended him against his detractors—notably scary Aunt Hester when she's going off on one. Not that he hasn't learnt how to handle the old biddy. He grins fleetingly at the memory of various battles waged and won (largely by him) in the kitchen. The memory, though, is bittersweet, accompanied as it is with his constant companion these days: guilt.

'Ben!' It's his dad this time, summoning him from the foot of the stairs, the impatience in his voice unmistakable. Ben levers himself to his feet and shoves a stick of gum in his mouth. Time to descend into the lion's den and get it over with.

⌣⌣⌣

'Here he is!' says George with forced bonhomie as Ben ambles into the sitting room. Ralph leaps to his feet, hand outstretched, his bony wrist protruding from a tweed jacket that must surely have belonged to his grandfather. Ben almost does a double-take. What is this? A Benedict-Cumberbatch-at-his-most-nerdy lookalike contest?

Ralph blinks behind his thick lenses and says, 'Hi, Ben,' in a strangulated voice that sets his Adam's apple bobbing. 'How's it going?'

''Kay,' says Ben, dragging his appalled gaze away to see, to his horror, that Isabelle has baked her famous—or, rather, infamous—chocolate fudge cake: an almost impenetrable slab of dense sludge, enveloped in a granular icing of gag-inducing sweetness. Why don't they offer the poor sod a beer?

'Ralph was just telling us about his first year,' says Isabelle brightly, using both hands to force the cake slice through her concoction as though carving a particularly unyielding cheese.

'Not for me, Mum,' says Ben quickly. 'I'll have mine later.'

'Not long had breakfast,' jokes George to Ralph, with a nod in his son's direction. 'All you youngsters are the same: you'd sleep until suppertime left to your own devices. Ha ha.'

'Ha ha,' says Ben.

Ralph resumes his seat, while Ben perches on the arm of the sofa nearest the door in readiness for the quickest getaway he can effect.

At George and Isabelle's urging, their guest begins to expatiate on the joys of university life. The spellbinding lectures, the testing tutorials, the mind-expanding hours spent in the library, the midnight oil burnt so that assignments are handed in on time, the nerve-racking wait for results . . .

'What's the social life like?' asks Ben, when a pause for breath offers him an opening.

His parents give identical uncomfortable laughs.

'Social life?' says Ralph, trying out the unfamiliar phrase.

'Yeah.'

Ralph looks nonplussed.

'I think Ben's asking about extracurricular activities,' says George. 'When you let your hair down with your chums.'

Chums! thinks Ben. *As you well know, I'm asking about bars and parties and having a good time.*

Ralph's face clears. 'Ah! Right. Of course.' He beams. 'Well, there's the most marvellous ChemSoc. We had a Wacky Scientist bop last term. You know, people all dressed up as—'

'Wacky scientists?' suggests Ben.

'Right! And you'll never guess who most people went as!'

'Einstein?'

'Oh . . . yes. How did you guess? Still, some of the wigs were amazing.'

'I bet,' says George stoutly. 'That sounds fun, doesn't it, Ben?'

'Epic,' says Ben.

'Indeed,' says Ralph. 'It's not all slogging away day and night over the old books, you know. I mean, one does have a pretty lively time of it.' He runs his finger around his collar.

'Yeah?' says Ben. 'Doing what?'

'Oh ... well ...' Ralph rapidly searches his extensive database of debauchery. His eyes glitter suddenly with remembered pleasure. 'Ah! Well, for instance, I'm not only a member of ChemSoc, but I also belong to ClassicSoc and we have some pretty amazing adventures there, I can tell you: museum visits, toga parties—that's where everyone dresses up in—'

'Togas?'

'Right! Have you been to one, then?'

Ben shakes his head.

'That's something to look forward to, eh?' says George heartily, with a pointed look at his son. Ben stares back guilelessly.

'Any tips for our boy, Ralph? About the application process? You know, personal statements and all that?'

'Tricky,' says Ralph, brow furrowed in his young-fogeyish style. 'I mean, you want something that makes you stand out from the crowd because competition is pretty stiff, especially at the better institutions. Have you given any thought to where ...?' He looks questioningly at Ben. Ben stares back. 'Early days, perhaps ...' says Ralph, smiling uncertainly and shoving his glasses back up his nose with a knuckle.

'He's thinking maybe Bristol,' says George.

'No I'm not,' says Ben.

'Or Sheffield,' says George, as if Ben hasn't spoken.

'Hmm,' says Ralph. 'Don't know much about either of them. I mean, I know they have good reputations ...' He looks around as if for inspiration. 'It is definitely chemistry you're interested in?'

'Yes,' says George.

'Sort of,' says Ben.

'Sort of?'

'Applied chemistry,' says Ben.

'Oh,' says Ralph eagerly, 'in what area? Pharmaceuticals?'

'No.'

'Biotechnology—that's always interested me.'

'No.'

'Renewable energy?'

'No.'

'Ben . . .' hisses George, as close to menacing as he's ever likely to get, while Isabelle wrings her hands.

'Do tell!' says Ralph brightly.

'Cooking,' says Ben.

A sharp intake of breath from George; Isabelle's hand flies to her mouth.

'No, Ben—' starts George.

'Well, yes,' says Ralph, his face brightening. 'And why not? How marvellous. Chemistry is the bedrock of food, after all.'

'It is?' says Isabelle faintly.

'Absolutely!' says Ralph enthusiastically. 'Sir Humphry Davy's *Elements of Agricultural Chemistry*—about 1810, 1812, if I remember rightly—that was all about food. I expect you know it, Ben? And Frederick Accum, around about the same period, said cookery was a branch of chemistry. And look at Heston Blumenthal—his kitchen is a positive laboratory!'

''S what my Aunt Hester says,' gloats Ben, regretting his initial and wholly irrational dislike of their visitor, who, now he looks more closely, is working that whole Cumberbatch look pretty well. 'One of Heston's books is actually called *Kitchen Chemistry*, you know.'

'Is it really? Well, there you are! This is jolly exciting,' Ralph rushes on. 'It's so encouraging to find someone who understands what chemistry is *for*. So many of my peers are only interested in abstracts, but you've absolutely got it! You'd need to choose your course really carefully, though. Don't want to go off down a blind alley. Unless—here's a thought—unless you got some practical experience before applying. They do seem to like more mature students these days, and if you'd been at the coalface as it were—I mean, actually getting hands-on experience in a restaurant, say—I'd bet that would stand you in really good stead against the opposition. Plus, you'd have a little money in the bank, which these days is no bad thing. Might that be something you would consider?'

Ben has spent hours in his bedroom practising expressions in front of his mirror. He assumes his best poker face.

'Practical experience? Instead of applying straight to university? Wow, that's a thought. Isn't it, Dad?'

A less controlled individual than George might at this stage have reached out a hand to encircle his son's throat and squeezed hard, if only to dislodge the look of smugness that hovers around Ben's features and that, try as he may, he is unable to suppress completely. George's carefully constructed plan to persuade his son of the inadvisability of his current career intentions by parading before him the paragon that is Ralph Pickerlees lies in ruins around him. But George is a patient man, a mild man and, most importantly, of the school that keeps its dirty linen entirely under wraps, so he merely gives a rather thin smile and offers their guest more tea. Ralph, while not averse to tea, is extremely anxious to avoid the risk of having to accept more chocolate fudge cake—having almost broken a tooth on his first helping—so he swiftly refuses and mumbles something about needing to meet someone in town shortly. Within seconds, he's out on the street, waving his goodbyes.

⌣⌣⌣

'That was helpful,' says Ben, as George closes the front door behind his guest. Were Ben not a teenager in the eye of a hormonal hurricane, whose parents are incapable of ever saying, doing or thinking the right thing, he might have found in his flinty heart a smidgeon of pity for a father so comprehensively trounced. Isabelle clutches her husband's arm sympathetically as he morosely begins loading the tea crockery onto the tray. 'Early days,' she whispers.

George rallies. 'Nice boy,' he says. 'I must thank Victor for persuading him to call by. Still, it's only one opinion. Be helpful to have a chat with your careers master at school, Ben.'

'Smatterson? You're kidding, right? He's the one who suggested I became a maths teacher! I hate maths!'

'We'll always need maths teachers,' says Isabelle timidly.

'We'll always need dustbin men and firefighters; it doesn't mean I'm going to become one!'

'Don't be cheeky, Ben,' says George automatically, putting an arm round Isabelle's shoulders. 'We only want what's best for you.'

Ben manages by superhuman effort to control his desire to scream: this conversation has played out dozens if not hundreds of times in exactly the same way and unless he's very careful it is certain to end precisely as it has always ended—with his mother in tears, his father apoplectic and him barricaded in his bedroom. To forestall the inevitable, he turns on his heel, takes the stairs two at a time and thunders down the hallway. The slam of his bedroom door goes some way in compensating for his powerlessness.

CHAPTER 9

Dinner is an awkward affair. Awkward for Harriet, anyway. Hester is in high spirits—*almost too high*, thinks Harriet, then chides herself immediately for her churlishness. Why shouldn't Hester let her hair down once in a while? She ought to be pleased to see her sister having such a patently good time after the rocky few months they've endured. She notes the spots of colour on Hester's normally pale cheeks and the uncharacteristic flamboyance of her gestures, the readiness of her laugh at Lionel's witticisms. *Why*, thinks Harriet, *she's flirting!*

Lionel's decorum is exemplary. Attentive to both sisters, he is clearly anxious that Harriet shouldn't feel excluded. But it can't be helped. How can she be included when Hester keeps steering the conversation back to their eventful day in the kitchen, when besides Hester's own run-in with the maestro, Riccardi had also laid into some other unfortunate student?

'She simply mentioned that someone on *MasterChef* had said there was nothing wrong with using dried pasta for *linguine con vongole* if you were pushed for time,' explains Hester indignantly.

'He's a purist, I imagine,' Harriet says, scratching around for something to contribute.

'A purist?!' Hester explodes. 'He's a tyrant! The poor woman was practically cowering under the counter. Lionel had to ride to the rescue.'

'Oh, Hester, I didn't!'

'Don't be so bashful. He did, Harry. He just said to Franco very quietly, "That's enough." And Franco subsided like a punctured balloon and went back to massacring red peppers.'

'Did he apologise?' asks Harriet, surprised that unassuming Lionel should have stood up to a bully. *Still waters*, she thinks.

'Oh, good grief, my dear, he wouldn't know how to!' Lionel laughs. 'Pampered by their adoring mamas, Italian men are never wrong.'

He catches Hester's eye and they smile broadly at one another. 'Anyway,' he continues, 'tomorrow we get to make our own pasta, so stand by for more fireworks.'

'Can't wait,' says Hester, eyes shining.

Harriet addresses herself to her *osso bucco*, over which her companions are now waxing lyrical.

'So nice to see it served traditionally,' says Hester.

'Absolutely,' says Lionel, savouring his mouthful. 'It's never the same without gremolata, don't you agree?'

Frankly, thinks Harriet, *I wouldn't care if it were served with chips. It's only a bit of meat, for heaven's sake!* But she smiles dutifully and agrees that, yes, gremolata makes all the difference. She wishes suddenly that she were back at The Laurels in front of the fire, Marmite on toast at hand, a crossword on her lap. It's hard work being a gooseberry.

Across the table, Hester eyes Harriet surreptitiously between forkfuls. Whatever is the matter with her? Poor Lionel is being a real trooper, gamely trying to maintain the conversation and getting the bare minimum in response. Is it her fault that Harriet's not able to join in the conversation about the course? She is fully aware of her sister's frequent glances in her direction. *I will not feel guilty*, she thinks. *If I want to have a private conversation with someone, why shouldn't I?* She is not thinking of Lionel; she is back in the garden, conducting that very difficult phone call. It was unfortunate the call had come through at that moment, with Harriet all ears. If anyone ought to be feeling guilty, it's Harry, sitting opposite looking like a week of wet Wednesdays . . .

'Do you have children?' asks Harriet, watching Lionel watching Hester.

'Sorry?' He drags his eyes back to look at Harriet, thoughts clearly elsewhere.

'I was just asking if you had any children.'

'Oh, no. Sorry. My wife and I, we . . . it somehow never happened. I think in some ways it was a blessing: Connie never enjoyed the best of health, unfortunately—a weak heart—and I think perhaps a child might have been . . . well . . . it's been ten years now since she. . .' He tails off with a brief smile that nevertheless signals clearly the end of his disclosures. Harriet nods neutrally. Hard to read his response: is he regretful? Thankful?

'How about you?'

She toys with a spoon. 'No, unfortunately.'

'Unfortunately?' says Hester sharply. 'I've never heard you say that before.'

Harriet is taken aback. This conversation, out of nowhere, suddenly feels horribly intimate. She shrugs self-consciously. 'It's never really occurred to me before.'

'How can it not have?' snaps Hester.

'Well, do you regret never having children?' asks Harriet, ruffled.

'We were talking about you.' Hester stamps on a distant memory hovering on the edge of her subconscious.

'And I'm asking you.'

Lionel clears his throat. The sisters stare coldly at one another. Harriet is the first to look away, aware of Lionel's discomfiture.

'I expect Hester has told you about Daria and Milo,' she says to him, hoping even as she asks that Hester hasn't.

'Oh, yes, the waifs and strays you took in,' smiles Lionel, relieved at the apparent change of topic, but affronting Harriet instantly. *Is that how Hester talks about them?*

'If you like,' she says stiffly. 'And our nephew Ben.'

'Second cousin,' corrects Hester.

Harriet ignores her. 'It's just that over the past few months, we've had a great deal of contact with all three of them—inevitably—and I've realised what a lot they bring to life. Especially a baby.'

'Like what?' says Lionel.

'Oh . . .' Harriet struggles for a moment.

'Yes, like what?' presses Hester.

Harriet actively dislikes her sister in that moment.

'Well . . . joy, laughter, tenderness and a tremendous protective-ness, if that doesn't sound too mawkish,' she says to Lionel. 'I realised with rather a shock when all the terrible things were happening over Christmas that if anyone had harmed a hair on Milo's head, I could most probably have killed the perpetrator.'

'I say!' Lionel sits back, shocked.

Hester, too, is taken aback by the violence of Harriet's response, then with a jolt realises she feels much the same.

Harriet gives a brief, embarrassed laugh. 'All I'm saying—' she is careful not to look at Hester '—is that I realise what a blessing it's been having the three of them in my life and I feel very privileged at my age to have become a sort of surrogate grandmother.'

The silence that greets this revelation is unsettling. It is as if she has unwittingly introduced an unwelcome solemnity to a riotous party: no-one quite knows how to respond.

'More wine?' says Lionel.

⌣⌣⌣

Harriet lasts until coffee and then makes her excuses to leave Hester and Lionel alone.

'Forgive me, but I must go and prepare myself for tomorrow.'

'That sounds intriguing. What on earth does the morrow hold?' asks Lionel.

Harriet supposes it is unease that moves him to employ such archaic language.

'The morrow—' she stresses the word deliberately and earns a frown from Hester '—promises a hike up a mountain, followed by strenuous artwork trying to capture something of the beauty of nature. That's according to the esteemed Gervais.' Gervais is their highly talented but ineffectual tutor, for whom the whole experience of trying to impart a glimmer of his own abilities to his class is manifestly proving a wearisome burden. He struggles to mask his appalled reactions to most of the students' work. 'It did say no experience required,' Harriet had hissed at one of her fellow students who, like her, was finding the experience a mixture of shame and hilarity. 'Yes, but not no experience gained,' Mary had hissed back; they had dissolved into stifled giggles at the back of the class, a position that Harriet fears serves as a metaphor for the pair of them for the entire course.

Lionel makes a valiant attempt to get her to stay: 'But the night is young, Harry! Do have a digestif, at least.' *Harry?!* When did she invite him to call her Harry? She glares at Hester, who is carefully inspecting the backs of her hands. But she is torn: she doesn't want the evening to end on a sour note and an Armagnac might restore the balance. On the other hand, despite Lionel's blandishments, Hester appears quite indifferent to as to whether Harriet stays or goes. Or has Hester's invitation to Lionel been a ruse to ensure she doesn't have to be alone with her sister? Suddenly, she is tired of the whole situation. Pleading fatigue, she declines Lionel's offer and makes her stiff adieu, conscious of their eyes on her retreating back as she makes for the foyer.

'We're off to the bar,' one of her new painting acquaintances calls over to her as she comes out of the restaurant. 'Care to join us?'

'Oh.' Harriet hesitates. She really would like a drink and the group is a good mix of personalities. But having just refused Lionel's invitation . . .

'Oh, come on. We can all get a bit wasted and slag off Gervais,' says Guy, a balding accountant from Surrey, here on holiday with his extremely attractive—and artistic—wife, Bella. She now loops her arm through Harriet's and frogmarches her towards the bar and a large

Vecchia Romagna—'No, you absolutely may not have an Armagnac—
we're in *Italy*! Shame on you!'—and a little light grilling about Lionel.

'Is it a holiday romance?'

'Bella!' says Guy with mock severity. 'Don't be so nosy. Look,
Harriet's embarrassed.'

'No, she's not. You're not, are you, Harriet?'

Harriet shrugs but keeps her counsel. 'The only thing I'm embarrassed about is the standard of my painting,' she says.

'Join the club,' says Guy morosely. 'I thought doing this course
might bring the pair of us closer together, but all it's done is prove
to me what I always suspected.' Bella starts laughing and tries to put
her hand over her husband's mouth, anticipating what is to follow. He
is considerably taller than her and easily fights her off. 'That I am a
talentless drone and she, my wife, the light of my miserable life, is a
refulgent star glittering in the company of the greats.'

'Stop it!' says Bella with a snort.

'Did you or did you not say my attempt at water lilies bore more
than a passing resemblance to fried eggs floating on a sea of oil?'

'I would be delighted if I could draw even a fried egg.' Harriet,
relaxing, starts to laugh. 'I hadn't realised until now how hopeless I am
at anything artistic.'

'Ah, but,' says Bella, whom Harriet now realises is more than a little
inebriated, 'the thing is, the only thing that really matters: are you
having a good time?'

'I am, actually,' says Harriet, surprising herself. 'Well, I am *now*.'

'Then who cares?' shouts Bella. 'Who gives a flying f—'

'Bella!' Guy's hand is clamped over his wife's mouth, his face a perfect
picture of feigned outrage. Bella winks at Harriet, struggles free of his
restraint and mouths a careful 'sorry' before turning back to signal to
the barman. Guy puts out a cautionary hand, then withdraws it.

'We don't get away often,' he says quietly to Harriet, as though
asking her pardon. He looks lovingly over at his wife. 'Our little lad,
Jack. Down's. My parents are looking after him for the week.'

'Ah,' says Harriet softly, suddenly sober. 'Sorry.'

'Don't be. We aren't. It's just, once in a while, we both need a break. Kick over the traces. You know.'

'Yes,' says Harriet, aware that she doesn't know, can't begin to know, nobody can. But it puts a lot of things in perspective. She drains her glass. 'I'll leave you to your lovely wife, then. Thanks for the company. And the drink.' She squeezes Guy's upper arm and he bends down to give her a swift peck on the cheek. He smells of wood shavings, vanilla and wine. Nice.

''Night, Bella,' Harriet calls, but Bella is deep in conversation with the barman. Guy rolls his eyes and sketches a wave, then goes to join her.

As Harriet slips across the foyer on the way to her room, she sees out of the corner of her eye the last two diners in the restaurant, heads bent close together, deep in conversation.

CHAPTER 10

'Sorry,' says Hester, reaching for her glass. Lionel dribbles the last few drops of wine into it. His own glass is still half full. He holds the bottle aloft.

'Another?'

Hester shakes her head. 'Better not.'

'Sorry for what?'

Hester pulls a face, flicking a glance across the restaurant. 'My sister.'

'Oh, Hester, really there's no need . . .'

'She was barely civil.'

'No, come now, that's not fair. After all, I think I put her back up, didn't I? Calling her Harry.'

Hester barks a laugh. 'A bit. Close friends and family only, you see.'

'Oh dear.'

Hester leans across to squeeze his hand. 'Honestly, don't worry about it. She's been in a peculiar mood for weeks and was just looking for something to take offence about. If it hadn't been you, it would have been something I said.' She smiles reassuringly but a little worm of guilt wriggles inside: she knows she's being treacherous to her sister. Harriet has her moments, to be sure, but is of a far more equable disposition than Hester herself and doesn't easily take offence; Hester recognises her own culpability in her sister's present unhappiness.

'Perhaps I ought not to have joined you for dinner?'

'No, not at all. Don't be silly. It was a pleasure.'

'I'd hate to put anyone's nose out of joint, least of all your sister's. It must be tricky for you, though.'

'For me? How?'

'Well—forgive me—but I get the impression that she's used to having you to herself.'

'We're not married to each other!' says Hester with some of her usual tartness. He's making Harriet sound like a clingy toddler.

'No, no, no . . . I apologise. I didn't mean to suggest—'

'Lionel, do forgive me. No, no. Please. I was very sharp. It's just—' oh, the perfidy! '—I feel sort of responsible for her.'

'Well, of course! You mustn't blame yourself. It's only natural you would be protective towards her and it does you credit but might I suggest there may be a smidgeon of—dare I say it?—jealousy involved?' Lionel's face flushes at his presumption.

'Jealousy?' stammers Hester, staring at him in disbelief. 'You mean . . .?'

He sits back. 'Oh no . . . Hester, my dear,' (she doesn't miss the endearment), 'I don't mean *me*. Not about *me*! Good heavens, no; I wouldn't dare flatter myself. I meant with your talents, your purpose . . . perhaps she feels—has always felt—a little overawed?'

Hester drops her gaze, inspects the tablecloth, rolls the stem of her wineglass between her fingers. Perhaps that's it. Perhaps Lionel, in his diffident way, has hit the nail on the head. It assuages her guilt to think so. For who, after all, does not relish a little flattery from time to time? She supposes she is a natural leader; her career successes attest to that. The older sister, the role model . . . Fragments of their childhood float into focus: Harriet always following in Hester's wake, the acolyte. All of which makes her conduct, her duplicity, the harder to stomach . . .

'Hester?'

'Mmm?' Lionel's concern draws her back to the present.

'I'm so sorry. Have I upset you? Perhaps I ought not to have—'

Hester waves his anxiety away. 'Oh for goodness' sake, let's stop talking about my wretched sister and enjoy the moment!'

Lionel beams with relief. 'I'm all for that. Shall we go through to the bar?'

Hester seizes the initiative. *You're a long time dead*, she can almost hear her father growling.

'Won't it be rather crowded? I just happen to have a bottle of Remy in my room, if you're game.'

'Oh, I'm game,' says Lionel. 'I'm most definitely game.'

〜〜〜

Harriet punches her pillow yet again in an attempt to wrestle it into shape. Curious how pillows can morph from supreme comfort one minute into a lumpy clump the next. She snuggles down irritably into the hot sheets and tries to immerse herself once more in her book, but for some reason Jackson Brodie is failing to charm, despite the lightness of Kate Atkinson's touch. She tosses her Kindle aside and pads over to the window to edge the shutter open. Below, at the bottom of the terrace, a couple are embracing, arms around each other's shoulders as they look out over the valley, their heads haloed in the light from the garden torches. At this distance, and without her glasses, she cannot distinguish their identity—not that it matters; it's their closeness that irks. Snatches of indecipherable conversation drift up, accompanied by the occasional shout of laughter from the bar. Harriet curses Hester, curses Lionel, curses the heedless couples, smug in their coupledom. It's not often that she feels sorry for herself, but tonight she's at a particularly low ebb, so totally at odds with Hester, the holiday that was meant to bring them closer together appearing to have quite the opposite effect. Jim has been much in her thoughts ever since they arrived, that long-ago trip to Venice conjured by the warmth and smell of Italy and now burning bright in her memory, along with the feel of his strong, dry hand in hers. She manages her widowhood well enough usually, and it's been a while since she has missed him so painfully; she knows her present ache is exacerbated by Hester and her new companion, but that awareness doesn't ease the wound. In a tiny, shameful part of her heart, she feels aggrieved that it is her prickly sister who, unaccountably, seems to have captured Lionel's affections. A tear leaks out; she brushes it away angrily and retreats to her mussed bed, to lie for hours staring sightless into the darkness.

~~~

'This is very nice,' says Lionel.

'The Remy or my bedroom?' says Hester coquettishly, enjoying the novelty of a man's company.

Lionel wags a finger. 'You're a dark horse, Hester.'

'Hetty,' says Hester, bestowing a rare honour on him did he but realise. 'Do you make a habit of this?'

'What do you mean?'

'Chatting up strange women.'

'Is that what I'm doing? And are you? Strange?'

'You should probably ask—' she had been about to say *Harriet*, but swiftly corrects herself '—my friends.'

'And how would they describe you, do you imagine?'

Hester thinks for a moment. 'Forthright, waspish, opinionated . . .'

'Irresistible,' says Lionel, laughing.

The bedrooms at Il Santuario, while luxuriously appointed, are not designed for entertaining. Once the single armchair is occupied, the only other place to sit is the bed; Hester had initially perched on the edge, nursing her tooth mug of brandy, then, as they got comfortable and lost their inhibitions, she had kicked off her shoes and shuffled herself up the bed to lean against the headboard, cushioned by pillows. The situation reminds her of her university days: the hours spent in lengthy disquisitions on life, ambition, the future, fuelled largely by black coffee and the occasional cigarette. Oh, the agonies of those juvenile love affairs, the terrible, terrible poetry written at dead of night after too much dirt-cheap supermarket plonk (any amount was too much, she recalls, still able to conjure its horrible metallic aftertaste). What privileged self-indulgence!

'Did you go to university?'

'Alas, no,' says Lionel. 'We weren't that sort of family. Straight to work as soon as possible, wage packet on the table Friday evening, pocket money doled out by my mother, who held the purse strings very, very tightly.'

'Good grief,' says Hester. 'It sounds positively Lawrentian.'

Lionel laughs. 'What, tin baths and coal dust? Not exactly. My father was an insurance clerk. Not very romantic.'

'But you escaped.'

'After a fashion. Although I'm not sure it was much of an escape, becoming an actuary.'

'Steady, though. Secure.'

'And dull, dull, dull. It's why I love cooking. The risks. The uncertainty!'

'Going off-recipe?'

'Exactly! Breaking the rules. Experimenting. Living dangerously.'

'You could bungee-jump. Abseil. Go white-water rafting.'

Lionel grimaces. 'God, no. Substituting crème fraîche for yogurt is about as daring as I get. Not like you.'

'Me?'

'All that business with . . . Dara, is it?'

'Daria.'

'I mean, that was terrifying.'

'Yes,' says Hester. 'Yes, it was.' A memory of her assault by Teddy Wilson—of all unlikely villains—in her own home assails her. She shudders. Her phone buzzes in her bag. As she reaches for it, Lionel checks his watch.

'Late,' he says. 'I hope it's nothing urgent.'

Hester checks the message, goes pale, inhales deeply. 'Sorry,' she says automatically, before painstakingly replying, spelling out each letter separately.

Lionel leans towards her, smiling at her ineptitude. 'Don't you use predictive text?'

Hester shakes her head, frowning, rereading her message on the screen, while shielding it with her other hand.

'Everything all right?'

She hesitates.

'Hetty?'

Hester sends the text, then weighs the phone in her hand, mouth drawn. 'How do you know you're doing the right thing?'

'About what?' Lionel is mystified. 'Is there a problem? Can I help?'

She sighs wearily.

'A trouble shared . . .' says Lionel.

'I think I might be about to make the biggest mistake of my life,' says Hester, voicing at last the worry that has dogged her for weeks. 'I might. But I can't just sit back and do nothing!' She turns to Lionel, her face stormy with anxiety and anger, eyes bright with unshed tears. The longing to unburden herself is unbearable.

'Suppose,' he says gently, reaching for her hand and closing his own around it, 'suppose you tell me what's going on, eh?'

And Hester, grateful, apprehensive, and just a little bit tight, does.

WEDNESDAY

CHAPTER 11

'Morning!'

Regina Pegg marches purposefully over to where Harriet is sitting on a boulder in the hotel garden, tying the laces on her hiking boots. Well, she may call them hiking boots but they're actually indeterminate footwear of uncertain provenance bought at a knockdown price at the local nursery. For two women with little interest in the garden, she and Hester spend a surprising amount of time at nurseries, pottering about and buying plants haphazardly, plants that rarely survive much more than a week once brutally wrenched from their cosseted environment and roughly transplanted into their neglected flowerbeds. They are, however, suckers for the bargain bins at such establishments, as these boots bear witness.

'Golly!' exclaims Regina. 'Frightfully bright, aren't they? Not much chance of getting lost in those!'

Harriet inspects the virulent green boots with orange go-faster stripes along the sides more closely now Regina has drawn attention to them. They are admittedly pretty hideous; their saving grace, however, is that they are remarkably comfortable. 'Not a pretty sight, I confess,' she murmurs. 'Still, they do the job.'

'That's the ticket,' says Regina heartily, hefting her rucksack onto her back. 'How's that sister of yours enjoying bashing the old pots and pans?' Regina possesses an uncanny ability to worm out everyone's life histories within seconds of meeting them that puts Harriet in mind of Peggy Verndale. In fact, with her ample bosom, wiry grey hair and capable hands, she bears a striking resemblance to Hester and Harriet's bridge foe: she bets Regina plays a mean game herself.

'Loving it,' says Harriet, grunting with the effort of securing the second boot. These days she's finding it increasingly difficult first thing in the morning to bend much past her knees.

'Give it here,' says Regina, hoisting Harriet's leg up between her thighs like a horse's hoof and deftly knotting the lace. 'It's a right bugger getting old, isn't it?' she says cheerfully, dropping the leg with as little ceremony. 'Need a hand to wipe our bums before we know where we are.' She changes tack without a breath. 'I see your sister's thick as thieves with that rather natty Lionel. Good for her, eh? Oh well, best be off. I see Sir's on the march.' As Harriet levers herself gingerly to her feet, Regina is already striding after their tutor, alpenstocks biting into the path purposefully. Harriet notes with a smile that it has taken Regina mere seconds to start a conversation with another of the would-be painters, Mary Martindale. She won't know what's hit her.

The lengthy walk to their painting spot this morning allows her once more to reflect on the events of the previous evening. Not that the bulk of the night hadn't been spent in much the same way. She had finally dropped off about four, plunging vertiginously into nightmarish dreams of Hester pushing her violently off her feet, while Daria, Artem and Lionel, inexplicably holding Milo, sneered from the sidelines. She had been relieved that their outing necessitated an early breakfast, so she had not had to encounter Hester—and undoubtedly Lionel, her constant shadow—so far today.

'Glorious, isn't it?' says Bella, drawing abreast, Guy on her other side. The younger woman turns her face up to the sun; Harriet notices the tiny crow's feet beside her eyes and a fine tracery of veins on her cheeks. She must be older than Harriet first thought. Bella lays a hand on Harriet's arm. 'Sorry about last night,' she says with a little laugh. 'I got a tiny bit smashed. I'm in the doghouse this morning.'

Harriet glances over at Guy, who winks before turning a censorious face towards his wife. 'Disgraceful,' he says with a poor attempt at gruffness, before giving Bella an awkward hug. They both stumble on the uneven path.

'Steady,' Bella warns. 'Harriet will think I'm still pissed. I promise you, I haven't had a drop since breakfast.'

Guy rolls his eyes.

Harriet feels inexplicably emotional.

~~~

They stop for coffee in a little hillside village, the only café opening on to the tiny square, shaded by gnarled olive trees; across the cobbles, an ancient crumbling stone fountain rimed with moss trickles fitfully.

'Gosh.' Panting, Harriet flops into a rickety metal chair. 'How much further is it? I'm not used to all this yomping.'

'Yomping? This is a mere stroll,' bellows Regina. 'Goodness me, Harriet, you should try a sketching holiday in Crete. That would really sort you out!'

Harriet is not the only one of their small party to blench; Mary, out of Regina's line of sight, pulls an appalled face, while Bella draws her hand swiftly across her throat and nods in Regina's direction.

'What's so funny?' Regina booms as the three women erupt with laughter.

'Nothing,' splutters Bella. 'I think we're all a little light-headed from the altitude.'

'Wimps!' cries Regina good-naturedly, on her way into the gloom of the unlit café in search of a lavatory.

'We ought to be ashamed of ourselves, being so unkind,' whispers Mary, staring after Regina, her contrition somewhat undermined by her gleeful grin.

'Nonsense.' Bella is unabashed. 'She gives as good as she gets. She's a real sweetheart under all that bombast. Anyway, Harriet's right. I'm absolutely knackered already. I signed up for painting, not The Long March.'

Gervais, who had plonked himself in a chair with his back to everyone on their arrival, is unable to ignore his pupils any longer; from under his panama, he growls, 'Fifteen minutes from here. You'll thank me when we get there.' He shrinks back into his jacket, tugging the collar around his neck and muttering to himself (but not so quietly that they cannot hear), 'Pathetic.'

⌣⌣

The view is spectacular; Gervais hadn't been exaggerating. The wide valley lies before them in a multitude of subtle greens; distant red-roofed stone farm buildings surrounded by umbrella pines pepper a steep hillside; rows of vines crisscross the landscape. The sun sparkles on a small lake barely visible in the late-morning haze, the air heavy with the resinous scent of the cedars that line the crooked roads beneath them. Fragments of an aqueduct punctuate the horizon like a run of decaying teeth.

'Just sketch your initial impressions—pencils only at this stage,' Gervais calls out brusquely, as though affronted by the necessity of instructing his charges. 'I'll be round in due course to have a look at what you've done. Remember what I explained yesterday about landscape composition.'

Regina wastes no time in erecting her portable easel and settling down on her collapsible stool. The other artists obediently set to. Sketchpads emerge from rucksacks and cloth bags, pencils and charcoal are readied and, tentatively at first but with growing confidence and verve, lines and whorls, shade and delineation start to mar the virgin paper. Gervais stamps off to a spot as far from his little group as he can manage without losing sight of them altogether, grunting, 'Less is more,' before cloaking himself in a solitude that no-one dares disturb.

I'm glad this cost me so little, Harriet thinks irritably, having been offered, unasked, a substantial discount by Alfonso 'to make up the numbers' when deciding which activity to pursue. She is beginning to suspect that this particular course, far from being the select group Alfonso so beguilingly described, is in fact composed of unfortunates only now becoming fully cognisant of their tutor's idiosyncrasies.

Mary spreads out a small rug and invites Harriet, Guy and Bella to share it, but Harriet demurs with thanks, preferring to climb a little higher to take advantage of the shade offered by a rocky outcrop. She kicks aside some cigarette butts, a Pellegrino bottle and a ball of cling film littering the dusty ground, then cautiously lowers herself onto her bottom. The boulder offers support of sorts for her back. She tugs her sketchpad and pencils out of her knapsack and opens the pad to a blank sheet. Her pencil hovers over the page. And remains hovering.

One of the many quirks of advancing age Harriet has come to accept, however reluctantly, is the tendency to overdramatise. During her long teaching career, she had always secretly prided herself on her no-nonsense handling of potentially serious situations. Young people had never alarmed or discomfited her as they had so many of her colleagues; their irrational rages, and occasional eruptions into abuse or violence, she knew were prompted mainly by fear: of an unfamiliar situation, of appearing small in front of their peers, of lacking the wherewithal to respond rationally to a perceived threat. So Harriet had become by default the member of staff most frequently called on to defuse a possible or actual confrontation. Perhaps it was her motherly approach, perhaps her diminutive stature, perhaps her apparent fearlessness—whatever the reason, she would wade in without a second thought, separate the would-be miscreants and demand an immediate cessation of hostilities. And generally succeed. Huge testosterone-fuelled youths would meekly desist at Harriet's firm intervention, sheepishly ambling away to cool off, accompanied by their equally chastened mates; the extravagant threats of teenage girls, high on bravado, bitchiness and—increasingly in recent years—alcohol or worse, would drain away in the face of Mrs Pearson's grim disapproval. And more often than not, those same troublemakers would surface in later years as respectable and biddable citizens, greeting Harriet warmly if their paths crossed.

But the persona she had created and cultivated in her career has slowly, year on year, eroded in retirement. At times, she attributes this to both her loss of profession and of spouse, as if Jim had provided some unacknowledged backbone to her own resolve. She is more circumspect these days, avoiding conflict in the main and leaving most battles to her more combative sister. Injustice and prejudice still rouse her liberal soul, except that that these days her responses are more muted, less hot-headed. The iniquities of politicians revealed in the media or through their own maladroit words continue to prompt outbursts at the paper or the radio, but her days of active protest are long gone. Or so it feels. And with this growing powerlessness, imagined or real, certain events can assume irrational proportions. As now. Seated on an Italian hillside, surrounded on all sides by evidence of her personal good fortune, Harriet feels nothing short of despair. Were she younger, she might attribute her present mood to the vagaries of her hormones, but surely all that emotional and physical upheaval is now firmly behind her?

The speed with which Hester seems to have succumbed to Lionel's charms—and she is not blind to his attractiveness herself—alarms her. She wonders if Hester's behaviour is in part a provocation, a response to their ongoing estrangement, but at the same time her innate fairness acknowledges that there is no reason why her sister should not enjoy a romantic adventure. Nothing in the decision to share their lives following the loss of their husbands had precluded a love life—for either of them. And while Harriet has not met anyone to set her heart alight since Jim's death, Hester's previous fondness for Teddy Wilson, despite his appalling reputation and manifest untrustworthiness, suggests that under her snippy exterior lies an openness to the possibility of love. There, she's articulated it: love. She ought to be rejoicing for her sister if so, not drowning in self-pity. Even as she acknowledges this, her eyes fill.

As is increasingly her wont, her mind leaps ahead. Suppose this is more than a holiday romance? Suppose Lionel is as susceptible to the lure of a relationship as Hester seems to be? Suppose he too is seeking companionship, closeness, something more than friendship . . .

The sun has moved around; her little piece of shade has shrunk to almost nothing, leaving her squinting in the brightness, the suspicion of a headache nagging away beside her right eye. She ferrets in her bag for her sunhat, then remembers seeing it lying at the foot of her bed that morning. Damn. The inside pocket produces a dog-eared Nurofen packet: empty. A tear trembles in the corner of her eye.

'You okay?' Mary staggers up the slope, sketchpad in hand. 'Gervais is finally doing his rounds so I thought I'd scarper before he got to me. God, he's a misery! How's it going?'

'It isn't,' says Harriet, rubbing the tear away swiftly with the heel of her hand and blinking furiously. 'Gosh, it's making my eyes water, this sun. Bright, isn't it?'

Mary drops down beside her. 'I love it. After the winter we've had . . . Mind, there's still the odd cloud.' She points across the valley to a clutch of wispy clouds threaded through the blue. 'Anyway, I've just decided to stop mithering about my total lack of talent. I'm a lost cause.' She holds up her rudimentary sketch in evidence. Harriet takes one look at the muddle of lines and shapes and starts laughing. Mary joins in.

'Let's see yours, then.'

Harriet displays the blank pad. Their laughter redoubles, nudging Harriet's headache into the background.

'Forgot my damned hat.'

Mary tuts. 'You'll have Regina on your back, you naughty girl.' She laughs again, but when Harriet does not join in, she turns and peers into her face, before saying, 'Always takes everyone by surprise.'

'What does?'

'People falling for one another at our age.'

'Oh!' says Harriet, startled by her companion's directness.

Mary continues blithely 'Seems slightly indecent. Don't know why, really—feelings don't stop as you get older.'

'Er . . . no, I suppose not.' Harriet's discomfiture increases but Mary continues with a rueful smile, 'I promise you they don't.' She scuffs her feet in the dust.

'Can I tell you something?' she asks, as though she's just reached a decision.

Harriet tenses. She's not sure she's up to someone else's confidences right now. Mary hugs her knees and turns to look into Harriet's eyes. *She's really rather pretty*, thinks Harriet, taking in the faded blonde hair, the blue eyes, the quirky smile. *I wonder why I didn't notice that before.*

Mary says, 'I'll tell you my secret. You tell me yours.'

'I don't have a secret.'

''Course you do. Everyone has secrets. Okay, then. If not a secret, then tell me what's bothering you.' Without waiting for a response, she says, 'I'm having an affair. With my neighbour. It's been going on for two years.'

Harriet flounders for an appropriate response for a moment, since Mary's quizzical look seems to be inviting one. 'Are you married?' is the best she can muster, prompting an immediate thought: *What does that matter?*

'Yes.'

'Is he?' Harriet's not sure why that's important: she has no intention of judging Mary either way.

'She. Yes.'

84

'Oh!'

Mary laughs, a rich, deep-throated laugh, her hand up to her mouth. 'Have I shocked you?' She watches with amusement as Harriet digests the information.

'No...' says Harriet uncertainly. 'Surprised me, I think.'

'I know,' says Mary, unfazed. 'I look like a proper little hausfrau, don't I? All WI and homemade cakes. I was as surprised as you obviously are when it happened. So was Rhona. But, oh, Harriet, the joy of it! You have no idea!' She stops. 'You haven't, have you?'

'What? Oh,' says Harriet, realising. 'No, I haven't. Not that I ...'

'No, well,' says Mary cheerfully, 'that's why I told you. I just needed to tell someone. Thanks.' She sighs happily and then without any warning yells at the top of her lungs, 'Life is too bloody short! Seize the day!' Her shout echoes around the valley, followed by a cry from below: 'Are you okay up there?' Slightly shamefaced, Mary gets up and shuffles over to the ledge's lip and waves down reassuringly, then returns to sit beside Harriet. She grins. 'Frightened the pants off them. Nothing beats a good old yell, trust me. There. The heavens didn't fall in. Your turn now.'

Harriet stalls. 'Why did you come on holiday by yourself?'

Mary screws up her face to the sun. 'Thinking time.'

'Oh?'

'Things are coming to a head. The kids are all settled, don't need us any more. Time to regroup. Consider the options.'

'And have you?'

Mary's trainer kicks a pebble away. 'I think so.'

Harriet waits.

'Nope,' says Mary, grinning. 'Not ready to say it just yet. Not out loud. Your go.'

Harriet shakes her head.

'Okay, then,' says Mary. 'I'll make an educated guess. You're scared.'

'Mary, I—'

'I know; I should mind my own business. But I like you, Harriet. I think under different circumstances, we might be friends.' She registers Harriet's frown. 'I mean, if we hadn't simply met on holiday. Chances are, we'll never see each other ever again after this little interlude. So—' she shrugs '—you're unhappy and that saddens me.'

'I can't see why.'

'Jesus, you *are* having a wallow, aren't you? No, don't get on your high horse. It's your sister, isn't it? All I'm saying is, give her a chance. Let her have her bit of fun. God knows how few chances we get at our age. Possibilities shrink by the minute.' She glances sideways at Harriet. 'I'll shut up now.'

Silence falls, but it's not uncomfortable. Below them, they hear the light buzz of voices, presumably Gervais skewering some hapless student.

'You're right,' admits Harriet reluctantly. 'I think perhaps I'm jealous.'

'I didn't say that.'

'No, not jealous exactly. Frightened, I suppose. I've suddenly realised that the things I took for granted—well, they're not as solid as I'd thought. I don't begrudge Hester a chance of fun, of happiness—'

'Good.'

'All I'm saying is, it's made me think about . . . what it might mean. You know, if it were serious . . . Hester and I live together, you see.'

'Ah. I didn't know that. That complicates matters.'

'And I can't help worrying—'

'Harriet,' says Mary, laying a hand on her arm. 'One day at a time. They only met on Sunday! Whatever happens, you'll cope. You know that deep down.' Harriet shrugs noncommittally. 'Don't be such a Cassandra! Face your fears. Think about alternatives. Trust me, the worst thing you can do is let your worries control your life. Take control. Carpe diem.'

'Oh, I know . . .' says Harriet unconvinced, yet grateful for her companion's concern.

Mary struggles to her feet and holds out a hand to help Harriet up. 'Come on, you. Enough soul-searching. We can't hide away forever. Time to go down and face the music.'

As they slip and slide back down the dusty path to join the others, her headache surging back, Harriet wonders whose music Mary has in mind: Gervais's or her sister's?

CHAPTER 12

If Ben thought he had problems before, they were nothing to the potential catastrophe now on his hands.

'Shall I wash these for the weekend?'

Ben, unkindly wrenched from sleep at dawn (well, ten thirty), had groaned and shielded his eyes from the cruel sunlight pouring into his room from the landing window. His mother was standing in the doorway to his bedroom, ringed in brilliance, her features unreadable.

'Wash what?' he had mumbled.

His mother had waved a pair of his jeans—his best jeans, a pair of extremely tight-fitting Diesels—at him. 'These, darling. They really could do with it.' Isabelle holds them away from her with an expression of distaste.

Ben, befuddled as he was, was able to do a quick calculation. 'They'll be dry by Friday night, yeah?'

'Oh, darling, now don't be difficult. You're not wearing these on Friday night!'

Ben's stomach flipped. How the fuck did she know about Friday?

'Why not?' he croaked.

Isabelle sounded uncharacteristically firm. 'I'm not having any nonsense, Ben, so don't start. You are not wearing jeans to Auntie Lynn's do. You will wear those nice chinos we got you at Christmas and that Ralph Lauren shirt.'

And with that she had pulled his bedroom door shut with, Ben thought, unnecessary force, leaving him curled into a ball of misery.

Auntie fucking Lynn! She's not even a real aunt; she's just one of his mother's close friends who's having some sort of party for her birthday. How could he have forgotten? His parents have been wittering on about it for weeks: Isabelle has, God help them, volunteered to provide a dish for the festivities. Please, please, please, let it not be her Coronation Chicken.

And it's not just that the party is on Friday—it's much worse than that. 'We can make a weekend of it,' his father had said brightly all those months ago when the invitation arrived. He and Isabelle had spent a happy evening scrolling through websites in search of what George considered 'a good deal', plumping eventually for a gloomy country house outside Bakewell. 'Excellent walking country!' he had exclaimed excitedly. 'And, Ben, look, they even have a swimming pool!' He had revealed this facility with great glee; Ben, looking over his shoulder, had been treated to the sight of an ancient pool, shrouded by trees, with a wonky diving board hanging forlornly over the leaf-strewn water. Even at the time he had regarded the whole weekend with dread and had promptly consigned it to the back of his mind, as he did anything he wanted to avoid. Except now it had come back to bite him, and with particularly sharp teeth. How crap is it that Auntie Lynn's party should be taking place on this very Friday, the one day in his life when he might at last get close—perhaps very close—to the object of all his desires? How is he supposed to remember the date of every shitty thing his idiot parents try to inflict on him? Somehow, he's got to come up with a reason why he has to stay behind.

⌣⌣⌣

'Studying?' hisses Jez into his phone, fully aware of his mother's scrutiny through the patio doors. Other people may underestimate Deirdre Nairstrom, misled by the blonde hair, the ditzy manner and flamboyant clothes. But not her husband, and not her sons. She's as shrewd an operator as Brian, controlling her small but extremely lucrative interior design company with absolute ruthlessness. Now, scarlet nails cradling a mug of coffee, she is staring implacably at her offspring as he wanders down the gravel path deep in conversation. Jez turns his back on her. 'You could always say you've, like, promised to come over to mine to go over something together. My lot will be out at this poxy dance thing.'

'Like what?' whispers Ben from under his duvet. 'We're not even doing the same subjects!' He keeps an ear out for his mother; he wouldn't put it past her to be lurking around outside his bedroom door. Anyway, he's none too sure she or his father would be persuaded that any useful educational purpose would be served by Ben and Jez revising together; on the one occasion George and Isabelle had found themselves at the same social event as Jez's parents, Brian Nairstrom had spent their entire short conversation banging on about both his sons' slothfulness and the improbability of either of them having the gumption to succeed him in his multi-million-pound IT business.

'We are so! English, French and maths.'

'Yeah, but I don't need any help with them, do I, you knob?! It's the sciences I'm struggling with, dickhead, and you're only doing biology—and you're crap at that, anyway.'

'Ta very much,' says Jez hotly. 'Just trying to help. Look, you gotta come up with something or we'll have to go ahead without you.'

Ben goes cold. 'You can't do that! Jesus! Anyway, you haven't got a key.'

Jez sniggers. 'Don't need a key, you div. Ryan's coming, in't he?'

Ben goes even colder. Ryan Riddell is famed for his ability to pick locks, having once accepted a challenge to open every locker in the changing room in under ten minutes. He'd done it in five. Ben fights his way up through his tangled sheets to gulp in some slightly less foetid air. He cocks an ear towards the door. Silence.

'You know what, Jez? You are so not helping. 'Course I'm gonna be there! No way am I not gonna be there, am I? I just gotta think of something.'

'Good luck with that, loser.' Jez snickers. 'Let me know how it goes.' For a split second, he contemplates updating Ben on numbers, then thinks better of it. Ben'd only go mental.

CHAPTER 13

'Where the hell is she?' hisses Hester, peering around the foyer and down the corridors that radiate off it. 'Did you check the garden again?'

Lionel nods, his face creased with concern. 'No sign of her. Hester, my dear, you really mustn't upset yourself. I'm sure she'll be here any minute.'

'Yes, well, she's not the only one!'

'Would you like a drink?'

'Just water,' says Hester abstractedly, head swivelling anxiously. 'Ah! Alfonso!' as the manager appears behind the reception desk. 'Thank heavens. Have you seen my sister, by any chance?'

The Italian, suave as ever today in a crisp striped shirt, designer jeans and loafers, checks his watch. 'Due back very shortly, *signora*.' He smiles winningly, teeth dazzling in his tanned face.

'Back?'

'*Sì*. Today is the mountain outing.' At Hester's frown, 'Foothills, really. We say mountains to make it more ... impressive. In the brochure, yes? But still, quite a climb. The painters always come back exhausted. But happy!' When his smile fails to elicit one in return, he says solicitously, 'There is a problem? Can I help?'

'No, no,' says Hester. 'It's just I'd forgotten ...'

'About the trip?'

'Yes. She did mention it, but we didn't see Harriet at breakfast this morning.'

Alfonso, never one to miss a clue, registers the 'we'. These English can be surprisingly fast workers. He tries to catch Lionel's eye—no harm in giving him a congratulatory nod, one man to another—but his guest is now anxiously scanning the entrance for the party's imminent return.

The reception phone rings. 'Excuse me, *signora*, *signor*.' He lifts the receiver. '*Pronto*.' Starts. Raises a hand in alarm.

'Please. Please. Signora Pegg, more slowly, please. Again, if you will . . . Yes . . . Yes . . . And the others? Okay. To be clear then. Signora Martindale, *sì*? And Signora Pearson?'

Hester spins around at the sound of her sister's name.

'What? What is it? What's happened?'

Alfonso's finger goes up to silence her. 'Okay, okay. Thank you. I will pass on the news. The minibus should be with you—' he checks the clock opposite '—in ten minutes. I am on my way too.' He swiftly replaces the phone in its cradle, free hand reaching behind him for the car keys. 'Signora Greene, I am very sorry, I have to go . . .'

Lionel strides over to Hester's side, puts a hand under her elbow. She feels the blood draining from her face.

'What?! What's happened?'

He is already running towards the car park as he calls over his shoulder, 'I'm afraid there's been an accident.'

〜〜〜

Mary is holding Harriet's hand. Clutching it. She has been since the moment when, twisting on the narrow path in mid-conversation, she'd lost her footing, reached out instinctively for anchorage and, pulling Harriet after her, tumbled down the almost vertical slope, their fall arrested only by a narrow ledge a dozen or so feet below the path. Harriet shivers recalling the sickening crunch of Mary's head on the protruding boulder; the stunned silence that followed before the panicky shouts from above.

They are now waiting for the ambulance; thank heavens Regina, a frequent visitor to Italy, knew the emergency number and had rung 118 immediately. Guy is hugging a distraught Bella, her face buried in his shoulder, while Regina chivvies the others into moving away out of sight of the two women on the ledge below them. Gervais stands to one side, out of his depth, distracted and ineffectual. Mary's hand tightens on hers; her lips move.

'What?' says Harriet, her headache spearing her skull with shafts of astonishing pain. She feels sick, her tongue too big for her mouth. Water would be a mercy. Mary murmurs something again but Harriet cannot decipher what she is saying; instead she tries to quieten her with comforting noises, conscious of the need to stay perfectly still, all the while clutching Mary's slight body to her. She watches a tiny spider picks its way up the sheer rock. Distantly, the wail of a siren pierces the late-afternoon quiet; feet shuffle above them on the dusty path in anticipation of help and rescue, little murmurs of relief breaking out.

'I think that's the minibus right behind.' Regina's voice sounds louder than ever, cutting through the silence. 'Let's just move ourselves out of the way.' The scuff of feet on the move. Regina's face looms over the edge, dislodging a trickle of dust and grit. 'Ambulance on its way,' she calls down. 'They'll have you out of there in a jiffy. Hang on.'

There is little else that Mary and Harriet, trapped above a sickening drop to the valley floor far below, can do.

⌣⌣⌣

'She's not answering!' Hester stares impotently at her mobile. 'Lionel, she's not answering!'

Lionel slides into the wrought-iron chair opposite her own and pushes a glass of water across the table. Marco's head pokes out into the garden through a side door for a second, then disappears.

'Marco!' Hester leaps to her feet, knocking the tumbler off the table onto the tiled patio, where it explodes with the impact. 'Go and ask him if there's any news, will you?' she begs, heedless of the shards of glass all around her feet.

Lionel turns to do her bidding, as one of the barmen, alerted by the crash, runs towards them with a cloth and a dustpan and brush. 'Hester, I'm quite sure if he knew anything—'

'Lionel, please! Just go and ask him!'

The waiter bends down to clear up the broken glass, straightening up almost immediately, to exclaim, '*Signora! Sanguini!*' Hester looks down as he gestures at her sandalled feet; dots of blood speckle her skin like tiny, but expanding, rubies. She feels queasy; she's never been good with blood.

'*Scusi . . .*' says the waiter, crunching over the glass with her chair and indicating she should sit. Numbly, she does so, to find Lionel instantly beside her, a voluminous white handkerchief at the ready. He kneels, peers at her feet, removes his glasses, eases her sandals off and, eyes inches from her skin, gingerly begins picking out the slivers of razor-sharp glass. She gives a cry of pain as Lionel teases one adherent fragment out from the fragile skin skimming her bones.

'It's all right,' she gasps, flinching, gagging.

'It's not all right,' mutters Lionel, intent on his task. He eases her foot back into its original position as Hester steels herself for the next extraction.

'Did you—ow!—find him? Marco?'

'No. For goodness' sake, Hester!' From her vantage point above him, Hester notices how thin Lionel's hair is at his crown; the wind catches at it, exposing a patch of pink, freckled scalp. He reaches up a hand automatically and flattens it into place.

Hester tries her phone again. To her indescribable relief, this time it is answered.

'Harry? Oh, thank God! Are you all right?'

The reception is poor, the line crackly.

'It's not Harriet, Hester, it's Regina. Regina Pegg? . . . Can you hear me? I've got Harriet's phone.'

'Well, where is she? I've been ringing and ringing.'

The phone hisses in her ear. '. . . lost her footing and fell . . . ambulance to the hospital . . . said there's no . . . hit her head . . .' More crackling and hissing.

'Hello? Regina? You say Harry's hit her head?'

Totally unintelligible sounds ensue. Then the phone goes dead.

'Aargh!' It feels as if Lionel is searing her foot with a brand. She gulps in air to try to quell the nausea. 'She's hurt, Lionel! She hit her head!'

'This needs a doctor, this foot.'

'Did you hear what I said?'

'Yes. Did you hear what *I* said?'

'Oh, never mind my bloody feet! What are we going to do? Can we get a taxi to the hospital? Can you find out how far away it is?' She realises the waiter is still hovering at her shoulder. 'The hospital—is it far?'

The boy spreads his hands in ignorance. 'I do not live . . .' He gestures at the surroundings. 'Sorry. I go . . .' And before they can protest, he sprints back towards the hotel.

Lionel gets awkwardly to his feet and checks his watch. 'That's the best I can do for now. What time are you expecting—?'

Hester grimaces as her feet meet the gravel. 'Six thirty. What time is it now?'

'Ten to.' Lionel frowns. 'Look, why don't I go to the hospital and you stay here to meet—'

'I can't! I can't stay here! She's my sister, for God's sake! I have to go!'

'But I don't even know—'

'You'll have to explain!' Hester feels everything slipping away. All her careful planning, the secrets she's kept at such cost from Harriet, all seem irrelevant in the face of this calamity. How can everything have gone so wrong so quickly? Unfamiliar tears threaten. She grabs for Lionel's hand, grateful for the warmth of another's skin, yet simultaneously ashamed of her neediness. Why, she barely knows this man!

Lionel encloses her hand in both of his and bends down to look into her face, his own full of solicitude. 'You're right, Hester, of course you are. You must go to Harriet. I'll stay here and wait for—'

The tears spill. Hester dashes them angrily away with her free hand. 'Oh God, thank you. I'm sorry, I'm ... Could you just ...' pointing towards her bloodied feet but managing not quite to look at them, '. . . some plasters ... bandages, anything ...' She takes a ragged breath and manages a weak smile of gratitude. 'Thank heavens you're here, Lionel.'

He hurries towards the hotel reception, smiling faintly.

⌣⌣⌣

Harriet sees a sign reading PRONTO SOCCORSO as the stretcher is whisked through the automatic doors after swift and efficient unloading by the paramedics. Mary is still holding Harriet's hand tightly, her face the colour of putty, eyes closed, lids flickering. They and the medical team hurry down the corridor towards double doors at the end that lead to the emergency treatment rooms. On the threshold, the senior nurse lays a hand on Harriet's arm and shakes her head.

'But . . .'

'No. *Scusi, per favore, signora.*' And before Harriet can respond, the nurse has waved the stretcher through the doorway and is disappearing after it. She's not sure, but amid the clatter of metal, the squeak of wheels on the lino and the urgent commands in Italian, she thinks she hears Mary cry out her name. She realises she is still clutching Mary's bag; feeling the shape of her mobile in an outer pocket, she pulls it out.

⌣⌣⌣

Six twenty. Hester's phone rings as she is being helped across the foyer by Lionel to the waiting taxi. Her feet sport assorted plasters; Lionel has insisted on encasing her right ankle in a bandage. Ridiculous how painful a few cuts can be. She stops and ferrets in her bag.

'Hester?'

'Harry! Oh, thank God! How are you? What's happened? I'm on my way!'

'No, no need. I'm coming back myself.'

'Back?'

'Yes, in the next few minutes. I just need to—'

'They're discharging you? Is that wise?'

'Hetty, I'm fine.'

'But they said you'd had a fall.'

'Not me, Mary. Well, I did fall, but it was Mary who—'

'I thought it was you!' Hester feels a surge of fury: all that panic—guilt, even—about Harriet and she's not even hurt! 'Alfonso said there'd been an accident! He mentioned your name. I thought—'

Harriet says wearily, 'I'll explain when I see you. I'm just waiting to find out if I'm allowed to see Mary before I leave.'

'Never mind Mary! You need to get back here!'

There is a moment's silence on the line as Harriet digests Hester's outburst. Lionel eases Hester to one side as a new guest arrives at the reception desk. The taxi driver hovers outside on the step, the door of the cab open, waiting.

'I'll get back as soon as I can,' says Harriet tonelessly. The least she might have expected is a touch of sympathy. If not for herself, then at least for poor Mary. Why is Hester being so *horrible*?

'Okay. Right. Good. We'll wait for you here then.' Staccato. Unyielding.

We. *Oh no*, thinks Harriet, *not Lionel, not now. I just want my bed, not the continuation of hostilities.* Her head pounds.

'Okay, then. Bye.'

Hester snaps her phone shut. Lionel squeezes her upper arm and whispers in her ear, pointing to a figure behind them.

'Five minutes,' says the doctor, the only one of the team who seems to speak English. He nods towards Mary, diminutive in the large bed. She's hooked up to various wires and monitors; there is a large pad taped to her head just behind her left ear. Her eyelids, veined and bluish, flutter. Harriet bends over her.

'Mary?'

The eyes open slowly. There's a puzzled frown, then a flare of recognition.

'It's Harriet,' says Harriet gently, grasping her hand.

Mary smiles faintly, then looks puzzled as she takes in her unfamiliar surroundings.

'You're in hospital. You had a fall. We both fell. But you're going to be fine,' says Harriet, more robustly than she feels, staring down at this insubstantial, shrunken Mary. 'I ought to get back.'

Mary's eyes darken into panic.

'Is there anything I can do? Ring home?'

Mary's face relaxes a fraction. She tries to speak.

'I've got your phone,' Harriet continues. 'Oh, and your bag. Shall I leave it here, or hang on to it?' She holds it up so Mary can see.

'Keep it . . . please. Call Ron . . . the number's in my phone.' The voice is wispy; Harriet has to lean in to catch the words.

'Okay. I'll do it right away.'

'Tell him . . . not to worry. And Rhona. Ring Rhona, will you? Tell her . . .' Mary closes her eyes for a second. Harriet waits.

Mary's faded blue eyes spring open, glittering. 'Just give her my love.' She squeezes Harriet's hand tightly, then releases it, a shadow of her old self in the crooked smile. 'Carpe diem, remember?'

CHAPTER 14

'Wotcha.'

'Ben!' Daria cries with pleasure, abandoning the washing-up and quickly drying her hands. 'How nice to see you! We think you have forgot us.'

Milo grabs up an orange plastic brick in triumph from the pile around him on the floor and extends it towards Ben.

'Hello, matey.' Ben squats down and takes the offering. 'This for me? Ta.' He ruffles Milo's hair, to the baby's delight. To Daria, 'What d'you mean, forgotten you? I was only here Sunday.'

Daria waggles her forefinger playfully in front of Ben's nose. 'But now is Wednesday and every day Milo cries, "Where is Ben? I want Ben!" You are his favourite person, for sure.'

'Yeah?' Ben could do with some more admirers like Milo: uncomplicated, undemanding. Unquestioning adoration. Unable to talk: even better.

'Busy?'

Daria sweeps a hand around her tiny kitchen; it is, as ever, spotless. 'Of course. I have been cooking—no!' As Ben advances on the rectangular tin by the oven, 'Not ready. Too hot.'

Ben pokes at the lightly browned and uneven cake-like confection. 'What is it?'

'Apple pie, of course.'

Ben scoffs. 'Apple pie! Apple pie is made with pastry, Dar. You know, pastry?'

The girl narrows her eyes angrily. 'Of course I know pastry! This is Belarusian apple pie, idiot. With *antonovka* apples. Except in this country, no-one knows this apple. The man at the shop, he say, use these.' She picks up a Granny Smith. Pulls a face. 'Tch! Not the same. Too sweet. What kind of country has not *antonovka* apples, eh?'

Ben grins. Daria is constantly outraged by the fact that the village shop does not stock Belarusian staples. 'Ought to test it, though, shouldn't we? Make sure it's okay?'

'Test? Test! I no need to test. Is beautiful, of course.'

Ben holds his ground, smirking, knowing that Daria will relent.

She does, snatching up a large knife and swiftly cutting the cake into sixteenths. She levers a corner piece out and slides it onto a plate.

'There! Now tell me is not wonderful!'

Ben takes a huge bite. It is still blisteringly hot. He flaps a hand frantically in front of his mouth as Daria nods with satisfaction and Milo stares up at the agitated visitor in wonderment. At length and with an almighty gulp, Ben finishes the mouthful.

'Well?'

He shrugs carelessly. 'It's okay. I guess.'

'Okay?!' Daria goes to snatch the plate out of his hand, but not before he has managed to grab the rest of the cake. He retreats to the other side of the kitchen to finish it with relish. Milo reaches up a fat hand, wanting a taste.

'Aw, too late, my little mate,' says Ben, dusting the crumbs from his hands. 'Best ask your mum for a slice for your tea.'

'Hmm,' says Daria darkly. 'Milo has had his tea. You are *nyagodnik*. Bad boy, Ben. Bad . . . what is it?'

'Influence?'

'*Tak*. Teaching Milo naughty things.'

'That's me,' says Ben happily.

'Why you are not studying?'

'Give us a break, Dar! Been at it all day.'

This is an exaggeration. True, Ben has been at his desk in his bedroom ever since breakfast (just after noon), staring unseeingly at his textbooks and notes, but his mind has been anywhere but on *Romeo and Juliet* and the dramatic significance of Mercutio's Queen Mab speech. His thoughts, as they have been ever since his mother's bombshell, have been on the Friday night quandary. Finally, driven to a near frenzy by his inability to fathom a way out of the crisis, he had grabbed his bike and cycled over to see Daria and Milo. Whizzing down the lanes, skidding around corners, he had felt his misery lifting and hope beginning to sprout like a tiny seedling. There simply has to be a way out of this mess.

He spots one of Jez's flyers on the kitchen counter and picks it up. A crudely drawn couple dressed in an approximation of country and western gear as envisaged by someone who has never been within a million miles of Nashville, holding hands with arms crossed, are swinging one another around in a circle.

Daria picks up Milo from the floor and comes to Ben's side, looking over his shoulder. '*Karagod.*'

'You what?'

'Is like Belarusian dance, I think. Different cloths, of course.'

'Clothes.'

Daria sighs. 'Dancing . . . I do not dance since . . .' She bends to kiss Milo's head. 'Well! I am mama now. No dancing for mama.'

'Don't be daft,' says Ben. 'Being a mum don't stop you dancing. You should go.'

Daria gives him an exasperated look and bobs her head at her son. 'With Milo?' She buries her face in her son's neck and he gurgles joyously.

Ben studies the spinning couple again and the germ of an idea takes root. A smile spreads slowly across his face. 'Not necessarily . . .'

'*What?*' says Ben.

'You heard,' Jez replies. 'I can't go. Someone found the leaflets I chucked in the bin and my dad has gone mental, hasn't he? He reckons I have to wait tables on Friday at his sodding barn dance.' He adds gloomily, 'Dressed appropriately.'

'You insane or what? I'm not holding a fucking party by myself! The whole thing was your idea—you got me into this, you twat!'

'All right, all right. I'll think of something. Anyway, you said you can't go either—'

'Yeah, but I got a plan now, haven't I? An idea. Unlike some people, I don't just drop my mates in it.'

'I haven't dropped you in it! It's my fucking parents!'

'Jez!' calls his mother from the landing.

'Look, I gotta go.'

'Hang on!'

'Ben?' calls Daria, knocking on the kitchen window.

'I gotta go.'

～～

'Listen, Dar, I been thinking—'

'Hold Milo for one minute, please. I must fill bath.'

'About that dance . . .' Ben follows Daria up the stairs. 'You should go. I mean it. You never go out. Artem could go with you.'

Daria squirts bubble bath into the water as Milo wriggles excitedly in Ben's arms.

'Artem!' Daria laughs throatily. 'My brother? Dance? Are you mad?'

'Yeah, but all you lot dance, don'tcha?' Ben has a vague recollection of some tedious documentary about Eastern Europe his parents forced him to watch. It was full of moustachioed peasants and buxom girls prancing about in gingham dresses. Or was that the programme on the Amish . . .?

'And who will look after Milo if I am dancing?' Daria lifts Milo out of Ben's grasp and, laying him down on his back on the bath mat, quickly divests him of his clothes.

'Yeah, well, I mean, I was thinking, like . . . *I* could.'

'You?' The baby's nappy, last to come off, is sodden but, to Ben's considerable relief, not soiled. 'Come on, *soneyka*, into the ocean!'

Milo screams with ecstasy as Daria swings him high into the air and plonks him into the suds, spattering herself and Ben in the process.

'Yeah! Why not? Come on, Dar, I've looked after him, like, loads of times. We have a right laugh, don't we, mate?'

But Milo is too entranced with the bubbles clustered all over his chubby body to respond.

Daria grabs a flannel and sets to with some vigorous scrubbing.

'Fact is, my lot would probably be dead pleased 'cos they're away for the weekend. Some party thing. 'Course I can't go, can I, 'cos I gotta revise. But the olds don't wanna leave me alone in the house—I dunno why, I'm nearly sixteen! If I could stay over at yours, though, that'd shut them up. Then you needn't hurry back and you and Artem could make a night of it.' He's thinking fast—get to The Laurels first off and make sure everything's organised, nip in here and see Daria and Artem on their way, shove Milo in the buggy and then settle him in one of the bedrooms back at the aunts' cottage, few drinks and that, get back here in time for Daria and Artem's return and then creep away to rejoin the party once they're asleep. Yeah, that works. Sort of.

Daria's hand slows in its journey over Milo's body. She's tempted, Ben can tell.

'Come on. You deserve a break, Dar. After all you been through. Well, the pair of you. Plus, it'd be a sort of celebration for you getting your visa, yeah?'

'I suppose . . .'

'Brilliant! I'll just clear it at mine and you tell Artem. Where is he, by the way?'

Daria, already mentally flicking through her paltry wardrobe, says absent-mindedly, 'He's finishing job for the cross lady—you know: very loud, she play card with Hester and Harriet.'

'I know,' says Ben, who doesn't, and cares even less.

'Then I ask him to check house on way home.'

'House?' Ben's heart bucks in his chest.

'Your aunts' cottage. Collect post. You know.'

This time Ben does know. And he cares. He cares a great deal.

'He will be home soon. Ben? Where are you going? Ben!'

Milo, startled by the banging of the bathroom door and his mother's raised voice, and bored now the bubbles have mainly dispersed in the fast-cooling water, begins to wail.

∼∽∼

It's only half a mile to The Laurels, but it's mainly uphill and the final approach is hazardous, with potholes and an uneven camber. By the time Ben arrives, he is pouring with sweat, legs weak from both the exertion and his blind panic. If Artem has arrived ahead of him and entered the house, then the game is over. There is a tiny corner of Ben's mind that would not find such an outcome wholly unwelcome. Of course there would be no end of grief and a considerable number of chickens would come home to roost, but perhaps the anxiety that has nagged away in his gut ever since that dickhead Jez got him into this nightmare would be over. He would drag his sorry arse along to this stupid reunion, sit glumly through the weekend, and he would never get to be kissed by Louisa Jellinek ever again, but at least all his worst imaginings would remain just that: imaginings.

But the both longed-for and feared sight of an open front door does not materialise. The cottage is deserted when he screeches up to the gate. He leans the bike against a tree and cautiously approaches the front door, feeling for his keys in his pocket.

'Ben?'

Artem looms over the hedge beside the gate. He looks filthy, his hair matted and coated with sawdust; a labourer returning from his toils, not the highly educated polyglot he in fact is.

'Artem . . . hi. How's it going?'

Artem fails to answer Ben's question. Their relationship has been edgy from the off. Artem considers Ben to be something of a chancer who exploits his aunts and is insufficiently deferential to his elders; Ben considers Artem a pompous, interfering foreigner, albeit one who in principle deserves his respect as a dissident. He just wishes that Artem were a little less . . . *perspicacious*. His English teacher had untypically praised his essay on George Orwell for this quality and having googled it (as indeed he had much of his essay content) Ben had decided it fitted Artem to a T. And not in a good way.

Artem is staring at the windows, upstairs and down.

'What?' says Ben, heart in his mouth. He never knew hearts could *hurt* so much.

'The curtains. Why are they closed?'

Ben gulps. 'Ah, the sun,' he says, improvising rapidly.

'Sun?' Artem advances up the path. He really is a big bloke: like, huge. Ben instinctively recoils.

'Yeah . . . Spoke to Aunt Harriet last night and was telling her what amazing weather we're having and how sunny it was, and she's like, "Sunny? Oh my God, can you go round ours and pull all the curtains?" And I'm like yeah, 'course I can. So I get on my bike and I just got here and done it and you turn up. But it's all sorted now, so no worries.' He finishes in a rush, his heart thumping like it's attached to jump leads or something. He can smell his sweat and it's not a pleasant smell.

Artem's eyes remain narrowed. He couldn't look more disbelieving.

'Yesterday? You spoke to your aunt yesterday?'

Ben instantly sees the trap he has set for himself. 'Yeah, and straight off I'm like, I gotta go to The Laurels to sort something and my dad's all, no way, you gotta revise, and so I had to leave it until just now.'

'I see,' says Artem. 'Well—' grudgingly '—at least you've done it now. I wonder, though, why they did not phone Daria or me, as we are so much closer . . .'

''Cos it was me that was talking to her, wasn't it? And she never knew how sunny it was till I told her. Plus she trusts me.'

Ben might as well have dipped the blade in salt as he twists the metaphorical knife. Teenagers are said to lack empathy as their brains mature; either Ben still has this phase to come or he is already through it, because his treachery bites deep even as the words leave his mouth. His lies are like poison on his tongue, made worse by his immense debt to those he is betraying. He is convinced his guilt must be written across his face, but Artem merely regards him closely for a few more seconds and then, shrugging, retreats down the path.

'See you, then, Ben.' And with a wave, he disappears down the lane. Ben slides down the door to the ground with a groan of relief. He's not sure how much more of this he can take. It's doing his head in.

CHAPTER 15

Harriet sits on a bench outside the hospital, weighing Mary's phone in her hand, grateful for the faint warmth of the late-evening sun. She feels she had handled the call to Ron Martindale as well as she could, given the news she had to impart and the resurgence of her headache, which is making her feel increasingly nauseous.

Mary's husband had, understandably, reacted with alarm but proved a decisive man, not given to histrionics.

'I'm most grateful to you . . . Harriet, did you say? And Mary is being well cared for? Do you have the name and number of her consultant? And the hospital? Thank you. You have been most kind.'

'No, really—'

'I shall phone this number immediately, but is there any chance you could get a message to Mary that I'm on my way? I don't suppose I can ring her myself? No . . . I see. Of course. No matter. Just tell her, would you, I'll be on the first flight out.'

'Ron, it's not for me to interfere, but might it be better to wait until they've finished their tests? For all we know, she'll be right as rain tomorrow.'

'Thank you, Harriet. But I want to see my wife.'

'Of course.' Harriet wishes she had kept her mouth shut.

Ron Martindale's reaction had been businesslike, cold even. Now for Rhona.

〜〜〜

'Mary! Darling!'

A throaty, warm voice on the edge of a laugh.

'Rhona, it's not Mary. My name is Harriet. Harriet Pearson. I'm a friend of Mary's.'

'Friend?' Not so warm, now; there's caution, a hint of suspicion.

'Let me explain. I'm on this painting course with Mary—'

'Right.' Definitely suspicious now.

'I'm using her phone. She asked me to ring because there's been an accident.'

'Oh my God!'

Harriet gives her the details as quickly as she can, finishing with, 'She asked me to give you her love.'

A moment. It sounds such a banal message, not freighted with the meaning it had had at the bedside. She adds, 'Ron's on his way out.'

'Oh, is he? Of course. Is there a flight tonight?' Now tears threaten; Harriet can hear them in the other woman's voice.

'I don't know. I'm not sure they fly—'

'I'll ring the airport now.'

'You're coming here?'

'Of course I'm coming!' A beat. 'Sorry. I'm so sorry, Helen.'

'Harriet.'

'Harriet. I'm all over the place. Sorry. Sorry.'

'Won't Ron be a bit . . .'

'Bugger Ron. Will you tell Mary I'm on my way? And give her . . . no, tell her I love her.'

〜〜〜

Hester is playing bridge. She's still at a loss to explain how this happened. One minute she was engaged in one of the trickiest conversations of her life, the next Regina Pegg was hallooing from the foyer and waving Harriet's bag at her.

'Hester! Over here. Have you spoken to Harriet? Good, good. She's a bit shaken up—well, who wouldn't be? Few scratches and the odd bruise, I dare say. Her bag fell over the ledge; got caught on a branch, thank heavens. Guy scrambled down to retrieve it, bless his heart. I don't think anything's broken. And she would insist on going in the ambulance—poor old Mary looked a bit of a mess, it must be said.' She had lowered her voice theatrically. 'Of course, Gervais was worse than useless—went completely to pieces. Probably frightened to death he'd be sued.' She paused for a moment to take a swig from her water bottle. In the hiatus, Hester's visitor had touched her lightly on the arm—'I'll be back at nine o'clock'—and before she could reply, was gone.

Lionel had returned at that point to insist they eat, Guy and Bella had joined them, and somehow they had got through the meal, Hester barely tasting any of it. Then Regina, indefatigable (surely there was something of Peggy Verndale about her?), had reappeared to suggest a few hands of bridge, and with patent relief everyone had exclaimed with extravagant enthusiasm that that was a splendid idea. Bella, not a player, had pleaded fatigue and retired to her room to read, leaving the four of them to their cards.

〰

Hester finds the discipline of bridge a surprisingly effective antidote to the worry gnawing away at her. She checks her watch. Eight thirty. Beside her is a large Campari and soda that Lionel had pressed upon her, admittedly with little opposition. This, coupled with the two large glasses of wine at dinner that she had somehow found herself drinking without really noticing how assiduously Lionel and Guy topped her up, have induced a sort of equilibrium, her painful foot notwithstanding. Without, she is relieved to discover, impairing her play. Regina, judging by her swift dealing and brisk bidding, is, as suspected, a seasoned player; Guy, who partners her, competent if cautious. But Lionel! Hester cannot recall playing with someone who is so extremely hesitant in trying to make a contract and teeth-clenchingly slow in play. Even Tippy Limbush at the Bridge Club is quicker than Lionel; he's not so bad when they are defending a bid, but seems paralysed with indecision when Hester is dummy. So far, they have only bid twice, their cards being on the whole pretty disappointing, making only one no-trump (Hester) and going down in two hearts (Lionel). Their opponents already have a game in hand and sixty on to rubber. Play continues in this vein, so that it is a great relief when Regina, mid-deal, glances over to the lounge doorway, and says, 'Oh, look who's back!'

And Hester, grabbing her sister's bag from a startled Regina, scrambles gratefully to her feet to hurry over to the doorway, where weary and dishevelled Harriet waits.

'You look awful. What took you so long?' Hester is appalled by herself as the words emerge: Harriet looks like she's in need of a hug not censure.

Harriet, weak from exhaustion and hunger, in thrall to her pounding head, shrugs, as though barely registering her sister's heartlessness. She starts to stagger in the direction of her room. Alfonso hurries over, all solicitude, making Hester feel even more of a heel. 'Signora Pearson! How are you? I have just spoken to the doctor about poor Mrs Martindale. What a tragedy! Would you like something to eat? We have saved you some dinner.'

'Thank you,' Harriet manages. 'Just some tea, if that's possible, please.' She finds her legs unable to carry her any further and subsides onto one of the sofas in the foyer, as Alfonso hurries off towards the kitchens.

Hester sinks down beside her sister and takes her hand. 'God, I'm sorry, Harry. Truly. I didn't mean to snap. But what on earth happened?'

Harriet laughs mirthlessly. 'We slipped. Well, Mary slipped. Grabbed me. I slipped. We both fell over a cliff. Can you imagine anything more ridiculous?'

'What? Are you sure you're all right? Did they check you over? I've been so worried.'

'We all have,' interjects a male voice beside them.

Oh good grief, think the sisters as one. *Just leave us please, Lionel, will you, for five minutes?*

Irritated both by the interruption and the recent bridge debacle, Hester says sharply, 'Give us a few minutes, would you, please, Lionel?' She turns back to Harriet, but not before she has registered his hurt look. He taps his watch meaningfully and jerks his head towards the entrance, then trudges morosely back towards the lounge, a picture of rejection. Hester is smitten with remorse. A car rolls into the car park. Hester squints at the figure climbing out and hesitantly making for the brightly lit reception. It looks like . . . yes, it must be. *Damn.*

'Harry, let's get you to your room and freshen you up.' She virtually lifts Harriet to her feet, marching her down the corridor as quickly as she dares, praying the newcomer hasn't spotted them. Perhaps Lionel will intervene. Assuming, that is, he hasn't taken umbrage at her sharpness. When will she learn? 'Regina kindly rescued your bag, so I've got your key. We need to get some food inside you. Here we are.'

'Too tired to eat,' murmurs Harriet. She longs to curl up under those crisp white sheets, her aching head cradled by the soft pillow, slipping into oblivion to escape this relentless pain . . .

'Nonsense,' says Hester briskly, unlocking the door and steering Harriet over to the armchair by the window. 'Bite of supper and you'll feel so much better.' She pours her a glass of water from the carafe and Harriet gulps it greedily. 'I'll get Alfonso to bring you a tray in a minute.'

'Soon as he likes,' says Harriet, 'or I'll be in bed.'

'No you won't!' Hester hadn't meant to sound so sharp. She adds, a shade more softly, 'Not just yet. For goodness' sake, it's not even nine.'

'Hetty,' says Harriet piteously, face drawn, 'I've had a hell of a day. My head's pounding. I'm shattered. All I want to do is sleep.' Then, hurt, 'You haven't even asked after Mary.'

Hester, wrong-footed and in the wrong, defaults to her usual defensive position: attack. 'Well, it's you I'm worried about. I barely know the woman! Obviously, I hope she's going to be all right. But she's in hospital now. There's nothing more you can do this evening.'

'Exactly. I'm going to get a good night's sleep—or try to—and then tomorrow ... Oh God!' She notices Hester's plaster-dotted foot and the bandage. 'What on earth ...?'

There is a light knock on the door.

'Doesn't matter. A little accident.' Hester, limping slightly, opens the door to discover Alfonso holding a beautifully arranged tray on which is a single rose beside a generous plate of antipasti, with bread on the side, and the promised pot of tea. Behind him, Lionel. She declines Alfonso's offer to bring in the tray, carrying it over to Harriet herself. Lionel, waiting in the corridor, beckons her to join him and starts whispering hurriedly, as Hester pulls the door to behind her.

Harriet stares at the plate of meats, sundried tomatoes and fat olives glistening with oil and feels sick. Averting her head, she tears off a small piece of bread and forces it clumsily into her mouth. The effort of chewing almost defeats her. She closes her eyes as Hester returns, shutting the door firmly.

Hunched in the chair, one hand to her forehead, clutching her glasses, Harriet shields her eyes from the overhead pendant. Hester switches it off and goes over to the window to look out over the garden, bathed in the light thrown by the outdoor lanterns. Her back to Harriet, she says, 'Harry, I'm sorry you're feeling so lousy, but I'm afraid you can't go to bed right away.'

'What?'

Hester looks down on a solitary figure sitting in the shadows on the far corner of the terrace. 'Someone's been waiting to see you. For hours.'

'To see me?' Harriet looks at Hester, confused, eyes dark with fatigue and pain.

'Yes.'

Harriet groans. 'I can't, Hetty. Whoever it is, they'll have to wait until morning.'

'No, Harry—'

Harriet levers herself out of the chair en route to the bathroom. She feels battered, unsteady, hollowed out with pain. Even the pads of her fingers hurt.

'Hetty, I'm sorry but—'

Hester grabs her arm. 'Hang on. Down there. Look.'

For a moment she thinks Harriet is going to resist. Then, awkwardly, she pushes her glasses back on with shaky hands, turns back to the window and peers out into the darkened garden.

'Where?'

'Over there? See? Far side of the terrace.'

Harriet just manages to make out a distant, blurred silhouette. Testily, the nausea resurfacing now she is on her feet, she asks, 'Who the hell is it?'

An infinitesimal pause: Hester's last chance to stop the avalanche she set in motion all those weeks before when the letter arrived. They are standing at a crossroads, she knowingly and her sister unwittingly. After tonight, their lives will change forever.

'Your son,' she says.

CHAPTER 16

'So?'

'Waddja mean, *so*?'

'You got me into this,' Ben snarls. 'You better be there . . .'

'I told you! My dad—'

'Speak to your mum, then! Jesus!'

Ben shovels the heel of the French stick into his mouth for want of anything better to do. He's beside himself with rage and anxiety. The crust is hard, the piece overlarge. Too angry to chew, he attempts to swallow it whole; it sticks in his throat and he starts coughing, then thumping his chest furiously to dislodge the wedge, to no avail. The blood starts singing in his ears; tears spring into his eyes. He gesticulates wildly to Jez to do something, but Jez, lost in misery as the promise of the impending party evaporates and his own shortcomings and powerlessness are laid bare, has his gaze fixed on his own plate.

Ben, choking and now beetroot-red, yanks at Jez's arm and his friend finally cottons on to the emergency. He leaps up from his stool and starts dancing around the kitchen in panic. 'Shit! Shit! What the fuck's wrong with you?'

Ben is pointing desperately at his back, trying to indicate that Jez should try hitting him there, when Deirdre Nairstrom sails in through the garden door laden with several designer carriers, karate-chops Ben smartly between his shoulder blades and frees the obstruction, which shoots out of his mouth and skitters into the island sink.

'Honestly, Jez,' she says, barely breaking her stride, 'you are worse than useless in a crisis. You okay, Ben?'

He nods weakly, tears streaming from his eyes.

'The pair of you couldn't organise a piss-up in a brewery.' And she disappears into the hall, calling to her son, 'I've just bought you a new shirt for Friday night.'

'See?' says Jez in despair. 'It's hopeless.'

'Maybe,' rasps Ben, clutching at straws and his throat, 'we could ask Louisa if she's got any bright ideas?'

⌣⌣⌣

And, of course, she has.

'Chill, babes,' she purrs down the phone. 'Ask Jez what time his village hall crap is due to end, yeah?'

Midnight.

'Okay, so you gotta be back at your crib by then, and Jez takes over from you for a bit till you can sneak out again. No probs! And don't forget, I'll be there.'

Ben knows. Oh God, he knows.

'Okay, so, like, me and Kat and Els will be there from the off and, trust me, babes, we won't stand for any shit.'

He bets they won't.

'Yeah? So, like, you don't need to worry. It's all good.'

It's so good, in fact, that Ben risks telling her about Milo. Jez's eyebrows shoot up.

'A baby!' squeals Louisa. 'This is, like, that Russian bird's rugrat? Mint.'

'Belarusian, but yeah. Still . . . maybe I shouldn't bring him. You know, the noise and that? And, like, if his mum found out—'

'Yeah but, babes, she won't, will she? Oh! No, hang on a minute!'

Ben waits for Louisa to reveal her next brilliant idea. 'Tell you what! Nats could sit instead.'

'Gnats?'

'Nats, my sister Nats. She sits for, like, everyone. Babies love her.'

'Yeah?'

'Sorted! I'll get Nats to, like, look after the baby while you party. Am I a genius or what?'

You, thinks Ben, *are not only a genius, you are the most wonderful, beautiful, glorious creature who ever lived.*

'Totally,' he says.

'What about me, though?' whines Jez as Ben ends the call. 'How'm I gonna get out of doing this fucking barn-dance thing?'

Ben, still glowing from his conversation with Louisa, is utterly devoid of sympathy. 'Best get your shit sorted then, bro,' he crows, 'or you're gonna miss all the fun, n'cha?' The party that had loomed ahead of him as a potential *Titanic*-proportioned disaster has now assumed the aura of a paradisiacal dream. With Louisa Jellinek on his team, why worry? He can't wait for Friday. Piss-up in a brewery? He is so going to prove Mrs Nairstrom wrong.

All that remains to complete the master plan is effect his escape from the weekend in Bakewell. He wishes he'd asked Louisa for some suggestions.

Then he has a brainwave of his own.

〜〜〜

'Saturday?' says George doubtfully. 'Although with your exam on Monday . . .'

'I know,' says Ben, nodding furiously. 'Goes back to uni on Sunday. I mean, it's dead good of him to give up his last day with his rents.'

'Rents?'

'Parents.' Ben watches his father closely, can see him weakening. Then, casually, as though it has only just occurred to him, 'Plus, you and Mum can have a weekend on your own. Which you deserve, no question. And I mean, it's not like Auntie Lynn will mind if I don't go, not really, not when it's my future at stake. I'll be revising most of the time anyway.'

Has he overcooked that one? Apparently not, because George is nodding, albeit with knitted brows.

'Top of which, I bet I get more out of a couple of hours with Ralph than a whole term in class. I mean, it'll be quality.'

He stops. Experience has taught him not to overegg his arguments. George considers the proposition, chewing his cheek absent-mindedly. Ben can hardly breathe.

'The only thing that worries me,' says George eventually, sending Ben's hopes into a nosedive, 'aside from Auntie Lynn being disappointed, is we'd be leaving you alone in the house over the weekend. I don't think your mother would be too happy about that.'

Ben frowns, as if acknowledging a valid parental concern, then says with disarming reticence, 'Thing is, Dad, wasn't gonna mention it, but I was asked if I could, like, help out Daria and Artem this weekend.'

'Oh?'

''Course, I explained we were going away . . .'

'Help out? How?'

Ben smothers an incipient grin. If there's one thing George—and indeed Isabelle—cannot resist, it's the opportunity to render help whenever and wherever it's needed. And even whenever and wherever it isn't.

Careful! Ben cautions himself, heart hammering. 'Oh . . . some event in the village they were invited to on Friday evening. I mean, they don't get out much, what with the baby and that, plus all the worry about their asylum applications . . .'

George assumes a sympathetic expression, as Ben had anticipated. Despite his initial reservations when the events over Christmas had been laid bare in all their danger, coupled with his patent disappointment that Hester and Harriet had failed to seek his help from the beginning, George had quickly assumed his habitual champion-ing of the underdog. No-one could have been more assiduous since in researching how and where support for Daria and Artem might be found.

Ben, buoyed by his success so far but ultra-sensitive to the workings of his father's mind, swiftly pre-empts a possible further reservation. ''Course, Daria won't leave him with, like, anybody, I mean, a random babysitter or whatever. . . understandably . . .'

George understands.

Ben presses home his advantage. 'But me, I'm different, 'cos Milo knows me and she can totally trust me with him.'

George acknowledges his son's surprising facility with the infant with a further serious nod.

'So Daria suggested, like—I mean, this was before I told her I couldn't—that I could stay over at theirs and look after Milo. You know, while they were out having a bit of a break. Probably let me stay Saturday night, too, if I asked . . .'

For a moment, things hang in the balance, George's lingering doubts about his son's integrity warring with his unquenchable goodness of heart and, frankly, his desperation to see Ben succeed in his studies.

'I must admit, the chance of one-to-one tuition with Ralph Pickerlees does seem too good an opportunity to miss. A masterclass, almost. And far be it from me to deny a little pleasure to poor Daria and Artem—God knows they've been through the mill these past few months, bless them. I'll just need to check with your mother . . .'

CHAPTER 17

Harriet's headache has bloomed into an exquisite example of the crawl-up-the-stairs-on-all-fours, kill-me-now variety, every beat of blood sending shafts of agony through her skull. Vision blurred, eye sockets on fire, stomach in revolt, she eases her head back onto the armchair, willing herself not to vomit but to concentrate somehow on the words spewing out of Hester's mouth. If she could only cross that couple of yards, roll onto, into, under—she doesn't care which—those white, white sheets, sink her head into the pillow ... but Hester is firmly ensconced on the edge of the bed and looks in no mood to move or, indeed, go anywhere.

Hester regards her whey-faced sister with little pity, so great is her agitation. All very well for Harriet to plead a headache and fatigue, but what about that poor man outside in the dark? He has been waiting forty-three years for this encounter and Hester is damned if she is going to make him—her nephew!—wait a moment longer than necessary.

It is, she allows, a measure of how poorly Harriet is feeling that she hasn't said a word since Hester dropped her bombshell. Well, she's certainly not going to waste the opportunity ...

The tablets Harriet had taken on her return are starting with agonising slowness to make inroads, nibbling away at the periphery of the pain. Cushioned by the chair, she feels the hawser-like muscles at the back of her neck relaxing ever so slightly; she can now move her head, albeit not very far, without that instant rush of nausea. She finds she can just about control it if she breathes shallowly through her mouth. Across the room, oblivious, Hester continues her diatribe.

'. . . arrived a couple of months ago. The end of April, in fact. You were out at the shops or somewhere. The post came. A letter addressed to Miss H. Ribbleswell, which was a bit of a shock. Very odd. I thought, old school friend? University? Anyway, I opened it, saw straight-away that it was meant for you.' She ferrets in her bag, withdraws the crumpled envelope she has been guarding all this time, and thrusts it across the void.

Harriet, unwilling to risk sitting forward, remains where she is.

Exasperated, Hester tosses the envelope into her sister's lap. 'Read it.'

Harriet tries to say something, fails, weakly flaps a hand.

Hester huffs noisily. 'Well, I'll tell you what it says, then, if you can't be bothered! I swear to God, Harriet, I would never have believed this of you. I can't tell you how much I . . . All these years! Did Jim know? I only hope for his sake he didn't.'

Harriet makes an indecipherable noise that Hester reads as an interruption.

'Let me finish! So I scanned it—hard not to, really, it's pretty short—and I couldn't believe what I was reading. Stephen—that's his name; I don't know what name you gave him—had managed to trace you, but—and this shows you how thoughtful he is—he'd deliberately used your maiden name to alert you in case your husband was around when the letter arrived. Of course he didn't know Jim had . . . Anyway, he thought it was much less likely anyone else would open it that way. That's the kind of person he is.

'I'll let him tell you everything in due course, but the long and short of it is, I decided I would contact him myself. Now, don't look at me like that!'

Harriet isn't aware she's been looking any way at all; she has had her eyes closed most of the time.

'. . . I know you of old. Anything you don't want to face up to, you back away. Run away, if you can.'

Do I? thinks Harriet. *Do I really? I like to think I'm one of life's copers . . . Is that what she really thinks of me?*

'. . . always fought your battles for you. No, don't argue, I have!' Hester, disconcerted by the unreadable silence from her sister, is feeling ever more aggrieved, an emotion that always brings out the worst in her. Harriet's lack of denial or explanation is stoking the fires of Hester's anger. 'We spoke several times on the phone, and the more we spoke, the more convinced I became that he was genuine, that it was true, that you'd been lying to me, to everyone, for years. Unbelievable. I kept thinking, how did she do it without anyone knowing? Then I checked the dates. I was in France, wasn't I? That six months at the Sorbonne. And Ma and Pa, of course, were in Germany. How very convenient!

'I suggested several opportunities for Stephen to come and confr— meet you, but they didn't work out for one reason or another. If you want my opinion, I think he's scared. And who can blame him? Mother abandons him, makes no attempt to find him—I assume you didn't? He must be in knots. Anyway, finally we establish we're both in Italy the same week—he's over on business—and he and I agreed that neutral territory might be best. So I arrange everything for tonight and then you get caught up in this wretched accident and start running all over the place after a woman you don't know from Adam, while your own son is sitting out there in the dark waiting for you to deign to show up!

'And . . . and . . .'

Harriet lifts heavy eyelids and looks across the gloomy room at her sister, who is now tearing a tissue to shreds.

'And I have been nursing this awful secret for weeks and you just blithely get on with your life as if nothing has . . . playing grandmother for Milo and sounding off about other people's children and all the while . . . oh!' Hester raises the last scrap of tissue to her eyes.

The room falls silent but for Hester's ragged breathing.

Harriet stares in astonishment at her sister. Is Hester *crying*? Brusque, armour-plated, battle-axe Hester?

'Hetty . . .' she starts, but Hester is on her feet, sniffing furiously and pointing at the envelope on her lap.

'I don't want to talk to you! But I tell you this: we've had our moments over the years, God knows, and there have been times when I could cheerfully have throttled you, but through it all, through everything, I always respected you. But this! This! Now read that bloody letter and then do the decent thing and get down into that garden and meet your son, you selfish, wicked woman!'

And then, with a slam of the door that reverberates viciously through Harriet's head, she is gone.

⌣⌣⌣

Harriet doesn't read the letter. She sits for a few more minutes staring sightlessly into the dark and then very, very gingerly feels her way into the bathroom, where she is violently sick. She washes her face in cold water and delicately teases a comb through her tangled hair, each pass of the teeth grating against her tender scalp. She can't bring herself to look in the mirror above the basin. Instead, she gropes her way semi-blind to the bedroom door and, inching it open, slides into the corridor, shielding her eyes from the light. Mercifully, there's no-one about. Distantly she hears muted chatter from the bar, the chink of glasses. Hugging the walls, grateful for their solidity, she slips towards a side door and out into the garden.

CHAPTER 18

'Ben? Ben! There's someone to see you.'

Ben surfaces from the complexities of Ted Hughes's poetry, head full of hawks and hooked feet. 'What?' He glances at the clock on his computer: nine thirty-five pm.

'Someone to see you,' repeats his mother, calling up from the foot of the stairs. There is a muffled exchange between her and the visitor on the doorstep—Jez, presumably.

'Tell him to come up,' he yells. 'I'm working.'

'Ben!' This time his mother's voice is tempered with a little steel. 'Will you come down, please. Right now.'

Ben, irritated, plods to the top of the stairs. 'What?' Peering past Isabelle, he sees a diminutive figure, swamped by a voluminous hoodie.

'This is Natalie,' says Isabelle, as though she's not at all convinced by what she has been told. 'She'd like a word.' She frowns a question up at Ben, who, equally puzzled, lopes down the stairs. 'Ta,' he says to his mother as he passes her, then waits until she retreats to the lounge before turning to the caller. 'Wotcha.'

The girl throws back her hood to uncover cornrows with bead-threaded braids and extraordinarily large almond-shaped eyes behind outsized glasses. 'Hiya,' she says. 'I'm Nats.'

Ben stares in astonishment.

'You know—Nats? Lou's sister?'

'Oh,' Ben manages. 'Right ...' Befuddled by hours of relentless revision, he's unsuccessfully trying to reconcile this tiny black girl with the leggy wonder that is Louisa.

Nats laughs, revealing blindingly white perfect teeth. The laugh has a definite edge to it. 'I guess Lou never said. She's such an airhead. I'm adopted. Mum's a sucker for racial integration, if not miscegenation.'

Ben has no idea what she is talking about, nor can he ask; words, even the most banal, have deserted him.

'We going to do this all on the doorstep?' She looks up at Ben combatively. 'You want me to help you out or not?'

Ben, still mute, steps back and ushers her in. Where to take her? She looks towards the lounge door but he quickly makes for the kitchen, shutting the door smartly behind them. He finds a voice. 'Want a Coke?'

'You kidding? Teeth rot. I'll have a coffee—or a glass of water, if that's too difficult. You're the cook, right?'

'What? Oh, yeah,' says Ben, caught between the sink (water) and the kettle (coffee).

'Water's fine,' says Nats, amused. 'I read your blog. Or I did. You haven't posted much recently.'

'Revision,' says Ben glumly, filling a glass. 'Haven't cooked anything for weeks.' That's not strictly true: he's cooked plenty of workaday meals recently but nothing that he feels warrants an audience. 'Here. Have a seat.'

Nats downs the water in one long uninterrupted gulp. 'That's better. Okay. Lou says you need a babysitter Friday—'

'Shh!' hisses Ben, glancing towards the lounge.

Nats glances in the same direction, pulls a face. She lowers her voice. 'Okay. So. You want me eight thirty to, what, eleven thirty?'

''Bout that.'

'She said Pellington?'

'Yeah. That a problem?'

'No. Got a bike.'

'How old are you?'

Nats looks put out. 'Old enough to ride a bike!'

'No, I meant your parents—you know, you out at night . . .'

'It's cool. They're off to this dance thing.'

'Great!'

Nats shoves the glass across to him for a refill. As he gets up, she says, 'Okay, then. Twenty quid.'

'Sorry?'

'To sit.'

'What?!'

'Twenty.'

He stops, glass halfway to the tap, while she stares up at him, mouth set.

'You're kidding, right? You thought this was a freebie? No way, José! Don't tell me Lou promised—'

'No, no,' says Ben quickly, flushing.

'But you assumed.'

'No, no I didn't,' he stammers, face aflame. 'I just—'

'Yes you did. Don't bullshit me. Anyway, that's my rate. Take it or leave it. And since chances are you're not the dad, I'll want to meet the parents and the baby first.'

'Meet . . . like, face to face?'

'I'm looking after someone else's kid, numbskull. Would you want some random girl you've never met looking after this Milo?'

Ben shakes his head, realising that he most certainly wouldn't. 'Thing is—'

Nats groans theatrically and drops her head onto the table, allowing Ben to marvel at the extraordinary symmetry of her rows. He looks away embarrassed when she raises her face to him, eyes flinty behind her glasses. 'Why do I get the impression that, as per, there's something my darling sister hasn't told me? I thought it was a bit odd from the off, you booking me. What's the deal?'

And Ben has no choice but to tell her.

'So,' reflects Nats, draining her second glass of water, 'basically, you want me to be complicit in this conspiracy? Right?'

Ben hears the strains of the BBC *Ten O'Clock News* from the lounge; any minute now his mum'll be coming through to make tea . . .

'It's not a—'

She bats away his denial. 'Whatever. Way I see it, you're deceiving your aunts, deceiving your parents and deceiving this poor Milo's mother. Nice. And all so's you can get in Lou's good books. Or into something else. Are you crazy or what?'

'I'm not trying to—'

Nats inspects the ends of one of her braids. 'I can tell you now you're on a hiding to nothing.'

'A what?' This girl does use the weirdest vocabulary.

'With Lou. You're going nowhere.'

Blotches of colour spatter Ben's neck and cheeks. 'What do you know?' he snarls.

Nats laughs. 'What do I know? That my sister —whom I love dearly, though that doesn't prevent me seeing all her many faults—is what in common parlance is called a prick tease. That she would no more look at you than she would eat meat.'

'She's a vegetarian?' says Ben, bewildered, certain that he once saw Louisa chomping a huge bacon butty in the café near school.

'This month,' says Nats sourly. 'Driving the rest of us up the wall. Anyway . . . what I'm trying to tell you is that Lou will do whatever it takes to get what she wants. Which in this case, by my reckoning, is not your lanky, somewhat spotty self—have you tried toothpaste, by the way?—but the chance of a—'

'Toothpaste?'

'Yeah. Supposed to dry them out. Leave it on ten minutes, they say. But I'm telling you, all she's really after is a party. So don't get your hopes up, sunshine.'

Ben wants to argue, to tell this really irritating little squirt that her divine sister had actually kissed his pustular face, so there! But somewhere deep inside him, the hateful truth has hit home. He could accuse Nats of jealousy—and who wouldn't be jealous, forever living in the shadow of Louisa's beauty?—but he suspects she is speaking from bitter experience. Not that he has any intention of giving her the satisfaction of acknowledging that right now. That tip about the tooth-paste is a new one, though . . .

'Whatever,' he mutters with feigned nonchalance.

Nats impatiently shoves her glasses up her nose, as though thor-oughly bored with the negotiations. 'So. Deal or no deal? Twenty quid and I get to meet Milo and his mum?'

'Deal,' says Ben, wondering how much money is left in his account this close to the end of the month.

'Cash,' says Nats, getting up. She gives him her mobile number. 'Text me tomorrow about when and where. I'm free after school until seven.'

'School? It's half-term.'

'Rehearsals. End-of-term play. Be done by four.'

'And what happens at seven?'

'Flute.'

'What school?'

Nats shakes her head in disbelief. 'You really are a piece of work! Same as you—I'm in the year below you.'

'Really?'

'Yes, really. Not that someone of your exalted status could be expected to notice a mere Year 10. We learn to hug the walls when you go by. Not.'

The television falls silent: presumably his mother has consumed as much of the world's awfulness as she can stomach for one day. The lounge door opens. Time to send his visitor on her way.

'We're done, yeah?'

'For the moment,' says Nats, making it sound more of a threat than an affirmation.

Isabelle enters, obviously surprised to find the kitchen occupied. 'Oh, I didn't realise . . .'

'It's okay. Nats is just on her way.'

'Do you live locally, Natalie?' asks Isabelle politely. 'Only my husband's out with the car at a parish council meeting or I'd offer you a lift.'

'No worries, Mrs . . . er . . .'

'Fry.'

'Of course. Sorry. Thanks, Mrs Fry, but I've got my bike.' Is Ben imagining it, or is Nats suppressing a smirk? 'I'll be on my way. Bye.'

She follows Ben to the front door.

'What's so funny?' says Ben, as he turns the handle.

'Serendipity.' Nats grins. 'I just realised. Your name. You had to be a cook or chef or whatever, didn't you?'

'Did I?'

'With a name like Fry? Well . . . duh! Nominal determinism.'

'You what?'

'Look it up. Text me.' She starts wheeling her bike down the path.

'Oi,' hisses Ben. 'How'm I going to explain you to Daria tomorrow?'

Those perfect teeth gleam under the streetlight. 'You could always tell her I'm your girlfriend.'

CHAPTER 19

Hester watches Lionel over the rim of her glass, taking in his attractive but seamed face (not that she's in any position to pass judgement, given her own wrinkles), the thinning hair, the soft lips. He looks as she does, as most of their generation do, blurred around the edges, fading into pleated skin too large for their frames. Still a good-looking chap, though. She sits a little straighter, upends the final dregs of brandy into her mouth.

'Better?'

She nods, not trusting herself to speak just yet, the fury still hot in her breast, but perilously close to tears. She who never cries. Her ear is cocked for the sound of footsteps down the corridor: surely Harriet will have the decency to come out and face what must be faced? Lionel had stopped her going out into the garden when she had emerged from Harriet's room, boiling with indignation. Now, calmer, she recognises the wisdom of his intervention. The situation is bad enough; she doesn't want to exacerbate Stephen's anxieties with more vituperation directed at the woman whose appearance he awaits. But her head is filled with that lonely figure sitting so patiently in the darkness.

'You've done all you can, Hetty,' says Lionel softly, laying his hand on hers. 'It's over to her now.'

In the garden, the night air is warm on Harriet's skin. She feels light-headed, distanced from her surroundings, as though seeing everything through gauze, so that she has to concentrate hard to plant her feet accurately. Every step rings through her, her headache still beating its persistent drum. Her shoes on the gravel sound unnaturally loud in the stillness, despite the thrum of humanity behind her, but the shape in her sights does not move, does not turn. She imagines Hester standing tall and thin like a stork at the hotel window, watching.

Lionel places another glass of brandy in front of Hester. She doesn't want it, but hadn't the energy to stop him when he got up to go to the bar. Thankfully, he had managed to intercept Marco bustling over to enquire about Signora Pearson and with a brief but courteous update had deflected him. What a comfort it is to have someone else take charge for once. She resists the temptation to go over and look out of the window, afraid that nothing will have changed, that Stephen will still be sitting alone, still waiting.

'Stephen?'

She has stopped a few yards behind him, her feet unable to carry her any further. She digests the bulk of him, the halo of springy hair. Her voice is weak, tremulous not with age but apprehension. Has he heard her? She tries again, this time with a little more emphasis.

The man pushes his chair backwards, sending gravel skittering across the path. He gets awkwardly to his feet, steadying himself on the edge of the table, then turns to face her, the light bleeding from the hotel illuminating his face. It's a plain face, slightly chubby cheeks, a small mouth pursed with anxiety, deep-set dark brown eyes, a smudge of bristles on his jawline. But a kind face.

'I'm Harriet.' Her name has never sounded so *wrong*. 'Hello.'

The greeting hangs in the air, demanding a response. It is a long time coming.

What is he expecting? Tears, embraces, excuses? What is *she* expecting?

Stephen seems paralysed, mouth slightly open, breathing heavy and erratic. His lips move, but no sound emerges. An arm swings out so suddenly and violently that she almost flinches, until she realises he wants her to sit. Somehow her feet make it to the table and she thumps down into an adjacent chair.

Stephen resumes his seat, feeling his way into it, his eyes never once leaving her face, his expression unreadable.

They face each other like two boxers readying themselves for a bout.

⌣⌣⌣

'Some good news at least,' says Lionel, smiling faintly, his voice a touch uncertain. 'Well, I hope you'll think it's good news. I do hope you don't think I'm being presumptuous, but these last few days . . .' He waits for some response; when none is forthcoming, he stumbles on. 'I just thought I'd ask. Alfonso, you know. About next week. It being high season and everything. Well, not quite high season but near as damn it. I thought they'd be fully booked but—' a little laugh '—lucky old me, one room left. Not the one I'm in now, but all the same . . . And, very good of him, no single supplement. Curse of the lone traveller. As we both know only too well. Ha! Still . . .'

He waits; Hester is looking in his general direction but he sees her thoughts are anywhere but on him. He ploughs on. 'Phoned the airline, changed my ticket, and—hey presto!—I'm staying until Monday too. So I can help you get to the airport and we'll have another couple of days together.'

Silence.

'I hope you're pleased? I know it might seem a bit . . . sudden. I mean, we only met on Sunday, but . . .' He trails off, forehead knotted.

Hester reaches automatically for her glass.

'Hetty?'

She blinks, starts, recovers, hand in mid-air. 'Sorry . . . it's just . . .' She processes what little she heard of his speech. Manages a feeble, 'That's great, Lionel. Really.' Then, pulling herself together, chastened by his hangdog countenance and aware he deserves better, 'Forgive me . . .' She injects a little more enthusiasm this time, manages a smile. 'That *is* good news, Lionel, truly, although I don't deserve your kindness. I'm hardly the best company at the moment.'

He seizes her hand; for a moment, startled, she imagines he is going to bring it to his lips. Instead he strokes it with warm, dry fingers, looking down, seemingly too shy to meet her eyes. 'I don't mind, Hetty. Not in the least. I'm here for you, you know that. Whatever you need.'

And Hester, who would ordinarily scoff at such an overworked platitude, finds herself deeply comforted by Lionel's devotion. She squeezes his hand in return, and, neither wanting to be the first to pull away, they remain for some moments thus coupled.

～～～

'Forgive me . . .' begins Harriet, just as Stephen finds his voice to say, 'I'm sorry . . .'

They both stop, each willing the other on. Harriet, heart hammering along with her head, holds out longer.

'I was going to say, well, sorry for springing this on you. Your sister explained about the letter . . . I didn't mean to ambush you like this.' A pleasantly modulated voice, with a distinct cadence: northern certainly. But east or west? She's never been awfully good at placing accents. There's something familiar about it, though, some echo of . . . she's got it. Landlord at the local pub.

'Liverpool?' she manages.

'Wha'? Oh, yes.' His eyes light up momentarily. 'Hoylake.' He registers her ignorance, sketches a map with his finger. 'West of Liverpool, on the sea. But, yeah, Liverpool originally.' He gives a short laugh. 'Can't escape, no matter wha'. You can take the boy out of Liverpool, bu' . . . et cetera et cetera. Still work there. City not United.'

'Right.'

A hiatus, as though both have simultaneously registered the incongruity of this conversation mimicking two casual acquaintances passing the time of day. Stephen coughs self-consciously. Harriet waits. He takes a breath, examining his hands on the table in front of him.

'Can I just . . . ?'

'Stephen, listen—'

He cuts across her interruption. A wave of nausea rises suddenly and she subsides, riding it out. He reads it as a signal to continue.

'Sorry. Look, this isn't meant to be a confrontation. I want you to understand that.'

Harriet nods; wishes she hadn't.

'It's not like I've been wanting to find my . . .' he pauses; looks at her '. . . birth mother all my life. I haven't. My adoptive parents were wonderful. Brilliant. I had a happy childhood. I was a happy child. I never wondered . . .' Again, that fleeting glance, the throat cleared. 'You get dealt a hand. I was dealt a good one. Okay?'

'Okay. But . . .' She takes a deep breath; her stomach settles, but the dull thud in her head pulses on.

He nods briefly, satisfied with her acquiescence, hurrying on to silence her. 'I don't want to come back into your life, disrupting it or whatever, if that's what you're worried about.'

A distinctly challenging note here that pulls her up short. She's not at all sure how to respond.

'No, I—'

He holds up a hand. 'Please . . . I've been sitting here for hours thinking over what I wanted to say. So I just want to say it.' He gestures with both hands. 'Get it out in the open.'

He looks at her for a reaction. She inclines her head, manages to restrain herself.

'This wasn't my idea. You ought to know that. I mean, me, I would have just let things lie. I don't want you to think my life's been blighted by . . . you know, because it hasn't. I'm not bitter, I'm not angry, I'm sure there were perfectly valid reasons why you did what you did—no, please, let me say this. But, you see, Mum died last year—I mean, no way would I have done this while she was still alive—and I'm about to get married . . .'

'Oh!' says Harriet instinctively. 'Congratulations.'

'Yeah.' A bashful smile. 'Taken me long enough. Emily. She's a teacher. Bit younger than me. Well, a good ten years, truth be told.'

'My husband was eight years older than me.' Harriet regrets sharing this even as the words emerge. Why on earth would he care about Jim? 'Sorry,' she says.

He shrugs. 'Thing is, Emily had a sister who died when she was eight. She had this thing called progeria.'

Harriet looks puzzled.

'Hutchinson-Gilford progeria syndrome. Horrible disease. I've become a bit of an expert, unfortunately. Premature ageing, dislocated joints, heart problems, stroke. Lucky if you make your early twenties. Lucy didn't. Anyway, it's made Emily a bit paranoid. I mean, progeria isn't an inherited disease—it's just bloody awful luck. But as a consequence Emily's sort of neurotic about genes and all that. We want to start a family in due course—well, pretty soon, in fact—and understandably she doesn't want to take any chances. So she insisted I find out everything possible about my birth parents. Just so we can be sure that there's nothing . . . we ought to be concerned about. Health-wise. You see?'

Oh, Harriet sees. Of course she sees. Her heart goes out to Stephen and his wife-to-be.

'So you'll understand why I've got in touch after all these years. I think your sister thought I wanted some emotional reunion or something, and I have to say she seemed pretty furious—not with me, but with you—so I'm assuming you never told her anything. Which is . . .'

He falters. 'I guess you had your reasons.' He pauses, biting his lip. Decides. In a small voice, trying to sound nonchalant, 'Have you got any other children?'

'No, no . . .' Harriet's heart feels too big for her chest. 'Stephen, listen—'

He exhales as though he's just reached the end of a very long and draining race. 'Had to ask . . . you know, you wonder. Any other family out there. What if you bumped into them one day? God! I never expected to feel so nervous! The waiting and anticipation has been torture.'

There's nothing she can say.

'Haven't been able to sleep for weeks. Wasn't at all sure about this plan of your sister's—thought it might backfire. But hey! It's done. We've met, nobody's got overexcited, we're both adults, we—'

'Stephen—'

'Sorry, sorry, always do this when I get uptight. Talk too much. I'll shut up. Let you say . . . whatever.' He is kneading his left cheek. 'Please, tell me what I need to know.'

'There's only one thing you need to know, Stephen.'

'Yeah?' Hope and fear war in that one word.

'I'm not your mother.'

CHAPTER 20

'What a charming girl,' says Isabelle, who is filling the kettle, when Ben returns to the kitchen after a quick stop in the bathroom. Delving into the cookie jar, he locates half an oat crunch. One of his. He crams it into his mouth.

'Who's been at these?' he demands, thwarted, looking around for something else to satisfy his sudden hunger.

'At what, love?'

'My biscuits.'

'I thought you made those for your father.'

'I did, yeah.'

'So . . .?'

'What, he's eaten the lot? Greedy—'

'Ben!'

He grabs a packet of Frosties and starts shovelling them into his mouth straight from the box.

'Ben, honestly!'

'I'll have to make some more,' he says, ignoring his mother's protests and making for one of the cupboards. 'Could do with a break.'

'You're going to start cooking at this time of night? It's a quarter past ten!'

'Yeah?'

'You need to get some sleep.'

'Not tired.'

'You're always tired!'

'I'm not tired *now*, am I?' He starts pulling down flour, oats, ground almonds, dried fruit.

'Well, if you went to bed earlier . . .'

'Oh here we go. I told you, there's piles of research that shows—' He yanks open the fridge door. 'Oh, Mum, not again!'

'What, darling?'

Ben thrusts a block of butter under her nose. 'This is salted. How many times? *Unsalted.* Jesus!'

'Language!' barks George, coming in unexpectedly. Neither of them had heard the car. 'What's going on?' George habitually returns home like a soldier returning to the battlefield. Tonight seems no exception.

'Butter,' mutters Ben, head buried in one of the lower cupboards in search of the mixing bowl.

'Butter?'

'I bought the wrong sort apparently,' murmurs Isabelle, torn between contrition and indignation.

'Again.'

'Butter's butter, isn't it?' says George mildly, stepping squarely on a mine.

'Oh, George, please don't get him started—' cries Isabelle, leaping in to change the subject. 'How was your meeting?'

'So-so,' says George absently, weighing up the pros and cons of tackling his son's bad manners. He decides the cons, as usual, outweigh the pros. 'Peggy Verndale turned up.'

'Peggy . . .? What, that loud woman from Pellington? Plays bridge with Hester and Harriet? She doesn't even live here.'

'Wanted to give us the benefit of her vast experience dealing with the planning authorities. You know, all that business of the field behind her house?'

Isabelle vaguely recalls seeing something about it in the local paper. 'Doesn't that belong to—'

'Teddy Wilson, yes.' A glance in Ben's direction, but he's busy weighing ingredients, humming away contentedly, earbuds blotting out the parental conversation.

'Practically hijacked the entire meeting,' George continues irritably. 'I tried to explain as courteously as possible that, while we appreciated her generosity, we had our own campaign plan—but would she listen? Starts distributing reams of photocopies—we did this, we didn't do that—while I struggled to maintain order. Then Brian Nairstrom puts in his penn'orth and they end up practically having a slanging match.' George is still smarting from Nairstrom stepping in; he could have sorted things out perfectly well if only the other man had given him time. There was absolutely no excuse for that sort of language. 'Next thing, he's asking why we weren't supporting this dance he's organising. Thank heavens I was able to plead a prior engagement.' He notices Ben turning on the oven. 'What on earth are you up to?'

'Making biscuits,' says Isabelle quickly, rolling her eyes in a 'please don't start anything' appeal.

George wilts, shrugs, reaches for his tea and starts for the stairs. ''Night, Ben.' He taps his son on the shoulder.

Ben whips round as if he's been bitten.

George repeats his adieu. He can't stop himself adding, 'Not too late, eh?'

Ben sighs dramatically and addresses himself once more to his task. Isabelle tentatively comes to his side and reaches up to kiss his averted cheek. Ben, exulting in his imminent freedom and a whole parent-free weekend, relents, and, in a lightning change of mood that totally wrongfoots his mother, turns to wrap his lanky frame around her. 'Sorry.'

Isabelle's heart melts, resentment and rancour vanishing in the comfort of his embrace, his distinctive minty, slightly oily smell, overlaid with deodorant. He's a good boy, really, under all that bluster and attitude. Just a typical stroppy teenager in thrall to his hormones. 'I liked your little friend,' she says shyly. 'Lovely manners. And what extraordinary hair.'

Ben curbs an immediate riposte that she's not his friend, that she's a money-grubbing little smart-arse, that she's not fit to kiss the feet of her adorable sister whose hair is spun from pure silk and wreathes her in glory. It's never wise to give Isabelle any ammunition; she's terrier-like if she gets the bit between her teeth. 'Yeah,' he says grudgingly, 'she's all right. S'pose.' Capitalising on this rare accord with at least one parent and in a bid to assuage his nagging guilt over the enormity of his subterfuge, he says, 'How about I make that pineapple tarte tatin again for you tomorrow?'

'Oh, darling!' Isabelle beams, touched beyond words. 'You are such a love. Isn't it a lot of bother?'

'Not for you, Mum.' Ben is doing a very convincing impression of a doting son.

'That would be gorgeous.' A thought. 'Oh, I know! Could I take it with us? To Auntie Lynn's party? Seeing as you can't be there yourself, it'd be a sort of present for her. She'd be thrilled.' Ben doubts anything he does is likely to thrill the old bat, but he smiles his agreement anyway.

Isabelle squeezes his arm. 'Well, night-night then, darling. Enjoy your cooking.'

Ben nods, reaching past her along the counter for the tablespoon.

'Oh!' she says, stopping in the doorway and pointing at first her face, then his. 'Sweetheart, I think you've got toothpaste or something on your . . .'

THURSDAY

CHAPTER 21

With the dawn comes pity and anger. Pity for Stephen, doubly bereaved. Anger at Hester, so self-righteous, interfering, destructive. Harriet's resentment bubbles up, accelerating her heartbeat, tightening her chest. In the aftermath of her terrible headache, in that state of woolly recovery, the full import of Hester's accusations the night before hit her afresh, as sharp and wounding as Hester had undoubtedly meant them to be but which, in Harriet's state at the time, had not always found their mark. She reviews their conversation—hardly a conversation, she had barely opened her mouth—forensically, reconstructing it word by hateful word. It feeds her fury. Is that what Hester really thinks of her? Her own sister? The demands of her bladder force her to pad through to the bathroom, where she takes a couple of paracetamol, just in case. She looks in the mirror at a stranger's grey face, eyes shadowed with more than fatigue. Five past five. She crawls back into bed and closes her eyes, desperate for the annihilation of sleep.

It does not come. But Stephen's face does, by turns sorrowful, mistrustful, heartbroken. Her physical pain—awful yes, but mercifully transient—had been nothing compared with his, a pain of such loss and bewilderment that for one mad moment she had almost lied, said, 'Yes, yes, it's me'—anything to expunge that look of despair when she had gently pushed the birth certificate back over the table to him. There in careful loopy handwriting was her name, Harriet Grace

Ribbleswell, listed plainly as the mother of Stephen Mark. There too the date: 3 August 1972, Liverpool Maternity Hospital. It is then that a door cracks open a fraction in her memory. She needs time to consider the implications. Speaking softly and quietly in the seclusion of the garden, she had held his desperate gaze, washed afresh with regret for the children she and Jim had never made, though not from choice. She could see in Stephen a solid, decent, lovable man, someone she would have been proud to call her own. But he is not and she cannot.

'I know how bitterly disappointed you must be, Stephen. But I'm not the woman you are looking for, despite what that says. I'm happy to take any test you like to prove that to you.'

He had shaken his head briefly, eyes glittering. She had stumbled on. 'I don't think this is a case of mistaken identity, I really don't. Would you be prepared to give me a few days? To try to find your mother for you?'

'Then you know—?' he had started, but she cut across him.

'No. Not definitely. I need to be certain. I don't want to send you down another blind alley. I have my reasons. Good reasons, Stephen, I swear. Trust me.' And with that scant comfort, broken, he had gone away.

Tears track down the side of Harriet's face and soak the pillow.

～～

'Good morning, Hetty,' says Lionel, sliding once more into the seat opposite. '*Caffè, per favore*,' to the hovering waiter. He leans across the table, face crumpled with concern. 'Have you spoken?'

Hester shakes her head. 'Not a peep. I thought she might have the common decency to come and see me once Stephen left.'

Lionel, recalling his own whereabouts last night, is privately thankful Harriet hadn't.

He glances at Hester's phone beside her plate; she intercepts the look. 'I thought he might text.'

'Stephen?'

'Considering all the trouble I went to, arranging the rendezvous.'

'He must be in a bit of a state—it can't have been an easy encounter. Perhaps you could contact him . . .'

'I hardly think so!' she snaps. He recoils as if slapped. 'I beg your pardon, Lionel. There's no reason for me to take things out on you. But I'm rather out of sorts.'

'Not at all. Quite understandable. I'll just get myself some . . .' He hurries away in the direction of the breakfast buffet.

Hester toys with the remains of an apricot cornetto, brooding. Her antipathy towards her sister hardens. She's prepared to bet Harriet will wait until she and Lionel are out of the way at their class before she creeps down to breakfast. Coward! *I will never forgive her for this*, she thinks darkly. *Never!*

━━━

Harriet wakes, dry-mouthed, stiff-necked. She squints at her watch, then groans. How on earth can it be nearly ten o'clock? From the corridor comes the squeak of the maid's cleaning trolley. Stumbling into the bathroom, she stands for a few blessed moments under a shower just the wrong side of comfortable, masochistically enjoying the jets pummelling her still-tender scalp. She rakes a comb through her towel-dried hair (*must get Ben to give me a trim when we get home*) and slips into a loose dress and sandals. She is just picking up her room key before setting out in search of a cup of tea when she spots Mary's phone beside her bag. The events of yesterday come flooding back. She must get to the hospital and ensure her new friend is prepared for the arrival of her husband—and lover. She must start to fulfil her promise to Stephen. She must—eventually—talk to Hester . . .

But first, she must find some tea.

━━━

Franco Riccardi is in an inexplicably good mood this morning. He is—it hardly seems credible—beaming, his little red lips stretched wide in the vastness of his beard.

'*Buongiorno, signore, signor! Come state?*' Unusually, he is in the kitchen ahead of his students, treating his assistant Enrico, they note to their astonishment, with near civility, even affection. The hapless lad is, admittedly, extremely slow and clumsy (four glasses and three plates down so far this week), but Hester attributes this more to his state of perpetual terror than any innate personal shortcomings. She must remember to tell Ben about Enrico to disabuse him of any notions he may have of waltzing into a position with an experienced chef and expecting to enjoy a comradely partnership. All she has ever read about the most successful in the field suggests that they are stern taskmasters who, like consultants with their housemen in hospitals, mete out to their unfortunate underlings the sort of treatment they received in their own apprenticeships, almost as a rite of passage.

But this morning Franco is bubbling with goodwill, primarily because he has just received news that in a few months he is to host a new, highly lucrative TV show, which means that he will no longer have to endure the purgatory of tutoring any more classes of idiotic amateurs like this. Unless, that is, they take place in front of the cameras. His bonhomie extends not only to Enrico, utterly disconcerted by his *padrone*'s volte face, but also to Melanie, who has borne the brunt of his criticism and insults throughout the week with a resilience that has astonished both Hester and Lionel and earned their respect. At each setback, the slight, nervous girl has simply shouldered the opprobrium heaped upon her and patiently repeated the procedure until she has mastered it. 'I'll never get another opportunity like this,' she had whispered to Hester after one particularly bruising encounter with the great man over her holey lasagne. 'I mean, cooking to my mum means beans on toast. When I won the competition, my friends were all, "You're never going?" and I'm, like, "Yeah, too bloody right I am." I won't give that bugger the satisfaction, neither.' Now Melanie is wearing almost the same expression of mistrust and suspicion as Enrico, watching Franco dancing around the counters with a grace that belies his bulk, showering everyone with Italian endearments. Hester raises a quizzical eyebrow at Lionel, who shrugs his own bemusement.

Hester had been in two minds whether to attend the course at all this morning. As minute after frustrating minute ticked by in the dining room and Harriet failed to appear, her apprehension and anger had grown, not helped by the lack of news from Stephen. At five to ten, Lionel had said tentatively, 'Should we go across? I mean, it might take your mind off . . .' And Hester, conflicted, anxious, had decided that it might.

'So!' exclaims Franco theatrically, 'we are all experts now—yes, even you, Signora Melanie!—in the bread, the pasta, the fish, a little meat, the antipasti. Very good! But today—' he pats his prodigious belly—'is dessert day.' He kisses his fingers. '*Sì, sì!* I love!' He picks up a short metal hollow tube and brandishes it. 'You like cannoli? Of course! But we don' buy cannoli, no, we make dough, we roll, we fry, we fill. Beautiful! So! Today is cannoli, is *struffoli*, *zeppole* and real Italian hazelnut biscotti, plus maybe gelati. I will see. We work hard, yes?'

Hard work is what Hester wants, what she needs. She dons her apron and sets to.

~~~

'No, no, really, I'm fine,' Harriet lies. 'Well, a tiny bit stiff. And bruised.'

'But you managed to sleep last night?' Alfonso could not be more solicitous and Harriet is happy to accept his concern at face value, not to attribute it to thoughts of compensation, reputational damage or fears about negligence claims.

She nods and smiles, unwilling to tell an outright falsehood. 'Could you call me a taxi, please? I want to go and see Mrs Martindale.'

'Of course. I rang first thing. She had a comfortable night. But no need for a taxi, *signora*. One of the boys will drive you over in the minibus. No trouble at all. Five minutes, please.'

Guy, crossing the foyer, spots Harriet as Alfonso hurries away.

'Harriet!' He hugs her. 'How are you? Bella and I have been so worried.'

'Bless you. No, I'm . . . well, I'm still a bit shaken up, but I'm off to see Mary.'

'Are you sure that's wise? One of us could go.'

'No, really, I'd like to see her. Her husband's on his way, too. And a . . . friend.'

'Okay,' says Guy doubtfully. 'If you're sure . . .'

When he has left, Harriet dials Stephen's mobile. 'Can you talk?'

'Oh! Harriet! I was expecting . . . Yes, just for a mo'. Between meetings.'

'How are you?'

There is a long pause; in the background she can hear voices, footfalls, a distant telephone ringing. Finally, 'I'm not sure.'

'As soon as I get back, I'm going to see . . . someone. On Tuesday, if I can.' From the silence, she assumes he knows who she's referring to. 'Did you speak to Emily?'

'Yeah. Soon as I got back to the hotel.'

'What did she say?'

There it is again, that hesitation, as if he's picking his way carefully through a minefield.

'Stephen?'

'She said, why would anyone do something as wicked as that?'

⌣⌣⌣

'Bravo!' says Franco, inspecting Hester's *zeppole*. He picks up one of her tiny, custard-filled doughnuts delicately and pops into his mouth. He savours it. 'Ver', ver' good, Hester,' he praises her, using her name for the first time this week. He points at the array of different pastries and sweets at her station and says to the class in general, 'This *signora* is ver' good. She watch, she learn.'

Hester squirms as her fellow students applaud politely. As the great man moves away, Lionel whispers, 'Teacher's little pet,' and pats her back affectionately.

'Try one,' Hester offers, but Lionel pulls a face.

'Bit too sweet and greasy for my taste—for most people's, I'd have thought.'

She looks at the fruits of her labours. She can think of one person who would love them.

⌣⌣⌣

'Harriet!'

Mary's face lights up and she pushes herself higher up her pillows. She looks horribly battered, her hair flattened and a large padded dressing behind her ear, held in place with a lopsided bandage.

Harriet pulls up a chair. 'I'm not really supposed to be here,' she whispers, trying to make herself inconspicuous by crouching. 'It's not visiting hours yet. The nice nurse sneaked me in. Anyway, how are you?'

Mary spreads her hands. 'No idea. All a bit muddled last night, then they gave me something and I went out like a light.'

'But you've had a scan?'

'I think so. I remember you saying something about it before you left but, frankly, everything's a bit of a blur. I wish I'd known you were coming in; I'd have asked you to grab my nightie and wash bag.'

'Oh, what an idiot: I should've thought. Is there a shop in the hospital?'

'Don't worry,' says Mary, taking Harriet's hand. 'I'm just glad to see you. Wish to God I'd done Italian at school—my sign language isn't up to much. Anyway, never mind me, how are *you*? They did check you over too?'

Harriet nods. 'I'm fine.'

'You don't look fine. You look bloody terrible. Worse than me.'

'Have you looked in a mirror this morning?'

Mary laughs. 'Listen, did you say when Ron and Rhona are arriving, 'cos I've forgotten.'

'They're coming *together*? Is that wise?'

'Well, I assume they are—there's only one flight a day, if that.'

'But how will Rhona explain her presence to Ron?'

'No idea,' says Mary airily. 'You know what I realised this morning when I was lying here staring at the ceiling? Ron is just Rhona with "ha" taken out, which says it all.' She laughs feebly at Harriet's puzzlement. 'No sense of humour, our Ron. How did I bear it for so long? I've been thinking: close shave, life's too short et cetera. In fact, I've decided my best bet is to let things take their course. *Que sera.*'

'Lordy,' says Harriet, dismayed and impressed in equal measure by her new friend's chutzpah. *I could do with a bit of her attitude*, she thinks.

'What?' says Mary, smiling.

'Very brave.'

'Hmmm. We'll see. But what the hell—I could be *dead*, Harriet. Then where would I be?' She examines Harriet closely. 'What's up? Another row with your sister?'

It's the suddenness of the question, the lack of preamble, that undoes her. Tears spring from nowhere.

'Hey! Hey . . .'

'Sorry . . .' Harriet tries to shield her face, mortified. Hearing voices in the corridor outside, she goes to rise. 'That's probably the doctor.'

Mary grabs her hand.

'You are going nowhere until you tell me what the matter is.'

CHAPTER 22

There's something buzzing over by the window. A fly? A wasp? It's really annoying. Sunlight knifes its way through the curtains where he failed to pull them tight last night. Well, this morning, in fact: he'd finally fallen into bed at two am, having baked three different sorts of biscuits and then waited for them to cool so he could dip the ginger ones in chocolate.

His fingers find his face and the patches of tightened skin where he'd dabbed on more toothpaste in the early hours. Judging by the furry feel of his teeth, the toothpaste hadn't quite made it as far as his mouth. The buzzing continues. As he finally surfaces from the dregs of sleep he realises it's his phone; groping blindly on the floor, he locates his abandoned jeans beside the bed and scrabbles in the pocket. Eyes still shut tight against the blinding daylight, he doesn't bother to check the caller's identity.

'Yeah?'

'Morning, boyfriend,' says Nats, warm and intimate in his ear, 'hope I'm not interrupting anything . . .' She makes it sound decidedly suggestive. Ben lifts both hands out from under the bedclothes. He opens one eye, squinting at the Pepsi clock over his desk.

'Fuck me! Man, it's a quarter to frigging nine.'

'On a beautiful spring morning,' sings Nats. 'I know. Just back from a run and checking we're still on for later.'

A moment of confusion, then the fog clears. Right. Meeting Daria and Milo. 'Yeah. It's all good.' Another cog engages. 'You've been out for a run? Already?'

'Yep. Just a quickie. Five k.'

'Five . . .?!'

'Psychs me up for the day. So, we meeting or what?'

'Meeting?' Ben is still trying to process the thought of anyone going running at all this early in the day, let alone running five whole kilometres. What is this girl on?

'Yeah,' says Nats, giving the word three syllables at least, as if speaking to an imbecile. 'Duh . . . like to go over and meet the baby and his mum? And for you to give me my money?'

'Ben?' calls his mother from the landing. 'Darling? Would you like a cup of tea? I know you're awake.'

I'm only awake, thinks Ben, fuming, *because this birdbrain girl, who is one of the most annoying people I have ever met in my life, has woken me at some fucking ridiculous hour when I've only been in bed five minutes!*

'Yeah, ta, Mum,' he croaks, not wanting Isabelle to linger long outside his door eavesdropping. He waits for her to retreat down the landing; the floorboard at the top of the stairs creaks reassuringly. 'Listen, you'll get your money,' he hisses. 'I said, didn't I? Get out of my face, will you? I'm supposed to be revising.'

'Then get out of bed,' snaps Nats. 'See you five o'clock by the bandstand this evening or I'll come round to yours. We'll cycle over.'

'Bandstand,' he says quickly.

'And my twenty quid.'

'Look—'

'Twenty quid. This evening. Or no deal. And just remember, babes, you need me. Ciao.'

She is a total nightmare and then some. If he didn't know there wouldn't be a cat in hell's chance of wheedling a replacement from his parents, he'd have hurled his phone at the wall.

~~~

The morning doesn't get much better. His mother brings him in a mug of tea, moans about the state of his room ('I'm revising, all right?'), moans about the state of the kitchen ('It was late, okay?') and reminds him he'd promised his father he'd clean the car for a tenner ('Yeah, yeah, I know! Gimme a break!'). Personally, Ben thinks leaving the Lada camouflaged by as much dirt as possible goes at least some way to concealing both its make and age, but he really needs the money. Especially with loony Nats on his case. He'd checked his account online last night; it holds the princely sum of thirty-nine pounds. Out of that he has to pay his blackmailer, get hold of some booze for the party and—in his dreams—get a new T to wear. Like that's gonna happen. Where does the money go? He starts the month pretty flush, thanks to the parental standing order, but it sort of *evaporates*. It's not like he's profligate, despite that accusation being levelled at him periodically by his father. Jeez, if he thinks Ben is bad, he should see Jez! Despite getting boatloads of cash, he's always skint and has to go crawling to his scary dad. Ben shivers at the thought of confronting Brian Nairstrom. Or even Deirdre. Thank God his mum is such a soft touch. Maybe she's worth a punt . . .

Groaning, he tips himself out of bed, makes a half-hearted attempt to straighten the duvet, kicks assorted pants and socks out of sight and staggers into the bathroom. Showered, teeth cleaned, he peers at his skin under the unforgiving light over the mirror; yeah, that definitely looks a bit smoother. He rubs more toothpaste into the most protuberant zits, taking care to blend it in, but it still looks patchy. He tries a dab or two of his mother's foundation. That seems to do the trick.

~~~

'Gosh, you look rather flushed, darling,' says Isabelle as Ben reaches for the cereal packet. 'You're not going down with anything?'

'No, just done my face with really hot water.'

'You poor lamb, it does look sore. Are you still using that new lotion I bought you?'

Ben grunts something that might be read as a yes, unwilling to go through yet another post-mortem on the state of his skin. Almost every time his mother goes shopping she returns with more potions and unguents, each one featuring ecstatic youngsters with flawless faces gurning at their unhappy spotty contemporaries who have yet to experience the wondrous effects of the container's contents. He shovels cornflakes into his mouth, noting that the kitchen has already been restored to order and its customary cleanliness. Isabelle might not have a clue about cooking but she certainly knows how to tidy up after her errant and extremely messy offspring.

'Ta, Mum,' he says, jerking his head towards the sink.

'Don't tell your father,' whispers Isabelle, 'he was pretty cross with you this morning when he came down. Got chocolate on his sleeve.' While applauding his son's unlikely talents in the kitchen, it is George's unbending rule that Ben should learn to clear up after his frequent experiments. But Ben knows perfectly well that if he waits long enough, his mother will cave in, her horror of mess and disorder trumping her desire to toe her husband's line.

'Gonna make that tarte later.' His mother's face falls at the thought of another tsunami of flour and sugar deluging her pristine surfaces. But she's a doughty soul, Isabelle, and a doting mum. She summons a bright smile. 'Super, darling! I'm off shopping in a bit: anything you need?'

Ben has had the foresight to check his ingredients the night before. 'No, ta.' He decides to risk it. 'Don't suppose you could let me have a couple of quid on account, could you?'

'For the car?'

'No, Dad's paying me for that. Just for stuff and . . .' Ben looks at her with hangdog eyes. 'Thing is—' he's thinking fast '—I thought it would be nice to get Ralph a little thank you present for helping me;

you know, with my chemistry and that? I thought maybe a . . .' A what? What the frig would a nerdy bloke like Ralph Pickerlees want? 'A nice pen or something,' he finishes lamely.

Isabelle's heart fairly bursts with pride. What a thoughtful son they have raised! First the tarte tatin for Lynn and now a present for Ralph. She wishes George were there to see. She reaches for her handbag.

'That is a lovely idea, Ben. I'm sure Ralph will be really touched.'

You bet, thinks Ben, scarcely believing his success.

His mother extends a ten-pound note. 'There.'

'Oh!' He doesn't want to push his luck, but she is looking so thrilled . . .

'I meant a really *nice* pen. You know?'

'Oh!' says Isabelle, blushing faintly. She'd hate Ralph to think Ben *mean*. There are few things worse in her book or George's than being thought stingy. She pulls out another tenner and then, for good measure, a third. 'You should be able to get something pretty decent with that, shouldn't you?'

'I reckon,' says Ben, whipping the extra notes out of her hand before she can reconsider. 'Thanks, Mum. 'Course, I'll pay you back.'

'Oh, no,' says Isabelle automatically, basking in the warm glow of her son's vicarious beneficence.

'You're a star, Mum,' says Ben with a huge smile, transforming himself in an instant into an adorable and rather attractive young man. That's worth thirty quid of anybody's money.

CHAPTER 23

'Unbelievable!'

'I know.'

'Your own sister!'

Harriet looks away, eyes shining.

'And when did this letter arrive?'

'Beginning of April.'

'My God! She's known about it all that time . . . been in contact with . . . God! And that poor man, how must he be feeling? And you! Oh, Harriet . . .' Mary clutches her hand in sympathy; Harriet returns the pressure, once again perilously close to tears. She swallows them.

'Well . . . there it is. The damage is done. Now we—or rather I— have to try to undo it. Stephen deserves nothing less. As for Hester . . .' Mary is shaking her head, incredulous. For what is there to say? How to explain Hester's behaviour, her immediate assumption of Harriet's guilt? Has some poisonous resentment been simmering beneath Hester's stern exterior for years? Some residual childhood rivalry that has lain dormant for decades, waiting for evidence of her sister's duplicity, her amorality? How else to explain the silence, the subterfuge, the cruelty inherent in the ambush?

Harriet catches Mary's eye, tries a feeble smile. 'Sorry. You've enough to worry about.'

'Don't be daft. My problems almost pale into insignificance . . .'

Something occurs to her. 'You share a house, don't you? You and Hester. I mean, you can't just walk away.'

Walk away? The thought appals her. Leave The Laurels, their shabby but comfortable home? Leave the village, their friends? Leave Daria, Milo and Artem? Ben? Even George and Isabelle? Can she? And why should she?

'You mean . . . ? No. Golly. Early days. First, I've got to sort out this mess for Stephen.'

'Of course. I didn't mean to upset you. Can I help?'

'You?' says Harriet on the edge of a laugh, looking at the battered and bandaged figure in the bed.

'Yes!' says Mary, aggrieved. 'Why not? A couple of days and I'll be raring to go again. You need someone to bounce ideas off. You don't want to be tackling this all by yourself.'

No, I don't, thinks Harriet. *And I would never have thought I'd have to. Something like this, I'd have expected to have Hester by my side . . . and* on *my side*.

Mary's phone buzzes. As she reaches over to her cabinet for it, it buzzes again. She reads the messages aloud.

'*Just landed. See you very soon, darling. All my love, Rhona.*' She smiles happily, then opens the next one and laughs. '*Arrived. Ron.*' She loses the smile, gives Harriet a wry look. 'See? D'you suppose he's spotted her? He must have, don't you think?'

'Perhaps they'll share a taxi,' Harriet suggests with a flash of her old mischief. 'Exchange notes.'

'Or blows. Oh God. Can you imagine?' Mary looks up at the clock on the wall. 'Listen, I expect you need to get back, do you?'

'Oh,' says Harriet. Is this Mary trying to get shot of her? 'Yes, I suppose . . .'

'No, you nitwit, I don't want you to go. Honestly! It would be great to have you here when the two of them arrive. UN peacekeeper. Besides which, you can back me up about what happened.'

'The accident?'

157

Mary nods, sighing irritably. 'Ron'll be looking for any opportunity to allege negligence. The route was unsafe, there was no guardrail, blah blah blah. He's a solicitor, works for one of these bloody no win, no fee outfits. You know, the sort who are forever phoning you when you're dishing up supper, asking if you've tripped over a paving stone.'

'Oh, so infuriating! Ron does that?'

'Well, not personally. But there's nothing he likes better than sticking a knife—only metaphorically, of course, as far as I'm aware, but who knows?—into some luckless sod who has the misfortune to cross his path. I can't bear to think of him having a go at Alfonso or Marco or suing the hotel. Or even Gervais, for that matter.'

'Really?'

'Well, okay, maybe I'll make an exception for Gervais. But seriously—I want Ron to understand from the off that it was my own stupid fault. Oh, and that I pulled you down after me, before he accuses you of shoving me off the path or trying to crush me to death by falling on top of me.'

Harriet starts laughing. 'He might have me there, the size of me. I can't wait to meet him now.'

Mary smiles broadly. 'That's better. First time I've seen you looking even vaguely happy all visit. Now, be a love, would you, and see if you can rustle us both up a coffee while I stagger to the loo and try to make myself look vaguely presentable? After all, got to look my best: I'm expecting my lover. And my husband.'

～～～

'Hospital.'

'No!'

'One of the staff drove her over. Alfonso says she left about eleven. Not a word. Not a note. Nothing.'

'And nothing from Stephen?'

'No.' Hester forces a smile. 'Well! No point hanging about here. We might as well go back and get cracking on our ices. Unless . . .'

'What?'

'Quick drinkie first? Buck us up?'

'At this hour? Don't you think it's a bit—'

'For heaven's sake! I could do with a drop of Dutch courage.'

'Are we talking Franco or Harriet?'

~~~

'I wonder if I might have a few moments alone. With my wife.'

Rhona and Harriet exchange a complicit glance, then silently rise from their respective chairs.

'See you in a bit,' says Mary with a tiny wave like a cry for help. Behind Ron's sizeable back, Rhona spreads her hands as if to say: *What else can we do?*

'Coffee?' says Harriet outside in the corridor. 'There's a café on the ground floor.'

'She looks dreadful,' says Rhona, glancing back towards the room. She rakes her thick black curls back from her forehead with strong fingers, exposing a widow's peak. Her gold-flecked brown eyes are dark with worry. Harriet thinks of a panther. 'Do you think they're looking after her properly?'

'I'm sure they are.'

They start walking towards the stairs. Harriet searches around for something neutral to break the silence, then Rhona says abruptly, 'You do know about me and—'

'Yes.' She hadn't meant to reply so baldly. Or so brusquely.

'He knows too. Ron.'

Harriet looks across at her. Rhona flushes. 'He's known for months, truth be told. Confronted me outside the house one night. Late. Been drinking. He had, I mean. He wasn't aggressive. He was tearful, which was worse. The fact is, I've never had much time for him. Even when

159

my husband was around and we used to do things together—go down the pub, the odd meal—I found him hard going. Always thought he led Mary a hell of a dance. Controlling, you know?'

Harriet doesn't really, but she nods.

'Makes it worse somehow. I mean, him caring. Minding. I thought he'd just turn a blind eye, hope the whole thing would burn itself out.' She stops on the stair, looks down at Harriet on the tread below, voice hardening. 'It won't. Something like this, it's . . .' Her eyes glisten; she wipes an impatient hand across her nose. 'Sorry.'

'No, please,' Harriet reassures her, her own eyes prickling. It's hard to fathom who deserves her sympathy most. 'Does Mary know? About the confrontation?'

Rhona hesitates. They've reached the café in the foyer, busy with visitors, one or two ambulant patients enjoying a break with their families. No instant coffee in paper cups here; the tantalising aroma of freshly ground beans hangs in the air. Harriet's stomach suddenly awakes to its emptiness; a vague dull throb above one eye warns her she ignores the signals at her peril. She indicates a seat. 'You sit. My treat.'

When she returns with two black coffees and a tomato and goat's cheese bruschetta for herself, Rhona having declined food, Harriet finds her companion in a mellower mood. 'Thanks. That looks tasty.'

'I can easily get you—'

'No, really. Listen, Harriet . . .' Rhona leans forward, hands entwined on the table; Harriet admires her toned, muscular forearms. 'I can be a bit . . . abrasive at times, sorry.' Harriet bats the apology away. 'No, please. I know you've been caught up in all this mess by accident. You're supposed to be on holiday, for God's sake!'

Some holiday, thinks Harriet.

'And in answer to your earlier question: no. I haven't told Mary about Ron. About him knowing. Call me deceitful, call me cowardly, but I was afraid—that it would force her to choose.' She looks down into her coffee, says in barely more than a whisper, 'I thought I might lose her.'

CHAPTER 24

Ben and Nats are staring up at the bedroom windows, she with barely contained irritation, he cursing the fact he hadn't thought to check first. What a cretin.

'You didn't think to ring her, then?' says the girl. 'Check she was in? Before we biked all the way over here.'

'She's always in,' mutters Ben. He's trying not to show how out of breath he is, having struggled to keep up with his companion's apparently effortless rhythm on the ride over.

'Well, patently not,' says Nats. 'Unless she's hiding.'

'Why on earth would she be—'

'Joke.'

'Oh.' He tries the bell again.

'Did you give the toothpaste a go?'

'The what?' He'd heard perfectly well.

'Toothpaste. I wondered if it works.'

Ben is wondering too. He thinks his skin looks marginally better, feels smoother, but he's not going to ask for her opinion. No way.

A faint snatch of song from along the road saves him from having to respond. He sprints out on to the pavement. 'Wotcha!'

Daria is wheeling the buggy towards him, upending it periodically to sing the refrain of a nursery rhyme—at least he assumes that's what it is, as it seems to be in Belarusian—into Milo's face. He is squealing with delight, legs kicking in ecstasy with each repetition.

'Ben!' She stops singing and bends down to Milo, pointing. 'Look, *soneyka*, is Ben!' The baby, deprived of his game, had been about to roar his displeasure, but the sight of one of his favourite people sends him into further paroxysms of joy. He stretches out his pudgy arms as far as the buggy straps will allow, straining for release as the teenager swoops towards him like an aeroplane.

'We wondered where you'd gone,' he says, pressing the little snub nose like a button.

Milo gurgles.

'We?' Daria peers past him.

'Yeah, I brought my . . . a mate. To meet Milo.'

'Only Milo?' says Daria with feigned hurt.

'What ? Oh, you an' all. 'Course.'

'We are visiting Finbar, are we not, Milo? With no Harriet and Hester, I think: poor old man, he will be lonely. I take him piece of my *antonovka* apples pie—except not *antonovka* because your country does not—oh!' They have reached the gate and she is staring with astonishment at the girl sitting cross-legged on the doorstep. 'Hello?' says Daria, suspiciously, unwilling to push her son towards the stranger until there is some indication of her intent.

'Oh, yeah,' says Ben, squeezing past her and the buggy. 'This is Nats. My—'

'Girlfriend,' says Nats before he can finish. She dares Ben to contradict her, eyes dancing with mischief behind her glasses. 'Ben's always talking about you and Milo, and I really wanted to meet you. Hope you don't mind? Oh, isn't he the cutest thing?!' And before Ben, Daria or Milo have a chance to react, Nats has leapt to her feet, freed Milo from his harness with one snap and is holding him at arm's length, pulling faces. For a brief moment Milo, eyebrows comically raised, regards this apparition with alarm, then he reaches out and takes firm hold of one of her braids. Nats mimes first wide-eyed surprise, then mock terror and finally elation, and Milo, entranced, is lost.

'Sorry. Better let you get the door open,' she says, stepping aside, as Daria, speechless, finds herself wheeling the buggy up the path, and fumbling in her pockets for her keys, all the while staring at her visitor, now engaged in a pretend tug of war with her son, still clinging triumphantly to his prize and trying to grab another with his other hand, while Nats swings her braids tantalisingly from side to side.

Ben and Daria lift the buggy into the hall, she hissing, 'Ben, that is a black girl!' as though he might not have noticed.

'Really?'

'Do not be *durylka*!'

'You what?'

Daria scrabbles for the epithet. '*Idiot!* This girl, she is your—'

'Yeah. Well, no . . . well—'

'For real?' Now Daria has got over the shock, she finds herself rather relieved; there have been times when she has thought Ben was looking at her . . . not as Ben should. Artem, unsurprisingly given the rocky nature of his relationship with the youngster, has hinted as much more than once. 'Well, she is . . . she is very pretty girl. What is the name again?'

'Nats,' says its owner, following them into the kitchen, having overhead Daria's judgement. She has Milo on one hip as though she has carried countless babies before. 'Short for Natalie.' She pulls a face. 'Grim, eh?'

'No,' says Daria. 'I have cousin Nataly. Pretty girl, pretty name.'

'Thanks,' says Nats, turning her attention back to Milo, who is still looking at her intently, and sucking the end of one braid.

From across the kitchen, Ben regards her with a mixture of exasperation and jealousy. Barging in as if she owns the place. Making eyes at Milo. *It's only the novelty,* he thinks. *It's not like she's spent the amount of time with him that I have. Bet she hasn't the first idea about what he eats, bedtime and all that. He'll soon get bored with her.*

'Kettle, Ben?' says Daria. 'I think Natalie will like some tea?'

Nats would.

'And I have special Belarusian biscuits—you would like to try?'

Nats would.

Ben turns the tap savagely, spraying his jeans with water as it hits the bottom of the kettle.

'I make these,' says Daria, prising open the tin. 'But I must hide from Ben. He is very greedy, no?'

'Oh, absolutely,' says Nats. 'Ooh, these look delicious. I'm always saying—aren't I, Ben?—*leave some for me, will you!*' She laughs gaily and Daria joins in.

Ben slams the kettle back on its base and glares at Nats. She reaches across and neatly flicks the switch to turn it on. He could murder her.

'I hope it's not inconvenient, us just dropping in like this, Daria.' Nats breaks off a tiny piece of biscuit. 'May I?' Ben waits for the explosion of horror from Daria; she has always been adamant about not feeding Milo between meals.

'Well . . .' says Daria. 'Little treat, yes? Just for special times.'

Milo crams the fragment into his mouth and gums it deliriously. Nats and Daria laugh.

Mugs crash down onto the counter, one, two, three.

'Careful, Ben!' cries Daria crossly. She shakes her head at Nats: men, eh? They exchange a conspiratorial smile.

'You are in class with Ben?'

'Oh, no,' says Nats, sounding suitably awed, 'he's older than me.'

'So you do not study your books as hard as poor Ben?'

'I wouldn't say that.' A blinding smile at poor Ben. 'I work pretty hard most of the time.'

'Ben, he work hard because he is going to be famous cook one day.'

'Chef,' says Ben quickly.

'I know,' says Nats reverently. 'How brilliant is that? A famous cook.'

'*Chef!*' Are they deaf or what?

164

'And you?' asks Daria. 'You have a dream, too?'

'Well . . .' says Nats with apparent reluctance and modesty. 'Not nearly so exciting as Ben. I just want to be a lawyer. A barrister.'

Ben slops boiling water onto the counter.

'A barrister?' breathes Daria. 'Like on the TV? With the white . . .' She flaps a hand.

'Wig, yeah.'

'And the black . . . er . . .'

'Gown, yeah.'

'You hear this, Ben? You have very clever girlfriend.'

'Yeah,' says Ben wringing the dishcloth viciously into the sink, 'don't I know it.'

⌣⌣⌣

Nats is careful not to outstay her welcome. She stops just long enough to comprehensively charm Daria and Milo, whose face crumples when, gently loosening his grip on her hair, she gets up to leave.

'Aw, don't cry, little one,' she says, caressing his head as he sobs on his mother's shoulder. 'See you soon, I hope.'

'I hope too,' says Daria, smiling broadly.

Ben noisily drains his mug and reaches for another biscuit.

Nats picks up her bag and slings it across her body. 'Have a great time tomorrow night, won't you? Ben says you're off to a *céilidh*.'

'A what?' asks Daria in bewilderment, saving Ben the trouble.

'A *céilidh*. Barn dance. That's what they call them in Scotland and Ireland.'

'Well, we're in England, aren't we?' says Ben sulkily.

Nats widens her eyes at Daria, who laughs.

'You staying?' says Nats to Ben, with an infinitesimal jerk of her head towards the front door.

'Yeah, just for a bit . . .'

'You are letting Natalie ride alone?' says Daria, frowning.

'No worries,' says Nats. 'I ride all over. 'Sides, I cycle way faster than Ben.' She laughs. 'Don't I, *babes*?' Ben glowers. Nats beams. 'Bye, Daria; bye-bye, Milo . . .' She blows the baby a kiss.

Ben follows her out to her bike. 'All right then?' he hisses.

'Beautiful baby,' she says, fastening her helmet. 'You got the hots for his mum or something?'

'No!'

'Just asking,' she says, wheeling the bike out to the road. She stops. 'You're a rubbish actor, you know. No one in their right mind would believe we had a thing going.'

'We haven't!' he says hotly.

Nats throws back her head and laughs. 'Thank fuck.'

Daria appears in the doorway, Milo in her arms. 'Natalie,' she calls, 'I am thinking. You want to come and look after Milo with Ben tomorrow evening? He would like very much.'

'Ben or Milo?' Nats calls back.

Daria wags a playful finger. 'Naughty girl! Both! Both the boys love you!'

'Yeah, right,' mutters Ben.

'I know,' shouts Nats, pedalling away. 'I'm irresistible. Thanks, Daria. I'd like that. See you!'

Ben slouches back into the house, shutting the door firmly.

'What a lovely girl,' says Daria, making for the stairs. 'Good manners. You are lucky boy, Ben.'

He grunts noncommittally.

'Though why she likes grumpy boy like you . . .'

'I'm not grumpy!'

'He say he's not grumpy, Milo. Do we believe him? No. Lovely Natalie, she is not grumpy, is she, *soneyka*? But poor Ben has exams, he has to work so hard. Perhaps this makes him—oh, you are going? Not staying for bath time?'

'No,' says poor Ben, shrugging on his jacket. 'On second thoughts, gotta get back to my books. See you.'

'Oh . . . okay. Say goodbye, Milo. Hey, Ben, you ride fast, perhaps you catch Natalie, eh?'

Catch Natalie? Some hope.

CHAPTER 25

The cooks are clearing up, hindered rather than helped by the unfortunate Enrico, restored once more to his position as metaphorical punchbag for Signor Riccardi, whose good humour has lasted only until mid-afternoon. Remaining cordial and charming is clearly too much of a challenge for the great man, even as the end of his torment approaches. One day to go. One more day of squandering his immense talents on these dabblers. It is infuriating that the final day of the course—*mio dio*, why had he agreed to this all those months back?—involves his students preparing dinner for the other guests, supposedly to display the wealth of experience they have acquired over the week spent worshipping at his feet. It would be quicker and safer by far to do the entire meal himself, even with *cretino* Enrico by his side, rather than risk the trashing of his reputation by these halfwits. *Al diavolo!* He looks at the eager faces now gathered around him, awaiting his pronouncement. Perhaps if he keeps things really simple . . .

'So, tomorrow is big day, no? Tomorrow you are cooking like in real restaurant for real diners. People are dreaming already of wonderful dishes, food of the gods.' He kisses his fingers theatrically. 'There will be flavours, beautiful. There will be 'erbs, a little spice, *piccolo, si*? Too much and the dish is . . .' He rotates his pudgy hands through the air as he searches for the word.

'Overpowered?' suggests Hester, increasingly wearied by his shtick

168

and anxious to get away. Surely Harriet isn't still at the hospital? She can't hide forever . . .

Franco masks his irritation; it's adulation he's after, not participation. Still, the *signora* is his star pupil. 'Overpower, yes. This we don' like. No, no, no. So. The menu tomorrow.' He pauses dramatically. 'We start with the pasta. Always the pasta!'

What about antipasti? thinks Hester.

'You and you—' he points at Lionel and Melanie pugnaciously '—will prepare the linguine, yes?'

Hester, whose almost transparent linguine had been fulsomely praised by the maestro, is disappointed not to be chosen for this dish. 'Remember, we use special flour—'

'*Farina di grano tenero,*' says Lionel eagerly.

Franco frowns at the interruption. 'Yes, correct . . . We serve with the mussels, the clams, the baby squids, like I show you. Okay? And the parmesan, if we must, for the English. Pah!' He considers the remainder of the class at length, eyes flicking from one person to the next appraisingly—aping, thinks Hester impatiently, the ridiculous judges on the TV cookery programmes whose deliberations take aeons. After a lifetime, the reliable teacher from Woking is allocated the making of the ciabatta, to be followed by gelato. He jabs a finger at the two middle-aged women who have gossiped and giggled their way through the course on the farthest stations. 'Yes! For you, *pollo ai semi di finocchio.*' The women frown uncertainly at Franco, then exchange panicky looks. '*Finocchio?* You remember?'

'Fennel seeds,' offers Hester, to spare the women's blushes, disappointed not to be chosen for something savoury herself; she guesses what's coming her way.

'Of course!' says Franco, a little coldly. 'Thank you. Fennel. Ver' popular in Italy. With the chicken. Enrico will assist with vegetables. And you, Hester *cara*, you are our queen of the puddings and pastries! So . . .' He makes an exaggerated moue of regret as if to say, what did you expect?

Hester accepts her fate, wanting only to get back to the hotel.

Franco leads a desultory round of applause. 'Tomorrow, then, is the showcase. Much excitement. Much pressure. Here prompt at nine o'clock. No sleeping in! Early breakfast, much coffee and then we start. It will be great fun.' Somehow he makes this sound more like a threat than something to look forward to.

∽∽

'Hester.'

Harriet steps away from the shadow of the wall, a glass of wine in each hand. Hester stops in mid-stride, blinking in the bright sunlight and almost overbalancing; Lionel, a few steps behind, puts out a steadying hand. The other students flow around the blockage on the path on their way back to the main building.

'Can we talk?' says Harriet. She holds up one glass. 'Barolo.'

'Hetty—' starts Lionel.

'Excuse us,' says Harriet firmly, her eyes fixed on Hester's face.

Lionel hesitates, then, at a nod from Hester, reluctantly slopes off towards the hotel. Harriet gestures to a nearby table below a vine-clad balustrade threaded through with wisteria with its distinctive vanilla and honey scent. 'Shall we?'

The sisters sit facing each other across the wrought-iron table, Harriet sweeping aside a drift of fallen purple petals, shrivelled in the sun. They each raise their glasses to their lips in an awkward toast.

'So?' says Hester, swallowing, unable any longer to quell her indignation. 'You took your time.'

Keep calm, Harriet cautions herself. Her jaw muscles tighten. 'Do me the courtesy of hearing me out, will you.' It's not a request. 'Without interruptions.' She can see Hester fighting not to launch into a vituperative attack, opting instead for a gulp of wine. She takes this for acquiescence.

'So . . .' she begins.

~~~

'Oh, God,' whispers Hester, the wine turning to acid. She pushes her glass away with an unsteady hand. She looks across the table at Harriet: the mussed hair (*it needs trimming*, she thinks distractedly; Ben pops into her mind), the papery eyelids, the dark shadows under her eyes. Her gaze drops away. *What have I done?*

Harriet stares levelly at her sister, wondering what is going through her mind now everything is out in the open. Well, not quite everything . . . For herself, the fact that they are now on speaking terms and the events in the garden the previous night have been revealed is a huge step forward, but the hurt and bewilderment induced by Hester's extraordinary conduct remains. Why the secrecy? Why hadn't Hester—the minute Stephen's letter arrived and, opening it, she realised her mistake—why hadn't she confronted Harriet there and then? She can almost hear Hester's astonished tones: *What on earth is all this about? Harriet? What's going on?* Why hadn't she reacted in her customary way, leaping in with both large bony feet, all bombast and umbrage? Saved herself the weeks of suspicion and worry, and Stephen and Harriet the awfulness of that midnight confrontation?

'Why, Hetty?' she says softly, and Hester is felled by that familiar diminutive. Her eyes prickle; she sniffs desolately, snatching a broken breath. Her fingers shred a withered leaf, its fragments skittering around the table with each downward exhalation.

'I don't know.'

Harriet stiffens. After all the trouble and heartache she's caused! 'Not good enough.'

Hester thrashes about for the words, any words, that might go some way towards explaining what propelled her down this catastrophic path. Finally, shamefacedly, brokenly . . .

'We'd just had a bit of a row about Ben—another row, I should say—about you covering for him . . . something to do with Isabelle, I can't remember exactly, something Ben was keeping from her. It got

171

rather heated. You said I was being a prig: "What harm will it do? She needn't know." And I thought: you've changed your tune, goody-two-shoes who hates to tell a lie. And then—look, I know how stupid and petty it seems—but I went into the larder and all the biscuits had gone. And I thought: why do I bother? Why do I try to stop you piling on the weight—it's not good for you, not at your age, you know what the doctor said—when all you do is go behind my back, shovelling all the wrong things into your mouth, and—'

'This is all down to some *biscuits*?!'

'No! You're not listening. I'm trying to explain.' Hester's customary bite begins to bubble up through the self-flagellation. 'I'm trying to be honest.'

'Try harder.'

Hester's voice toughens. 'All right!' A pause while she damps down her rising temper. 'Look, I was shocked. The letter. You'd gone out to the supermarket or something. With Ben. I read it and I felt sick. I had to sit down. I mean, why would anyone contact you out of the blue, unless it was true?'

'Unless it was—'

'Okay!' A deep breath. 'Please. Look . . . you've read it. It's . . . heart-felt. Convincing. It convinced me, anyway. But I was shocked to the core! I wanted time to think about it, so I . . .'

'Concealed it.'

'. . . delayed telling you.'

'And never once in the days that followed did you think to say: "Look at this, Harry"?'

'Of course I did! But the longer I delayed the more impossible it got. Besides, things were so tricky between us . . .'

'And now we know why!' Harriet snatches up her glass.

'I persuaded myself that you'd buried this, you'd purposely kept it a secret—and I was sure you'd just deny it.'

'Why would I?'

'I don't know! I haven't felt myself for months. The slightest thing . . .

I was angry with you, jealous—' The hot, tangled mass of emotions are tumbling out now, as though a dam has burst.

'Jealous?!' Harriet's glass stops halfway to her mouth.

'Yes! I know how stupid it sounds.'

'Too bloody right! Jealous of what? What on earth is there to be jealous about?'

'Everything. You, your relationship with Ben, with Daria, Milo . . .'

'Hetty! What are you—'

'I know, I know! I can't explain it. I hate myself. I look in the mirror sometimes and I think: who is this woman? I used to be so sure of myself, Harry—too sure at times, I know. Bossy old Hester, never knows when to shut up. No, don't laugh. Don't you ever have those horrible thoughts in the middle of the night: What am I doing? I lie there and it's all so . . . *frightening*. What's going to happen to me? If I start losing my mind, if my health goes . . .'

'Oh, Hetty . . . you silly, silly . . .'

Harriet is up, she's round the table, she has Hester in her arms, that familiar bony frame now shaking with sobs, and she's cradling her sister as they weep together, a single knot of grief and regret.

⌣⌣

Lionel, alone in the bar, his face inches from the glass, watches the two women embrace. His face tightens.

CHAPTER 26

'What time you off then?'

Ben's just got to the trickiest part of the recipe: turning the tarte out of the baking dish without leaving any of the caramelised pineapple stuck to the base. He holds the plate tight over the dish, turns it over swiftly, gives it one violent shake, places it on the counter and gingerly lifts the dish away. The inverted tarte sits exactly in the middle of the plate, every slice of pineapple in place, the pastry evenly risen and nicely browned. Perfection.

'Oh, darling!' gasps Isabelle. 'That is magnificent!' His mother, a stranger to the mechanics of the simplest of recipes, thinks all his cooking is brilliant, but even he has to admit this is one of his best. He whips his phone out and takes a photo, then sends it to Hester with a note: *And I made the pastry!* His aunt will appreciate the effort involved in making puff pastry from scratch. Only amateurs buy it ready-made, she has sniffed on many occasions. He'll update his blog later. He knows he's been a bit lax in recent months but Nats' approbation, much as he hates to admit it, has rekindled his interest in it.

'Tomorrow?' he prompts.

'Oh,' says Isabelle, still lost in wonderment. 'Mid-morning, I expect. Your father will want a swim in the afternoon, I dare say, and I'll pop this over to your Auntie Lynn and see if she wants a hand with anything. Do you want to write a card or something?'

Ben doesn't, but he supposes it's politic to play the game. His mother ferrets in the study and returns with a gruesome notelet featuring two improbably fluffy kittens gambolling around a flower-stuffed basket. 'Seriously?' he says, appalled.

'She'll appreciate the thought.'

'Yeah, but she might think I chose it.'

Isabelle laughs gaily. 'Oh, you teenagers! It's what you write in it that matters.'

'Like what?'

'Goodness me! Do you want me to write it for you?' Ben thinks this wouldn't be a bad idea, but realises that his mother is attempting sarcasm. He grabs a biro and scribbles: *Dear Auntie Lynn, Sorry I couldn't make your party. Have a good one. Hope you like pineapple!!! Bx.* Somewhere at the back of his mind he remembers the aunts grizzling about exclamation marks but he can't remember why. That'll do.

'Oh, Ben.' His mother's eyes are moist. 'What a thoughtful boy you are. She'll be over the moon.'

Anyone less likely to be over the moon than sallow, morose, hypochondriac Lynn he can hardly imagine, but whatever. He gives Isabelle a brief hug and sets off for his bedroom. He's got some serious planning to do and he's already running through recipes, ingredients and timings for tomorrow's cooking. He leaves Isabelle to fathom how best to transport the large, sticky tarte safely to Derbyshire and closes his bedroom door firmly behind him.

He checks Facebook, reassures himself about the numbers for tomorrow night, has a quick look at his Twitter account, uploads the picture of his tarte, retweets a neat quote from a chef in California he's following, then texts Nats to tell her he has the money and will give it to her tomorrow night. An instant reply: in her hand first thing tomorrow at the latest or no deal. Ben's face bunches with exasperation and anger. Nobody in the history of the whole world has ever pissed him off so much. He knows what Nats' 'first thing' means: no way is he going to get up early tomorrow. Not for her, anyway. He fires back a terse text saying he'll be over right away. *Be still my beating heart!* comes the reply. What the fuck?! He grabs his jacket and wallet and thunders down the stairs.

'Going out!' he yells, making for the garage and his bike.

Isabelle hurries to the front door. 'Dad'll be home any minute! What about supper? What about your revision? And where's your helmet? Lights!'

The reply is a perfunctory wave as Ben powers down the street and disappears from sight.

⌣⌣⌣

His temper improves slightly as he gets into his cycling stride. It's only a mile or so to Nats' place; he whizzes around parked cars and weaves his way to the front of the queue of traffic at the crossroads, then scoots across on a red, earning a furious horn blast from the brick lorry bearing down on him. The speed and the cool air rushing at him is invigorating and then it comes to him in a sudden, heart-stopping flash: where Nats is, there too might, just possibly, be Louisa. The thought of her—that hair, those legs, that intoxicating musky scent—erases her sister in an instant: he replays their recent encounter frame by wonderful frame, so caught up in it that he only just avoids ploughing into a bloke shambling across a zebra crossing. Slamming his brakes on, Ben slews to an ungainly halt and is about to shout some ill-deserved abuse when the startled man, now safely on the pavement, calls his name.

'You're in a hurry,' says Ralph Pickerlees with commendable friend-liness, given the fate he has just so narrowly avoided.

'Sorry, mate,' says Ben, breathless from both his exertions and the close shave. 'Lot on my mind. Miles away.'

'Ah,' says Ralph kindly, 'revision, eh? How's it going?'

'Yeah. Good. Well, you know . . .' He puts his foot on the pedal, scanning the road for a gap in the traffic.

But Ralph's in no hurry. 'Any time you want to talk, I'd be glad to help.'

Ben's face floods with colour as he recalls his deception. He feels a right shit. The man may be a nerd and boring as fuck, but he means well. 'Yeah, ta for that.' An idea bursts in his brain. Dare he? 'Matter of fact . . . Ralph . . . I was, like, wondering. Coupla things I'm not sure about, you know, chemistry and that. Don't suppose I could have a word sometime?'

'Of course!' Ralph smiles broadly. 'I'd be only too delighted.'

'Yeah? Say if I give you a bell Saturday?'

'Saturday's fine. What time?'

'Two-ish?'

'Brilliant.'

'Awesome.' Ben sketches a wave, starts to pedal away.

'Ben!'

He stops. Now what?

'My number?'

'Oh yeah . . .'

Ralph reels it off and Ben taps it swiftly into his phone. Then Ralph insists on taking his.

'Can you give me a rough idea what you're struggling with? So I can mug up before we speak?'

Ben flounders around for anything remotely convincing. 'Well, there's, like, quite a lot of things . . .'

'For instance?'

'Er . . .' He tries to conjure the jumble of books on his desk. 'Dynamic equilibrium?'

'No sweat. Anything else?'

What is this? An exam? 'Er . . . Le Châtelier's thingy?'

'Principle. Okay. Honestly, there's really not that much to—'

'Ta ever so, mate. Gotta go,' says Ben, desperate to escape before he's called upon to remember anything else. 'I owe you big-time. Laters.' He pushes off; Ralph's response is lost in the roar of traffic.

Ben smiles to himself: now he really does have a revision tutorial with the man, so he isn't lying to his parents at all. And if he has to cancel, well, that's how it goes . . .

⌣⌣

'You look hot.' Nats smirks at Ben from the doorway and holds out her hand. 'As in, sweaty, before you get overexcited.'

'Been cooking.' He shoves two tenners at her.

The smirk disappears to be replaced by something that might almost be mistaken for respect. Almost. 'Like what?'

He describes the tarte tatin.

'Nice. Should've brought some over.'

She's made no move to invite him in. He's trying to peer past her, listen out for voices; the television's on and all that's audible is the manic cackle of a studio audience.

'Don't suppose I could have a glass of water?'

Nats shrugs, a little smile playing around her lips. 'I guess. Won't be a mo'.' She steps back into the hall and half closes the door. Ben seethes, ears pricked for the slightest evidence of Louisa's presence. Seconds later, Nats is back with a glass, coming out onto the path this time to pass it to him, pulling the door nearly shut behind her. Eyeing him with amusement, she says, 'Anyway, thanks for coming over. I could've dropped by on my run first thing in the morning.'

'It's cool. Needed to stretch my legs.' He drains the glass, gives it back.

'What time tomorrow? To go over to Daria's?'

'Meet you seven at the newsagent's?'

'Okay.' She pushes the door open a fraction and slips into the house.

Ben reads this as a farewell and turns his bike around, flinging one leg over to walk it down the path. He sets off back the way he came, downhearted; someone calling his name brings him to an abrupt halt. 'Ben? Babes?'

Louisa! Circling swiftly, he races back. Nats is standing at the gate. Alone.

'What? What?' He knows she knows what he was hoping for.

'Just thought you might be interested. She's out with Joe. At a gig.'

Nats retraces her steps to the front door.

Ben gulps. 'Joe?' he says to her retreating back.

'Yeah. Anyway, see you tomorrow. 'Bye-ee.'

The front door slams.

～～～

Nats listens for the click of Ben's wheels slowly turning for home. The look on his face! Their American cousin Jo visits very rarely; she's over on business, was offered two tickets for One Direction at the last minute and Lou and Nats had tossed for them. (Nats, to her relief—and Lou's jubilation—lost.) Well, there's no-one to blame but himself if he's going to wallow in misery and jealousy all night. Shouldn't jump to conclusions, should he?

CHAPTER 27

Hester feels light-headed and in a vague but not wholly unpleasant way purged, as though the boil of her suspicions and bitterness has been lanced. Her primary emotion, however, is one of horrible embarrassment. At her conduct, her misreading of the situation from the outset and, perhaps worst of all, at having succumbed to such a storm of weeping, clinging to Harriet's comfortable bulk in mortification. She sniffs hard once more and fumbles for a fresh tissue. Harriet quietly eases the wineglass closer to her and Hester obediently takes a sip, waiting for Harriet to break the silence, conscious that this is the first time in months they have sat together so ... well, companionably. *God, how I've missed her!*

Harriet, ostensibly looking out across the sweep of the gardens dappled in late afternoon sunshine, the distant mountains hazy, watches Hester out of the corner of her eye. The almost absurd melodrama of the past two days has exhausted them both; for the moment she is happy to let the silence wash over them, cleansing away the enmity—no, not too strong a word—that bubbled so viciously and swiftly to the surface. What does this reveal about the true state of their relationship? An irrevocable rift? Of course, she would be the first to admit that, like most people living in close proximity, they have had their differences in the past, some alarmingly vitriolic, especially where politics is concerned. But nothing in their history, those sudden irruptions of ill humour if not outright anger, had prepared her for the shock of Hester's full-throated denunciation of her character, her morals, her integrity. It wasn't so much the fact of the assault but the obvious relish with which Hester had delivered it, as though she had been storing up this mountain of bile for years . . .

And yet, and yet . . . that attempt to articulate the inexplicable, the sense of life slipping by, anchors loosed, time rampaging into a dark and terrifying future, she can empathise with that. No-one, surely, is immune from those insidious thoughts that worm their way out of the recesses of the mind in the small hours: what have I done? What mark have I left? Rightly or wrongly, everyone wants their life to have had some scintilla of meaning, some influence, however tiny, on those left behind. She thinks: *I should say these things. Tell her I understand. Tell her I forgive her—*

'We all need to matter, Hetty.' Words come before she's quite ready. 'It's part of the human condition.'

She might not have spoken.

'Such a fool,' says Hester, head averted, her voice harsh. She purses her lips as though trying to corral unwise words. 'I never cry.'

'Perhaps you should,' says Harriet gently. She doesn't like this defeated, deflated sister; she wants her old cantankerous sparring partner back. Hester's diminution threatens her own sense of self, the certainties that keep the shivers under control.

'It's not just about us,' she says.

'Stephen.' It's not a question.

'Yes.' The pause lengthens. 'I promised him. We owe him that.'

'Do you know where to start?'

'Oh, yes, I think so,' says Harriet with a robustness she does not wholly feel. What she does feel, though, is the first stirring of indignation, if not anger, at being an unwitting pawn in a decades-long deception.

'Care to tell me?' The words edged with doubt, as though Hester does not believe herself worthy of her sister's confidence.

Harriet hesitates. There is something about putting her surmises into words that worries her: what if she's barking up not only the wrong tree but ferreting in entirely the wrong forest?

'Fair enough.' From the hurt in Hester's voice, Harriet might just as well have slapped her.

'No! I didn't mean . . . Hetty, it's not that I don't want to tell you, simply that I don't want to set hares running unnecessarily.'

'As I did, you mean.'

Harriet snaps. 'Hetty, once and for all, will you stop it! This isn't you: self-pitying, self-regarding. You got it wrong. Okay! Live with it. Whatever's happened, it's over, you hear me? Over.'

Hester looks at her sister in astonishment; an astonishment that swiftly turns to pique, if not anger. Hasn't she just apologised? Since when did Harriet get so self-righteous—

'I do hope I'm not interrupting?'

Hester spins around, intent on sending whoever has had the temerity to interrupt a private conversation packing. What confronts her is Lionel, who has somehow managed to emerge from the terrace's foliage without either of them noticing. He carries two large glasses of wine. His expression is anxious.

'I thought perhaps . . . a refill?'

The Ribbleswell girls were well taught by their exacting parents, particularly the major. That there is nothing more reprehensible than the laundering of private matters in public had been drummed into them from infancy. Hester swallows the compulsion to dismiss Lionel peremptorily and send him scurrying back to the hotel; Harriet with effort steadies her breathing, takes a deep breath and manages to conjure a smile. 'How kind.'

Lionel's tense muscles relax a fraction. He had waited in the bar as long as he could bear, but finally his innate curiosity and his genuine concern for Hester had overridden his fears of a rebuff. He so wants Hetty to realise how worried he is about her . . . He hovers hopefully.

'Please . . .' says Hester, indicating a chair, avoiding Harriet's gaze.

Lionel swiftly sits, eyes darting cautiously from sister to sister. A rather uncomfortable silence falls. Lionel shreds a desiccated leaf between his fingers in unwitting echo of Hester's earlier destruction.

The two women reach forward simultaneously to sip the fresh wine, which is palatable, if somewhat lacking in body.

Lionel hurries to explain, covering himself. 'It was someone's birthday . . . he stood everyone a glass. Is it—' he gropes through the new vocabulary Hester has taught him over the past week for the right word; fails '—okay?' Much as he has enjoyed the different wines he has sampled under Hester's tutelage over the past days, and much as he has learnt about vintages, regions, terroirs, he is at heart and knows he will ever be a beer man, though he is careful to conceal his predilection from Hester lest it adversely colour her opinion of him.

'Hmm,' says Hester with mild but unmistakable distaste. 'Perfectly acceptable. If you like this sort of thing. What do you think, Harriet?' Everyone notes the *Harriet*. Hester stares challengingly at her sister, who has no option but to continue the banalities.

'Very refreshing. Perhaps a trifle thin, but for an aperitif . . .' Harriet remembers her manners. 'Thank you, Lionel. Very thoughtful.' *Not that you had to pay for it*, she thinks, instantly chastising herself for her mean-spiritedness. He's a pleasant chap; if only he weren't so . . . *ubiquitous.*

Silence descends again, this time a deadening pall that repels conversation. The three people around the table nurse their individual grievances: Hester still smarting from Harriet's censure, Lionel put out by the indifferent response to his gesture, and Harriet irritated by his insensitivity. Can't he see they don't want to be interrupted? She wants to clear the air with her sister after the weeks of subterfuge and deceit, to restore the equilibrium that characterised their shared lives until Hester, for reasons still not properly explained, set in train the disastrous events that have brought them to this juncture.

But Lionel sits on, apparently oblivious. Harriet's indignation hardens. Can he really be this obtuse? She glances at Hester, but sees from the set of her face and her averted profile that there is no help to be had from that quarter. The thought of sitting over dinner making polite, stilted conversation is more than she can bear. Perhaps she could ask for a tray in her room, pleading a not wholly fictitious fatigue.

She gets to her feet.

'Oh!' says Lionel, suddenly animated. 'Are you going? Don't say I've driven you away!'

It is with a considerable effort that Harriet presses her palms down hard on the table and contrives a smile. 'Not at all,' she manages. 'I need to . . . avail myself of the facilities.'

She hears across the table an infinitesimal intake of breath that anyone else might have taken for relief. It is not. It is Hester wordlessly fulminating at her sister's deliberate use of a phrase that she abhors, a phrase much employed by Peggy Verndale, whose propensity for euphemism is a perennial source of guilty mirth between them.

'See you at dinner!' calls Lionel after her as she hurries up the steps towards the hotel.

Two more evenings, Harriet thinks. *Just two more evenings until Saturday and he goes home. I can do it.*

FRIDAY

CHAPTER 28

'Hello?'

Ben, key halfway to the lock, freezes.

'I say, hello? It's Bill, isn't it?'

Ben turns slowly. Peggy Verndale, face aquiver with curiosity, is peering over the top of the hedge. He sidles swiftly in front of the carrier bag containing two six-packs of lager beside him on the step.

'Ben,' he says.

'Ben! Of course. Silly me. The Flower Pot Men,' trills Peggy, to Ben's utter mystification. 'Before your time, no doubt. The nephew?' There is a flurry of movement, some growling, a yippy bark and she disappears from view momentarily. 'Stop it, Seth! Behave! Gideon, get off him!' Her face, somewhat redder, reappears. 'These wretched dogs. Worse than the grandchildren. Are they back then? I thought they said—'

'Monday,' says Ben quickly, still frozen on the doorstep.

'That's what I thought. I had to get a couple of the girls to fill in for them on Monday morning, that's how I know.'

'Fill in?'

'What? Oh, bridge.' She looks up at the windows. 'Why are all the curtains drawn?'

'Sun,' says Ben.

'Sun?'

'Yes. Protect the furniture.'

187

'The—? Good Lord,' says Peggy, clearly picturing, like Ben, the dilapidated decor of The Laurels: saggy-bottomed sofas, wonky chairs and tables whose acquaintance with wax or even spray polish, until Daria's arrival, has been slight. 'Well ... I suppose ...' Peggy, forthright as ever, cuts to the chase. 'What are you doing here, then?' The question sounds to Ben's guilty ears extremely accusatory.

'I ... they ... Aunt Hester ...' he scrabbles, 'asked me to ... yes, clean out the fridge.'

'Clean out the—?' Understanding dawns. 'Of course, you're the cooking boy, aren't you?'

'S'pose,' says Ben, offended.

'Marvellous! Too many young people these days ... I must say I'm surprised Hester didn't think to do that before they left. I always clear mine top to bottom before we go away. Mind you ...' The image of festering food hangs in the air. 'Some people are not quite so particular, I suppose.' Seth or Gideon barks impatiently. 'All right! Walkies in a minute.'

Would she never go?

'Don't let me hold you up.' Peggy waits. Ben reluctantly inserts the key and turns, trying to slip through the tiniest of gaps and shield the cottage's interior from view. Peggy, gimlet-eyed, still manages to peer past him. She recoils. 'Where's all the furniture? The hall table? That dreadful old chair with the needlepoint seat?'

Fuck.

Peggy's hand is on the gate, the dogs' heads pushing eagerly through the slats. She reaches for the latch.

Ben swivels in the doorway. 'Carpets.' Genius!

Peggy has her head down, trying to unlatch the gate. 'Carpets?'

'Yes! They've just been cleaned.'

'Cleaned?' repeats Peggy, unable to disguise her astonishment. She has finally managed to raise the latch; she hovers at the bottom of the path. 'What, with a—?'

'Yeah. Daria, like, shampooed them last night. With one of them—you know. We had to move all the stuff into the kitchen. Took us forever, especially the sofa,' says Ben, the memory of the event still vivid. 'That is well heavy, I gotta tell you.'

Peggy, frowning, takes a step forward, the dogs straining on their leashes.

'No! You can't come in! They're still a bit damp—the carpets,' says Ben desperately, swiftly heeling off his Converses. 'Daria's coming over this afternoon to hoover them. Long as they're dry. Then we'll move everything back, me and Daria. And Artem. Nice and tidy. Clean as a . . .' He snatches up the carrier, waggles it in her direction. 'More cleaning things!' He starts to tiptoe backwards in an exaggerated fashion in his socks towards the kitchen, then realises his error and just as carefully moves back towards the front door, miming as best he can a person squelching across a damp floor. 'Nice seeing you, Mrs . . . er . . . Bye!'

He pushes the door shut, sliding down it into a relieved heap on the coir mat, hugging the lager, ears straining for the sound of Peggy's retreat, the snick of the gate and the diminishing yelps of the dogs as she continues up the lane. Racing into the sitting room, he eases the curtain aside to watch her disappearing around the bend in the lane, his heart jumping painfully. This frigging party had better be worth it, the grief it's causing him.

⌣⌣⌣

An hour later Ben is reflecting that he is nothing if not his culinary aunt's nephew (although he vaguely recalls a thoroughly confusing lecture from Aunt Harriet one evening to the effect that neither sister is actually his aunt, nor is he truly their nephew, but WTF) as he magics some cheese scones out of soured milk and a rind of parmesan and then concocts three different flans, one out of frazzled bacon and a handful of sorry-looking mushrooms in a just-the-right-side-of-rancid cream cheese filling, one from eggs and chives, topped with tomatoes, and one—his most ambitious—from the unrotten end of a large courgette mouldering in the vegetable drawer, a tin of shrimps and a thick hollandaise sauce. *Eat your heart out, Delia*, he thinks happily as the kitchen fills with delicious aromas. He finds half a very stale loaf in the bread bin, soaks it for an hour or so, then revels in mixing a spicy bread pudding rich with dried fruit and bitter marmalade with his bare hands, the mixture slithering in a most satisfactory way through his fingers. Aunt Hester would never miss a few store cupboard ingredients and, anyway, he's doing her a favour making use of things that would otherwise get binned; he knows how she loathes waste. By the time he's finished, cleared everything away, popped the scones, quiches and bread pudding in the larder out of sight and disinfected the entire fridge, he's feeling almost virtuous. If people want to order in pizza, let them, but he's betting they won't be able to resist his homemade food.

The numerous messages he's received throughout the day from his mates, as well as the lengthy text from his mother reassuring him of their safe arrival, the loveliness of their room, his father's delight at the leaf-clogged pool, Aunt Lynn's ecstatic reception of the pineapple tarte tatin (he imagines a sour, grudging smile) and the repetition of the maternal injunction to be sure to have something to eat, get an early night and thank Daria for putting him up and Ralph Pickerlees most especially for his kindness, have almost entirely assuaged any lingering worries about the coming party. He stows the booze out of sight, checks the rooms once more and, light of heart and wallet, jumps on his bike to cycle round to Jez in the hope he will have finally found a way to extricate himself from his duties at the barn dance.

⌣⌣⌣

No such luck. Jez is morosely picking at a limp salad (cooking not featuring among Deirdre Nairstrom's many talents) that seems to comprise packet ham and rock-hard tomatoes dotted in a landscape of undressed leaves. Ben filches a flabby crust from a white loaf and,

unable to locate any butter, liberally smears it with hydrogenated vegetable fat masquerading as a cholesterol-busting miracle spread. It is
disgusting.

'Got any jam?'

'Jam?'

'Yeah. Fruit boiled in sugar not the punk rock band.'

'Ha fucking ha.'

Ben ferrets among the various jars in the cupboard and finally,
in the absence of anything vaguely sweet, settles on Marmite. 'I'm
guessing you're still playing waiters.'

Jez grunts and turns over a forkful of vegetation.

'Be able to do a runner when it's finished?'

'What's the point? Be all over by then.'

'Hope not! Jesus, the thing finishes at eleven. That's when I'm
expecting Daria and Artem back.'

'Yeah,' says Jez mournfully, 'but then the bastard'll expect me to
collect glasses and wash up and all that shit.' He stabs a slab of wet
ham despondently.

'Serious?'

'Bet you.'

The two boys reflect in silence on the iniquities of parents. 'Least
you got rid of yours,' says Jez eventually. 'Least you get a couple of
nights off.'

'What's that, darling?' says his mother, sashaying in silently on
cork-soled mules, wearing a diaphanous kaftan; Deirdre Nairstrom
possesses a spooky knack of appearing without warning as though
borne, witch-like, on the wind.

The boys hurriedly review their conversation for anything incrim-
inating: neither knows how long she's been in the vicinity, but they do
know she can sniff out a conspiracy as unerringly as a police dog.

'Who's got a couple of nights off? Ben?'

'Yeah,' says Ben, immediately on his guard. 'My folks are away for
the weekend.'

'They surely haven't left you all by yourself? You poor lamb, you must stay here—we've plenty of room. Come to think of it, you could give Jeremy a hand this evening at the do. I'm sure he'd enjoy the company. It'd be fun, wouldn't it, Jeremy?'

Jez stares at his mother, dumbstruck, fork and its meat cargo aloft.

'Thanks all the same, Mrs N,' gabbles Ben, 'but I'm babysitting tonight and staying over.'

'Babysitting! You hear that, Jeremy? Glad to hear someone has the nous to earn some pocket money rather than sponging off their parents. Perhaps tomorrow night, Ben?'

'I'm staying over then too.' Could it get any worse? First the Verndale nightmare and now ball-breaker Mrs N on his case. He makes his excuses and flees, the Marmite and pappy bread like ashes in his mouth.

CHAPTER 29

'She's avoiding me.'

Lionel glances up at the dining room clock—ten to nine—then girds his loins. 'We ought to be getting across, Hetty. He warned us not to be late.'

Hester sniffs. 'As we're paying for the privilege of cooking the wretched meal this evening, I hardly think he's in any position to order us about.'

Lionel, who feels Franco has done little else *but* order them about all week, keeps his counsel. He's learnt very quickly to keep his head down when Hester is verging on the splenetic. Yesterday's uneasy truce between the sisters doesn't seem to be holding very well. Harriet had pleaded fatigue immediately after a dinner of awkward pauses and forced conversation and retired to her room, taking with her, he noted, a generously replenished glass of the very good Lacrima di Morro d'Alba that he had ordered (on the sisters' advice) in an attempt to smooth the pair's still clearly very ruffled plumage. It had had little effect except to add a hefty sum to his hitherto modest bar bill. He is in truth torn: much as he wants to support Hetty, and prickly as Harriet can sometimes be, he can't help feeling that she has been done a grave injustice by her sister and that a little more, well, *humility* on Hetty's part might not go amiss. Wisely, he does not articulate this, judging by the set of his companion's features that, as far as she is concerned, yesterday's fractious confrontation in the garden is behind her and resolved, and she is in no mood for contrition today.

'I said I was sorry!' she says for the third time.

The clock now reads eight fifty-three. Lionel makes a decision and rises. 'I'm just going to—'

'Please don't!' barks Hester.

'I'm sorry?' Lionel, conscious of several heads swivelling in their direction, reddens.

'Don't,' says Hester, in a slightly lower but nevertheless still penetrating voice, 'say you are going to see a man about a dog, use the facilities or other such nonsense. If you mean lavatory, then just say it, for heaven's sake!'

Someone sniggers on the far side of the room. Lionel, beet-red, gathers his tattered dignity and, leaning across the table, says quietly, 'I was going to say, clean my teeth,' then weaves his way swiftly through the tables towards his room.

Hester, mortified, watches his retreating figure for a second or two then grabs her bag and hurries out of the garden door in the direction of the outbuildings. Were a hairshirt to hand, she would don it in an instant. That she has merely been condemned to a day of pudding-making seems poor penance for her seemingly ungovernable ill humour.

⌣⌣⌣

Harriet wakes late. That is, she rises late, having lain for hours as dawn strengthens into day, reviewing recent events, longing to be at home, in her own bed, the familiar creaks and groans of The Laurels about her. After last night's disagreeable meal, she simply cannot face Hester and Lionel across the damask this morning. *I am such a coward*, she thinks, watching the hands of her alarm clock inch round to nine thirty, by which time she is confident that Hester and her shadow will be busy on their course. Sunlight courses through the window as she folds back the shutters; despite herself she feels her spirits lift as she raises her face to its warmth. She is just trying to find her phone to ring Daria when a text arrives with a picture: Milo standing triumphantly, hanging on to a stool, nappy sagging.

'Hello!' yells Daria seconds later. 'You got picture? Little *soneyka*, he is on his feet! I am washing the clothes, I turn round and he is standing. I say, clever boy, we must show the *babulki*, they will be so proud. You are having good time? Hester is loving the cooking? Yes, of course! Oh! No, no, Milo, not that! Sorry, Harriet, I must go—he is trying to open—oh! *Nyagodnik*, no! See you soon. Bye!'

Fifteen minutes later Harriet, considerably cheered, is seated alone in the dining room with a basket of rolls, butter and chestnut compote, accompanied by a tiny cup of eye-wateringly strong espresso, as the serving staff clear the tables around her.

Alfonso glides to her side. 'Ciao, Signora Pearson! Another beautiful day, yes? But you are not drawing today?'

Harriet laughs; there is a polished geniality about this man that is irresistible. That and his easiness on the eye . . . 'I was never drawing, I'm afraid, Alfonso. I was simply despoiling perfectly good paper with my scribbles.'

He laughs too. 'Despoiling . . . ah, yes, a perfect word.' Then, realising how this might be construed, 'Oh! Forgive me, I did not mean . . .'

'Trust me, I did,' says Harriet dryly. 'I think Signor Gervais will be counting his blessings this morning.'

'I cannot believe that for one moment,' says Alfonso, gallant as ever. 'So, today, how will you amuse yourself? Your sister of course is busy preparing our wonderful feast for tonight. There is much excitement, much—what is it?—anticipation, I think. Perhaps you will visit Signora Martindale? I can easily arrange—'

'No, not today,' says Harriet swiftly, recalling her uncomfortable encounter with Ron and Rhona the previous day. She can do without a repetition of that just at the moment. 'Maybe tomorrow . . .'

'Of course. More coffee?'

⌣⌣⌣

'Lionel, I am so sorry. I really don't know what—'

He holds up the knife with which he has been carefully chopping chillies while the pasta dough is resting. The thin uniform slices lie glistening on the board. Melanie tactfully crosses to another station to use the sink. 'Hetty, my dear—'

'I am a hateful old crone, Lionel, who doesn't know when to shut up. No, don't argue, I am. You have been nothing but kind—no, let me finish, please. You have held my hand through a very difficult week and I repay you by humiliating you with snide comments in public. I am thoroughly ashamed of myself—oh!' Hester finds her apology cut short as Lionel grabs her to his chest and thrusts her head onto his shoulder to silence her, while carefully holding the knife, sharpened to stiletto keenness moments earlier, well away from them both.

'Shh, shh, Hetty.' He feels her relaxing ever so slightly against him and reaches up a daring hand to stroke her hair.

A pregnant silence, then Hester pulls her head away from his disconcertingly comforting embrace. She rallies. 'No, Lionel, listen—'

'Hetty . . .'

'I want you to know—'

'Hetty!'

'What?'

'Shut up.' Said softly, kindly, but very firmly.

Hester is astonished. Who does he think—She is even more astonished when he plants a hard kiss on her open mouth.

A stunned moment and then the entire kitchen bursts into applause. Franco Riccardo bustles over, brandishing a cleaver. 'What is this!' he cries in mock fury. 'No time for all this *passione*. Cook! Cook! Hungry people are waiting! *Mio dio!*' He manhandles a flustered Hester back towards her station, murmuring under his breath to Lionel with a wink, 'Hey, Casanova, *bel lavoro!*' His rumbling laugh is echoed by the other students.

As she struggles to regain her composure, ostensibly checking her recipes but in truth unable to take in a single word, Hester suppresses a smile. Well! Good Lord. Lionel!

The lothario, nonchalantly scraping chillies into the pan, wills his thumping heart to settle, hoping fervently that his beta-blockers are doing their job. Still, it had been worth it, if only to see the look in Hetty's eyes. Not to mention Franco's. It is with some difficulty that he controls the urge to burst into song, contenting himself with a little light humming.

～～～

A shadow falls across Harriet's Kindle. She looks up, squinting, to find Regina's considerable bulk blotting out most of the sun.

'At last! Here you are,' says Regina, plonking herself down on a stone bench.

Harriet sighs inwardly; here she indubitably is. She checks her watch: it's just before one.

'We thought we might see you today. In class. It being our last day, you know.'

Harriet feels as though she's been caught playing hooky. 'No, I thought . . . well, I'm so behind already, I decided to have a quiet morning in the—'

'She's over here!' bellows Regina, leaping to her feet and waving enthusiastically. 'Guy and Bella,' she says to Harriet by way of explanation. 'We've all been scouring the place for you.'

'Oh,' says Harriet, ruing the truncation of her escape into her book—a surprisingly engaging crime caper written by a disgraced former minister—but at the same time touched by her fellow students' concern. She smiles brightly as Guy and Bella crunch up the gravel path to join her and Regina. 'You're very kind.'

Regina grunts dismissively. 'Like to look out for our gang, don't we, chaps?' she says.

Out of her line of sight, Bella rolls her eyes at Harriet.

'You okay?'

'Fine.'

'We hear Mary's making good progress,' says Guy. 'Have you seen her today?'

'Not yet.' Why does everyone assume she's glued to Mary's side?

'We thought we might pop in to the hospital this afternoon,' says Bella. 'Seeing as we've got the car. Though why we bothered to hire one, I'm not sure; we've barely used it.' Judging by the tightening of Guy's face, this is not the first time she's made the point.

'Ah, well ...' starts Harriet, on the verge of sounding a note of caution, but catching herself just in time. It's not for her to dissuade people from visiting Mary; she's not her keeper. And, who knows, if the atmosphere at the hospital is as strained today as it was yesterday, Mary might be only too delighted for some new visitors to divert her and relieve some of the tension.

'I hear,' says Regina, with the air of someone revealing secret information, 'that her husband's been making a bit of a song and dance about what happened. I overheard Alfonso quizzing Gervais about the state of the path. Did he warn everyone to take care? Was he supervising the group properly?'

'For heaven's sake!' says Guy with some warmth. 'We're all adults. It was perfectly obvious you needed to exercise a bit of caution.'

'Well, of course,' continues Regina, undeterred, 'you won't be remotely surprised to hear that Gervais was flapping about like a wet fish—the man is simply hopeless—so I felt I really must intervene. I told Alfonso there was absolutely no doubt in my mind that it was an accident. Mary slipped, lost her balance, whatever. That's the size of it. These things happen, unfortunately. No-one's fault. Jolly bad luck, that's all it was. A mercy that she was able to grab hold of you, Harriet. Otherwise, she might have plunged all the way to the bottom and that would have been a very different story. I said to Alfonso, Mary's husband should be thanking his lucky stars that she got off so lightly, instead of pointing fingers.'

'I can still hear her scream.' Bella shudders. 'I'd just taken a picture and was following you down—I was looking at my feet because it was so uneven—and Mary and Harriet were right behind me. I sort of saw them out of the corner of my eye. Then Mary cried out as she slipped. The next thing I knew, she and Harriet had disappeared over the edge.'

Harriet throws her mind back, remembers the care they were all taking as they picked their way down the pebbly path, sliding occasionally in the dust, the scent of the ox-eye daisies as they brushed against them, the splash of poppies like daubs of crimson paint, the distant hum of traffic on the unseen road, the fragmentary conversations . . . then that terrible sudden moment when they fell. She shivers in spite of the sun.

'I couldn't agree more,' says Guy.

'I was ahead of you all at the time so I didn't see. She must have just felt herself go,' says Regina decisively. 'You know, you miss your step, oh crikey, then . . .'

'Yes,' says Bella. 'Horrible. Still, makes you think, doesn't it? How transitory everything is . . .'

Guy squeezes her shoulder.

'That's all it takes,' declares Regina. 'A moment's inattention . . . Had a school friend years ago who leaned out of the carriage just as the train entered a tunnel. Very nasty. Blood all over the shop. She never really recovered. Bright girl, too, top of the class often as not. Except in geography. Anyway, let's not dwell on it. Sounds like everything's going to be fine. Come along, Harriet, we're determined to drag you in to lunch, whether you like it or not. This is no time to be skulking in the shrubbery.'

Harriet, outgunned and in no mood to argue with anyone, least of all Regina, surrenders without demur and tucks her Kindle away. At least there's no danger of running into Hester and Lionel over lunch: the cookery course participants are hard at their labours the whole day. And in truth, she realises she is feeling a trifle peckish after her meagre breakfast; perhaps she could just manage some antipasti, maybe with cheese and figs to follow.

Regina grabs her elbow, hauls her to her feet and starts propelling her along the path towards the hotel. 'Incidentally, our course appears to be over—the maestro graciously announced this morning that he only ever does a half-day on the Friday, which frankly I could have done with knowing earlier. I mean, I might have wanted to make other plans. Anyway, assuming we can find a fourth, I thought we might try for a few hands of bridge this afternoon. You won't mind lending us Guy, will you, Bella dear? In fact, why don't you pop over to see Mary while we're playing? Speaking of bridge, Harriet, how is your sister's amour with that Lionel fellow coming on?'

CHAPTER 30

'Everything all right, sweetheart?'

'Mum! You only texted like an hour ago!'

'Yes, but you didn't reply. I thought something might be wrong.'

'Like what?'

'Well, I don't know . . .' Isabelle falters. 'But I'm worried about leaving you on your own.'

'I won't be on my own, will I?' says Ben. 'I'll be with Milo, and then with Daria and Artem.'

'But you're on your own now, sweetheart.'

'That's because I'm revising, Mum! Or trying to. Only people keep phoning me to check if I'm still alive.'

'But I'm your mother!' wails Isabelle. 'It's only natural for me to be concerned about you!'

Ben switches tack. If indignation doesn't work, he'll try filial solicitude. 'Mum, honestly, you mustn't worry about me. I'm fine. The only thing I'm worried about—'

'You see! I knew there was something!'

'—is that you'll spoil your well-deserved break worrying yourself to death about me. Please, just forget about everything except having a lovely weekend with Dad and a great time at the party.'

'Oh, you are such a good boy,' says Isabelle, melting. 'I know I shouldn't get so wound up.'

'No, you shouldn't.'

'But I can't help thinking about you all on your own—'

'Mum!'

'—nose stuck in your books, while we're enjoying ourselves at a party.'

Not as much as I'm going to enjoy myself at mine.

'There'll be plenty of time for partying once my exams are over,' says Ben sanctimoniously. 'In the meantime . . .'

'Yes, yes, I'll let you get on, sweetheart. Sorry to be such a fusspot. I'll phone you—'

'Tomorrow,' says Ben quickly. 'You ring me and tell me all about it tomorrow. Not tonight. *Tomorrow*. Promise?'

'Promise,' chirps Isabelle. 'Bye, darling. Love you.'

Ben mumbles something similar and ends the call. He resists the temptation to check for messages or tweets and reluctantly returns to his mathematics textbook. He has set himself a target of two hours' revision of his least favourite subject today and there's only twenty minutes' torment left. Then he's going to shower and get ready. Six o'clock can't come soon enough.

~~~

'Hiya.'

Nats looks good in a skimpy T-shirt and lace shorts, with a sweater knotted round her middle, braids under her helmet cloaking her almost to her waist. For such a tiny frame, her legs are surprisingly long, ending in silver flats. She catches Ben's glance and smirks. 'Lou's. She'll go ballistic if she finds out.'

'What, the shoes?'

'No.' She flicks one sleeve of the pink sweater. 'This. Her prized cashmere. From Macy's.'

Ben looks blank.

'In New York? You must've heard of Macy's! Really? You've never been to New York?'

Ben, ashamed of his parochial life, ashamed of having parents whose idea of foreign travel is the Isle of Wight, sets off. Within seconds, Nats is beside him. He concentrates resolutely on the road ahead for fear of catching her giving him a pitying look.

'You should wear your helmet,' she calls over her shoulder as she overtakes him.

'What are you, my mother?' Like he's going to ruin his hair—that he's just spent a whole five minutes styling—with a helmet.

'I'm just saying. Don't you read the stats?'

'What stats?'

'About cyclists and head injuries.'

He doesn't reply; puts all his efforts into keeping up.

A minute or so later, she shouts, 'All ready, then?'

'What?'

'The party, what else?'

'Yeah, guess so.' What's it to her? He's having to pedal faster and faster.

'What music you playing?'

'Lou's sorting it.'

'Oh God, really? You're kidding.' She snorts and puts on a spurt. 'Good luck with that. Hope you're a Harry Styles fan.' She shoots off and he has to work doubly hard to catch up.

'Anyway, what you gonna do till she arrives?' She doesn't even sound out of breath.

'What d'you mean?' he manages. Jesus, she's fast!

'Well, knowing my darling sister, she'll waltz in about three hours late. It's what she always does, so she can make an entrance. Or she won't pitch up at all. You didn't seriously think she'd be there from the off?'

This is exactly what Ben had thought. All day, all week, he's nursed a picture of him and Louisa at the door, welcoming people to a party already throbbing with music. In his wilder moments, he's even imagined Louisa draped seductively over his shoulder, proclaiming to all the world the status of their relationship ... or wrapped around him in a slow dance, hips swaying provocatively ...

'Look out!' screams Nats as Ben, in a world untroubled by road safety and oblivious to a tanker thundering down the hill, turns directly into its path at the junction. She accelerates from a standing start at the crossroads, and with a mighty shove sends Ben and herself hurtling into the hedgerow. The tanker scorches past, missing them both by inches, spitting dust and stones in its wake, its horn sounding with ear-splitting fury until it disappears from sight.

'What the fuck?'

'You wanker! You nearly got yourself killed!' Nats is practically lying on top of him, both bikes in a tangle beneath them. She pushes herself up and starts dusting herself down as he gets unsteadily to his feet.

'I told you to wear—oh, great!' Nats flaps a pink sleeve at him, now sporting a jagged rip and plastered with wet mud. 'Jesus wept! What the fuck am I going to tell Lou? This is your fault, you moron!' Her face is a mask of fury.

'My fault? I never asked you to run me off the road! Get out of my face, will you, you little gob—'

'Oh right! I should have left you to get flattened by the lorry, should I? I wish I had now, you ungrateful shit!'

'Ah, *proprium humani ingenii est odisse quem laeseris*,' says a sonorous voice behind them. 'A lucky escape for you both, if I may say so.'

'Finbar!' cries Ben, alerted immediately by the newcomer's pungent body odour.

'Yes, he *has* injured me,' snaps Nats, seemingly unfazed by the appearance of an elderly Latin-speaking tramp, accompanied by a battered tartan shopping trolley festooned with price stickers. 'Look!' And she points at her knee, now beaded with blood.

'Ah!' says Finbar, beaming, ignoring her wound, 'a linguist! Remember, dear child, *omnia causa fiunt*.'

'You what?' Ben is lost.

'Everything happens for a reason,' translates Nats with a contemptuous eye roll, turning back to Finbar. 'Although, frankly, I'm at a loss to believe that right now, the way this tosser is behaving. I'm Nats, by the way.'

Finbar extends a filthy hand. Nats takes it without hesitation.

'An inestimable joy to meet you, Nats,' he says, enclosing her small hand in both of his, 'even under these inopportune circumstances. Finbar. Rare it is indeed to meet someone so young with such facility in the ancient tongue. Do you, perchance, also speak Greek?'

''Fraid not. At least, not yet. But I might give it a whirl.'

'Give it a whirl!' says an enchanted Finbar. 'Yes, yes, do, do, my dear. Any assistance I might render in that regard would be an unalloyed pleasure.'

Ben has by this stage untangled the bikes and is dolefully inspecting his. The front wheel looks decidedly out of true. He is muttering under his breath, 'I'll kill her, swear to God, I'll kill her . . .'

'Problem?' says Nats combatively.

'Duh. You've only buggered my bike—'

'I think, young Ben, if I may,' interrupts Finbar sternly, 'you are being more than a little ungenerous here to your guardian angel. Shaken though you be, I feel you owe heartfelt thanks to this young Soteria, who, not to put too fine a point on it, saved your life just now.'

Nats smiles smugly; she, at least, knows who Soteria is.

'Saved my—'

'Yes, indeed. I was witness to the entire episode en route to my redoubt yonder.' He points towards the decommissioned bus shelter a few yards up the road that doubles as his accommodation.

Nats, intrigued, limps over to inspect the mountains of books and carrier bags stacked on the seat and the squalid sleeping bag, with its clumps of wadding protruding, lying underneath.

Ben, despite his present hostility, has to admire Nats' sangfroid; he's seen grown men blench at the stench.

She limps back. 'Cool,' she says. She rights her own undamaged bike. 'We'd better be on our way. Lovely to meet you, Finbar. May I call you that?'

'I would be honoured, my dear Nats,' says Finbar, sketching a slight bow. 'Are you going far?'

'Just to Daria's,' says Ben, who has that moment noticed the knees of his relatively new jeans are wet with something viscous he'd rather not investigate too closely at this point.

'Ah! The lovely Daria and her little cherub! I am not an aficionado of infants as a rule,' confides Finbar to Nats, 'but there is something about Milo . . .'

'Oh, I know,' says Nats, dabbing her bleeding knee with a tissue. 'He's almost edible, isn't he?'

'Much as I enjoy my food,' says Finbar hastily, 'I wouldn't go that far. Do leave your bike, Ben, I'll fix it.'

Ben looks at him in mute astonishment.

'I see you doubt my abilities,' says Finbar huffily, readjusting his grimy jacket and unleashing a noisome waft of his unmistakable odour. 'I'll have you know, young man, I was the 1962 junior twelve-mile cycle champion for my county and I did all my own maintenance! No-one could hold a candle to me for speedy puncture repairs. But of course if you prefer to squander your money on—'

'No, no! Don't go off on one. I just never knew.'

'Quite,' says Finbar, slightly mollified, adding darkly, 'there is much about me that you do not know, nor ever will, if the gods allow. Now, just wheel it over to my abode and I shall begin my ministrations. I will return it to you at Daria's later.'

Alarm bells ring instantly. 'No, honest, no worries. I'll pick it up tomorrow on my way home, yeah? I'm staying over tonight. Baby-sitting.'

'Indeed? Babysitting, is it? I must say that has always seemed to me the oddest terminology. One wonders at its derivation or should I say provenance—'

'Yeah, right, ta, Finbar. You're a mate.' Ben hastily leans his bike against the shelter and starts up the hill. 'I owe you.' He knows Finbar too well; once the old codger gets talking it's like trying to stop a juggernaut.

'Bye, Finbar.' Nats waves, then wheels her bike up beside Ben, who has set such a cracking pace she almost has to run to keep abreast of him. If he's going to be an arse, she'll just ride on ahead and leave him to it. Except then Daria might wonder if they've had a row and that would put paid to the love's young dream fiction . . .

Back at the shelter Finbar watches them hurrying away. A mate, young Ben had said. A mate. He considers the epithet for a while; decides he likes it, is flattered almost. And that young friend of his with the Medusa-like hair: she is a marvel indeed. He very much hopes she does decide to give Greek a whirl; he has a primer somewhere in his collection he'd be only too glad to lend her. Whistling contentedly, he begins ferreting through numerous carriers for his tools.

CHAPTER 31

There is a very small man sitting beside Regina Pegg. The staff have fashioned a vast banqueting table by amalgamating all the individual tables so the guests dine *en famille* to share the fruits of the cookery course's labours. Seated directly opposite Harriet, the little man is painstakingly picking over the contents of his plate and, as far as she has observed, has not uttered a single word all evening. Regina has answered for him at every serving, the entire company privy to her remarks.

'Not for Charles, thank you.'

'Charles will just have a little.'

'Don't eat it all if you don't want to, Charles.'

'Not a great fan of mussels, are you, Charles?' A rhetorical question only as Charles, whom Harriet cannot remember ever seeing before, simply smiles meekly and addresses himself to his modest meal.

'Has he just arrived, the chap next to Regina?' she whispers to Bella, who on her return from the hospital—where she had found Mary in good spirits, clearly itching to be discharged—had commandeered Harriet and marched her to the bar, just as a triumphant Regina was proposing a fourth rubber. She and Harriet had decisively trounced Guy and a perfectly serviceable player, Tony, who had spent the week on an archaeological tour of the region and whom Regina had bullied into joining them. Harriet, finding Regina's bidding and play thoroughly intimidating and feeling that their opponents had suffered enough, was relieved to be rescued and had thanked Bella effusively over a bottle of pre-prandial wine. Now, the pair of them are just the tiniest bit squiffy and Guy, under cover of refilling his neighbour's glass, has moved their current bottle out of reach.

Bella splutters into her glass. 'Harriet, honestly! He's her husband!'

'Really?' Harriet peers across at the silent diner, eyes narrowed. These spectacles are hopeless. But squint as she may, the little man looks no more familiar. She supposes he must have been engaged in some course or the other that took him away from Il Santuario most of the time.

Regina intercepts the look and waves gaily. 'Absolutely marvellous!' she booms, gesturing with her fork across the contents of the table.

The cooks, duties done, have relinquished the serving of the food to the regular waiting staff, while Franco, in his element, wafts around them daintily, hoovering up compliments. Hester and Lionel are seated some distance from Harriet, with whom, not apparently by design, they have barely exchanged a dozen words in all the brouhaha—champagne, cocktails and the rest—surrounding this much-anticipated final evening. Now Harriet raises her glass to her sister in a silent toast and mouths, 'Well done.'

Hester, heart-warmed, bobs her head in thanks as Regina, never one to miss a trick in bridge or life, takes Harriet's lead and leaps to her feet, glass aloft. 'To the cooks!' she roars, pre-empting Alfonso, who has been waiting for a lull in in the hubbub to propose a vote of thanks to the chefs and Franco in particular.

There is a startled pause, then the company rather raggedly follow Regina's lead, whereupon Alfonso, who is determined to regain the initiative, initiates a round of warm applause. He clears his throat.

'May I on behalf of the management extend our personal thanks to our wonderful and so talented cooks . . .'

More applause.

'. . . and the incomparable maestro, Signor Franco Riccardi . . .'

Even more applause.

'. . . who has guided them so expertly through the . . .' he searches for, finds and pronounces with understandable satisfaction the right word '. . . intricacies of our beautiful Italian cuisine.'

Assorted cheers and the thunder of numerous fists thumping the table.

'So we hope—Marco, myself and all the staff here at Il Santuario—that you have each in your different ways enjoyed your time here with us.'

Various 'absolutely's and 'I should say's ring out; more reserved heads nod.

'Good, very good. Don't forget, please, to tell TripAdvisor!' A volley of laughter. 'And tomorrow we have to say goodbye to many of you.'

'Shame,' shouts a lone voice.

'Thank you! We shall be sad to bid *arrivederci* to those who leave us. But first, before we enjoy the rest of the evening, an announcement. You know that earlier this week, we had a small . . . let us call it "misfortune", with Signora Martindale on the mountain.'

Low rumbles and mumbles of regret around the table; behind Alfonso, Marco shakes his head sorrowfully.

'Where Signora Pearson—yes, yes,' as spontaneous applause, to Harriet's embarrassment, breaks out, led by Bella, 'of course, our heroine, was so brave, although also injured! Well, today we hear that the *signora* is to leave the hospital. Tomorrow. Yes!' A scattering of applause. 'She will spend a few days here before she is allowed to fly home. So! This is—is this the correct expression?—the cherry on the cake, I think. Yes!'

Sustained applause and several whoops of appreciation as Alfonso beckons to the staff to bring more wine and serve the cheese. Conversation springs up once again around the room. Harriet finds herself almost tearful.

'What a relief!' she murmurs to Bella. 'Did you know?'

'About her being discharged? No. They were waiting for the consultant to come round when I left. Ron—that's his name, isn't it, the husband?—he was wittering on about flights tomorrow. I thought he was being a bit previous.'

'Was Rhona still there?'

'The sister?'

Harriet doesn't disabuse her.

'Yeah. She seems very nice—but not much love lost between her and Ron, is there?'

'No.'

'Can't say I took to him personally. Shame we'll miss Mary, though. Our flight's at eleven and the minibus is collecting us at eight. You'll have to give her our love.'

'Of course.' Harriet grasps Bella's hand, mellowed into uncharacteristic tactility by the alcohol. 'I've really enjoyed our time together.'

'Me too.'

'I think I'm a little bit tiddly.'

'Me too.'

They giggle.

'Listen,' says Bella, 'I'm not a great one for holiday friendships but I'd really like to keep in touch, if you want to.'

'Oh,' says Harriet, moved. 'Yes! Yes, indeed. I'd like that very much.'

Bella's face clouds, tightening her features and ageing her instantly. 'And perhaps you could meet Jack one day.'

'I'd love to. How old is he?'

'Six.' Bella's eyes fill. 'Just six. He's . . .' Her hand creeps along the table, finds Guy's. Harriet thinks, *Poor loves, thank goodness they've got each other*. Guy extracts himself from his conversation with his neighbour and turns to smile at his wife, eyes searching her face as though there is no-one else around. *What a comfort*, thinks Harriet, *the way he knows instinctively*.

'Bit of air?' he says. Bella nods.

'Excuse us,' says Guy quietly, arm around his wife's shoulders as he guides her towards the garden, leaving Harriet feeling suddenly bereft and very alone.

⌣⌣⌣

Regina ambushes Harriet as she is on her way around the room to reach her sister. 'What a success, my dear! I had my doubts, I must confess. All eating together—my first thought: positively bohemian! But we enjoyed it, didn't we, Charles?'

The little man, dabbing a wetted finger at the crumbs on his plate, nods, smiling down.

'You have met Charles?'

'I'm afraid I haven't had that pleasure,' says Harriet, extending a hand.

The hand over the plate stills, trembles, flexes, relaxes. Regina leans close to Harriet's ear. 'Stroke,' she whispers. 'He can't . . .' She covers Charles's hand with her own. Reaches down from her considerable height and plants a kiss on his head. Manages a tight smile, saying brightly, 'But we manage, don't we, my love? We manage very well. And we still have lots of fun. You keep me in check, don't you, my darling?' And there is so much loss, love and history in the embrace she gives her husband that Harriet has to turn away.

⌣⌣⌣

'Beautiful meal,' she says to Hester, slipping into the chair Lionel has just vacated en route to the bar. 'Especially those little dumpling things. Gorgeous. I had far too many.'

'*Struffoli*. I made those,' says Hester, with not a little pride. 'You didn't find them too sweet?' Personally, she thinks them utterly sickly, slathered in honey and strewn with citrus fruit and almonds.

Harriet laughs guiltily. 'Too sweet? Me? Sorry—what was the question?'

They both smile, relieved to have found neutral ground.

'So. Was it worth it?'

'The course? Absolutely. I've learnt so much.' Hester, on edge for so much of the evening, wondering if Harriet has deliberately kept her distance, relaxes.

'Seriously?'

Hester eyes Franco across the room, the picture of bonhomie. Hard to credit what a monster he can be in the kitchen. 'I may not like his methods, I may not like him very much, but the man can cook, no doubt about it.' She turns back to her sister, flushing. 'Sorry I was such a pig when we arrived. It was a wonderful gift. I am thoroughly ashamed of myself.'

Harriet leans across to squeeze her hand. Thank God. Perhaps the fracture between them is beginning to mend. Her sense of loneliness diminishes a little; the comforting coupledom she has so unthinkingly relied upon these past few years with Hetty seems suddenly within reach once more.

'It's been quite a week,' she says quietly.

'Hasn't it?'

'Stephen and I have spoken a couple of times.'

'Oh?' says Hester, thinking, *Well, I haven't heard a word. But, then, I deserve no more.* The memory of the whole episode and her behaviour makes her cringe afresh. She waits for Harriet to continue.

'I need to go and see someone. For Stephen. Soon as possible. I asked Alfonso to check if he could get us on an earlier flight—'

'Oh,' says Hester, thinking immediately, *Well, you might have asked me first!*

'But no joy. So it looks like we're stuck here until Monday in any event. So I'd like to try and go on Tuesday ideally. To see . . . ' She still doesn't want to say the name. 'I don't want the poor boy waiting a moment longer than necessary for news.'

Hester waits some more.

Harriet, put out, continues, 'I know we'll only just have got back but—'

'You know, if you'd like company . . .' says Hester hesitantly. Something in Harriet's expression stops her. 'What?'

Harriet stares hard at her sister. There's something different about her face, about her whole appearance. It isn't just that she's looking uncommonly smart this evening in her pearls and burgundy cashmere sweater, her tousled hair curling attractively; it's more than that. There's a luminosity to her complexion, a heightened . . . good God, she's wearing makeup! Hester's lashes are indubitably mascaraed, and isn't that a smudge of eye shadow? And surely it can't be . . . but yes, she's plucked her eyebrows! The faintly Kahlo-esque bridge between her brows has disappeared entirely. Harriet tries hard not to gawp. The sisters have never been disposed to comment on each other's appearance, but on one fateful occasion Isabelle had ventured to suggest that tweezers might be employed to, as she had put it, 'tidy up' Harriet's eyebrows; to this day Harriet shivers to recall the icy blast of scorn that had greeted the proposition. It had taken their chastened cousin-in-law a good month to summon the courage for another visit. Harriet is flabbergasted to realise that somewhere in Hester's capacious and shabby sponge bag must presumably lurk not only ancient and surely dangerously out-of-date cosmetics but also *a pair of tweezers*.

'What?' repeats Hester, pointing to her teeth. 'Have I got . . .'

'No, no,' says Harriet quickly, thinking: *Makeup. Tweezers. And is that scent?* Is Harriet's last-night armoury all for Lionel's benefit? She says distractedly, 'So anyway, I was wondering if I shouldn't hire us a car on Sunday. Go for a bit of a drive and see something of the country-side. Might take our minds off things. What do you say? Seems a pity to come all this way and—'

'Oh, that's funny. Lionel had the same idea.'

'Lionel?'

'Yes.'

Lionel . . . here . . . still . . . on Sunday?

Oh God, thinks Harriet.

Oh God, thinks Hester.

'Care for a top-up?' says Lionel beside them, beaming. 'I managed to snaffle one of the last bottles of red.'

CHAPTER 32

'Pooh! What is that smell?'

Daria, ready for action in her dancing clothes—a tight-fitting white blouse and flared gingham knee-length skirt courtesy of Oxfam—enters the kitchen to find Ben scrubbing furiously at the legs of his jeans with a cloth. Nats watches from the table, shaking her head despairingly. Her face lights up in a wide smile as she gives Daria's outfit the onceover.

'You look great; I'm loving the fifties vibe,' she says, before turning her attention once more to Ben's activities. 'I told him they'd need washing.'

'Thank you, Natalie!' The older girl smooths the skirt fabric self-consciously. She bends down to inspect Ben's saturated knees and recoils. 'Ben! What is this horrible ... *Boža moj!*' She rushes over to throw open the window, theatrically flapping her hands about to clear the air.

Ben, given the proximity of the accident to Finbar's shelter, has a very strong suspicion that he knows what the yucky gunk might be, but he has no intention of letting on.

'Come on!' barks Daria, returning with hand outstretched.

'What?'

'Take them off.'

'Take them—? No!'

'Told you,' says Nats.

'Washing machine!' orders Daria, with a face that brooks no argument.

'I can't wash them!' cries Ben. 'How will I get them dry in time?'

'For what?' says Daria.

Nats smirks and raises an eyebrow at a cornered Ben.

Daria sighs with exasperation. 'We put on line, nice wind, no rain, will be dry by morning. Now, come!' She thrusts her hand out again.

'What am I supposed to wear instead?'

'I don't know . . . Yes! I give you pair of Artem's trousers for evening.'

'Artem? But he's, like, ten feet tall!'

'Ben! We will be late!' Daria, nose wrinkled in disgust, is now very cross indeed. Ben cannot deny that there is still an extremely unpleasant smell in the room.

There's nothing for it. He slouches sullenly towards the hall.

'Where you are going?'

'To take the shitty things off.'

'*Skatsina!* No swearing, please. Baby in house!'

Nats turns her snort into an unconvincing cough. Ben glares at her. Daria rummages through a basket on the counter and pulls out a black garment. 'Here. Now, take off. In here. I don't want smell out there. We look away.' She turns her back on Ben and Nats does likewise. The girls exchange exasperated glances. 'Hurry, Ben, please! We are not wanting to be late.'

'All right! All right!' Ben tears off his sodden, stinking jeans, hurls them across the kitchen towards the washing machine and thrusts his legs into Artem's chinos. Daria, grimacing, gingerly picks up the offending clothes between thumb and forefinger and drops them into the drum, loads the drawer with a large scoop of detergent and sets the machine going, before disinfecting her hands at the sink. She turns back, towel in hand, to find Ben angrily trying to prevent the oversized trousers from falling down by bunching the spare material in one fist, Nats head in hands weeping with silent laughter and Artem, ready to go dancing in denims and a checked shirt, taking in the scene from the hall doorway.

'What's happening?' He does a double-take and points at Ben's lower half, frowning. 'Are those mine?'

There is a muffled hiccup from Nats, whose small frame is vibrating like a tuning fork. 'Hello. Are you okay?'

Nats, head bowed, nods furiously, incapable of speech.

'This is Natalie, Ben's friend. I tell you about her.'

'Ah, Natalie, of course. Welcome!' says Artem warmly. 'I've heard a lot about you.'

'Hello,' Nats manages.

'So why *are* you wearing my trousers?' Artem asks Ben, but before he can explain, Daria says irritably, 'I am having to wash his jeans. Ben! Get rid of stinky cloth!'

'Oh my God, what is that smell?' gasps Artem, setting Nats off on a fresh paroxysm.

'Ben had accident,' says Daria.

Artem looks at the boy, over to the washing machine, then back again. His face changes from bewilderment to revulsion.

'Not that kind of accident!' shouts Ben, dropping the cloth in the bin. 'Jesus! Sorry,' to Daria, before she can protest. 'I fell off my bike into some sh— . . . muck, that's all.'

Artem shakes his head. He'd been in two minds about this jaunt but Daria was insistent, and now the sooner they escape this house—and the smell—the better.

'Go! Go!' says Ben desperately, having just caught sight of the clock. He shuffles towards the door to usher Daria and Artem on their way, the hems of the chinos caught under his feet. Nats stuffs her sleeve into her mouth.

'Okay, okay,' says Daria, miffed. 'But we would not be in hurry if you had not—'

'All right! I'm sorry. Now go and have fun, will you,' snaps Ben, swiftly cutting off Daria's usual litany of childcare advice. 'Yes, I know where the nappies are, I know he has water not milk if he wakes, I know he's not allowed any biscuits! Now off you go!'

Startled by Ben's vehemence, brother and sister grab their coats and keys and leave.

Seconds later, Nats and Ben hear Harriet's ancient car—on loan for the duration of her absence—rattle off down the street after some inexpert gear selection on Artem's part.

Ben collapses onto a kitchen chair. 'Shit, shit, shit!'

Nats is wiping her eyes. 'Problem, boyfriend?'

Ben is so stressed he doesn't even bother to argue with her sarky endearment. 'What do you think? I've got a load of mates turning up at the house for a party in—' he checks '—just under an hour, my bike's busted to buggery and I'm dressed like a frigging clown. No, no problem at all.'

Nats strolls over to the laundry basket. 'Lucky I'm here then, isn't it?'

∾∾∾

'Serious?' says Ben, looking at himself in the hall mirror five minutes later.

Nats shrugs, biting on a nail as she eyes him up and down. 'Best I can improvise in the time available. Think of it as a sort of retro *Misfits* tribute.'

'You what?'

'*Misfits*. It was this great show about—'

'Oh, yeah.' He looks at himself again. 'You sure about this?'

He is wearing Artem's ripped boiler suit belted with rope, undone to the waist to display his white tee. The legs are rolled over several times to bunch over his trainers. 'But weren't theirs orange?'

'Well, duh,' says Nats. 'We don't have orange, do we? We have *blue*. I guess, in a poor light and from a distance, if you ignore the colour, there is a very—and I mean very—faint resemblance to Robert Sheehan.'

'Yeah?' repeats Ben, instantly feeling a whole lot more cheerful. 'Robert Sheehan, eh . . .' He supposes, now he comes to think of it, that his currently mussed hair—the earlier styling totally ruined by his encounter with the hedge—does look a little bit like . . .

'Don't start getting up yourself. Like I say, from a *very* great distance. Anyway, it's all about attitude, clothes. Look like you feel comfortable, you can wear anything,' says Nats. Then she remembers. 'Except, maybe, your sister's totally fucked cashmere sweater.'

'Sorry,' says Ben, meaning it.

'Yeah, well, I'll have to think of something, won't I? While you're off enjoying yourself. Talking of which, you better scoot. Wanna borrow my bike?'

Ben, in spite of himself, is touched. 'Nah, ta all the same. It's only five minutes. Look, I'll be back just before eleven, okay? Please God they don't decide to come home any earlier.' He takes one last look at himself in the mirror. Truth is, the get-up really doesn't look half bad.

Nats regards him thoughtfully. He's a bit of a muppet sometimes, but . . .

'You know what? Here's an idea. Why don't you not come back at all?'

'Eh?'

'I'll tell them you went to bed early with a headache or something. They won't check, will they? Then I'll get myself off home as per. And you creep in whatever time you like. What d'you think? Is it a plan?'

Ben, rapidly running through the implications of her suggestion, is speechless with admiration. Not only is it a plan, it's pure genius. No danger of getting back too late (he knows where Daria hides the spare key), no danger of getting caught if Artem decides not to go to bed the minute they get back from the dance. It'll mean he can go and enjoy himself without busting a gut to sneak back. He won't have to risk leaving the cottage in his friends' unreliable care. He won't have to hold back on the booze either. As ideas go, it rocks. It's awesome! She's awesome! He could kiss her. Even though she's a total smart-arse ninety-nine per cent of the time, he could kiss her. Almost.

'Ta,' he says, restraining himself—just—from high-fiving her instead. He has a feeling she might consider that less than cool. 'Ta very much. I owe you. Big-time.'

⌣⌣

By eleven pm no-one has gatecrashed, thrown up or kicked off. Ben's outfit has been deemed well cool by several of the girls, his food vanished the moment it appeared and sufficient alcohol has been consumed to make everything and everyone pleasantly mellow. Some-one's iPod is playing a mournful Brother & Bones song, a few couples shuffling in unsteady circles in the denuded sitting room, arms looped around each other's necks, with further pairings making out in corners and on the stairs. Ben and two of his similarly partnerless classmates, more than a little bored in truth but determined not to show it, are trading harmless insults about the merits of their respective football teams in the kitchen, with Ben vaguely wondering whether he has the makings of some pancakes in the larder. Most of the guests had brought giant bags of crisps and Wotsits—now long gone—and he has a sudden craving for something sweet. He also has something much stronger than a craving for a sight of Louisa, who, as predicted, has not turned up. He can't bear the thought of Nats' face when next he sees her. Or Jez's, come to that. Assuming he ever shows.

He reaches down the side of the fridge where he had secreted his cans to meet only air.

'Oi, you lot snarfed my booze?' He turns on his companions, suddenly furious.

The two boys step back, muttering denials: 'Weren't me.' 'I got my own.'

'Well, someone has!'

'Maybe,' says Tom unwisely, 'you finished it.'

'Oh, yeah? Or maybe some scumbag's been helping themselves.'

'Hey, don't go off on one!'

'Don't tell me what to do!'

With some part of his brain, Ben is aware that this manufactured spat is not about cans of lager, nor about needing sugar: it's about Louisa, or the lack of her. If it weren't for her and Jez, there'd be no party; a party that, if he's really being honest, largely sucks. He wouldn't have to lug furniture back in from the garden all day tomorrow and replace all those shitty books and other crap—probably single-handed, as Jez'll no doubt find some excuse not to help out. And as for Louisa Jellinek: fuck her. Fuck her blonde hair, her hot hard bod, her flirty little giggle . . .

'Man!' breathes Tom, staring over Ben's shoulder down the hall to the front door, which has just opened. 'Man alive! How awesome is that!'

Three identical slender figures sashay into the hallway, coronas of bright fuchsia like enormous peonies around each immaculate face, bodies sheathed in bright green jumpsuits with spaghetti straps and cinched belts, the ensembles completed with gravity-defying heels. Ben cannot find words at all.

'You like?' Louisa pirouettes in the kitchen doorway, her two friends posing like caryatids either side of her. She points at her head. 'Clock the wigs! Fantabuloso or what?' Then her eyes light on Ben and his outfit. 'Yo, Ben my man, neat gear!' She blows the thunderstruck trio a kiss. 'Brought you a little pressie,' she cries, waggling a bottle of Grey Goose in Ben's direction. 'Let's party, babes!' And she and her entourage totter over to the paper cups on the counter.

'Jeez,' whispers Tom, 'she must be loaded. That's thirty-five quid of anyone's money. You are one lucky fucker, Ben Fry.'

Ben, himself more than a little bombed, can see that Louisa and her besties Kat and Els, unsteadily filling the flimsy cups with vodka, are indeed loaded, if not quite in the way Tom meant. The world is suddenly a much, much better place. 'Hey,' says Lou confidingly, leaning in his direction so that he can smell her sweet intoxicated breath, 'this is like really good shit, babes. You wanna try? Yeah, 'course you do. Give the man some voddy, Els.' The girls hoot as Els, struggling to pour while keeping her balance in her towering heels, sways dangerously trying to line up bottle and cup. Lou grabs the vodka from her and, snickering, holds it to Ben's unresisting mouth and upends it. In his surprise he gulps a huge mouthful, the alcohol hitting the back of his throat like a wave on the way down. He swallows, chokes, coughs, feeling the fire punch his chest and stomach. His eyes fill involuntarily.

'Don't drink it all!' shrieks Kat. The other boys look on open-mouthed as Louisa's arm glides round Ben's neck to cradle his head between her perfect breasts. He takes in her scent, her heat, that almost imperceptible tang of sweat that ought to be a turn-off but so isn't. He could stay here forever. Then a damp hand is pressed to his mouth and his lips open automatically like a puppy snaffling a treat. In goes something round and small, followed immediately by the neck of the vodka bottle. Another torrent of alcohol chases the pill down his throat before he can protest. The girls explode with laughter.

He staggers, rights himself, tries to focus on the three flowers whose heads are now bobbing to the saccharine but oddly compelling beat of Katy Perry's 'Last Friday Night', which has miraculously replaced the earlier music, with Louisa, Kats and Els performing a highly rehearsed routine and singing along raucously to the chorus. He steadies himself on the counter, hooking his fingers through the handles of the drawers behind him for stability, only for one to detach itself from its mooring and clatter to the floor.

The girls, still dancing and passing the bottle from one to the other, whoop like banshees. Kat reaches down to retrieve the handle and starts spinning it round and round on her forefinger as part of her routine. This, apparently, is the funniest thing her friends have ever seen, if their hysteria is any guide.

Ben, desperately trying to stop the world from sliding out of true, watches Kat's gyrating finger with its metal girdle going round and round like a fairground ride, his head trying desperately to keep pace with it. His eyes seem to be on an orbit of their own, sneaking off in all directions no matter how sternly his brain speaks to them. Something tells him he would do better to close his eyes.

'Oi, wake up, babes!'

With a superhuman effort he wrenches his lids apart to find an enormous face in his, filling the universe, the lips moving like a sea creature, sounds he can't catch dribbling out. They're eeling away like ribbons in the wind; he puts out a hand to catch them but they are so slippery . . .

'Having fun, Benji-boy?' breathes the flower, fronds about his face like silk.

He wants to nod, but his head won't move. His legs, however, decide they've held him up for long enough: he slides neatly down the cupboard to the floor.

'Aw, bless him, that was quick!' says Louisa to her companions. 'He's well gone!'

''S good shit, babes,' Els says with a giggle. 'Hope you still got some left.' It's unclear whether she's referring to the vodka or Louisa's little pills.

Louisa is reaching into her bag when the doorbell rings. The noise cuts through the music, interrupts the chatter and the snogging. It rings on and on insistently, piercingly, imperiously. As though someone means business. As though someone has every intention of pressing it until the end of the world. Or someone answers it.

Someone does.

All the guests crowd into the hallway; those who cannot insinuate themselves into the throng peer around doorways and through banisters or stand on tiptoe at the back. Only Ben, spread-eagled on the kitchen floor, images whirling sickeningly behind his eyelids as the unaccustomed alcohol surges through him, remains oblivious as the door is flung open to reveal a mass of muscles, testosterone and machismo, fronted by a triumphant Jez, borne aloft on several beefy shoulders. 'Hey, guys, say hi to my bros! Look who's home!'

And the full complement (plus subs) of the Hatchets, one of the least successful but most feared of university rugby teams, armed to the teeth with bottles and six-packs, thunders through the doorway, scattering everyone in their path, led by their captain, Henry Nairstrom. Otherwise known as Hedge.

SATURDAY

CHAPTER 33

It's just past midnight.

The communal feast has ended, as such events usually do, with the company breaking into small groups dictated by proximity, friendships or—as time wears on—inertia. Some of those leaving tomorrow have already made for their rooms to finish their packing, get their heads down for the morrow's travel ordeal or engage in that time-honoured finale to a foreign holiday, muffled copulation.

Harriet is sitting by the window overlooking the moonlit garden with Regina and Charles and Bella and Guy, the last having been trying to persuade his reluctant wife for the past ten minutes that they really ought to call it a night.

'You'll be exhausted tomorrow.'

'Oh, tomorrow,' says Bella, leaning back in her armchair with eyes closed. 'Tomorrow can look after itself.' She opens one eye and inspects her glass. 'Besides, I haven't finished my drink.' The eye shuts sleepily.

Guy, smiling wryly in defeat, shakes his head at Harriet. *Bless her heart*, she thinks, *she just wants to wring every last drop out of this holiday.* She hopes they remain in touch, fears that life—and Jack—may make that difficult. *I must make the effort; it's up to me to ensure it happens.* She adds that resolution to the list of tasks awaiting her on her return home. Track down Stephen's mother—

229

'Your sister's little romance seems to be flourishing,' says Regina, peering through the window.

Hester and Lionel are seated close together outside on the terrace, backs to the hotel; in the half-light it's hard to see, but they may be holding hands. Harriet has been trying not to look too closely for the past half-hour.

'Getting serious, is it?' Regina sits forward eagerly. 'I only ask because a little bird told me that there was a very public display of affection earlier when they were cooking together. And we do like a happy ending, don't we, Charles?' Charles beams, whether in agreement or because that's the way he always responds to his wife's questions it's hard to say.

'Holiday romance,' murmurs Bella from the depths of her armchair, blindly reaching out for her glass. Guy gets to it before she can knock it over and wraps her fingers around the stem, earning a lopsided smile.

I hope so, thinks Harriet. She smiles neutrally at Regina.

'Ooh, cagey, aren't we? She must have said *something*.' Honestly, in the nosiness stakes, Regina would be neck and neck with Peggy Verndale. 'Don't be coy, Harriet.'

Harriet, now adding this new intelligence about her sister and Lionel to the earlier shock of his plans to stay on, manages a smile. 'I think they're simply good friends. Shared interests, that's all.'

Regina turns to Charles. 'Come along, my love, looks like we're not going to get another word out of the sphinx and it's way past our bedtime.' She gets to her feet and turns to extract her husband from his chair with the practice born of long experience. She places a steadying arm under his and, after an imperious goodnight that takes in the whole room, they make their way out of the bar, oddly dignified despite the disparity in their heights and his obvious infirmity.

'Funny old world,' says Guy, eyes coming to rest on his now-sleeping wife. He puts his arms around her unresisting body and pulls her upright. 'Will we see you in the morning, Harriet?'

She nods and rises to kiss his cheek, then his wife's.

Bella mutters, 'Nighty night.'

'Aspirin,' says Harriet in Guy's ear, 'before she goes to sleep.'

He smiles his thanks.

'Sweet dreams.'

～～～

There is a slight chill in the air, but neither Hester nor Lionel is minded to move. They sit in companionable silence for a few minutes, staring up at the stars, the bright moon spilling a path across the garden. A minute gecko darts up from beneath the table in front of them and quivers on the edge, regarding them quizzically with head inclined as if questioning their invasion of his territory. A second later, with a flick of its tail, it vanishes. Lionel clears his throat.

'What was he like? Gordon?'

Hester, thoughts far from her late husband, drags herself back from her reveries. She gives the question due consideration. Gordon. She tries to conjure him. 'Big man. Over six foot. It was one of the reasons I was attracted to him.'

'Oh,' says Lionel, conscious of his just-above-average height. He sits up a little straighter.

Hester laughs briefly at the memory. She hasn't missed Lionel's reaction. 'It mattered so much more then. Not sure why.' She recalls the years of adolescence, low heels or no heels according to her current boyfriend's stature, her apologetic stoop, before she grew into her character and her height and ceased to care.

Lionel relaxes.

'Kind man. Very kind. Would have made a wonderful father but . . . well.' She wonders not for the first time whether that's true. It's become one of her tenets, trotted out routinely. She can't remember now when she first said it: certainly not while Gordon was still alive. Perhaps it's simply what she wants to believe, part of her personal mythology.

'Where did you meet?'

'Oh, uni. As everyone did in those days.'

Lionel shifts in his chair; he didn't.

'He was a rugger bugger.' She registers Lionel's surprise. 'Oh no! Not one of those loud obnoxious ones—not a Bullingdon type. Dear Lord, what do you take me for?! No, more driven, training all the hours God sent. I used to trail round every weekend to watch him play.'

'You?!'

'I know. Hard to credit. Anyway, he got a decent enough degree, joined his father's firm.'

Lionel raises a questioning eyebrow.

'Stockbroker.' She catches his expression. 'Oh, don't get the wrong idea. This was before the height of the Thatcher boom in the City. Gordon missed all that. Comfortable, yes, but not silly money. Anyway, he hated it. Cooped up in an office all day behind a desk. He decided he wanted to strike out on his own.' She frowns at the memory. 'His father was furious. Incandescent.' The rows and recriminations, short-lived as they had been, had not been pleasant. She knew that initially Gordon's parents had suspected she was egging him on; nothing could have been further from the truth.

'What did he do? Gordon.'

A sort of embarrassment washes over Hester's face. Even now she finds it absurd. 'He . . . opened a shop.'

Lionel cannot mask his astonishment. He knows Hester made her career in local government, gathers she was quite a high-flyer; somehow he cannot reconcile that with a shopkeeper husband, especially one who, like her, had attended a prestigious university. 'A *shop*?'

'Uh-huh. Not what you were expecting, is it? Nor me. At the time. I thought he was completely barmy. I told him so in no uncertain terms. But he was so very unhappy and I was already making my way up the greasy public sector pole. I had a modest amount of money from our parents' estate and we invested that in the business . . .'

'What sort of shop was it?'

'Sports equipment. And shops, not shop. Within a couple of years, he had three of them. A little empire. Fact is, he was a brilliant businessman. It suited him down to the ground. Talking to customers all day, demonstrating equipment, trade jollies—best thing he ever did. I was so proud of him.' She realises, *Gosh, I was, wasn't I? So why did I never tell him that?* 'His father had to eat humble pie.' Which, to his credit, he eventually had. Although he had to the end enjoyed his little dig: never 'How's business?' when they visited, but 'How's trade?' It drove them both to distraction. But Gordon's first career had stood him in good stead; his knowledge of the stock market had helped him to build a very tidy portfolio in time.

'Well!' says Lionel, flummoxed. This wasn't at all what he had pictured. 'And so . . . were you sporty?'

'Not really. Could play a half-decent game of tennis if required and I'm not a bad croquet player, but I've always preferred indoor pursuits, preferably cards. Mind you, Gordon played a mean hand of bridge himself.'

Lionel, aware of his shortcomings in that department, shrinks a little. This Gordon sounds quite a character. Quite a . . . paragon.

A breeze ripples the leaves of the bushes beside them as ribbons of cloud scud across the face of the moon. Shivering slightly, Hester pulls the neck of her cardigan tighter around her throat.

'Want to go in?'

She lays a hand on his for a moment. 'Not particularly. I'm fine. You?'

Lionel wishes he had thought to don a vest under his thin shirt but shakes his head; he doesn't want to break the moment. 'I wouldn't want you getting cold.'

Hester's hand, warm and dry, returns. 'I'm not cold.'

⌣⌣⌣

Harriet cannot sleep. She knows she's had at least one glass too many. She knows too that she is starting to obsess again about the future, her temporary equilibrium unsettled by Regina's relentless probing. She's tried a shower, a few pages of her novel, an old half-completed cryptic crossword she'd found crumpled at the bottom of her handbag, a hot chocolate from the sachet in her room (watery and over-sweet) and—her activity of last resort—writing a list of her worries. So far it reads:

Stephen (? Marion—Tues)

Mary

Move?

Hester

Lionel

She underlines *Hester* heavily, almost scoring the paper through, then for good measure rings the name, noting the irony that in so doing she has half crossed out the words above and below. For Hester is the key, the spider at the centre of a web over which Harriet feels she no longer has any control. A wave of powerlessness tinged with self-pity assails her once more, bringing in its wake a hot shaft of anger. For hadn't it been Hester who first broached the idea of sharing a home? Hester who fixed on Pellington as the ideal location? Hester who had found The Laurels, chivvied Harriet into pooling their finances, laid down the ground rules for their co-habitation, assumed without discussion dominion of the kitchen and much else besides? She chooses to forget the many occasions when she herself had asserted her views and Hester had backed down without demur. It suits her for the present to lay at her sister's door all responsibility for her turmoil, to blame Hester for Stephen's dilemma, for her own potential homelessness, for upending what had promised to be a comfortable and secure retirement. And why? Because Hester is a back-stabbing, solipsistic snake-in-the-grass! Concealing that letter from Stephen all those weeks and jumping to wrongheaded and catastrophic conclusions! Carrying on with Lionel like a love-struck teenager! Pathetic! Harriet throws the pad and pen down on the covers, fired with righteous indignation. She won't be a victim. She doesn't have to dance to Hester's tune—and she won't.

She scrambles out of bed, throws on her dressing gown and hurries down the corridor towards the foyer. The light at the reception desk is still on.

'Ah! Alfonso, sorry to disturb you, but I wonder if you'd be so kind . . .'

CHAPTER 34

It's just past midnight.

Someone is hammering on Ben's head. No, not on: *inside* his head. With a tiny pickaxe. Whoever is wielding it has found the most tender part of his cortex and is relentlessly swinging away at it, like a miner attacking a particularly inaccessible seam of coal. Ben forces his eyes open, finds that he is not trapped in a mine but has fetched up on a ship in the middle of a ferocious storm, pitching and yawing as the horizon dips and slews amid stomach-dropping plunges. He feels very, very unwell. Clawing his way upright he feels metal, sees a void immediately below him and vomits copiously into it.

⌣⌣⌣

Hedge is bored. He and Louisa have been snogging energetically for ten minutes now and his tongue is flagging. He pulls away; the suction broken, Louisa droops to one side and is instantly asleep, snoring lightly. One of his mates sniggers from the other side of the room and salutes his captain with a beer can. 'Nice one, bro.'

Hedge slides his arm from beneath Louisa's body, extracting his left hand from the inside of her jumpsuit, where he had been enthusiastically kneading one breast, gently tips her onto the floor and stands, flexing his cramped limbs. This party is crap. The music's crap—he hates heavy metal; which lamebrain put that on?—he's got the munchies and the booze is running dangerously low. 'Jez?' he yells. 'Where the fuck is he?' It's thanks to Jez they all pitched up here: he's dangerously close to looking a right dickhead in front of his mates. He needs to sort something and soon. 'Jez!'

'In the garden,' someone mumbles. 'Asleep.'

'Fucking great!' snarls Hedge, flinging his empty can at the wall. It hits a shelf, falls over and the remaining few drops of beer trickle out, dribble across the glass and start to snake down the wall, blending none too prettily with the stems of the faded floral wallpaper. The can rolls to the edge of the shelf, teeters, rocking back and forth, but does not fall.

'Hey, man, good shot!' One of his mates, glad of the distraction, lumbers to his feet and staggers over to Hedge, adopting the stance of a darts player, and lobs his own can at the shelf. His, though, is half-full: the liquid arcs out as it flies, sketching a dark stain across the floor. The boy whoops as his projectile, still heavy with some beer, hits Hedge's and sends both of them clattering to the floor.

'Fuck off,' shouts Hedge good-naturedly, snatching up another discarded can from the floor and, as if playing boules, delicately aims it at the shelf. It lands with a dink, skids across the surface, ricochets off the wall and drops to the floor. His companion, now armed with two cans, crows with derision and flings his weapons in quick succession at the bottom shelf, lodging one firmly in the corner where the two walls meet. It's going to be harder to dislodge this.

Hedge rises to the challenge. 'Game on!' he yells, his battle cry penetrating the sodden brains of the rest of the team, who one by one rouse themselves from their various positions under and astride assorted girls or morosely sitting unpartnered on the stairs and rush to answer the call.

Brick, nineteen stone of muscle and fat, returning from the upstairs bathroom and too impatient to weave his way down through the knot of bodies on the stairs, decides to take a short cut, swinging his huge bulk over the banister at the top to drop down into the hallway. The Laurels' banisters were designed to facilitate the stately descent of modest gentlefolk, not to act as a vaulting horse for an ungainly prop forward; with a crack as loud as a gunshot, the aged wood, dried out by years of central heating, fractures neatly at the newel post. The spindles, freed from restraint and unable to sustain the torsion, snap like flower heads under a scythe and flop drunkenly over to hang precariously above the hall. Brick's brain, or as much of it as is still functioning, registers the hazardous nature of their position. He reaches up and neatly finishes the demolition job by snapping them off completely to a roar of approval and admiration from his teammates, now clustered around Hedge, each one with an armful of missiles, as they listen to the rules of the impromptu game he has just invented.

'One point for a direct hit. Two points for any part of the anatomy you knock off. Three points for an arm and five points for the head. Only one throw per go.'

The competitors as one squint at the probable distance, angle and velocity required to score points. The bone china shepherdess, her sanctuary at the back of the very top shelf a sanctuary no more, stares back with a provocative smirk, her fate sealed.

⌣⌣⌣

Ben has nothing more to bring up. He has spewed and retched himself into exhaustion, expelling every last drop of lager and vodka, every scrap of food and, buried among the steamy, stinking mess, most of Louisa's little white pill. The sour smell of vomit hangs over the kitchen, no matter how long he runs the tap, until in desperation he squirts the entire washing-up liquid bottle down the plughole and the sharp tang of lemon fills the air instead. Dark shapes float outside the window; once or twice he hears the unmistakable sound of someone else voiding the contents of their stomach in the garden. He tries hard to suppress the thought of what will be revealed when the morning comes. All he wants to do now is crawl into bed. He can't begin to imagine how he is going to make it back to Daria's, once he's turfed everyone out and locked up the—

There is a sudden eruption of noise from the front of the house: cheers, laughter, yells. If it weren't for the fact that they'd removed every scrap of furniture from downstairs and locked all the bedrooms, he'd swear that what he could hear now, accompanied by renewed yelling, was the splintering of wood. But the only wood left is the doors. Oh, fuck, no . . .

Ben gropes his way unsteadily across the sticky floor to the kitchen door and yanks it open. A fug of beer, sweat and cheap perfumes and aftershaves hits him. Followed by something rather more concrete as Brick flings one of the spindles airily over his shoulder and fetches Ben a painful clout on the arm. He is so appalled by the scene of devastation that meets his eyes that he doesn't even cry out. He simply blinks, hoping, praying, this is a mirage, a terrible, gut-wrenching nightmare from which he will wake any second. Please, someone tell him that isn't a vast ragged gap where the banister once stood? Please tell him people—his mates among them—aren't gleefully yanking the remaining spindles, like rotten teeth, out of their housing?

'Stop! Stop! What the fuck—' he tries to shout, but the words, feeble as a baby's, are lost in the cacophony of shouts and drunken applause. It is as though everyone has lost their reason, infected with a primeval urge for destruction, each fresh breakage greeted with atavistic roars of encouragement. And there, in the centre of the maelstrom, arm aloft, hollering and stamping in triumph, is Hedge, a headless, limbless figurine in his fist. His cronies begin an inept parody of a Maori war dance, circling their captain in a surging mass of sweating menace, their bellows drowning out all but the bass beats of the music. Hedge hurls his trophy into the fireplace, smashing it to smithereens.

The vibrations shake the old house to its foundations, pulsing through the floorboards, penetrating even the sleepers' unconsciousness; dizzy heads are lifted, uncoordinated limbs try to hoist their owners' bodies upright. Louisa, her jumpsuit splodged in a Jackson Pollock of beer stains, sits up groggily, then crawls through the forest of legs to begin mountaineering up Hedge's heedless body. As her arms finally loop themselves around his neck and she gazes up at Hedge in drunken adoration, Ben, watching in horrified disbelief, his dreams in tatters, his aunts' house being trashed before his eyes, beseeches any gods that might be witnesses to grant him instant oblivion, if not death.

He covers his eyes. All around him, before him, above him, the horror continues unabated. Behind his eyelids flit images of all the people he has betrayed: his parents, infuriating but well-meaning; his aunts, forbidding but unfailingly kind; Daria, so naive and trusting; innocent Milo; Artem—

A huge roar of fury explodes close by, overtopping the tumult. It slams through the house with stunning force, like a cannon fired into the midst of battle, disorienting the combatants and freezing them in mid-frenzy.

Ben's eyes spring open on a miracle. There, framed in light from the porch, filling the doorway from edge to edge, stands an avenging angel. Or rather angels, three of them, in descending order of height. As the shapes coalesce into definition, Ben sees first Artem, then Finbar, and finally Nats. All three seem to be staring straight at him with expressions of appalled disgust that cut him to the heart. Then they charge into action.

Collars are seized, bodies flung like rag dolls out of the front door to sprawl on the path as Artem and his companions advance relentlessly through the fray. One look at their merciless expressions and resistance melts away, people scurrying as fast as their rubbery legs will carry them out of the house, stumbling and trampling over still-prone bodies, bottles, cans and bits of wood, intent only on escape. Even rugby players quail before Artem's vastness and his rage; all, that is, except Hedge and Brick, who, scornful of their teammates' craven retreat, decide to make a stand.

Ben and the few stragglers still making their exit look on with mesmerised horror as the two beefy rugby players crouch down as for a scrum and begin circling their opponents, spitting defiance. They are almost as tall and broad as Artem, and Brick is undoubtedly heavier; beside Artem, Finbar looks suddenly frail and vulnerable. The element of surprise that initially carried them through the house, sweeping all before them, has now dissipated: this has become a straight fight. And in Ben's opinion, drunk though Hedge and Brick may be, an unfair one.

In a moment, the atmosphere has changed from one of mayhem and confusion to concentrated malice. Hedge's lip is curled in derision as his gaze rakes over the old man. Brick, with a similar sneer, is sizing up Artem. Ben stands helpless, mind racing with panic. His foot nudges one of the spindles littering the floor. Of course! He bends to pick it up, but before he can grasp it, it is snatched away. A streak of colour flashes past, darts between Artem and Finbar and launches itself into the air with a bone-chilling cry of menace.

There is a split second of silence and then, before everyone's astonished gaze, Hedge and Brick simultaneously drop like felled trees to the floor, where they lie clutching their groins, writhing and groaning in agony, as Nats, back on solid ground, stands over them, one foot on Hedge's neck, the spindle pressed threateningly against Brick's.

Her two victims initially stare up at her with a mixture of uncomprehending shock and then, as they take in the size and gender of their enemy, chagrin. She stares back impassively, then gestures towards the front door with her weapon. 'Now fuck off, the pair of you, or else.'

They need no second bidding. Crawling at first, then levering themselves into a crouch on the doorjamb, they shuffle out of the house, trying desperately to muffle their moans, their only consolation that most witnesses to their humiliation have long since melted into the night.

Nats strolls down the hall and gently closes the door after them. Artem and Finbar emerge from the sitting room, regarding her with undisguised admiration, Artem miming applause and Finbar raising a grimy thumb.

Then they all turn to face Ben.

CHAPTER 35

Nestling in the heart of this picturesque village, a magnificent character cottage (Grade 2 listed), beautifully restored whilst retaining many original period features. Hall, sitting room with inglenook fireplace, study, kitchen, breakfast room with bi-folding patio doors, two bedrooms, bathroom with separate shower cubicle, delightful south-facing rear garden with decked patio and small pond.

Grade 2, thinks Harriet, *no thanks*. Peggy has bored the sisters for years over many a bridge table with the restrictions placed on Standfast House by its listing. It had taken decades to secure permission for a conservatory and the sisters had heard all they ever wanted to—and more—about the Verndales' battles with the planning department and the local Civic Society, whose eagle-eyed members patrol their fiefdom relentlessly in search of actual or proposed infringements. And a pond . . . not ideal when an adventurous baby like Milo visits.

She clicks on the next possibility.

Set in a delightful spot on the eastern fringes of this much sought-after village, a rare opportunity to purchase a very pretty and tastefully presented cottage with a pleasant outlook to two sides (Pleasant . . .? Not stunning? Or delightful? What, then? Something commercial? Industrial? Derelict?). *The snug porch* (read, tiny) *provides the welcome to Bramble Cottage* (too twee by half), *leading through to the compact* (oh dear, oh dear) *open plan kitchen and homely* (Chintz? Knickknacks?) *sitting room. The modern high-spec kitchen is fully fitted while the sitting room reflects the cottage's historic past with beams* (low, undoubtedly; hazardous for tall visitors. Like Hester), *open fireplace with wood-burning stove, assorted nooks and crannies* (knickknacks, definitely, and probable dust traps) *and original stone floors* (cold, presumably, no matter what the outside temperature). *A door conceals a neat staircase* (i.e. narrow) *leading to a comfortable landing with pleasant views* (Oh God, 'pleasant' again—do these agents not have a thesaurus?). *The main bedroom has pleasant views* (aargh!) *over farmland* (Dust and smells all summer. That is, assuming it isn't earmarked for housing development). *Up further stairs* (With my knees?) *to another double bedroom, also with views* (Of course it has views! Unless it's a windowless cell. But views of what? Too hideous to reveal?). *The garden is all to the front of the house and enjoys a good degree of privacy* (and excellent cover for burglars) *thanks to the high hedges. A small garage* (built in the days of the Morris Minor and thus useless for any modern car) *is set back from the cottage. Viewing essential.*

Or not, thinks Harriet sourly, removing her glasses and rubbing her eyes. She sits back wearily from the computer, where—after Alfonso's help in getting her online in the games room (the computer at home being almost exclusively Hester's domain)—she's been trawling Rightmove for the past hour. *Just to be on the safe side*, she tells herself. Already, she's requested full particulars of four houses in their local area to be sent to her at The Laurels. Mary was right: better to do something, take charge of events and plan ahead than cower helpless in the face of others' machinations. And all this knowledge at one's fingertips, thanks to the internet!

A thought strikes her. Of course! With luck, she'll be able to set the wheels in motion before they get home. Seconds later, she types a name into the search engine and starts to scan the results. The hotel is silent as she pads past the now-deserted reception desk on her way back to her room.

∽∽∽

'Morning!' says Harriet cheerfully as she slides into a chair opposite Lionel some six hours later, having just made a brief but productive phone call, kept short on the pretext of avoiding extortionate overseas mobile charges. 'Beautiful morning, isn't it?'

Lionel looks a little nonplussed by the warmth of her greeting and half rises.

'You don't mind me joining you?'

'No, no, not at all,' he stammers, looking around anxiously as he sits again. 'May I order you some tea or coffee? I'm sure Hester will be down shortly.'

'I'm sure she will. I hear you're staying on until Monday too.' Harriet bestows on him her sweetest smile. She's feeling back in control once more, after her nocturnal activities and this morning's phone call.

He looks across the table nervously, like someone encountering an animal whose friendliness is in doubt. 'Well, yes . . . yes, I am as it happens. I had nothing urgent to hurry back for.'

'Oh?' says Harriet, still smiling. 'Lucky man.'

Lionel, on high alert now, looks desperately towards the door, the garden, anywhere Hester might conceivably be. What's taking her so long?

Harriet, face now cradled in the palm of her hand, waits.

'Oh, look! Here she comes!' Lionel's face is washed with relief.

Harriet notes that despite the hour Hester has applied a little makeup and the merest dab of scent. *Aha.* The sisters greet one another warmly, but Harriet nonetheless registers the subtle but unmistakable look of complicity that flashes between Hester and Lionel as he holds out her chair for her and then resumes his seat.

'You missed the others,' Harriet says, unfolding her napkin.

Hester raises her eyebrows—her *plucked* eyebrows—in query.

'On the minibus to the airport. They all left about half an hour ago. Regina, Bella and Guy send their best.'

'How kind,' says Hester, looking around for a waiter. 'I'm afraid I slept in rather. That's why I'm so late.'

But not so late that you didn't get made up and perfumed, thinks Harriet.

'We meant to say our farewells last night, but somehow . . . Lionel, dear, I don't suppose you could rustle up some tea for us?'

Unusually, there are no members of staff to be seen in the dining room, which, awaiting the next influx of guests, is empty but for their party. Lionel leaps up to do her bidding and disappears in the direction of the swing doors that lead into the hotel kitchen. There is a small hiatus.

'I thought I would walk into the town this morning, get a bit of exercise,' says Harriet. 'It's supposed to be well worth a visit. Besides, I'm almost out of shampoo. And I wondered if I might find a *Guardian*. I've got crossword withdrawal symptoms.'

'I have shampoo,' says Hester. 'In my room. You know, the complimentary sachets.'

'I know. So have I. But I'd like to stretch my legs.'

'I might come with you.'

'That would be nice,' says Harriet, silently adding, *as long as it's just you*. 'Lionel won't mind?'

Hester swiftly swerves around Harriet's trap. 'Lionel?' she says, as though astonished he should figure in the equation. 'I hardly think so. He'll be perfectly happy in the garden, reading.' Having tried to downplay his importance in the scheme of her own activities, she now realises she sounds as though she can predict if not dictate his actions. She vigorously smears greengage conserve onto a roll. Harriet reaches for the butter.

'Tea's on the way,' says Lionel, hurrying back from his mission. The sisters regard him brightly and chorus their thanks. Rather than reassure, their overenthusiastic response unsettles him further.

Gingerly, he lowers himself onto his seat and sets about splitting a roll, addressing the task with intense concentration. Harriet solicitously edges the butter dish over to him.

'Harry and I are just going to walk into Camerino after breakfast.' Hester smiles across at him. 'I told her you wanted to finish that book of yours.'

Lionel recognises the hint for what it is and nods.

Hester turns to her sister. 'Lionel's quite a reader,' she says, as though vouching for his credentials before a sceptical jury. It unfortunately comes out as a rather patronising does-he-take-sugar? comment, and Hester realises it the second she says it.

Harriet is unable to resist the bait. 'Oh. How lovely. What sort of books do you like?'

Lionel's bread and jam stalls halfway to his mouth. Something in the way both Harriet and Hetty are regarding him—the one with faint amusement, the other with what he reads as muted alarm—panics him. He senses that much hinges on his reply, that he has unwittingly been lured into a minefield. Should he lie? Pretend a fondness for some author he might imagine Harriet would approve of? He opts for the truth.

'Oh,' he says with what he hopes is a manly self-deprecating laugh, 'nothing highbrow, I'm afraid. Typical male stuff—all war, espionage, and blood and thunder!' He shovels the bread into his mouth to forestall any further comment.

'War?' says Harriet. 'We like books about the war, don't we, Hetty?'

Hester frowns. 'Do we?'

'Yes! *The Siege. The Greatcoat.* Helen Dunmore,' she explains to Lionel.

He gulps. 'A woman?'

Oh dear, thinks Hester. *Oh dear, oh dear . . .*

'Yes,' says Harriet levelly. 'Imagine! How on earth did she know what to write?'

⌣⌣⌣

The track—not worthy of the name of 'road', being unmade and heavily rutted—up to the main highway is steeper than either of them remembers. By the time they pass the crumbling pillars that mark the boundary to Il Santuario, Harriet is considerably out of puff, although struggling not to show it. Hester, in contrast, strides out purposefully, her longer legs forcing her sister to break into a semi-jog from time to time to keep up. *That'll teach her*, thinks Hester, still rankled, *humiliating Lionel like she did. Poor chap didn't deserve that.* She had parted from him in the garden with a whispered, 'Don't let her get to you,' but his wavering smile suggested he found that of scant comfort.

'Could we take it a little less energetically?' pants Harriet. 'I'd really like a chance to admire the scenery and take a few pictures.' Harriet pulls out her phone and readies herself to take a photo, forcing Hester to stop.

Hester smiles to herself. It seems to take Harriet an inordinate length of time to find an aspect that pleases her, by which time her breathing has steadied, although her forehead still glistens from the exertion.

The sisters stroll at a more modest pace along the edge of the road, the occasional passing car stirring up clouds of fine dust. Ahead, above thickly forested slopes, stand the honey-coloured medieval stone walls of Camerino encircling the ancient cathedral, the twin-towered Duomo, the churches and university of this tiny jewel of a town. Below them the valley swoops down to the river, the fields striped in a dozen shades of green, interspersed from time to time with expanses of huge yellow sunflowers, their broad faces smiling up at the sky.

As they trudge along in apparently companionable silence, Hester frets to herself, *Should I tell her?* Beside her, reviewing the events of last night, Harriet thinks: *Should I tell her?*

'Been a bit of a week, hasn't it?' says Hester finally, in an opening gambit, as she bats away a cloud of midges dancing over her head. She has decided to put this morning's little hiccup to one side for the moment; however, the words sound forced and banal. Not what she intended at all.

'A bit,' agrees Harriet, thinking: *Here it comes.*

'I feel so guilty.'

'Hetty, don't. You mustn't—oh my God, watch out!' Harriet yanks Hester up the verge out of danger as a bright red Maserati surges by and careers around the sharp bend ahead, spitting grit. Falling awkwardly in a heap against the bank, they crush a clump of wild flowers, releasing a cloud of drowsy bees. The fall takes Harriet momentarily back to that fateful drawing trip. 'That was close,' she says shakily, pulling Hester to her feet. The feel of her sister's skin under her hand provides an odd comfort, like their embrace in the garden a few days earlier. She squeezes Hester's arm, then slips hers through it and hugs it to her side. Together they clamber back down to the road and start to climb the hill again towards the town.

A breeze springs up out of nowhere, rippling across the fields in a shiver of leaves, sunflowers swaying in a shuddering dance. Hester glances up. 'Where the hell did they come from?' Two bulging grey clouds have materialised overhead, incongruous in the china blue, and almost instantaneously one or two fat raindrops splat down, sizzling on the hot tarmac. Another hits Harriet squarely on the crown of her head and trickles down the back of her neck, tracking refreshingly through the sweat. They have barely had the chance to register the abrupt change of weather and look around for shelter before rain is drumming furiously on the road, creating instant rivers that course down the hill, saturating their shoes. Peering through rain-spattered glasses, Hester spots a tiny ridge-tiled terracotta structure beside the road a little further ahead. 'Quick!' she yells, grabbing Harriet's hand and pulling her up the incline. 'Run!'

A lorry trundles by, sending up a spume of water that catches Harriet squarely across the midriff. They stumble, laughing, breathless and sodden, into the little sanctuary, both having to duck to avoid hitting their heads on its arched entrance. Inside, the roof is high enough for Harriet to stand upright; Hester is forced to adopt a comical crouch.

It's a wayside shrine, a simple Madonna painted on the back of the plaster niche, the Virgin's face and robes streaked and faded with time and damp, stubs of yellowing candles around her feet. Rubbish, blown in by wind or traffic, litters the floor: cigarette and crisp packets, squashed and torn, battered tin cans and a single sheet of newspaper; Berlusconi, his hand-sewn hair poking up like freshly planted saplings across his pate, smirks his wolfish smile through a patina of muddy footprints. A thin rusted metal bar runs the width of the shrine to protect the Madonna. The sisters test its strength and perch awkwardly on it, unpeeling wet clothes from damp skin and flapping them in an ineffectual attempt to get dry. Harriet heels off her walking shoes to remove her socks and wring them out.

'This feels faintly sacrilegious.'

'What, all this garbage?' Harriet stirs it with her foot. 'There ought to be some whiskery black-clad crone in permanent residence, armed with a broom, repelling all non-believers.' She sweeps a glance around their cramped temporary quarters. 'Or a bloke.' Both think immediately of Finbar, ensconced in his own not dissimilar sanctuary, and this brings in its wake the thought of home, and all the complications that now threaten their life in England. Both sense the change of atmosphere, an opportunity lost. The chance of reconciliation, of secrets shared and confidence regained, seems to have been washed away with the rain.

CHAPTER 36

Finbar, Artem and Nats impale Ben, frozen at the end of the hallway by the kitchen door, with identical contemptuous stares. Artem's eyes rise as cold as ice to take in the shattered staircase, then sweep across to the sitting room, to the floor strewn with discarded cans and bottles and shards of china, pools of beer and lager—and worse—staining the floorboards, the ruined wallpaper. He turns his unforgiving eyes back to bore into Ben once more. One word drops into the silence: not English but Belarusian; just a single word, but its meaning couldn't be clearer. It seems no words in Artem's extensive English vocabulary can express the depths of his disgust. Ben's roiling stomach churns.

'*Sceleris plenissime!*' growls Finbar, which must, despite Ben's incomprehension, surely be intended to heap more coals of shame on his head.

Only Nats says nothing, and somehow her silence is even more painful than the men's expletives. She flicks her glance away as though even looking at Ben offends her.

Artem jerks his thumb over his shoulder in the direction of the front door. 'Out.'

Ben's legs refuse to move. Leave? What about the cottage? What about the damage? What about . . . everything?

Artem reads him immediately. 'Tomorrow morning. In the daylight. We assess the full extent of this . . . *devastation*.' He virtually spits the word.

251

Ben, head down, eyes glued to his feet, shuffles down the hallway, hugging the walls so as not to touch, to defile, anyone. As he goes to pass Finbar, Artem leans forward and hisses, 'But you can at least thank this gentleman before you crawl away, you little shit. Thanks to him the house is still standing. Thanks to him we were able to get here in time to save your—'

'Sorry arse,' inserts Nats helpfully, looking anywhere but at Ben.

'Arse. Yes.' Ben has never heard Artem swear before, certainly not in English, and he is shamed afresh at the catastrophe that has driven this usually so contained of men to such lengths. He gulps down the bile of humiliation and manages to whisper through nerveless lips, 'Thank you, Finbar. Thank you all.'

'Now get in the car,' snarls Artem.

'No, I—' The thought of having to sit in close proximity to Artem, to any of them, is more than he can bear. As for coming face to face with Daria . . . He'd rather walk all the way home to an empty house and nurse his shame and self-disgust alone.

'Shut up!' Artem gives him a savage shove between the shoulder blades that propels him out of the door and onto the path, where he only just manages to keep his footing. 'Get in!'

Harriet's battered old car sits askew in the lane. Ben scrambles in and cowers in the back, trying to make himself as small as possible. He catches snatches of a short conversation between Artem and Finbar, then hears the latter start off up the lane on foot. Seconds later, Nats jumps in and slams the passenger door, Artem insinuates himself awkwardly into the cramped driver's seat, yanks his door shut and, executing a clumsy three-point turn, surges back towards the main road, waving at Finbar as they pass him.

No-one speaks. The tension in the little tin prison is unbearable. Ben buries his face in his hands trying to blot everything out, but he cannot escape the sound of Artem's ragged and enraged breathing. Nats' thin shoulders remain resolutely turned away from him, every line of her averted head a reproach.

They pull up outside Daria's cottage with a jerk. Light blazes from the doorway, where Daria waits, huddled in a dressing gown several sizes too large. She runs down the path and pulls Nats' door open, her face twisted with worry, a torrent of Belarusian tumbling out.

'Shh! Shh!' cautions Artem, indicating the adjoining cottages. 'The neighbours!'

Daria claps her hand to her mouth then, as Nats climbs out, continues her diatribe at a slightly lower volume, jabbing her index finger repeatedly towards Ben's huddled form.

Nats grabs her arm and hurries her back inside, whispering furiously.

Artem climbs out and comes around to tug Ben's door open.

The boy, not wanting to court further humiliation, stumbles out and, cold and sick at heart, stands uncertainly on the pavement.

'Inside,' snaps Artem.

'No, I—'

'Now!'

Ben shoots up the path, almost colliding with Nats, who, rucksack over one shoulder, is bidding a quiet farewell to Daria. She ignores Ben completely.

'Bye, Artem.' Nats stretches up, as if she has done it forever, to peck Artem on the chin, which is as high as she can manage on tiptoes. She reaches for her bike.

'No, no, Natalie! You cannot ride home alone at this time of night!'

'Artem, I can. I must. My mother will be—'

'I will drive you.'

'No you won't! Now get to bed. Trust me, I can look after myself.'

For a second it looks as though Artem might contradict her, then he recalls her extraordinary contribution back at The Laurels. He cannot deny it: this tiny girl can indubitably look after herself.

She flings a leg over the saddle, strapping on her helmet. 'See you first thing tomorrow,' she says sotto voce, steps hard on the pedals and is off.

Artem waves briefly at her departing back, shaking his head in admiration. Then his eyes light on Ben, cowering just inside the door. 'Bed!' he snarls, pushing him towards the stairs, just as Daria re-emerges from the kitchen, eyes blazing. Ben scoots up the stairs two at a time and tears into the tiny boxroom under the eaves, shutting the door swiftly but silently. God help him if he wakes Milo. He hears Daria and Artem at the foot of the stairs engaged in a furious exchange. No prizes for guessing the subject matter. Tears of self-pity threaten to overwhelm him; ripping off his clothes down to his underpants, he crawls in utter misery under the quilt, tormented by a kaleidoscope of images whirling around his aching head. And then, abruptly, miraculously, blessedly, he falls asleep.

〜〜〜

The jury sits facing him at the kitchen table as he staggers down, dry-mouthed, disoriented and crushed, the following morning. All three of his judges nurse mugs of black coffee and all three wear the same expression. Disdain and anger, yes, of course, but harder, much harder, to withstand: deep, undisguised disappointment. He has braced himself for their justifiable contempt, but seeing how low he has sunk in all their estimations makes him realise the true cost of what he has forfeited. And this represents just the tip of a horrible iceberg, for the real victims of his stupidity and duplicity have yet to learn of his betrayal. It is not his parents' reaction he most dreads, terrible though that will be; it is the aunts'. And not in truth Aunt Hester's stony-faced fury, but Aunt Harriet's infinitely more painful sorrow and regret that the boy she has championed and supported so valiantly for so long against an army of detractors has proved utterly unworthy of her love.

Daria rises without a word, pours him a glass of milk and slams it down in front of him, then sits again. Nats sips her coffee, watching him coldly over the rim of her mug. Artem consults a sheet of paper in front of him, then slowly locks his eyes on Ben's. 'Drink.'

Ben does as bid, imagining the milk curdling as it hits his still-tender stomach. His shaking hand fumblingly wipes the milky moustache off his upper lip. From the front room comes the sound of a heedless Milo playing with his bricks in the playpen. He waits for his sentence, all hope gone.

Artem clears his throat. 'Natalie and I have inspected the damage this morning.' He catches Ben's glance at the clock on the windowsill. Ten forty-three. 'Yes. While you were *sleeping*. It is severe.'

Ben swallows.

'The staircase must be totally rebuilt. There is little remaining that we will be able to . . .'

'Salvage,' murmurs Nats.

'Yes, thank you, salvage. The floors require thorough cleansing. With bleach, with disinfectant. The walls, perhaps, may be cleaned, but I am not hopeful. They are so badly stained. We may need to redecorate the best room completely.'

Ben gulps.

'Someone has vomited down the curtains. Daria will try to wash them. One of your *guests* has kindly smashed the washbasin downstairs. How?'

He looks genuinely bewildered. For a moment Ben thinks he is waiting for an explanation, then realises just in time that he is simply seeking to fathom the mindlessness of the demolition. 'Someone has . . . what is the word?' He turns to Nats, miming a knife.

'Scored their initials.'

'Yes, scored their initials on the kitchen door.' He shakes his head with incomprehension. 'Finbar is even now attempting to unblock the lavatory.'

'Finbar?' croaks Ben.

Daria, no longer able to contain her ire, interrupts, thumping the table with her fist. 'Yes! Finbar! Your . . . your . . . he rescues you!'

'Saviour,' offers Nats quietly.

'Yes! He saves you. He runs—an old man, in the dark!—he runs from the house of Hester and Harriet and he is bang, bang, bang on the door here! *Karavul! Dapamazhytse!* Help me! Wake up! Come quick! There are men, mad, mad men, throwing, breaking . . . and still he helps today!'

From the front room comes a startled wail; Milo has obviously heard his mother shouting.

'You! You see! Wicked, wicked boy! Even baby is crying!' She rushes from the room. 'Okay, okay, Milo, Mama comes!'

Artem straightens his list. 'So, this is the plan. I will phone Barry, my friend. I will ask him please to help.'

'Barry?' manages Ben, head now pounding.

'He is a carpenter. I will ask him to mend the stairs. If he can. If he will. At the weekend. The weekend, when he ought to be not working. Relaxing.' He juts his jaw at Ben to emphasise the huge sacrifice he will be asking of Barry. 'We—' he sweeps his hand over himself, Nats and Ben '—we will start immediately to clean the house as well as we are able. Then we will see what more we must do. And we will then try to put everything back together again. Somehow. Before poor Hester and Harriet return.'

He makes it sound almost possible.

Ben's face lifts; he cannot mask his relief. Hope flickers for a moment. 'Thank you, thank you. I can't tell you how sorry—'

'You twat!' Nats' face twists with incredulity; even her braids seem to be quivering with rage. She is a pulsing bundle of fury. 'We're not doing this for you! Are you out of your tiny half-arsed brain?! We don't give a stuff about *you*, you selfish prick, or what you think. This is for your aunts. No-one deserves what you've done to them. No-one! Just thank Christ there are all these people who really care about them, who really love them! I've never even met them but I want to help! Stop sitting there feeling sorry for yourself like the total dickhead you are. For fuck's sake, go and have a shower, will you, and clean your bloody teeth: you stink.'

CHAPTER 37

The rain stops as suddenly as it started. Only the steady *drip drip* from the shrine's eaves remains as witness to its visit. Harriet picks her way outside across the litter to look up at the sky, where a valiant sun struggles through the remaining cloud, twinkling on the puddled potholes. She wriggles her toes to the ends of her sodden shoes. She'll have to manage the rest of their walk without socks.

'We might as well get going. Perhaps we could get a bus back. Or a taxi.'

'A taxi!' To Hester, the height of extravagance. 'I thought you wanted a walk!'

Harriet resigns herself to a soggy trudge back to the hotel. 'Come on, you old skinflint, let's at least splash out on a decent coffee.' *And maybe,* she thinks, *one of those delicious little doughnuts . . .* It seems ages since breakfast.

～～

They find a trattoria in the town square, its striped awning still dripping, with a *padrone* more than happy to serve two damp English ladies with good strong coffee and, to Harriet's delight, a plate of tiny biscotti and pastries. Hester, eschewing anything but her coffee, tuts almost but not quite inaudibly as her sister reaches for her third biscuit.

'I'm on holiday!' protests Harriet, with a grin. She flicks back and forth in the dog-eared town guide she found on an adjacent shelf. 'This is brilliant. Listen. *Placed in a suggestive position between two mountain large and grand, the town is surprising.* Full stop.' She laughs delightedly. 'And we really can't leave here without a visit to the botanical gardens—'

'Stop it,' whispers Hester, glancing over at the *padrone*.

'No, seriously. *Botanic garden despite its little smallness and position in the centre that allows no widening yet offers to the eye hidden corners of suggestive delights to discover always new scenaries.* It's clearly a very suggestive place.'

'The worst kind of cultural snobbery, sneering at the natives,' says Hester sanctimoniously, but with a glint in her eye. For years, one of their mutual pleasures has been spotting and celebrating infelicitous translations.

The sisters share a complicit look. And both relax, sensing the beginnings of a return of their old easy camaraderie. Hester reaches over and snaffles the remaining biscuit on Harriet's plate.

~~~

The taxi draws up outside Il Santuario, the driver hurrying around to heave open the sliding passenger door and offer the poor lady a helping hand. Mary takes it gratefully and, supported by Ron and Rhona, carefully eases herself out of the vehicle, to be greeted effusively by Alfonso and Marco, who have run down the steps to welcome her. They usher her into the hotel and towards the room designed for disabled guests, sited close by reception.

'I'm fine. I'm fine!' Mary keeps insisting, embarrassed by all the fuss.

'Perhaps the *signora* would like to lie down?' Alfonso asks Ron, as though his wife's accident has deprived her of all volition.

'I'm okay,' says Mary plaintively, looking desperately to Rhona for support, only for Ron to ignore her interjection and agree with the hotelier that yes, she must rest and be left to sleep. Perhaps a sign requesting silence could be displayed outside her door?

'I'm sick to death of sleeping,' mutters Mary, fast losing all hope of the coffee she has been craving for the last two hours as they battled the impenetrable bureaucracy at the hospital before finally securing her discharge. Defeated, the reluctant invalid allows herself to be frogmarched to her room, the restorative view of the sun-bathed countryside to be hidden behind light-excluding shutters, her shoes removed and a blanket to be drawn over her. Her minders tiptoe noisily out and shut the door, leaving her in almost total darkness. She closes her eyes.

The beauty of the town's Renaissance architecture feeds the sisters' bonhomie as they begin to retrace their steps, on their way calling into the *pharmacia*, where Harriet purchases a bottle of Italian shampoo emblazoned with what looks like sprigs of rosemary. Regardless of its perfume and ingredients, it has a signal quality approved by both sisters: it is cheap. They marvel over the wealth of treasures contained within the narrow streets, agreeing that they really must return one day to do the town justice, as they make their way back towards the main road: at the geraniums spilling over wrought-iron balconies, the occasional cat sunning itself on pot-strewn steps, pedestrians raising a hand in greeting as they pass with a muttered '*Buongiorno*'.

'I could almost live here,' says Harriet.

'Really? You mean you'd seriously leave England? Leave Pellington?'

Harriet stiffens. Is that relief, hope even, she hears in Hetty's voice?

'No, of course not. Not really. It's just the sun ... the food ... the people ...'

'The rain ...'

'Yes, but look at it,' says Harriet, a sweeping hand taking in view and sky. 'It's over in seconds. Not like back home.'

'It snows here in winter,' says Hester, pointing at a symbol of snow tyres on a road sign.

'Good point,' concedes Harriet. 'Holiday madness, that's all.'

'And the politics?' Hester's face crinkles with disapproval. 'You wouldn't last five minutes.'

The sisters share a rueful laugh. This sort of conversation always ends up with the same conclusion: however bad life, society and politics may appear at home, it's better than anywhere else.

'Could *you* live somewhere else?' says Harriet, spotting an opportunity. 'Not abroad. I mean in England. London, say?'

'London?' Hester frowns in thought. Tries it out. 'London . . .'

'We're always saying we don't see enough theatre. Think of all of those galleries and exhibitions on your doorstep.' Harriet glances across at her sister. 'I mean, depending on where in London you lived.'

'Couldn't afford it,' says Hester decisively, 'even if we wanted to. What's brought this on?'

'Nothing,' says Harriet, with studied casualness, thinking '*we*'. *Who's we?*

They walk on in silence for a few more minutes. Harriet thinks: *the longer this goes on, the worse it's going to get. I hate all these secrets.* Did she but know it, Hester is thinking along almost identical lines.

'Hetty—'

'Harry—'

They both laugh apologetically.

'Sorry. Go on—' Harriet is almost glad of the interruption.

'No, you first,' says Hester, secretly relieved. She nods at her sister to continue.

Harriet takes a deep breath. '*Well*, you know what you were saying about Tuesday? About coming with me? To see Marion?'

'Marion?' says Hester. 'Do I know her?'

'No, I don't think so. Friend from uni.' *Friend*, thinks Harriet, *but was she?* 'She was on my staircase in college.'

'And you think . . .?'

'Yes.' There, she's put it into words. 'I don't know for certain or why on earth ... but yes. I spoke to her briefly this morning. Said I was going to be in her neighbourhood and could I drop in on Tuesday. Anyway, I'm sorry I was a bit iffy when you offered to come with me. I'd love you to. If you still want to.'

'Of course I will! It's the least I can do,' says Hester humbly. 'I got you into this mess.'

'I thought we'd agreed you'd take off the hairshirt, Hetty. But I'm glad, I truly am. I'm really apprehensive, if I'm honest.'

Hester grunts, Harriet's overture balm to her still-battered and guilt-ridden spirits. She gives her sister's shoulder an awkward pat in thanks.

'Thanks,' says Harriet. 'Thanks a lot. Anyway, what were you going to say?'

'Oh ...' *No*, thinks Hester, *not right now. Not when we've just got back on an even keel.* 'I can't remember. Doesn't matter. Gosh, it's hot, isn't it?!'

Harriet knows an evasion when she sees one. She decides to let it go.

'Mary should be back today,' she says, seeking a neutral topic of conversation.

'Presumably she'll fly back on Monday on our flight,' says Hester, as much from a desire to keep the conversation flowing as from any real concern for Mary. She's bubbling inside with relief.

'I guess. Let's hope they can all get seats.'

'And who's this other woman that came over?' says Hester. 'Her sister?'

'Neighbour.' It's not for Harriet to spill Mary's secrets. 'Best friend, that is.'

'Must be,' says Hester, with some asperity. 'Frankly, I'm not sure I'd muscle in, not when there's a husband to hand.'

'I'd've done the same for you.'

'Well, of course,' says Hester scornfully, 'but I'm your *sister.*'

They turn in through the entrance to the hotel.

⌣⌣⌣

The waiter lays out the plates of salami and hams, the pecorino, a basket of bread, pats of butter glistening with tiny drops of moisture, bowls of olives and thick slices of tomato sprinkled with torn basil and drizzled with oil. Plates, glasses, napkins, cutlery, a jug of water, a carafe of *vino bianco*, perfect for a light lunch. Alfonso and Marco, content that the necessities of life are at hand, that Signor Martindale has made no further mention of the accident, are at last returning to their duties: they have a business to run, fresh guests arriving any minute.

'*Bellissimo!*' says Rhona. '*Grazie.*' The young boy sketches a bow and scampers back up the steps, leaving Mary's husband and lover alone for the first time since they arrived in Italy.

Ron regards his rival sourly. His mind simply will not allow him to comprehend the nature of her relationship with his wife. *His* wife! It's an aberration, a test Mary has set him, a provocation. God knows why. Perhaps this accident, this blow to her head, will restore her to her senses. All he wants is for things to return to the way they were. Safe, predictable. They need never speak of it. If this bloody woman would just bugger off . . .

The bloody woman gets to her feet. Her face is transformed, lit as from within, with rapture almost. He's not a religious man but he's seen the pictures. She might be a saint transfigured in a medieval painting. He envies her that joy and whatever its cause with an inexplicable sense of longing. Turns and sees Mary carefully making her way down the steps, clasping the rail tightly, smiling a small secret smile of triumph. If he had the words, had the courage, he would tell her—

Rhona runs lightly up the steps and for one terrible moment he thinks she is going to kiss Mary. There, under this unfamiliar sun, in front of him. His heart tears, a hard hot pain, not with jealousy but regret. That she got there first. That it is her hands that are guiding Mary down those last few crooked steps.

'You shouldn't be up!' What he means as concern sounds like censure.

'Oh, Ron!' cries Mary. 'Do give it a rest!'

Rhona gently eases Mary into the nearest chair; sits beside her, still clasping her hand. She strokes her hair back from her forehead.

Two figures appear above them, indistinct in the shadowy doorway, then one of them steps out into the sunlight.

'Oh! Mary!' calls Harriet. 'Mary, my dear, how lovely!'

And Mary cranes her head sharply upwards, squinting in the brightness, the memory of the fall suddenly washing over her afresh.

She shields her eyes with one hand, the other flying up to cradle her head wound. 'Oh, no!'

Rhona and Ron both leap forward in concern.

Harriet stumbles down the steps towards her, calling her name. Mary cautiously opens her eyes; finds herself enclosed in a claustrophobic circle of concern. Her gaze lights on one face in particular.

'Harriet . . .'

CHAPTER 38

There are simple hangovers, dull, sickening, head-thumping hangovers, with an acid stomach and vicious stabs behind the eyes that leave the sufferer reeling and courting oblivion. But nothing he has ever experienced in his short and relatively sheltered life and his even shorter acquaintance with alcohol and drugs could have prepared Ben for those same ghastly torments exacerbated with even greater quantities of shame and humiliation.

He has twice already ducked out into the garden to throw up, even though he has nothing left to bring up but bile. His mother certainly, his aunts possibly, seeing him in such misery might have felt faint stirrings of pity for his condition. Indeed, his soft-hearted mother would almost certainly have relented, despite his crimes, and packed him off to bed. But not Artem. Not Daria. Not Nats. No word of sympathy escapes their lips as he staggers out and back. The only acknowledgement he has received in the three hours since they began the herculean task at The Laurels is Daria's frequent replenishment of his bucket with fresh water and cleaning fluid. He assumes that he is not even to be trusted with such a simple job. Each time, she slams the bucket down beside him and stomps back to her own work.

The silence from Louisa, Jez, all his mates in fact, has been thunderous, the only communication so far this morning a timid text from his mother asking for reassurance that he is still alive. He has dutifully responded, narrowly resisting the temptation to reply simply: *Just.*

At the moment, he is on his knees in the hall, scrubbing the floorboards, the hammering in his head complemented by the hammering and sawing from the landing, where Barry the carpenter, whistling and from time to time breaking into tuneless song, is cheerfully fashioning a new set of banisters. Barry, despite his initial damning assessment—'Jesus, Artem mate, you don't ask much, do you? A week's work, if it's a day'—has set to enthusiastically, sizing up the remaining fragments of the old staircase and using Ben's photos (which had briefly elicited the merest hint of admiration from Artem when he had revealed their existence) for comparison. Barry's enthusiasm is maintained by Daria's regular trips upstairs with chocolate biscuits and mugs of steaming, highly sugared tea, each successive mug prompting more and more effusive thanks.

Artem and Finbar are busy plumbing in a new basin in the downstairs loo after a lightning visit to the builders' yard, picking up some wood for Barry at the same time; Ben will not even start thinking about how much this is all costing. Nats has worked wonders on the sitting room walls and has now left the paper to dry out, moving on to the kitchen floor, having already sanded down the mercifully shallow marks on the door. With Milo secured in a makeshift pen in the garden, Daria has taken down the stinking curtains, hauled them through to the utility room and is washing them one at a time on the lowest possible setting, since they are both perilously threadbare and also labelled *Dry-clean only.* The barely readable label bears the legend *Marshall & Snelgrove.*

'I say! Hello?'

A face appears at the curtainless front window. All activity, save for Barry's sawing and gutsy rendering of 'I Will Survive' upstairs, is suspended.

Artem streaks down the hall, vaulting over Ben, and disappears through the front door, closing it swiftly after him. Nats creeps out from the kitchen and sidles up to the sitting room doorjamb, standing out of sight of the window, listening anxiously.

'Mrs Verndale!' Artem bends down to fondle her two dogs. 'How are you today?'

Peggy tries to peer past him, but he stands up, his bulk managing to almost completely block her view into the house. 'I was passing and I thought, good heavens, it looks as though The Laurels is being demolished!'

'Not at all!' says Artem. 'We are just preparing a surprise for Hester and Harriet. A—what do you call it?—a spring-clean?'

The unmistakable sound of saw meeting wood rings out, coupled with the dying chords, tortured almost to death, of Gloria Gaynor's masterpiece.

'Spring-cleaning?' sniffs Peggy suspiciously. She has always thought her friends naively trusting of these Eastern Europeans, appearing out of nowhere with their tales of woe. Not that she would dream of voicing her misgivings: the whole village seems smitten with them, everyone vying to champion their cause more energetically than their neighbours. She would hate to be thought xenophobic. 'Is that a saw I hear?'

'Precisely,' says Artem, lowering his voice confidentially and skilfully easing the dogs, and thus their owner, slowly back down the path. 'We discovered some . . . what is it? Little creatures in the stairs.' He looks to Peggy for help.

'Woodworm!' exclaims Peggy in horror, as Artem nods vigorously. 'Good Lord, it can run through a house like wildfire! The furniture will be ruined.' Not that in her opinion there's much decent furniture in the house to ruin.

'Exactly so. We thought—Daria and I—that if we simply sorted it out, Hester and Harriet need never know. It would only alarm them. My good friend Barry is just now replacing the bad wood with good.'

'It's a very *extensive* spring-clean,' says Peggy, her concerns largely allayed, but still conscious of her neighbourly duty to watch out for the sisters. 'The carpets. The curtains . . .'

'Oh, my sister!' Artem laughs conspiratorially. He has got Peggy and the dogs as far as the lane now. 'Once she starts! What is that English expression? If a job is worth doing . . .?'

'It's worth doing well,' finishes Peggy. 'My motto in life, too.' One of the labradors pulls at his lead. 'Well . . . I'd better get on. Leave you to it, then.'

'Thank you, Mrs Verndale,' says Artem, hand to grateful heart. 'I wonder, though, if I might request a favour?'

Aha, thinks Peggy. *I knew something was up.*

Artem bends forward from his great height. 'The ladies, the sisters, are so, so generous. As their dear friend, you will know this only too well. If they discover that we have been working so hard cleaning and repairing in their absence, there will be offers of money, of recompense. This we do not want at all. It is our gift to them, small though it is, for their many kindnesses. So, please, I beg of you, say nothing to them about—' he waves his hand at the cottage '—all this. Ever.'

Peggy is simultaneously chastened and ashamed at having harboured such doubts about his motives. 'Of course, of course. You are very good people. The best of luck to you.'

She takes a few steps, then turns back with a frown. 'The only thing is, Artem, won't they notice? You know, if everything is so spick and span?'

The idiom does not defeat him. He responds with a wry smile. 'Mrs Verndale, they have many virtues, the ladies, I'm sure you would agree. But . . .' he spreads his hands, 'being houseproud—that is the right term, yes?—forgive me, is not one I would put on the list. Would you?' He invites her complicity with the raising of a mischievous eyebrow.

Peggy is lost. 'You naughty man!' She giggles. 'How rude! But, I'm afraid, true!'

She trots off down the lane, still giggling.

〜〜〜

Nats claps him on the back in admiration as he staggers theatrically back into the house and closes the front door firmly behind him. Smiling, he returns immediately to the loo to find Finbar's feet protruding into the hall as he lies on the floor siting the pipework beneath the basin. Artem takes in a lungful of fresh air before plunging back into the foetid atmosphere that habitually cloaks the old man. Except that for once it doesn't. True, there is still an underlying whiff of ancient sweat and clothes unwashed for years, but the top note, though chemical and artificial, pleasantly recalls freshly laundered sheets. Artem cautiously sniffs again in perplexity as Daria taps him on the shoulder and, warning finger to lips, waves a canister of Febreze under his nose. He stifles a shout of laughter. Signalling silence, she then warily lifts a garment, so seamed and impregnated with grime it is impossible to determine its original colour, off the doorknob where Finbar has hung it while he works, and tiptoes away towards the utility room.

⌣⌣

They stop for a late and very welcome lunch of bread and cheese. Ben is famished but he hangs back, waiting for everyone else to fill their plates first. He collects several hunks of cheese, the heel of the loaf and retreats to the garden bench. Animated conversation issues from the kitchen, laughter, the bass rumble of Artem's voice, Daria's excited chatter and Milo's gurgles. Once, the baby crawls to the kitchen step, one hand clutching a plastic toy, which he holds out to the boy. Daria's arm appears and scoops him back into the kitchen, closing the door. Ben has never felt more alone.

He waits until he hears the scrape of chairs on the tiles as everyone returns to work, then quietly slips back into the kitchen to wash his plate. A fresh pail of water stands waiting for him in the hall. As he goes to kneel, he sees Nats standing in the sitting room doorway opposite the cleaned wall, inspecting it critically. She registers his presence. For the first time since her outburst in Daria's kitchen, she addresses him.

'Won't do, will it? Shit.' The wallpaper has dried in bubbles, the pattern rubbed almost to invisibility in places, residual beer stains spotting it here and there. Even with the pictures rehung, and however myopic both aunts may be, they would need to be virtually blind not to notice the damage.

Despair washes over him. All morning he's been clinging to the slim possibility of getting away with it, buoyed by Artem's detailed plan, all his faith invested in this disparate group beavering away so hard. He looks at the bare windows, at the streaked and stained floor, the remaining stumps of the wrecked staircase and across at the ruined wall. It's hopeless.

'Shit,' says Nats again, rolling her shoulders to ease her aching muscles. He longs to place a hand either side of those thin shoulders and massage the tension away, like he does for his mother sometimes. His hands remain where they are.

'Artem,' calls Nats, 'got a minute?'

Artem extracts himself from the cramped toilet and lopes down to join her. They regard the wall together for a moment or two.

Artem sucks his teeth; shakes his head. 'No. It will not do.'

'No,' says Nats sadly. 'Sorry. I tried.'

Artem lays a huge paw on her shoulder. 'You did your best, Natalie.' He sighs. 'I don't know what else we can—'

'Repaper,' says Ben quietly behind them.

'Repaper,' repeats Nats scornfully, rolling her eyes at Artem. 'Like anywhere still stocks this design? Looks like it's been up here for centuries. Like, even if we locate some, we can get hold of it at—' she consults her watch '—three thirty on a Saturday afternoon? Oh, and like anyone has the first idea how to redecorate a room? You volunteering?'

Ben holds his nerve. 'We've got paper,' he says.

Nats turns to look at him properly for the first time. 'We have? What, *this* exact pattern?'

'Think so. Yeah, I'm sure. In one of the sheds. There's a box with loads of rolls of wallpaper in it.' He remembers shoving it into a corner when he and Louisa were stowing the sofa.

'You sure?' Her flinty eyes soften a fraction in thought. 'Worth a try?' she says to Artem.

'Anything is worth a try.'

〜〜〜

There are dozens, hundreds, of YouTube clips showing complete beginners how to hang wallpaper. Ben and Nats huddle over his phone and watch a couple of them.

'How hard can it be?' says Ben, a little of his customary confidence seeping back. He had been right. They've found four rolls of the right paper, two of them a little damp-stained at the edges, but Ben reckons they can cut those bits off and patch if necessary. He's finding the challenge quite energising.

Nats sounds a note of caution. 'There's got to be a reason why people employ professional decorators.'

'Only 'cos they're too dumb or busy to do it themselves. Or too rich. I mean, you're just sticking a bit of paper to a wall.' It occurs to him that, thrifty as his parents are, they always get someone in when the house needs decorating. He decides not to share that.

'Oh yeah?' Nats is skimming through a discussion thread for DIYers. 'This bloke reckons it's the hardest thing he's ever done. Oh God, and there's a woman here says, whatever you do, don't start with a patterned wallpaper. Oh, great . . .'

Ben is determined not to be beaten. They'll just follow the instructions step by step and it'll be okay. Two intelligent people—for fuck's sake!

〜〜〜

An hour later, they've managed to get most of the old paper off the wall, having lost a good twenty minutes trying to remove the glass shelves. Barry had eventually come to their rescue with an electric screwdriver and whipped them in seconds. 'Don't forget to fill the holes,' he says, bounding back up to the landing. Thirty minutes later and they're on their third sheet of paper. The first piece Ben had cut too short. They had had words about that, so Nats assumed responsibility for measuring thereafter. Ben managed to tear the top of the second sheet. Now they are trying to line the third sheet up by eye, Ben having assured Nats they don't need a plumbline.

'Just use the top of the fireplace as a guide.'

'What if that's not straight?' says Nats.

'How can a fireplace not be straight?' says Ben. 'Everything would slide off it.'

'Depends on the slope,' says Nats.

Ben climbs the stepladder and offers the paper up. Weighted with wallpaper paste, it flops back over his head before he can smooth it into place at the top.

Nats laughs. 'What were you saying about a piece of piss? I wouldn't give up your day job just yet.'

Ben looks at the expanse of wall they have to cover and panic begins to stir. He retreats down the ladder and lays the strip glue-side up on their improvised pasting table. 'You're so clever, you do it.'

His phone rings. He doesn't recognise the number.

'Hello?'

'Ben? It's Ralph. Is this a good time?'

A good time? For what? Oh, shit, yes, his revision session.

'Oh, man. I'm, like, a bit tied up at the moment, Ralph mate.'

'Oh, right. Revising another subject?'

'Not exactly.' An expectant pause. 'It's just, I'm helping out a mate with some emergency decorating—you know, like, wallpapering . . .'

'Oh . . .' The guy sounds really disappointed. There's a moment's silence. Then he says tentatively, 'I've done a bit of decorating in my time. I could come over if you'd like a hand?'

CHAPTER 39

Harriet and Mary are whispering in Mary's temporary quarters.

'It's driving me round the bend!' Mary rolls her eyes. 'It's like being on suicide watch. It feels like they're trying to outdo one another in the compassion stakes. I could scream!'

Mary had managed to hiss, 'My room, fifteen minutes,' in Harriet's ear as Rhona and Ron had manhandled her up from her chair and hustled her back into the hotel after her little turn in the garden.

'Can't be too careful,' Ron had said.

'I told you not to do too much too soon,' Rhona had scolded.

Harriet had had the presence of mind to fill a plate with cheese, bread and olives and now the pair of them are guiltily consuming them like schoolgirls enjoying a midnight feast, ears pricked for any sound of footsteps in the corridor outside. Harriet had felt like a criminal sneaking into Mary's room. The dismay on both Ron and Rhona's faces when Mary had welcomed Harriet with such warmth (and, Harriet thought, relief) had been almost farcical.

'What are you going to do?' she asks through a mouthful of pecorino.

'God alone knows. I never did get my coffee! There's me saying seize the day, but now I don't know which day to seize. Whatever I do is going to create the most unholy mess.'

Harriet, privately wondering why Mary, apparently a rational, intelligent woman, hadn't thought this through before, can't help but agree: stay with Ron, and Mary has a constant reminder of her affair living the other side of the fence; choose Rhona and her marriage will implode, never mind the fallout in terms of domestic arrangements, finances, children—

She looks up to see Mary's eyes filling with tears. 'Hey . . . hey . . .'

'I'm such a selfish cow,' murmurs Mary. 'Dragging you into all this. As if you didn't have enough on your plate. It's just . . .'

Harriet squeezes her hand. 'I know: it helps to have a sounding board. How's the head, by the way?'

Mary flaps her hand dismissively. 'Flesh wound only. It'll heal. My hair will grow back. It's *fine*.'

'Okay. Sorry.'

Mary looks aghast and grasps Harriet's wrist. 'No, *I'm* sorry. I didn't mean to snap. It's just—'

'It's all a bit much, isn't it?'

Mary manages a shaky smile. 'You are an absolute brick, Harriet, as my dad used to say. Thank God you're here. Anyway, never mind me, I haven't even asked you about your own troubles.'

Harriet tells her about contacting Marion ('No, I didn't want to accuse her on the phone. It seemed too brutal'), then makes light of Hester and Lionel's burgeoning romance by regaling Mary with her abortive property search. This has them both helpless with laughter by the time she has finished describing, with outrageous embellishment, the hovel she is likely to end up in if her worst fears are realised.

They freeze as someone passes the door.

'I'd better be off before someone comes to check on you,' whispers Harriet. 'That really would put the cat among the pigeons. Anyway, I think you should rest.'

'Oh rest, rest! That's all anyone says to me. I've got another two days of this. Do me a favour, will you?'

'What?'

'Don't leave me alone with them. I haven't got the strength right now.'

Hilary Spiers

'But . . .' Harriet doesn't fancy being referee in this awkward love triangle.

'I know it's not fair to ask you, but please . . . please . . .'

And Mary looks so forlorn with her white face and her pleading eyes that Harriet gives in. 'It's not going to make me very popular—'

'They'll have to lump it,' says Mary with surprising vehemence.

But Harriet hadn't been thinking of Ron or Rhona. She'd been thinking of Hester.

～～～

'Harriet!'

Scuttling quickly along to her own room, Harriet is startled to hear Hester calling her name. Guilt, she's not quite sure why, assails her. 'Oh, I didn't see you,' she says lamely.

Her sister eyes her suspiciously. 'We've been looking all over for you, Lionel and I. Wherever did you get to? One minute you're in the garden, the next you've disappeared.'

'I went to have a chat with Mary.'

Hester gives an exasperated sigh. 'Hasn't she enough people fawning over her? Really, Harry, you're such a sucker for a sob story. Leave them to their own devices, for heaven's sake.'

'What did you want me for?' says Harriet in a conciliatory tone.

'Lunch,' says Hester. 'Lionel asked if he could have a go at his linguine again while the hotel is quiet, bless him, and he's been busy in the kitchen most of the morning. I thought it might be nice if we enjoyed the fruits of his labours together.'

'Oh, I've already—' Harriet stops herself just in time. She really mustn't rebuff Hester's overture. Not given their recent reconciliation.

'Already what?'

'—been wondering what delights there might be for lunch. Lionel's pasta! How delicious.' She beams at Hester.

Hester breathes out, only now aware how nervous she'd been about issuing this invitation. 'Ten minutes in the bar? Lovely! We can have a pre-prandial. Alfonso has just taken delivery of a local Montepulciano he's raving about. I thought we might give it a go.'

A glass of wine, thinks Harriet. *Exactly what I need*. Her smile broadens. 'Let me freshen up. I won't be a mo.'

～～

'Harriet?'

She's just picking up her room key from the dressing table when she hears the faint knock. What does Hetty want now?

She opens the door to find Rhona on the threshold. 'Oh! Hello.'

'Hello,' says Rhona, eyes darting over Harriet's shoulder and about the room. 'Are you alone?' Without waiting for a response, she steps forward, forcing Harriet back to allow her access. 'Could I have a word?'

'I was just about to—'

'Look, I'm sorry,' interrupts Rhona, 'but I really need to talk to you. About Mary.'

Harriet's heart sinks.

'I just wondered if she'd said anything.' Rhona has fetched up by the window, is peering out into the garden cautiously as though afraid of being spotted. 'About me. Us. I mean, you know: the situation. Since you seem to have her ear—' an unmistakable tinge of bitterness here '—I thought she might have confided in you.'

Harriet finds herself in a cleft stick. Mary has indeed been confiding in her, but admit that and she risks making their friendship (if that's what it is, after so short an acquaintance) seem something more to someone like Rhona, who is clearly feeling vulnerable and is unquestionably prone to jealousy. Harriet opts for an ambiguous sigh and shake of her head. 'I don't know what to tell you.'

Rhona spins around from her position by the window, eyebrows knitted fiercely. 'What do you mean by that?'

To buy some time, Harriet says, 'I mean . . . I think she's still shaken up by the accident. And having you both here, you and Ron, well, it's awkward.'

'Obviously,' snaps Rhona, then pulls herself together. 'Sorry. Sorry. Obviously it's awkward. It's awkward for all of us. But what else was I to do?'

Well, you didn't need to come tearing over here. You could have waited. Let Ron bring her home.

'I think,' says Harriet carefully, 'that perhaps she's still a little confused. The head injury, you know? She's finding it difficult . . . to order her thoughts.'

'Order her thoughts?' repeats Rhona, baffled, as though Harriet were speaking Chinese. 'What do you mean?' Clearly not one of life's optimists, she immediately puts the worst possible construction on Harriet's comment. Face crumpling in despair, she collapses onto the bed. 'Oh God, she doesn't want me any more, does she? I knew this holiday was a mistake! It's over, isn't it? Isn't it?'

〜〜

'She's on her way,' says Hester to Lionel happily, popping her head around the kitchen door. 'Everything under control?'

Lionel has been given a small station with a compact hob in the corner, so as not to disturb the staff's regular routines. The rest of the kitchen is filled with a band of sous chefs and kitchen porters, each of them busily intent on the task in hand, chopping, peeling, frying, basting, boning, filleting, as the head chef keeps a beady eye on them all. A hand on the shoulder here, a pursed mouth there, a brief but welcome nod: language appears superfluous as the well-oiled machine grinds on. Saturday lunch at Il Santuario is a buffet, to accommodate the different arrival times of those guests booked in for an activity holiday. The coming week offers photography, yoga, life coaching ('What on earth's that?' Hester had sniffed. 'Learning how to live? They'll be teaching breathing next!')

and mindfulness meditation ('Oh, ver' popular,' Marco told her. 'Many peoples!'), but no cooking.

Lionel transfers his linguine from the drying poles into the pan of bubbling water. He's bubbling himself after last night. 'Should be ready in about ten minutes.' He swirls the pasta around the saucepan, then turns his attention to the adjacent frying pan, filled with a creamy sauce speckled with green. Beside the hob sits a bowl of more chopped parsley.

'Ah!' says Hester, spotting a saucer of grated cod roe on the counter. 'Bottarga sauce?'

'Oh, Hetty! It was supposed to be a surprise. Off you go!'

'Sorry.' Hester goes to leave, then stops. 'But shouldn't the linguine be—'

'Made with squid ink. Yes,' says Lionel regretfully. 'They didn't have any.'

'Details, details,' breezes Hester, tastebuds already preparing themselves for the treat. 'Just remember—'

'No parmesan!' they chorus, laughing, smug in their companionship.

⌣⌣⌣

'Harriet!'

Harriet is en route to collect her handbag, having eventually coaxed a shaken, teary Rhona back to her own room, following several minutes of sobbing and importunate pleas for Harriet to intercede with Mary on her behalf. 'Honestly, Rhona,' she had said, disconcerted that this superficially feisty and resilient woman had fallen apart so comprehensively, 'it's really nothing to do with me. I barely know Mary!'

'But she listens to you!'

'Rhona,' Harriet had said gently, 'I'm sorry, but the three of you need to sort this out between you. I'm not a marriage guidance counsellor.' *I've troubles of my own, plenty of them, thank you very much.* And she had steered Rhona firmly over her own threshold and pulled the door closed before hurrying back towards her own room, conscious that Hester would be wondering where she had got to.

'Harriet, forgive me.' Hand on her door handle, she turns to find Ron beside her, anxiously scanning the corridor and crowding her into the room. He closes the door behind him and says in an urgent whisper, 'I'm sorry to ambush you like this, but I really need to talk to you. About Mary.'

Hester, two large glasses of Rosso Conero Riserva in front of her, peers over towards the restaurant entrance, expecting Harriet at any moment. *How long does it take her to freshen up, for heaven's sake? It's not as though either of us is prone to primping and preening*, she thinks, absent-mindedly fingering the unfamiliar smooth skin between her eyebrows. Why, on one of their Scilly holidays they had once both overslept and still managed to dress and pack in five minutes *and* made their ferry, albeit in a rather flustered and dishevelled state.

She sips the rich maroon wine, rolls it around her mouth, savours its signature cherry, plum and tannin notes, and then takes a proper mouthful. Alfonso had not been exaggerating its qualities. She is just about to rise and go in search of her sister when an aproned Lionel sashays through the kitchen's swing door, expertly using his hip, a tea towel protecting his hands from the two sizeable and steaming bowls. He stops in surprise, halfway to the table.

'Oh!'

'I know,' says Hester crossly. 'No sign of her. She said she was on her way.'

Lionel hesitates. 'Shall I . . .?' He gestures back towards the kitchen.

'Certainly not. No reason why ours should spoil just because she's late.'

Lionel, the heat rapidly penetrating the flimsy cloth, is only too pleased to set the bowls on the table.

'We might as well eat,' says Hester, picking up her fork. 'Don't want it to go cold.' She nudges the spare glass of wine across the table. 'Try that.'

Lionel, thinking of the third plate of pasta cooling by the hob, sits reluctantly. 'Would you like me to—'

'No,' says Hester. 'Just tuck in, Lionel. It's her own fault.' Disgruntled and embarrassed at her sister's rudeness, she twirls her fork into the middle of the pasta and lifts it to her lips. 'Smells gorgeous.'

Lionel waits nervously for the verdict. Hester chews and swallows. 'Absolutely delicious, my dear. D'you know, I think the squid ink might have been overkill. The roe and parsley really comes through. Great pasta, by the way.'

Lionel, gratified, digs in himself. 'Mmm. You're right. I think I'm really getting the hang of this pasta malarkey. It's very satisfying, making your own, don't you find? Not too much garlic?'

'Not at all,' says Hester. 'Just perfect. Do try the wine. It really complements the dish. Unless you'd rather have a beer?'

'No, no,' he says hastily, lifting the glass, 'wine's just the job. But what about Harriet?'

'What about her?' says Hester, reaching for her own glass.

CHAPTER 40

'Thing is,' says Ralph, smoothing out the paper on the pasting table and fingering the age-dried edges dubiously, 'ideally, you'd want to use lining paper first. 'Specially for a house this age. Was there lining paper on before?'

Ben and Nats exchange an uncertain look. 'Dunno,' says Ben, 'we just ripped it off quick as we could.'

'Do you still have it? The paper you took off?'

Nats hoicks a black plastic bin liner in from the hall.

Ralph feels inside, pulls out a long, curling strip and examines it. 'Yep, see? Lining paper.'

'We haven't got any,' says Ben, itching to get on with things. It's already five o'clock and they haven't got a single strip up yet—

'Hmm,' says Ralph, thinking. 'Well, the DIY places open at ten on a Sunday—'

'We can't wait till tomorrow!' Panic overwhelms Ben. His eye lights on the banister, still resembling an abstract sculpture—a very poor one at that. How long does it take to repair a simple staircase? Barry has been sawing and planing for hours with only a huge pile of wood shavings to show for it, as far as he can see. Plus a growing number of coffee mugs, courtesy of Daria.

'—line the walls tomorrow morning, day to dry out, start wallpapering Monday. Except I'm off back to uni tomorrow . . .' Ralph is talking as much to himself as to any potential listeners.

Nats takes control. 'Ralph, the problem is we really need to get this done, like, now? See, the aunts are back Monday and we've got to sort the wall, re-lay the carpets, move all the furniture back . . . so, see, we don't have time for lining paper and all that.'

'Pity,' says Ralph, 'it makes it look much more professional.'

'Done is what we're after, frankly—bugger professional.'

'Fair enough,' says Ralph cheerfully. 'Let's get cracking. Got a plumb-bob or spirit level, have you?'

Nats gives Ben a withering look that says unequivocally 'told you so'. 'Nope.'

'No worries. Find us a length of string and . . .' He looks round the space, frowns, settles finally to the right of Nats' face. 'Can I pinch that earring for five minutes?'

⌣⌣⌣

Ralph is marking plumblines at intervals along the wall with his improvised instrument, Ben holding the stepladder steady. Nats has disappeared, ostensibly to make some much-needed tea but also to spend some time with Milo, who is very vocally demanding entertainment. Nats' game of 'Catch my braids' is proving a source of huge fun, the baby's shouts of glee echoing around the house.

'So,' says Ralph, 'Le Châtelier's principle. No point wasting the opportunity, we can get this paper up and have our tutorial at the same time. Incidentally, what happened here?' It's the first time he's shown any curiosity about the activities taking place all over The Laurels.

'Long story,' mutters Ben, hoping Artem or Nats don't appear to reveal to Ralph the full and shaming extent of his idiocy.

'Okay,' says Ralph equably. 'Right, so what does the principle say?'

Ben observes with envy the confidence with which Ralph is tackling the job. 'Er . . . something about dynamic equilibrium—how come you know what you're doing?'

'Holiday job. Painting and decorating firm. What about dynamic equilibrium? Come on!' Ralph sounds suddenly uncharacteristically assertive.

'Oh! Um ... if a dynamic equilibrium is disturbed by changing the conditions, the position of equilibrium ...'

'Moves, yes ...'

'Moves to ... counteract the change,' finishes Ben, dredging the definition parrot-fashion from his shaky memory.

'Good.' Ralph starts measuring the paper. 'What sort of conditions?'

Ben rakes once more through his meagre fact store. 'Temperature ...' He pauses; Ralph nods, starting to paste the first strip. 'Volume ...' Another nod, more impatient this time. 'Concentration ... pressure ...'

'Why is it important?' barks Ralph.

Jeez, thinks Ben, *give us a break: he's worse than old Fishface at school. Why* is *it important?*

'Er ...'

'For goodness' sake! If you know the impact on equilibrium you can manipulate the chemical reaction. And why might you want to do that?'

Ben flounders, a thousand wild guesses pinging around his brain.

'Think of it in terms of cooking. Take ice-cream. What happens when you interfere with the core temperature? By putting it into a freezer?'

'It freezes?'

'Well, yes, obviously but what happens to its nature?'

'It ... changes?'

'Yes. And what happens to it if you take the frozen ice-cream out and leave it on the counter?'

'It melts.'

'Into what?'

A chink of understanding. 'The same as before.'

'So what's the reason for the changes of state—or equilibrium?'

'Oh . . . yeah . . .'

'Yes! Change of temperature. And? Its equilibrium . . .'

'Adjusts!' says Ben excitedly. *Awesome. Awesome!*

～～～

They have stopped for tea and biscuits. The chimney breast is now neatly papered, the flowery pattern lining up perfectly. 'Another couple of hours and we'll be done,' says Ralph, chomping on a garibaldi.

Milo is at their feet, draping the offcuts around his neck like cut-price leis, occasionally testing the taste before anyone can stop him. Daria has just rehung the washed, ironed and only slightly damp curtains ('They dry in here just as well as outside') prior to taking him home for bath and bed. She pulls the curtains closed and steps back to inspect them critically. Artem joins her.

'Too short,' she says. She mutters something under her breath that is unmistakably a curse.

Ralph wanders over to join the inspection party. 'How much?'

She holds up thumb and forefinger to measure perhaps an inch. Ralph reaches up to check out the heading. 'Move the hooks up,' he says. 'See? They're on the bottom channel. Move them up to the top and you'll gain about half to three-quarters of an inch.'

Daria sighs wearily.

'Leave it. You want to get off. I'll do it before I go.'

'You will?'

''Course. It'll only take a few minutes. Ben can help me. We'll have it done in no time.'

'Ben,' says Daria sternly over her shoulder, still not deigning to afford him a look, 'you are very lucky boy. First Natalie and now this lovely Ralph. You do not deserve such kind friends. I hope you are grateful.'

'Yeah,' mumbles Ben, flushing to his roots, 'dead grateful.'

'Thank you, Ralph, kind man,' says Daria formally, then reaches up to kiss his cheek.

Ralph's hand flies to the imprint of her lips. 'Oh, I say!'

He is still beaming as he ambles back to the pasting table. 'Now, Ben, about scum formation . . .'

Ben's phone rings. Everyone turns to look at him. He fumbles in his pocket, checks the screen. 'It's Mum,' he lies. 'I'll just take this . . .' Waving in the direction of the garden, he hurries out.

ᶜᵕᵕᵕᵕᵕᵕᶜ

'What?'

'Oh, babes, you sound so pissed!'

'I am pissed,' hisses Ben. 'Have you any idea the shit I'm in?'

'It can't be that bad,' breathes Louisa, but there's a palpable note of anxiety in her voice. 'Can it?'

'Well, thanks for asking!' spits Ben. 'Thanks for coming round first thing to see how I was! What damage your tosser friends have done.'

'I've only just got up,' wails Louisa. 'That was nasty shit we had last night. Didn't you think so? We've all had the most horrible—'

'Great! So you've managed to check with everyone else before you got round to calling me? Well, thanks for nothing. And no, I've no idea about whatever it was you forced down my throat last night— apart from the vodka—because I threw it up almost immediately. But it didn't stop me having the mother of all hangovers, thanks very much. And now everyone's on my case because the house is wrecked and my aunts are back in two days and I'm getting the blame for everything. And I'll tell you something else, Louisa Jellinek, you may think you're God's gift but your sister's worth a hundred of you any day. She's worth a hundred of any of your airhead mates, too, and as far as I'm concerned if I never ever see you again, it'll be a blessing.' He stabs the off button and stands quivering and panting with rage.

'You really shouldn't speak to your mother like that,' says Nats from the kitchen doorway. 'Show some respect, will you?'

Ben spins round, appalled. How long has she been standing there?

Nats gazes at him levelly and then gestures towards the interior of the house. 'Ralph wants you.' As he pushes past her in a maelstrom of fury and embarrassment, he could swear he hears her snigger.

CHAPTER 41

Hester is seething, despite Lionel's best efforts to calm her down. Their cleared plates lie empty and smeared before them.

'So rude!' she says for the umpteenth time, now on her second large glass of wine. 'I am so sorry, Lionel. After all your hard work.'

'But you enjoyed it, didn't you?'

'I did!'

'Well, that's all that matters. I suppose I could try reheating Harriet's over some boiling water—'

'Absolutely not. It would ruin the flavour—probably split the sauce.' Hester lowers her voice as a large contingent of new guests enter the restaurant, secure several tables and fall upon the buffet. Lionel nods a greeting to the one or two who look their way. 'Besides, I think the management have been extremely accommodating so far, letting you use the kitchen—you don't want to exploit their goodwill.'

'Good Lord, I should say not,' says Lionel, looking stricken. 'I really don't believe I got in anyone's way.'

'No, I'm sure you didn't,' says Hester abstractedly. 'I suppose I ought to go and see if something's happened. Chances are she's closeted with that wretched Mary again. Oh, Lionel, don't look at me like that. You're as bad as Harry. Far too soft-hearted. I know, I know, I'm horrible—but honestly, don't you think she has quite enough problems to contend with right now without adding to them unnecessarily?' Problems, she ruefully admits, that are largely of her making. It is that sense of responsibility that propels her out of her chair and, with a promise to return swiftly, sends her off in the direction of Harriet's room.

～～～

'Ron,' says Harriet, embarrassed at the sight of this overweight man in tears in her armchair and simultaneously fretting at the thought of Hester impatiently awaiting her arrival in the restaurant. If only she hadn't gone back for her bag . . . 'I really think you need to have this out with Mary yourself.'

'I can't!' Ron slumps in the chair, one hand ineffectually shielding his streaming eyes. 'I've never been able to talk about . . . things like that. Emotions and . . . oh God! . . . she thinks I don't care, I know she does!'

'Oh, I'm sure she doesn't,' says Harriet automatically.

Ron's habitual belligerence resurfaces. 'What makes you such an expert? You hardly know her.'

Harriet smiles grimly. 'If you recall, I've been trying to make that point for the last five minutes, Ron. This isn't my problem. I've simply got caught up—'

'Yes, yes,' says Ron, deflating. 'You have. You're right. Of course you're right. I oughtn't to have come. Ambushed you like that. Thoughtless. Selfish.'

Yes, huffs Harriet, *yes, you bloody well are. Now, will you, for pity's sake, go!* She reaches for her room key.

'The thing is,' Ron continues, 'I think she's trying to teach me a lesson. Mary. That's the only explanation that I can see. For having this . . . thing with that bloody woman. I mean, for heaven's sake, we've been married for twenty-five years—or is it twenty-six?—and she suddenly decides she's—' he finds it impossible to say the word '—whatever she thinks she is.'

'Gay?' Maybe she should simply walk out, go off to find Hester and leave him to talk things out alone.

'Gay!' He spits the word out like a fruit pip. 'She's not gay! Mary? She's just *experimenting*.'

So? thinks Harriet and says mischievously, 'Late-blooming lesbians, I think *The Guardian* call them.'

For the first time since he entered the room, Ron looks at her directly, aghast. '*The Guardian*? Do you read *The Guardian*?'

'Only behind closed doors and with the curtains drawn.'

Ron goes to reply, stops, looks at her afresh, brows beetling suspiciously, then heaves himself to his feet. Marching across the room, he flings open the door and halts. 'Well, I've obviously been completely wasting my time here.' The door slams shut.

〜〜〜

'Harriet? Harry!' Harriet knows that voice. 'Come in,' she calls weakly.

Hester flings open the door to find her sister curled up on the bed, clutching her stomach. Oh Lord, Lionel was right! While she's been guzzling wine and chomping her way through a plateful of linguine, mouthing off about her ill-mannered sibling, poor Harriet has been writhing in agony. She flies over to the bed and pulls Harriet to her bony chest.

'Oh, Harry! Whatever is it?'

Harriet tries to speak but the sounds are unintelligible. Hester's heart turns over. How could she have been so thoughtless? So callous? Why hadn't she come to look for Harriet straightaway when she failed to appear? How long has she been lying here alone?

'It's all right,' says Hester gently, trying to disentangle herself. 'You're going to be all right. I'm here now. I'm just going to call for a doctor.'

Harriet grabs her wrist. 'No, no,' she moans, face buried in Hester's now-damp T-shirt. 'Just let me—' She erupts in another paroxysm before flinging herself back against the pillows. 'I'm not ill,' she manages to gasp.

'Harry?' Hester searches her sister's face, takes in the reddened eyes spilling with tears, the heightened colour. 'Are you *drunk*?'

Harriet explodes a second time. 'No . . . no, I'm afraid not. Hetty, it's much, much worse.'

⌣⌣⌣

'Well!' Hester throws herself down in the chair beside Lionel, shaking her head in exasperation.

'Is she all right?' He presses his half-full glass of wine into her hand; she raises it to her lips unthinkingly. He waits until she has taken a gulp, then tentatively takes her hand. 'Is she?'

'She is *fine*,' hisses Hester. 'She is lying on her bed, exhausted—'

'Oh dear.'

'—from laughing.' She takes another gulp, heady with indignation. 'She has been convulsed for the last ten minutes. It took me all that time to get any sense out of her.' She looks down as if surprised to find her hand in Lionel's. He hastily withdraws it. 'It appears that she's been besieged by all the protagonists in the soap opera that is the blessed Mary's life and got trapped by each of them in turn. Somehow she allowed herself to get embroiled—typical Harriet! Ron Martindale ambushed her to talk about Mary and then discovered—horror of horrors—that she's a *Guardian*ista.'

'Mary is?'

'Not Mary!' snorts Hester, as Ron appears in the doorway, spots her instantly, throws back his head in contempt and marches out again. Suddenly the absurdity of the situation hits her. With laughter bubbling up, she sniggers, 'I mean my darling sister. You know, my muesli-gobbling, bearded, sandal-wearing sister.'

'Bearded?' frowns Lionel, trying to fathom what or who on earth she is talking about, as Hester splutters into her wine.

⌣⌣⌣

Harriet, thoroughly drained by the dramas in her bedroom, has slept most of the afternoon, leaving Hester and Lionel to a drowsy few hours in the garden, both ostensibly buried in their paperbacks but each catching periodical naps when they believed the other to be engrossed. Hester had crept back to Harriet's room in the late afternoon to find her deeply asleep, a smile still on her lips. Softly, Hester had drawn the thin blanket over her sister's sleeping form.

Now, the evening sun dappling the distant mountains and the air still warm with the day's heat, they are seated in the garden, all three enjoying the view and the quiet before dinner. Alfonso appears with a menu.

'*Buonasera, signore e signor. Come state? Bene, sì?* I am thinking, it is a beautiful night, you would perhaps like to eat out here? We have many new guests so is quite lively in the restaurant. We would be very happy to serve you here.'

They agree that to eat al fresco would be delightful and pore over the menu for a few contented minutes.

'I missed Lionel's wonderful pasta at lunchtime,' says Harriet, who has already apologised fulsomely for her non-appearance, 'so can I start with the calamari and then the tortellini Portofino, please.'

'*Gamberoni*, then the *branzino primavera*, Alfonso,' says Hester, handing back her menu. 'Thanks.'

Lionel hesitates. 'I know what I want for my starter: the *capesante*—'

'Oh!' says Hester. 'I missed that. Can I have the scallops as well, please, instead of the prawns.'

Alfonso corrects the tab and turns back to Lionel. 'And to follow, *signor*?'

Lionel looks across nervously at Harriet. 'Would it be unforgivable of me to have the veal?' He looks as though he suspects Harriet of being a rabid animal-rights activist.

She smiles inwardly. 'Please, have what you like, Lionel,' she says pleasantly.

Lionel gives an uncertain smile. Hester, seated between them, feels a tiny charge in the atmosphere, the faintest sense of unease.

Alfonso's pencil hovers.

'No. *Agnello*, I think, on reflection,' says Lionel, loosening his collar. 'Now what about some wine, ladies?'

He leaves the ordering to Hester, who opts for a Verdicchio dei Castelli di Jesi ('Okay with you, Harry?') that meets with Alfonso's approval: 'Excellent choice, *signora*, the jewel of Le Marche! Very good with shellfish but not, *signor*, with the lamb so may I suggest for you a Rosso Conero?' Lionel nods his agreement swiftly and Alfonso bounds back up the steps.

'Better to be out here, I think,' says Harriet, breaking the silence. 'I'm not sure I could keep a straight face if I bumped into Ron.' The remembered mirth bubbles up. She and Hester exchange a knowing smile. *Good*, thinks Hester.

Good, thinks Harriet. *Just like the old days—*

'We wondered if you'd like to join us tomorrow,' says Lionel. 'I've hired a car and Hester and I thought we'd take a trip through the mountains. Stop for lunch somewhere. Seems a waste to come all this way and not see a little of the environs.'

'Lionel says there's an old abbey up in the hills, which the guide-books say is a must.'

Harriet tenses. *Damn.* 'That sounds wonderful,' she says. 'I would have loved to but, unfortunately, I promised Mary—'

'That bloody woman!' The words slip out before Hester can stop them. 'She's already ruined enough of your holiday, hasn't she? For God's sake!'

Honestly, thinks Harriet crossly, *she might have let me finish my sentence and explain!*

A loaded silence falls as one of the waiters arrives with their wine, cutlery and glasses and proceeds to lay the table with agonising slowness. Hester glares at Harriet, then rolls her eyes at Lionel.

'Shame,' he says, as the waiter finally departs.

'Shame indeed,' fumes Hester, busying herself with their drinks. *Well, to hell with Harriet. We've extended more than enough olive branches! What more does she want?!*

Across the table, Harriet eyes her two companions with mixed emotions. *Damn, damn, damn. Hester's bound to take it the wrong way. Still, I daresay they'll be thrilled to have a day alone up in the hills. Just the two of them.* She catches Lionel's eye. He colours and looks away. *He'll be cock-a-hoop.*

CHAPTER 42

Milo is roaring. It is a source of endless wonder to Ben that a creature so tiny can generate such an astonishing volume. The baby is being egged on by Nats, who is matching him roar for roar as she teaches him how to make as big a splash in his bath as possible. Daria is downstairs in the kitchen, busy preparing supper, Radio 1 on full, drowning out her son's cacophony. In the doorway to the cramped bathroom Ralph and Ben stand watching Nats tease Milo into a state of shrieking ecstasy as she pours a torrent of water from on high into his splayed hands. He is beside himself as he is engulfed.

'Marvellous,' says Ralph. 'Never had much time for kiddies, but this little chap is—'

'I know.'

Ralph scratches his cheek. 'Well, I guess I'd better make a move. I've really enjoyed this afternoon. Hope our little tutorial helped.'

'You kidding? It was awesome. Seriously. You make it all seem so . . . obvious.'

Ralph ducks his head in embarrassment. 'Oh, I don't know about that. Just common sense, really. Once you find something meaningful to pin things on to . . .'

'It was sick, mate. Almost makes me look forward to the exam.'

'Really?'

'Almost.'

'Monday morning, is that right? Listen, you just go over what we discussed, and any questions, ring me.'

'Cheers. And about the wallpapering—'

'Oh, Ben! Forget it. It was my pleasure. I mean it.'

Daria appears at the bottom of the stairs and calls up, 'Everything okay, Natalie?'

Hearing his mother's voice, Milo yells all the louder.

'Brilliant,' shouts Nats. 'Should I bring him down once he's in his PJs?'

'No, no!' cries Daria. 'Nappy, then cot, please. For story. I will come—'

'I'll do his story,' offers Ben quickly.

Daria's face hardens; she's not at all sure she's ready to forgive Ben just yet.

Nats appears between the two lads, a flushed Milo wrapped in a towel in her arms, one fist triumphantly clutching several of her braids. 'We'll do it together, Daria. Give you a break.'

Daria surrenders. 'Thank you, Natalie.' She studiously avoids looking at Ben. 'Ralph, you are staying for supper, yes?'

'Oh!' Ralph's face is suddenly as pink as Milo's. 'No, really . . .'

'You don't like my cooking?' Daria plants a hand on each hip, glaring up at him.

'Stay,' hisses Nats.

'*Kalduny*,' says Daria. 'You don't like *kalduny*?'

'Er . . . I don't know.'

'Then you stay and try. Okay?' Without waiting for an answer, Daria returns to the kitchen, calling out to her son, 'Be good, *soneyka*. Mama will come to say *dabranach* after story.'

～～～

Kalduny, Ralph is soon to discover, are Belarusian dumplings, stuffed with mushrooms and onions and, in Daria's version, served in a rich beef broth. They are delicious. Milo, dried, dressed and read to (brilliantly, with loads of sound effects) by Nats, has dropped into an exhausted sleep even before Daria can make it upstairs to kiss him goodnight. Nats, Ben and Ralph are just settling down around the modest kitchen table on a mishmash of stools and odd chairs when Artem appears in the doorway.

'Room for two more?'

'Two?' says Daria, ladling soup and dumplings into various bowls at the stove.

Artem ushers a sheepish Barry into the cramped and steamy kitchen.

'Barry!' cries Daria delightedly. 'Sit, sit!'

Barry has shed his overalls and now sports jeans and a faded Led Zeppelin T-shirt under a leather bomber jacket. 'You sure? Only Artem wouldn't take no for an answer. I can easily get takeaway.'

'Takeaway!' spits Daria, appalled. 'No, you eat here. Good food. Sit!' She guides Barry over to her own place and seats him firmly, her hands remaining, in Ben's opinion, far too long on the newcomer's shoulders.

Artem returns from the hall with two more chairs and they all cram around the table, elbow to elbow. A companionable silence falls as, tired and hungry, they each concentrate on their supper. As bellies fill, desultory conversation starts up and, under Daria's tireless probing, they swiftly learn that Barry is Pellington born and bred, lives with his widowed mother, is saving up for a Harley—'Cool,' says Nats as Daria tuts—and has ambitious plans for his own carpentry shop and firm in a couple of years. Artem nods in approval; ambitious himself, he has nothing but admiration for self-starters like his new friend. Ben scowls over his supper as Daria plies Barry with second helpings.

'Cracking. What is this again?' he asks, chasing the final dumpling around his bowl.

'*Kalduny*,' mutters Ben before Daria or Artem can reply. 'Unleavened dough—flour, water, eggs, salt. You have to rest it, then boil in water or stock.'

'Soup,' says Daria sharply, affronted at Ben having the temerity to commandeer her national cuisine. 'I cook these in soup.'

A prickly silence falls, broken by Nats offering brightly, 'Ben's a bit of a cook himself.'

A bit, thinks Ben. *A bit!* Ralph gives him what he reads as a supportive wink.

Daria sniffs.

'Yeah?' says Barry, looking at Ben properly for the first time. He's aware that the boy is in deep doo-doo over events at The Laurels: Artem had explained to him on the way exactly what happened. 'Like *Bake Off*?'

'*Bake Off*,' says Ben contemptuously, 'is just cakes and that.'

'And pastry and bread. All sorts,' chips in Nats, unable to resist the opportunity to wind Ben up.

'Well, I cook loads more than that,' snaps Ben indignantly. 'Loads.'

Nats smothers a smirk but catches Artem's eye; they both look down, lips twitching.

Daria, still on her high horse, oblivious to the undercurrents, wades in. 'Yes, and who teach you to cook, huh? Wicked boy. Is *babulki*, yes? Hester, in the kitchen, helping, explaining always.' She turns to Barry. 'The house we are mending, yes? Is home of Hester and Harriet. They are kind, beautiful ladies. Take me in. Take Milo. And—' she points an accusatory finger at Ben '—him also. And what he does, this idiot boy?'

'Okay,' says Artem. 'He knows what he did.'

'Yes, but—' Daria hasn't finished.

'Daria, he's said he's sorry.'

'Sorry! Pah!' Daria shoves back her chair, noisily gathers up the crockery and thumps it on the draining board. She picks up the saucepan.

Ralph and Barry both inspect their empty plates.

Ben gets to his feet. Daria swings around, looking for a second as though she is about to brain him with the pan. 'Where you are going?'

'Home,' says Ben miserably, eyes glued to the floor. Tears prickle his eyelids.

'Home? No! You stay here. Your poor mama and tata, if they know what you done . . . Tonight, you stay here.' She stops suddenly as a thought strikes. 'Artem! We forget! Finbar!'

Finbar had refused the offer of supper at the cottage, to everyone's secret relief. Even after Daria's sterling efforts with the air freshener and her surreptitious washing of Finbar's filthy jacket, the thought of sharing close quarters with him for any length of time remains extremely unappealing.

'I promise to take food,' says Daria, momentarily deflected from her verbal assault on Ben. 'Poor man, he is waiting . . .'

'I'll go,' says Ben desperately, grabbing a loaf and starting to saw at it maniacally. He dashes to the fridge. 'Can I give him a bit of this cheese?'

Daria scurries over to a cupboard and extracts an old yogurt pot into which she starts ladling some broth and dumplings. She wraps it in cling film.

'Give him cake,' she says, pointing at the tin on the counter.

Ben cuts a generous slice and parcels it up in tinfoil.

In minutes, the makeshift picnic is assembled and stowed in a carrier bag. Ben snatches up his jacket and makes for the kitchen door. He can't get away soon enough.

'Want a lift?' says Ralph, getting up. 'I really should be making a move.'

'No, you're all right, mate,' says Ben quickly. 'Could do with a walk.'

'If you're sure . . .'

'Thanks for—you know. Be in touch.'

And he's away, out into the mild evening air, gulping down great lungsful to try to dissipate the sense of shame that dogs him. He stumbles up towards the main road, breath ragged, thoughts racing. There is nothing he would like more than to dump all this crap with Finbar, then crawl home, bury his head under a pillow and try to forget—

'Hiya, numpty.' Nats slides to a halt in front of him, her bike wheel blocking the path, forcing him to stop.

Oh, Jeez, this is all he needs . . .

'Back off, will you.'

'You're a proper pillock, Fry. You know that?'

'Am I.' He dodges around her and breaks into a jog, but she's beside him in seconds, cycling along with ease at his pace.

'You could stop feeling so sorry for yourself and try being a bit grateful. Everyone's been working their butts off for you today and you just sit there sulking and picking your spots.'

'I haven't—'

'Metaphorically. And stop making eyes at Daria, for Chrissakes. Get a grip, will you? And a move on. Finbar's not going to want cold stew, is he?'

With that, she steps hard on the pedal and surges off, her rear lights twinkling in the dark. He watches until she disappears from view.

⌣⌣⌣

'You took your time, young man. A person might die of hunger if reliant on your tender mercies.'

Finbar snatches the carrier bag and eagerly ferrets inside, withdrawing the leaking yogurt pot first. He fishes in his trouser pockets and finds a spoon. Ben shudders to think what company it has been keeping.

'What have we here?'

'Belarusian dumplings in beef broth.'

'The feast of kings.' The spoon dives into the pot.

'You say so.' Ben moodily kicks a pebble; it skitters down the road.

Finbar chews thoughtfully, then takes a further spoonful with relish. 'I am blessed with fine cooks. Hester. Daria. A man could die happy after their ministrations. Or, indeed, minestrone.' Finbar cackles at his own witticism. He dunks the end of the bread into the broth and, spraying food about, says, 'Well, you really are wallowing in the Slough of Despond, aren't you, you ungrateful wretch?'

'Oh, not you 'n' all.' Ben picks a globule of soggy bread off his sleeve. 'I'm off.'

'Were you not in such a bate and a potential danger to yourself and other users of Her Majesty's highway, you might like to ride back.'

Ben has forgotten all about his bike. Finbar, still eating, jerks his head towards the rear of the shelter. Picking his way gingerly over the piles of detritus, discarded plastic bags, sandwich cartons and old newspapers, Ben finds his bicycle tucked into the lee of the shelter, its front wheel restored to true. He trundles it round to the roadside.

'Thanks. It's brilliant. When you said you—'

'You didn't believe me. What, that old codger?' Finbar eyes him beadily. 'I may be old, I may be a codger, but I'm not blind. Unlike you, my boy, at times. This current debacle being a prime example. *Fronti nulla fides.*'

'You what?'

'Don't judge a book by its cover. Now bugger off, there's a good chap. I hate people watching me eat.'

SUNDAY

CHAPTER 43

'Are you sure about this?' says Harriet, all the while repeating to herself silently, *Drive on the right, drive on the right.*

Mary glances over her shoulder and slides down in the seat, pulling her baseball cap down even lower, wincing as she eases it over the pad taped behind her ear. 'Quite sure. Quick as you like, please, or one or both of them might discover I've scarpered.'

Harriet accelerates down the bumpy track towards the main road. The little Fiat wobbles from side to side on the uneven surface, its suspension groaning. It was the only car left at the rental garage in the town when she had asked the man on reception to arrange it the night before. Fortunately, no-one else was in the vicinity at the time. She and Mary had crept out of the hotel at seven am, eschewing breakfast in favour of a quick getaway before the others emerged.

Mist hugs the valley; the distant cedars ghost-like in the chilly morning air. The long ridge of the hills is softened by its shawl of cloud, as a valiant sun struggles to break through. A thin finger of light penetrates the mist, tracing a line across the valley floor to bathe the road in sunlight for a few seconds. Harriet fumbles around the dashboard, locates the right switch and turns on her lights, just in case.

'Did you leave a note?'

'Two,' says Mary. 'Identical. Just saying I was going out for the day and not to worry.'

Fat chance of that, thinks Harriet. *They'll be incandescent.* 'I popped something similar under Hester's door.'

The same thought strikes them. 'Thelma and Louise,' says Harriet, laughing, as Mary giggles. Then, 'Oh my God!' She flinches as Harriet veers around a goat that has suddenly leapt onto the road out of nowhere. 'Other side!'

A truck whips around the bend ahead and shaves past them, horn blaring.

Harriet is crouched over the steering wheel, concentrating fiercely, heart pounding. 'Sorry . . . I'm not really used to . . .'

'What?'

'You know . . . driving abroad.'

'Why on earth didn't you say?' cries Mary. 'I'd have driven.'

'With a head injury?' queries Harriet with unintended scorn, forgetting for a second that it's not her usual passenger beside her. 'I don't think so.'

Both women take deep, somewhat embarrassed breaths.

'Where do you suggest?' says Harriet as they approach a signpost.

'Ancona?'

Harriet imagines the perils of driving in a strange city, unfamiliar roundabouts, parking restrictions.

'How about exploring the mountains?' she says. 'They'll never find us there.'

'Oh, I know! How about San Ginesio—that's not far. It's got a Sunday market, I think. Might be fun.' Mary pulls a brochure out of her bag and consults it. 'I picked this up earlier in the week. Yes, here we go. Looks about twenty, twenty-five miles. What do you reckon?'

'That,' says Harriet, 'sounds perfect.'

⌣⌣⌣

'Hester, dear,' says Lionel, 'what's done is done. Let her get on with it.'

Hester, still fuming after discovering Harriet's note, bites back a retort and silently concedes that there is absolutely nothing she can do about her errant sister and she ought not to let her spoil the day. She relaxes in her seat as Lionel expertly and effortlessly guides the car along the winding route, the gear changes as smooth as silk. Such a pleasure not to be on constant alert for every hazard, hands clamped rigidly on the front of the passenger seat. Lionel had warned her it would take at least a couple of hours to reach the abbey but the time passes swiftly as they take in the breathtaking scenery, largely in companionable silence. The web of cloud has thinned, buildings and trees coming into sharper focus. The sun has dispelled most of the early haze and the heat is rising, but Lionel has set the air-conditioning to a perfect temperature. 'Isn't this marvellous?' He smiles. 'I do love driving.'

'The freedom of the open road.' Harriet smiles back. 'Although I can't imagine driving in London is that much fun.'

Lionel's face darkens. 'Oh, London. No, I don't drive like this there. It's all stop-start and diesel fumes.'

Hester closes her eyes. 'I've been thinking. I've hardly asked you anything—'

'Aha!' says Lionel. 'Here we go.' He points at a discreet brown sign bearing the image of a church and a cross, and eases the car onto a small side road. 'Look!'

Ahead, high above, partially shielded by clumps of poplar, the hillside below corrugated with olive trees, Hester sees an imposing collection of buildings, dominated by two square bell towers. Lionel pulls over to allow a coach to pass them on its way down, giving them both the opportunity to take in the spectacular view.

'It's open, then,' says Hester, spirits lifting even further. 'I did wonder, it being Sunday.'

'It's a working abbey. I checked.'

How lovely, thinks Hester, *to have someone else in charge for a change.*

~~~

They've had an enjoyable hour or so wandering through the Sunday market, sampling olives and cheeses, Harriet scoffing a huge slice of warm crostata filled with sour cherry jam. 'That looks sweet,' says Mary with a frown, looking for a second not unlike Hester. 'Very sweet.'

'Mmm,' is all Harriet can manage.

'We really ought to visit the church while we're here,' says Mary, looking around the square. 'It's supposed to be rather special. Oh, and the theatre.'

'Won't they be having Sunday services, mass or whatever?' says Harriet, just as the strident notes of an organ cut through the market's bustle and noise. 'Besides which, I don't have a hat and I'm not too sure your baseball cap sets quite the right tone.' She's just spotted some colourful clothes stalls and would rather like a mooch. 'But you go if you want. I'll wander round here.'

In truth, she really wouldn't mind a few minutes away from Mary's relentless dissection and re-examination of her love life. Sympathetic as Harriet had been initially, the constant picking at the scab of Mary's amours is beginning to become rather wearing. On a couple of occasions, she's been on the verge of suggesting her fail-safe—make a list of pros and cons—but her companion has barely drawn breath.

'No,' says Mary, 'that's all right. I'll come with you.'

~~~

They are overwhelmed with colour, opulence, the scent of incense, the thunder of the organ. Hester and Lionel sink down gratefully on a stone bench in the haven of the herb garden. An old monk at the far end of the hedged walk slowly sweeps up piles of privet cuttings with what looks like a handmade broom. It might be any century, any time. Distantly, they hear voices and traffic, but here in the sweet-smelling garden, the herbs perfuming the warm air, they might be cloistered from the world themselves. Arriving just too late for one of the guided tours, they had contented themselves with a leisurely exploration of the magnificent architecture: the soaring fluted columns, ornate painted ceilings, the intricate tessellated floor, the sun-flooded nave illuminated by a huge circular window set into an astonishing biblical fresco in vivid hues. And finally the extraordinary organ, flanked by painted saints, flooding the entire edifice from crypt to bell towers with notes so deep and rich they seemed to fill every atom of body and space with glory.

'I feel . . . cleansed,' says Hester quietly. She's not a religious woman, but something unexpected, spiritual almost, has touched her today, filling her with calmness.

Lionel's hand creeps into hers; their fingers lace.

'What was it again?' he says, almost as quietly. 'The abbey's motto?'

'Iste est quem tibi promiseram locus.'

He frowns. 'Remind me?'

'Here is the place—or *this is the place*—*that I promised to you.* Or *I promised you.* Something along those lines.'

Lionel's dry, warm hand tightens around hers. He clears his throat.

'Hetty, my dear, I know this might seem somewhat premature, but talking of places and promises . . .' he begins.

～～～

'What I'm beginning to think,' says Mary, twisting her wineglass round and round, as Harriet eyes it enviously, having not dared to risk even a drop given that she's driving, 'is that what I really want is simply not Ron. Just that. Not anyone else necessarily, just not Ron. Does that make sense?'

They are sitting under the awning of a crowded trattoria in the busy piazza, having managed by dint of some determined hovering to secure a table against stiff competition from a party of four.

'Uh-huh,' mutters Harriet, wondering, after her delicious *coniglio in porchetta,* if she can manage a dessert or if she should persuade Mary that they pay the bill and return to face the music. Hers and Mary's.

She's also worrying about the steep and winding roads she has to navigate again.

'The thing is, we get told, don't we, that we need other people, that we're always better off having someone in our lives. Which is true, in the main. And maybe I just needed to think that Rhona was that other person. And she was there, available, just the other side of the fence, neatly filling the Ron-shaped hole.' The waiter hovers with the menu. 'Oh, no thanks, *grazie*. We're not having puds, are we?'

Harriet surrenders. 'No, I suppose not. Coffee?'

'You know, I'll pass. I've still got my wine.'

Yes, thinks Harriet with a flash of bitterness, *you have, haven't you?* '*Un caffè, per piacere.*'

The elderly waiter pulls a mournful face, hesitates just a second or two in case the *signora* changes her mind, then shuffles off towards the kitchen.

Mary continues. 'The trouble is –'

Oh, please, not again!

'—what with the accident and everything, I've had time to think. And the more I do that, the more I start to wonder if I haven't rushed things. You know, not sorted out one mess before I get embroiled in another.'

Quite, thinks Harriet.

'I mean, don't get me wrong, Rhona is a wonderful woman, kind, loving, but—for God's sake don't tell her I said this—just a tiny bit overpowering. Do you know what I mean?'

She barely waits for Harriet's nod.

'And, frankly, I've had that for years with Ron, thank you very much; I don't want to walk straight into the same situation again, do I? Oh, do you know what, I think I will have a coffee after all.'

She signals to another waiter and orders a *cappuccino*; only Harriet notices his look of disgust as he moves away: milky coffee after a meal! These English!

'I'm sorry to keep going over and over it, Harriet.'

Not as sorry as I am.

'But you don't mind, do you? I'd hate to think I was being a bore. You are a love. Has anyone ever told you what a good listener you are?'

⌣⌣

'We should get back,' murmurs Hester, extricating her hand from Lionel's as they sit in the car in the car park, looking out over the panorama of hills and rivers and long avenues of poplars laid out below them as in a painting. She feels a mixture of happiness and excitement tinged with disquiet. Lionel's declaration, so sudden, so heartfelt, had elicited first surprise and then a sort of odd shyness. Her first thought had been: *I must tell Harry.* Followed almost immediately by the realisation of how difficult, if not impossible, that might be at this juncture.

'You do understand, don't you?' she says, stealing a glance at Lionel's profile, taking in the slight smile, the eyes crinkled against the sunlight. 'I mean—'

'There's a lot to consider. Yes. Don't think I don't realise that. You take as much time as you need. Only—' now he turns to her, cups her face in his hand in a gesture that makes her want to lean into him '—I meant every word I said.'

'I know you did,' she says, turning away, touched and suddenly tearful. Her heart flips. *Heavens*, she thinks. *Heavens above, I must be going soft in my old age.*

CHAPTER 44

By eight thirty, they are all back at The Laurels. Ben can't remember the last time he got up so early on a Sunday. Daria had thumped on his door at seven, although he'd been awake for at least an hour by then, listening to Milo gurgling in his cot in the next room, practising his rudimentary vocabulary, an exercise that clearly affords him much delight.

Breakfast is a silent affair but for Milo's shouts and experiments with feeding himself (largely consisting of introducing his porridge into any orifice but his mouth), Artem busy timetabling the repairs and renovations remaining and Daria studiously avoiding anything but the most minimal of conversations with Ben. Unasked he washes up, grabbing the tea towel before Daria can intervene, drying each piece of crockery and cutlery carefully and stowing it in the appropriate cupboard or drawer. He's not going to risk doing anything that might draw further wrath down on his head.

They pull up outside the house to find Finbar waiting on the doorstep, and Nats close behind on her bike.

'I thought you had a rehearsal today, Natalie,' says Artem.

'Yeah, but not until three. We're running lines, that's all.' She bends down to pinch Milo's cheek playfully. 'Hello, sweetness.' She swings her hair tantalisingly just out of his reach. 'We've work to do, little one. Work, then play, okay?' She pulls something out of her back pocket and presents it to him with some ceremony.

He grabs it and shoves it into his mouth automatically before removing it to inspect it quizzically.

Nats laughs. 'It's a toy, Milo! You don't eat it.'

Daria fingers the slightly damp fur and looks at the girl for enlightenment. 'My old rabbit,' says Nats. 'I thought he might like it.'

'Oh,' says Daria, 'what a kind girl. Say thank you, Milo.'

Milo gnaws at his treasure anew by way of gratitude. The two women laugh.

'What's the joke?' says Barry, peering over the hedge.

'Is Milo,' says Daria, grinning. 'Good morning, Barry.' And she gives the new arrival her widest smile.

Ben, pressed against the bushes at the back of the group, feels a sudden surge of jealousy at Barry's good fortune. And Milo's.

'Okay,' says Artem, squaring his shoulders as he unlocks the front door, 'let us get this task finished.'

⌣⌣

The paper looks as if it's been on the wall for decades, the precisely matched pattern bleeding into the slightly faded edges to perfection.

'That Ralph is one mean paper-hanger,' says Nats admiringly. 'We'd never have done it on our own.' She glances over at the rehung curtains. 'You wouldn't know, would you?' The hems now almost brush the floor; once the carpet is back in place, it would be an eagle eye that spotted anything amiss. Ben says nothing but a tiny flame of hope that they might just get away with this is rekindled.

Barry, belting out a horribly off-key but extremely enthusiastic rendition of 'Wind Beneath My Wings', is hard at work on the reconstruction of the staircase, with a deftness and speed that hearten them all. Finbar is back in the downstairs cloakroom, putting the finishing touches to the basin and taps, while Artem plans the order of play for the reintroduction of carpets, furniture, books and the assorted knickknacks, bric-a-brac and curiosities that make up Hester and

Harriet's home. Daria, never satisfied, is having another scrub of the kitchen floor, Milo penned in the corner behind an intricate barricade of kitchen chairs.

'If Barry would be kind enough to put those shelves back up . . . Barry!' yells Nats over the sound of planing. 'Barry!'

He peers over the landing balustrade through a cloud of wood dust. 'Yeah?'

'Don't suppose you could . . .' Nats jerks her thumb towards the far wall of the sitting room.

'Them shelves? Be right down.'

Minutes later the three glass shelves are back in place.

'Tidy,' says Barry, bounding up the stairs. He spins round at the top and hollers through to the kitchen. 'Artem, mate, I'll be making a mess for about another hour. Don't bring anything back in until then, okay? Thing is, however careful you are, the dust gets everywhere. Much better you let me finish, we hoover the whole shebang and then you get stuck in. You've got varnish, have you?'

'Varnish?'

'For the wood. It wasn't painted, was it, the staircase?' He examines what's left of the old one. 'No, look: varnish, that is. Be a bugger to match, though.'

Nats comes through to join Artem at the bottom of the stairs. They inspect the old varnish together. 'Shit,' mutters Nats. Then: 'Sorry.'

'No, shit is right,' says Artem. He gnaws his lip. 'Never mind the colour, how long will it take to dry?'

Barry's head reappears above. 'Depends. Minimum of four hours as a rule. Might be as much as twelve. And you'll need at least a couple of coats.'

Ben, listening to the exchange from the sitting room, feels his feeble hope trickling away. This is impossible. Hopeless. They might have got the curtains cleaned and the wall repapered, but there's all the furniture to reinstate, and now the necessity of getting the staircase to look as it had before the aunts had so blithely set off for their holiday. What's the first thing that will greet them when they walk in the front door? He stifles a groan. They might as well just give up now.

Nats puts her head around the door. 'Did you see any varnish in the sheds? Ben?'

He looks at her in abject misery.

'Come on! We need some varnish! Is there any outside?'

'Dunno.' He doesn't really care. Don't they know when they're beaten?

'Well, go and look, will you?' Nats glares at him until he shambles out through the kitchen into the garden. He yanks open the door of the nearest shed and stumbles into the gloom. In the far corner, tucked almost out of sight behind several armchairs and a nest of tables precariously balanced on top he makes out an assortment of paint tins piled high, webbed with grime, some smeared with rivulets of colour, lids frilled from repeated opening. He's pretty certain the aunts have never decorated the place themselves since they moved in, so God only knows how old the contents must be . . .

'Anything?' says Nats, close behind him.

'Can't see. We'll need to move these—'

'Oh, give me strength!' Nats shoves him aside and, nimble as a gymnast, works her way carefully across the obstruction to drop down in front of the paint mountain. She pulls her phone out of her pocket and, using it as a torch, inspects the tins carefully. 'No . . . no . . . Jeez, how much magnolia does anyone need?! Dashed Pebble, Caramel Camel, Crushed Oats . . . fifty shades of beige, in other words. Can't even read this one—oh wait! Yes! Burnt Oak varnish . . . oh, you are one lucky sod, Ben Fry, you know that? And look, someone has even written *Stairs* on it. Here.' She hefts the battered tin over the furniture to Ben and climbs back to join him.

⌣⌣⌣

Over coffee and biscuits, they inspect the aged varnish in the bottom of the tin. Barry shakes his head gloomily. 'Looks gloopy to me. Gone off.'

'Gloopy?' This is a new one on Artem.

'Yeah. Like, sticky? Too thick.'

'White spirit,' says Finbar, wolfing down a chocolate digestive. Daria's subterfuge with his jacket has markedly ameliorated his customary odour: he still smells, but not quite so pungently.

'Worth a try,' agrees Barry. He finishes off the last of his coffee and thunders back upstairs. The repaired and remodelled spindles are now in place; he lifts down the replacement banister from the landing to align it with them and, Artem and Ben holding it steady, begins the delicate task of securing everything in place. Daria, holding Milo, released from temporary immurement, looks on with undisguised admiration.

In very short order, the spindles are expertly fixed into position and Barry replaces the mercifully intact cap on the newel post. Nats and Daria clap their hands delightedly and Milo enthusiastically, if inexpertly, joins in. True, the staircase looks unfinished, but it is undeniably a staircase once more.

They all set to, sweeping, wiping and vacuuming in preparation for The Laurels' refurbishment. Finbar volunteers to apply the diluted varnish ('I've some experience in such matters') while the others, under Artem's direction, start the laborious task of reassembling the rooms. Barry elects to remain and help, even though his job is complete.

'No sweat. Got nothing else on today.' His smile lingers on Daria.

⌣⌣⌣

The photos on Ben's phone prove a godsend, since everyone has differing views on the siting of the furniture.

'No, no, table is in wrong place. There! There!' insists Daria.

'I am sure that chair is too close to the sofa. Let us move it just a little . . .' grunts Artem, dragging the offending article a few inches to the left.

'That rug is the other way round, I'm telling you,' says Ben, exasperated. 'The roses face the fire—'

But the photographic evidence is irrefutable and the protagonists have no option but to concede that, yes, okay, they might have been mistaken. The carpets seem none the worse for being rolled up and go down fairly smoothly. As the furniture is hauled back into the house, Daria anxiously watching for scrapes and bumps on the freshly washed walls and paintwork, The Laurels slowly assumes its habitual feel. The monumental challenge of replacing two lifetimes' worth of books and ornaments lies ahead and would surely have defeated them were it not for Ben's forethought.

'Dead clever,' says Barry, flicking through the images on Ben's phone. 'Would never have occurred to me. Blimey, got a lot of stuff, the pair of them.'

They have indeed. It takes a good three hours, Ben keeping an anxious eye on the time in view of his parents' imminent return, before they stand back, hungry, exhausted but triumphant. Piles of papers teeter on tables, books and magazines haphazardly carpet the floor around the armchairs, pictures hang (slightly askew, as is their usual mode, given the sisters' slipshod dusting) on the walls once more and Ben has even remembered to catch the corner of the hearth rug under the foot of Hester's chair.

Finbar, varnish tin and brush in hand, shuffles in to inspect their handiwork.

'Hmm,' he says.

'Is good, yes? Perfect,' says Daria smugly.

'I'm afraid it is,' says Finbar.

Artem frowns. 'Afraid?'

'Oh dear, oh dear. It just will not do.'

'Why not?' growls Artem testily. He badly needs some food.

'Come now, dear boy. Remember your Goethe.'

'*Goethe?*' stammers Nats. This time the old boy's lost her.

Finbar shakes his grizzled head, unleashing the familiar waft of stale sweat and beer. The circle around him widens. '*Certain flaws are necessary for the whole. It would seem strange if old friends lacked certain quirks.*'

'You what?' says Barry.

'Oh, of course,' says Artem as realisation dawns, with a sweeping glance around the room. 'I see what you mean.'

'I don't!' says Ben. He and Barry exchange a bewildered look.

Milo, playing at his mother's feet, somehow at that moment loses his balance, toppling sideways into one of the meticulously engineered piles of books. He lies, unhurt but winded, amid the scattered volumes, still clutching his new toy.

'Oh, Milo! Silly boy,' says Daria, cross with fatigue and hunger, as she bends down to right her son and tidy the mess.

'No, leave it,' says Artem, a hand on her arm. 'Finbar's right: it's too perfect. Everything's too clean, too tidy. It looks like . . .'

'No-one lives here,' finishes Ben. It doesn't take much for his heart to sink today and already he can feel the familiar plunge towards despair.

'Oh, no!' wails Daria. 'I cannot . . .!'

'Now, now. *Nil desperandum*, my dear!' exclaims Finbar, patting her shoulder. 'All can be remedied. Do we have perchance some sponges? Might some strong black tea be procured?'

Artem translates this quickly into terms Daria (and indeed Barry and Ben) will better understand.

'Black tea?' repeats Daria, mystified. '*Black?* Always I give you milk and three spoons of sugar.'

A rumbling laugh erupts. 'Not to drink, my dear girl. I need it for the walls. And perhaps you might get the vacuum cleaner out once more and—no need to switch it on—just drag it around willy-nilly.' Daria looks at him as if he has lost his mind. He carries on regardless. 'Bash it into the skirting boards with gay abandon. Even the odd bit of furniture if the spirit moves you. Barry, my dear fellow, you might care to wrap that hammer of yours in a duster, say, and give a few of those spindles a whack. Not too hard, mind, just enough to give them an air of genteel mistreatment: I'll apply the second coat afterwards. And, Artem, Ben and Natalie, throw yourself into those chairs and on that sofa. Kick your feet about a bit. I'm sure young Milo will be delighted

316

to help.' He looks around the haggard faces. 'But first, I fancy, some food . . .?'

'No, no,' says Daria. 'Please. Let us do it now. Quickly. Then we eat. Oh!' She puts her hand to her mouth, staring aghast into the far corner.

Following her gaze, all eyes come to rest on the contents of the top glass shelf: a small carriage clock (broken, its hands forever at twenty-three minutes to six), a jasperware vase presented to Harriet by a grateful parent whose son had miraculously scraped his O-level English Literature decades before, thanks to her good offices, a framed photo of George and Isabelle proudly nursing a scowling baby Ben and . . .

'Oh no!' cry Artem, Daria and Ben as the dreadful penny drops.

'What?' chorus Nats, Finbar and Barry.

Milo, wide-eyed, hugs his rabbit.

CHAPTER 45

Harriet sinks into the chair beside Hester in a secluded corner of the terrace. The minute they arrived back at the hotel, she had bid Mary a hasty adieu and hurried to her room, praying not to bump into either Ron or Rhona. She had been in the nick of time. Shutting her door, she had heard footsteps thundering along the terrace and Ron's furious voice, 'Where the hell have you been? Are you out of your mind, woman?!'

Hester jumps slightly. 'Oh! You're back!'

'Couple of hours ago. Had a quick lie-down. Did you have a good day?' Both decide not to mention Harriet's early morning flit.

Hester colours, recovers and says brightly, 'Oh, heavens, you know, nothing of consequence—bit of sightseeing, spot of lunch, a little snooze in the sun . . . how about you?'

'We drove to San Ginesio, up in the mountains. Enchanting little town with absolutely stunning views across the Sibillini Mountains. Masses to see but we just sauntered round the market. You should have seen the size of the peppers! And the figs! You'd have loved it.' *And a lot more than Mary: too busy rabbiting on about her woes.* Harriet can imagine her sister's reaction to the gorgeous displays of local produce, the spectacular flower stalls.

'Mary okay?' asks Hester, thinking simultaneously, *bloody woman!*

'Glad of an ear to bend,' says Harriet, with a half-smile, which,

318

to her guilty relief, Hester returns. 'That's really all she was after. I shouldn't be so unkind, but, you know, it's exhausting hearing the same thing for hour after hour. Especially when you know perfectly well that nothing you say will make a scrap of difference.'

Good, thinks Hester, suppressing a desire to smile smugly, *she's come to her senses at last.*

'I think you've been a saint.' Hester glances up at the hotel, hoping Lionel will emerge. Somehow she feels safer—protected almost—with him beside her.

Harriet casts about for a neutral topic.

'Did you make it to the abbey?'

Hester seizes on the question gratefully and launches into a detailed description of the architectural and artistic delights of the building. In her anxiety, she overdoes it. Lionel barely figures in her narrative. Harriet, who reads her sister only too well, listens with half an ear, her suspicions multiplying by the second.

Alfonso materialises at their side. '*Signore*,' he says, arms outstretched, taking them both in. 'I know it is early—' he checks his watch '—only a little early, nearly half past five, but perhaps a glass of wine to start your last evening?'

'To hell with how early it is, yes please, you dear man,' says Hester.

Alfonso grins a faintly roguish grin. 'I have a little treat for my two favourite guests. After all the excitements of your holiday, no?' He lopes up the steps.

'Ah!' says Hester, her face lighting up, a bloom of colour flushing her cheeks, 'and here's Lionel!' She waves vigorously. 'Over here, my dear!' Face crinkled in a huge smile, he swiftly picks his way down the broad stone steps to join them. As he skirts Hester's chair to take his own seat, his hand rests lightly on her shoulder for a brief moment. It does not go unnoticed by her sister.

'Harriet!' he says solicitously, 'how are you today? An enjoyable excursion?' He glances across at Hester to check the mood. She smiles back.

'Fine, thank you. Hester's just been telling me about your day.' She doesn't miss his instant and alarmed look at Hester. *Oho.* She continues, 'Alfonso has just gone to fetch us some wine. A bit early, I know, but after the week we've had, we thought . . . well, now we know Mary's going to be okay, if not exactly a celebration, then at least a toast to the future.' As Lionel and Hester exchange yet another almost shifty look, she silently curses her inelegant efforts: what made her mention the future? In an instant the problems crouching so patiently in the wings start once more to advance towards her: Stephen, Hester's decision, her own future at The Laurels . . .

Hester watches Harriet self-consciously reach for a stray sun-brittled leaf that is skittering around the table in the intermittent breeze and crush it into a thousand fragments. She sweeps them to the floor, then looks out over the valley, looks across the gardens at guests dotted hither and thither, looks up towards the hotel expectantly, looks at her hands. Looks anywhere, in fact, but at Hester or Lionel. Hester wills him to silence. The hiatus lengthens, balloons, envelops them, until mercifully broken by Alfonso's return.

'Ah! Signor Parchment, I anticipated you might join the ladies!' His good humour and obvious desire to please break the spell as he swiftly unloads the tray, carefully placing on the table four large glasses and a carafe into which he has decanted the wine. 'I hope you will permit . . .' He smiles winningly, seeking permission to join them in a celebratory drink, as he presents the empty wine bottle for scrutiny.

'Of course!' chorus the sisters, grateful for his company and the distraction it offers, as they both sit forward to peer at the label.

'Oh, goodness!' says Harriet.

'My word!' says Hester.

Alfonso beams. 'Yes,' he says proudly. He knows these ladies; knows he need say no more.

'Nineteen eighty-one,' breathes Hester reverently. She smiles up at the Italian. 'A great year. A Bersano!'

'Yes! At such a time, only the best will suffice.' He hands the cork first to Harriet, then Hester, to smell.

Lionel watches circumspectly; they might be talking Greek for all he can contribute.

With considerable theatre, Alfonso slowly pours the dark wine into one glass and hands it ceremoniously to Harriet. 'Signora.' He waits.

'No, please,' says Harriet, cradling the glass, tastebuds aglow, 'let us all drink together.'

Alfonso inclines his head gravely in agreement and pours three more glasses in similar fashion. In unison, he, Hester and Harriet insert their noses into the bowl and sniff; Lionel has taken a sip before he realises his blunder.

A collective sigh escapes the oenophiles; as one they tip the wine to their lips, allow the flavours to flood their mouths, and swallow.

Hester thinks she has never tasted anything more sublime. 'So firm,' she says in quiet ecstasy. 'And . . . is it roses . . .?'

'And tar, that is what they always say,' says Alfonso, taking another appreciative sip. 'Yes, for sure.'

'Dark chocolate,' says Harriet, momentarily beyond happiness, her worries temporarily forgotten. She rolls another mouthful over her tongue. Divine.

'And truffles?' asks Hester.

Alfonso nods. 'Very earthy.'

A thought strikes both sisters simultaneously. Hester voices it. She points at the bottle. 'How much . . .?'

Alfonso adopts a martyred look. '*Signore!* I would not dream . . .!'

Both sisters breathe an inward sigh of relief. In matters vinous, they rarely stint themselves, but this wine would be eye-wateringly expensive.

A further thought strikes Hester. 'Does Marco know?' Alfonso's partner, while expressing enormous sympathy for Mary and Harriet's plight and making all the right noises, has their business to consider. And now one of his most expensive wines has been opened . . .

Alfonso puts a finger to his lips. 'Shh . . . the cellar is my responsibility. How do you say: what the eye is not seeing . . .?' He laughs mischievously.

'Thank you, Alfonso,' says Harriet, getting up to kiss his cheek. He smells of lemons and expensive aftershave. 'I don't know what—'

'Please.' He takes her hand and raises it to his lips. 'My pleasure, *signora*, entirely, to be of service.' He drains his glass with evident satisfaction, then refills theirs, placing the now empty carafe with the bottle and his own glass on the tray. 'Destroying the evidence,' he says with a wink, before running lightly up the steps.

'Magnificent.' Hester holds her glass up to the light.

'The wine or the sommelier?' says Harriet.

'Both.'

Benign with wine, Harriet looks over to Lionel. 'How did you find it, Lionel? The wine.'

He jumps, and shifts uneasily. Hester looks out over the vista. 'Oh! Yes, very . . . er, pleasant. Very pleasant indeed. I wonder if I might propose a little toast?'

Hester and Harriet tense. Hester tries to signal to Lionel: *Not now. Please don't say anything . . .*

Harriet thinks, *Please, please don't.*

A shadow falls across the table.

'Oh, very nice. Very nice, I'm sure,' spits Ron Martindale, substantial chest heaving with indignation. 'You sit here, guzzling wine in the middle of the afternoon, while my wife is recovering in her room after gallivanting around the Italian countryside courtesy of your idiocy and irresponsibility! Mary has a head injury, for God's sake! It's only by the greatest good fortune that she didn't suffer a relapse while you dragged her off to some godforsaken market or something. You just stay away from her, do you hear, you interfering old—'

Hester gets to her feet. 'I beg your pardon?'

'Stay out of this, if you please. It's this woman—' he jabs a finger in Harriet's direction '—I'm talking to. This conniving troublemaker, who's been pouring God knows what poison into my wife's ears. I swear, if you come within a hundred feet of—'

Hester gathers herself to respond, all her instincts screaming at her to protect her sister against this bully.

Harriet, reading Hester's intent instinctively, wills her to silence, knowing that, once roused and particularly when anyone attacks those she loves, her sister's self-control evaporates. *Oh, Hetty, please don't.*

'I must ask you to stop shouting at Mrs Pearson,' says a quiet voice out of nowhere. 'You are making a spectacle of yourself and embarrassing us all. Now, kindly remove yourself or I shall do it for you.'

Ron's bulky frame seems to swell still further with fury. He looks around for the perpetrator of this outrageous interruption. Lionel pushes back his chair and stands up, slight but resolute, interposing himself between Ron and an ashen-faced Harriet.

'What the hell's it got to—' Ron's face is beet-red, flecks of saliva bubbling on his lips. A vein pulses on his forehead.

'You might like to ask yourself why exactly your unfortunate wife did not ask *you* to take her out for the day,' says Lionel in the same calm tone.

Ron's mouth drops open comically.

'Now, please leave. I shan't ask a second time.' Lionel makes an infinitesimal move towards the other man and Ron flinches visibly, falling back.

'You haven't heard the last of this,' he blusters in a failed attempt to regain the upper hand. Flinging one last contemptuous look at Harriet's averted face, he wheels around, throws back his head and stomps back up the steps, shouldering his way through a clutch of gawping onlookers, and disappears into the hotel.

For a moment, everyone is frozen in a shocked tableau, until Hester collapses into her chair, hand already reaching for her glass.

The hero of the hour maintains his flinty demeanour until Ron is out of sight, then, as if his legs can no longer support him, drops into his seat, a look of appalled realisation washing over his face. 'Good

Lord, Good Lord above,' he mutters almost to himself, one shaky hand to his brow. All around them, bright, over-casual conversation breaks out as their erstwhile audience melts away, eager to rake over events at a more discreet distance.

Harriet gently edges Lionel's glass towards him; when he fails to respond, she wraps his nerveless fingers around the stem and gives them a squeeze. 'Thank you, Lionel.'

'Lionel the lion,' murmurs Hester in something approaching wonderment.

She catches Hester's eye; there is a moment of confusion and uncertainty, then the smiles that start to creep across their faces mutate swiftly first into sniggers, then snorts of glorious, slightly hysterical laughter.

～～～

Their joint good humour lasts all through the evening. They ignore the surreptitious glances thrown at them by some of the other guests and each secretly sighs with relief when it becomes apparent that Ron Martindale has no intention of braving the restaurant that night. Of Rhona there is likewise no sign; Harriet can only imagine the grief both she and Ron will be visiting upon the embattled object of their joint affections. Weary as she is of the whole saga, she nevertheless continues to feel a certain responsibility towards Mary. But at Hester's insistence, she has agreed that she will let matters lie for the moment.

'I will leave her a note, though,' she says, regardless of Hester's frown. 'I don't want to her to think I've abandoned her entirely.'

Lionel puts out a restraining hand as Hester goes to protest; Hester subsides.

Harriet yawns extravagantly, washed with a sudden wave of fatigue. She pushes aside her half-eaten zabaglione. 'Golly, I'm exhausted. Forgive me, but I'm ready for my bed.' She gets unsteadily to her feet. 'Whoops! It's not the wine, honestly, it's just I'm utterly wiped out.'

'Early start tomorrow,' says Hester. 'You need a good night's sleep. Want me to come with you?'

'Don't be daft. You finish your meal. Sorry to be such a . . . anyway, good night, both. And, Lionel, can I just—'

He stops her with his palm. 'Honestly, there's no need.'

Harriet nods her thanks and, overcome once more, hurries from the restaurant, as Lionel reaches for Hester's hand.

☙

A good night's sleep, however, eludes her.

She tosses and turns, punches her pillow in frustration, wide awake still, although her eyes feel gritty with tiredness. The looks between Hester and Lionel that she tried so assiduously to ignore over dinner come back in all their significance: *something* happened today on their little outing, she's sure of it. *Thank God we're going home tomorrow*, she thinks. *Then it'll all fizzle out, with any luck.* She comforts herself with that thought and once more snuggles down into the sheets. But minutes later, her mind is racing again, unpicking her mental comfort blanket, running through increasingly disturbing scenarios. She recalls her conversation with Hester in the town yesterday, that oddly jagged discussion about living abroad, about moving to London—

'Oh, for heaven's sake!' She peers at her alarm clock. Just past midnight. Reading offers no hope of a solution to her insomnia and she's had enough of lying in the dark, worrying. She gets up, pulls on her dressing gown and creeps through the silent corridors to the room housing the computer, slipping past the deserted restaurant where two diners remain, faces illuminated by candlelight, their fingers entwined.

CHAPTER 46

They're on their sixth black bin bag. The first five have been emptied out onto the lawn, sifted through and then, at Daria's insistence, been carefully refilled. 'Put by gate,' she says. 'Tomorrow men come with lorry.'

'Thank God,' says Nats, heaving two of the bags around the side of the cottage. 'Wouldn't fancy having to hoick this lot off to the dump.'

The sixth bag discharges a mountain of bottles and cans. 'Were we in less of a hurry,' says Finbar, 'we ought to recycle these, as responsible citizens who cherish this fragile planet. As it is . . .' He stirs the glass and metal with his foot, stopping to peer closely at something half buried in the grass. 'What have we here?' Bending down creakily he retrieves a small fragment of—

'Is it?' implores Ben, hope stubbornly resurfacing. Heedless of the smell, he leans over the old man's palm to examine his find. 'It's the right colour. Yes! Look, that's a foot, isn't it?' Feverishly, he begins raking through the rest of the pile, but in vain. No further fragments of the shattered shepherdess emerge.

Finbar angles the remnant of china to the light, eyes inches from the surface. 'I fancy somewhere about my person is my loupe . . .' As the others exchange bemused looks, he ferrets in his jacket pocket and withdraws a jeweller's eyepiece that he screws into his right socket. 'Now then . . . ah! Is that a . . . no, perhaps not . . . I thought for one moment . . . yes, yes, here we go, the lion . . . and the crown . . . Oh, and unless I'm much mistaken that's the remains of an HN number.' He whips the loupe away and beams triumphantly. 'Royal Doulton, without a doubt.'

'Yeah?' says Ben eagerly. 'So we can—'

'Hold your horses, young man,' says Finbar. 'What we have so far is the manufacturer. What we need is the name of the piece, serial number ideally, its date of issue and possible retirement—'

'What was that number you said? HN?' says Nats, fishing her phone out of her pocket. 'What's that?' Her thumbs move like lightning.

Finbar considers for a moment, brow furrowed. 'I used to know . . . it's something to do with . . . was it a designer? No, perhaps it was . . .'

'Henry Nixon,' Nats says, reading the information on her screen. 'Innovative designer. Appears on any piece after 1913.'

'Great Scott!' Finbar is awestruck, looking from the mobile to Nats' grin and back. 'How on earth . . .'

'Welcome to the twenty-first century, Finbar,' says the girl, waggling her phone in his face. 'Now, any idea what this statuette thing was called?'

Daria, Artem and Ben look hopefully at each other, then give a collective shrug.

'Not a clue,' says Ben miserably. 'Woman in a dress. Was there a sheep?' He looks to the others for help.

'Sheep?' says Daria. 'No, no sheep.'

'Man,' cries Nats, staring at her screen, 'there's hundreds of them on Wikipedia. You sure it was a shepherdess?'

'I think,' says Daria.

'Okay, let's try that first,' says Nats, typing swiftly. 'There's a few on eBay. Here's one from 1991. Any good?' She holds out the phone for them to inspect the image. They shake their heads.

'Too recent,' says Finbar. 'I seem to recall Hester telling me it had been her mother's. So, working backwards . . . let's see . . .'

'Got one here from the 1930s,' says Barry, who has been following the conversation and quietly conducting his own investigations. He hands Daria his phone.

'Yes!' she gasps delightedly. 'Is the lady! Clever Barry has found her! Look, Artem, is same as Hester and Harriet's!' She thrusts the image in her brother's face. As his face creases in a smile of recognition, Ben feels his tightened muscles relaxing slightly.

'Can I see?' says Nats. She examines the picture for a second or two. 'It's pretty gross, isn't it? Still, takes all sorts.'

'I know,' says Daria solemnly, wrinkling her nose. 'Is old lady figure. I don't like. But Hester and Harriet do. Is their . . . history, yes?'

There's an air of both relief and excitement in the garden. Daria scoops up her son and makes for the kitchen to assemble lunch. Finbar, Barry and Artem set to shovelling the cans and bottles back into the bin bag. Ben edges closer to Nats, who still has hold of Barry's phone and is flicking from page to page.

'It's a Buy It Now as well as an auction,' she says. 'That's a relief.' She freezes, her smile dissolving.

Ben's stomach somersaults. 'What? What is it?'

'Er . . . seems this is a collector's item.'

'Yeah?'

She looks at him pityingly. 'It's four hundred and ninety-nine pounds.'

Ben's innards slide south. 'Four hundred . . .'

'And that's not all. It's collection in person. From Edinburgh.'

⌣⌣⌣

All three of them—Ben, Nats and Barry—have checked and rechecked every single site that lists the figurine. Three of them are in the States, so completely out of the question given the timeframe, although iron- ically all three are cheaper (in one case considerably cheaper) than the Scottish one. Over a lunch of bread and cheese, the trio sit hunched over their mobiles until Ben, exasperated by squinting at a tiny screen, goes upstairs to use Hester's PC. The search results inevitably remain the same. He slumps in the chair, beyond despair, beyond any solution. Nats pokes her head around the door.

'I'm just off. Rehearsals. Sorry about the shepherdess. Bummer, eh?'

Sunk in misery, Ben is barely able to summon a nod. He needs to get off too: his parents will be home in a couple of hours and he's promised to have a meal waiting for them.

'You could just fess up. Tell them you were mucking about and—'

'Who with? Doing what?' It comes out as more aggressive than he intends.

'It was just a suggestion. Suit yourself.'

He hears her running lightly down the stairs. Wants to call out, 'Sorry!', thank her for her help . . . He hurries to the landing and leans over to see her disappearing through the front door, fastening her helmet.

'Hey!'

Nats turns, looks up. Waits.

'I didn't mean—'

'Forget it. Gotta go.'

'This play you're in . . .'

'What about it?'

'I might come.'

The tiniest of pauses. 'Okay.'

The door snicks shut.

᠆᠆᠆

Finbar is applying the second coat of varnish to the banister as Ben eases past him on the stairs. Viscous trickles run down some of the spindles like sticky raindrops. *Clever,* thinks Ben, recalling now the slipshod varnishing of the originals. *He's very observant. And kind.*

'Ta, Finbar,' he mutters humbly, squeezing past.

'For what, dear boy?'

'For . . . you know, like, helping and that.'

'My pleasure entirely. Very little is needed to make a happy life; it is all within yourself.'

'That so?'

'Marcus Aurelius.'

'Right. Well, ta anyway. Just gonna . . .' He flaps a hand in the direction of the kitchen.

He repeats his thanks to Daria, Artem and Barry, then makes his excuses, explaining about his parents' imminent return.

'Cook, then study,' says Daria sternly. 'No more parties.' She sniffs with disgust as Milo shouts for attention.

Ben hoists him up and bumps noses. 'Gotta go, matey. Be good.' He turns to hand the baby over to his mother, is surprised to find Milo's sturdy little body lifted out of his grasp by Barry. Milo, no respecter of affections, immediately transfers his attentions to his new playmate, to Ben's chagrin.

'What about the shepherdess?' says Artem as Ben reaches for the door handle.

Ben shrugs. 'Dunno. I'll have to tell them, I guess.'

'About all this?' says Artem, alarmed.

'No, 'course not. Just the f— the china thing.'

Artem grunts and turns away, reaching for a biscuit.

Dismissed, Ben slouches out, raising a hand in farewell to Finbar on his way to the front door. The old man stops his brushwork and unfolds himself from the stairs, following Ben out into the front garden.

'Where's the bicycle?'

'Oh, back at Daria's. Just gonna collect it.'

Finbar puts his hand on the gate to stay him. 'My boy, we all make mistakes. "Though you break your heart, men will go on as before." Not a bad philosophy.'

'You say so.' Ben just wants to get away from all these witnesses to and reminders of his stupidity, to immerse himself in creating something in the kitchen, not trying to repair what he's helped destroy. The weekend's events are made worse by the fact that, of all the people in his life, it's his supportive and loyal aunts he has so grievously wronged. The annihilation of the cherished figurine is a tangible—albeit fragmented—symbol of everything he has ruined.

'It's many a year since I was last in Edinburgh,' Finbar is saying, scratching his beard. 'A fine city, Auld Reekie. Half alive and half a monumental marble, that's what Stevenson said of it, and I'm bound to say, I think he's right.'

'Yeah?' says Ben, baffled, trying to slide through the narrow gap between gate and hedge. Can't the old codger see he's in a hurry?

'So I'm thinking, a short sojourn in the Athens of the North might be just the ticket. The train ticket, in fact.' Finbar permits himself a spluttery laugh at his wit. 'I was considering, perhaps this very evening, if you catch my drift.'

Ben dimly begins to fathom the old man's meaning and after a day of false starts and setbacks finds his heavy-handed attempts to help serve only to exacerbate his ill-humour. 'But I haven't got five hundred quid! I haven't got five quid! I already owe Artem or Barry or whoever for all the wood and the basin and Christ alone knows what else and where the frig am I supposed to find the money to repay them—let alone pay for a trip to Edinburgh and then shell out shedloads of money I don't have on a shit piece of crappy pottery?'

There is a moment of ominous silence during which Finbar fixes Ben with an adamantine glare, before drawing back in cold fury, nostrils flaring, tugging his jacket down hard by the lapels to release a malodorous effluvium. 'Did I ask you for money, young man? Did I? Did I at any point even mention lucre, filthy or otherwise? Do you suppose that everything that has occurred since your ill-judged and utterly irresponsible decision to play fast and loose with your esteemed aunts' habitation has been executed for your benefit? What effrontery! No, it is for those fine ladies' sakes that we have toiled so assiduously to restore their hearth and home to something approximating its customary beloved state. To spare them the wounding disappointment that would surely ensue when the realisation dawned that the viper whom they had nursed in their bosoms had sunk its selfish, feckless fangs into their very hearts. That the waif who had inveigled himself into their affections had betrayed their trust, abused their hospitality and polluted their nest. Money is nothing, a mere bagatelle: all that matters is that those paragons of generosity should remain blissfully ignorant of the devastation wreaked by you and your soi-disant friends. So if I choose to journey north tonight, if I choose to use my money—not yours, note, but mine—to purchase a replacement figurine of questionable taste but one in which memories fond and sentimental are clearly invested, it ill becomes you to object. Or, indeed, to proffer any comment *whatsoever* on my proposed course of action. So do whatever is necessary to secure the shepherdess, apprise the seller of my intentions and do it NOW!'

'There's no way—'

'Did I ask for your opinion? Just do as you are bid, you impertinent whippersnapper!'

Ben hesitates for no more than a millisecond—there is something positively scary about the set of Finbar's features. He hurriedly calls up the site on his phone, navigates to the appropriate page and, under the old man's baleful glare, clicks *Buy It Now*, including a message stressing the urgency and that payment will be made on collection. 'In cash?' he checks with Finbar. 'Only it says no cheques.'

'In cash,' confirms Finbar grimly. Ben presses send.

'There's no knowing when this bloke will pick up the message. I've asked for a number but he mightn't, like, check it that regularly. I mean, eBay will let him know it's sold but what if he isn't online or whatever?'

'I've no idea what any of that means, but let us just see if the gods are with us, shall we?' says Finbar evenly.

'I'm just saying—' Ben's phone buzzes. He gawps at the screen. 'Jeez, it's him! That's amazing! Look!' He thrusts the phone in Finbar's face; the old man recoils.

'I take it from your intemperate response that contact has been established. Now kindly facilitate a conversation between myself and the vendor.'

'Ring him, you mean?'

'Unless you happen to know a more effective way of allowing us to converse?'

'All right! All right. You know sarcasm is . . .' Ben swiftly keys in the number and hands the phone to Finbar. 'Might go to voicemail.'

But the gods, it seems, are most decidedly on Finbar's side. The call is answered by Angus McWhitty of the New Town, Edinburgh, over-joyed to have found a buyer for Granny's bibelot, sympathetic to the urgency of the situation and yes, if the gentleman is serious, happy to wait up and complete the transaction—in cash, no cheques, regret-tably—this very evening, trains permitting. Finbar is all smiles and fruitiness through their brief exchange, but as he hands the phone back to its owner when arrangements have been completed, the smile disappears. Ben, on the verge of trying however inadequately to express his thanks, finds the words die in his throat under Finbar's glacial glare.

'Now you, young man, had best get about your business. I shall complete my ministrations within and then leave immediately for Scotland. You will keep your counsel about my plans, revealing only what is necessary to prevent alarm. You will never for any reason whatsoever apprise your aunts of these events because, be in no doubt, while I am generally a man of infinite sweetness of nature, you would not want even to the smallest degree to incur my wrath.'

And with that, Finbar turns on his heel and disappears back inside, closing the door with more than usual firmness, leaving Ben shell-shocked on the path. He hadn't understood everything the old man had spat at him, but he is in absolutely no doubt that he has just expe-rienced one of the worst bollockings of his life.

CHAPTER 47

'This is delicious, darling,' says Isabelle happily, forking in another mouthful of chicken pie. 'But really, you oughtn't to have neglected your studies. I could have rustled something up.'

Ben, raised on what his mother 'rustled up' from perfectly nutritious ingredients that somehow transmogrified into unidentifiable culinary monstrosities, smiles faintly.

George, sitting opposite, frowns. 'Your mother's right, son. You can't afford to slacken off, not with your exams starting tomorrow. Although the pie is truly excellent. First class. Tell me, how did your session with Ralph go?'

Isabelle sits forward eagerly. 'Oh, yes. We were telling your Auntie Lynn how hard you were working and what a nice boy Ralph is. Did it help?'

'Brilliant. Absolute genius.'

George recoils slightly in surprise: his son sounds positively enthusiastic. This is most encouraging. 'Good ... good,' he mutters uncertainly.

His wonder is exacerbated when, unprompted, Ben launches into a lengthy speech lauding Ralph Pickerlees' tutoring skills.

'. . . made it all, like, relevant. I mean, I could see what the point is. First time anyone's bothered to do that. At school it's all, learn this principle or equation or whatever. Ralph makes it make sense. Yeah.'

Ben cuts himself another hefty slice of pie. He's dead pleased with the pastry: he'd experimented with a tablespoonful of cornflour in the mix, reckons it makes it just that bit lighter. Must remember to tell Aunt Hester . . . The thought of his aunts brings Finbar suddenly to mind, possibly even now speeding northwards on his mission.

'. . . nice pen?' His mother looks at him enquiringly. Ben drags himself back to the moment. Oh, fuck, the pen he was supposed to buy Ralph with the money his mother had given him. The money he'd instead spend on booze, most of which ended up going down the drain. He thinks fast. Just then his phone buzzes beside him. He glances at the screen, ignores it. It'll be either Jez or Louisa, both of whom have been bombarding him with calls and texts for the past twenty-four hours; he's not talking to either of them.

Ben swallows his mouthful. 'Oh yeah, about the pen . . . You know what? We were having such a ball we thought we'd go out and get, like, you know, some food?'

'Really?' Isabelle looks doubtful. 'Did you have enough money? I only gave you—'

'No, we just went to . . . you know.' He hopes no-one presses him, that they're imagining a café, a fast-food outlet. 'So we could keep talking. 'Cos I was getting so much out of it.'

'Well,' says George, relaxing, 'I'm delighted to hear it. I did wonder how you two lads would get on, if I'm frank, but Ralph clearly knows what's what. I must ask his father to pass on our thanks tomorrow.'

Isabelle beams. 'I really don't know why I worried so much about leaving you on your own. You seem to have had a marvellous weekend.'

It takes a superhuman effort, but Ben somehow manages a weak smile. 'Yeah, so tell me about Auntie Lynn's party, then . . .'

His parents' voices advance, recede, peak and trough. He dimly registers that the pineapple tarte tatin had been a triumph—'Auntie Lynn was so touched! She had two helpings!'—that their hotel had been rather disappointing, with lumpy beds, and that they hadn't got to bed until after one, the dirty stop-outs.

His phone rings and he glances at the screen. 'Gotta take this.' And before they can protest, he's on his feet, through the kitchen doorway and halfway up the stairs.

'Wotcha, lover. How's tricks?' says a voice in his ear.

He's surprisingly pleased to hear Nats' voice. 'Yeah, good. You finished with the play?'

'Just. Had a thought while we were packing up: you ought to be at the cottage when your aunts get back—'

'Yeah, I—' The same thought had occurred to Ben.

'—sort of distraction you know? Like, first thing they see's you, not the walls. Might deflect attention.'

'Yeah, I—'

'Artem said they'd be back about six. Might come with you.'

'You?!'

'Yeah. Why not? Like to meet them and what could be a better distraction than me?'

She has a point. A tiny, black, corn-rowed distraction. All else will pale into insignificance if past experience is anything to go by.

'About the china thingy—had an idea.'

'Sorted,' says Ben, with more confidence than he feels. Where on earth would Finbar get that kind of money? And Finbar on a train? It seems highly improbable. He tells her anyway, the old man's words of warning still ringing in his head, and swears her to eternal secrecy.

'Serious?' For once Nats seems taken aback. 'Tonight?'

'So he said.'

'Respect. That Finbar rocks. You are one lucky dude, you know that?'

Oh he does, he does.

'Okay,' says Nats. 'Gotta get off. Oh, my birdbrained sis has been whingeing you're not answering her calls. You pissed with her or something?'

'Er . . . hello? 'Course I'm pissed with her! Her and her fuckwit friends. After what they did, are you kidding?'

'Yeah?' Nats' glee is unmistakable. 'I'll tell her.' She sounds as if she's relishing the prospect. 'Anyway, boo, best you get back to your books. Good luck tomorrow. Ciao!'

Boo? thinks Ben, throwing his phone on his bed en route to his desk. Is she just messing with him or . . .? He smooths his hand over the still uneven skin of his cheeks and forehead and reaches for the tube of toothpaste secreted in his top drawer.

His phone rings again.

'Hello? Ben?' yells Daria. 'You are working?'

'Trying to.'

'Good. I speak, then you work more. Is Tata and Mama back safe?'

'Yes.'

'Good.' A crash in the background, followed by a wail. 'Artem, quick! Milo, Milo, Uncle Artem is coming!' Her voice booms again in Ben's ear. 'Milo is pushing chair over. Now, Ben, Hester and Harriet are returning tomorrow. Artem is collecting from airport.'

'Yeah, I know. Me and Nats—'

'We are thinking, Artem and me, it will be good idea to be there when they come. At the house. Yes? We make lot of noise, laughing, then they are not seeing—'

'Yeah, we thought the same.'

'Oh . . .' Daria sounds the tiniest bit disappointed, the wind taken out of her sails. 'Well . . . is good idea, I think.'

'Plus I thought I'd cook them something for their tea.'

'Cook? You? No, no, no, I am making borscht. Right now. Hester loves my borscht. And Harriet.'

Now it's Ben's turn to be disappointed. 'I just thought . . .'

Daria is on it like a terrier. 'Oh yes, clever boy. I see your plan. Cook nice meal, smiling, look what nice boy I am, Auntie. Guilty, guilty heart trying to pretend all is a dream only. Is not dream, my friend, no, no, no. What about china lady? Heh?'

Ben leaps in as Daria pauses momentarily to draw breath, hissing into his phone in case either parent should be hovering on the landing, 'Don't worry about her.'

'Don't worry?' hollers Daria. 'He say, don't worry!' This, presumably, to Artem. 'I do worry, Ben. And why? Because Hester and Harriet will think I break this when I am cleaning! I do not break! Never, never. Always careful. Wash in warm water, dry with towel. Is precious.'

'No, Daria, listen—'

'Poor ladies, they do not expect—'

'Daria, just shut up a minute—'

'What? What!' Ben holds the phone away from his ear. 'Now he is telling me to shut it! Rude boy!'

'Finbar's gone to Edinburgh,' says Ben swiftly.

Silence.

'Daria? Did you hear what I said? He's gone up to Edinburgh to buy the shepherdess.'

'Finbar?' whispers Daria, appalled. 'He is walking to . . .'

'No, no! Not walking. He's catching a train.'

'A train?' says Daria, still clearly astonished.

There is a rapid exchange in Belarusian as Daria shares the intelligence with Artem. The next moment, it is Artem's voice on the phone. 'Are you sure?'

'He told me himself,' says Ben, omitting to share the rest of that painful conversation. 'Said he was leaving immediately.'

Artem whistles softly. 'He is a dark man.'

'Horse. It's a dark horse.'

'Of course. But where did he get—'

'The money? Dunno. Didn't like to ask.' Didn't dare, in fact. He glances at the clock on his screen. 'I'm not supposed to tell anyone. Will you make sure Daria knows? Not to say anything, I mean. Look, I gotta get on, Artem. Revision and that. What time you expecting to get back from the airport?'

'Perhaps six thirty. But Daria and I will check everything at The Laurels mid-afternoon.'

'We'll see you there then.'

'We?'

'Yeah,' says Ben as casually as he can, 'Nats thought she might call by too.'

MONDAY

CHAPTER 48

Harriet doesn't mind the hard plastic seat. She doesn't mind the watery coffee or the stale roll with its meagre slice of unidentifiable cheese. She doesn't mind the voluble Italian crammed into the seat next to her who has been gesticulating wildly for at least a quarter of an hour through what appears to be a very fraught telephone conversation. She doesn't even mind if they are delayed. They are on their way home; that's all that matters. And then she'll decide what to do.

'Two hours!' says Hester, head cocked to make out the garbled message crackling through the tannoy. 'Is that what it said? That was our flight number, wasn't it?'

Lionel, sitting opposite her, leans forward to extricate himself from two large ladies either side of him who are taking up rather more than their allocated seat space. 'Would you like me to go and check, my dear?'

Hester shakes her head. 'Thank you really, but no.' She glances over to where several dozen people are moodily regarding the lucky few who have secured seats. There has already been a very unpleasant face-off between a middle-aged businessman and a harassed mother with two toddlers in tow. Lionel had been on the verge of offering up his seat to avoid a violent confrontation when the man, finally shamed by the waves of outrage emanating from the onlookers, had grudgingly ceded the field, earning a mocking round of applause as he fled. 'Best sit tight. I'm sure they'll announce what's what in due course.' She nudges Harriet, glad of the excuse to avoid Lionel's beseeching eyes. 'Should I text Artem and say we'll be late?'

Harriet looks up from her Kindle, removes her glasses. 'Artem?'

Hester notes with concern how distracted Harriet seems. 'Yes. Shall I let him know about the delay? Don't want him waiting for hours unnecessarily. Not to mention the exorbitant price of parking at the airport.'

'Oh,' says Harriet, 'yes. I'm with you.' But she doesn't look it. 'Maybe wait until we're about to board?'

'I think I'll just warn him to expect us a bit later,' says Hester, scrabbling through her bag for her phone. She's all too conscious of Lionel's eyes on her, patiently waiting to learn his fate after their long heart-to-heart last night in the empty restaurant. She had made him a promise that they would talk today.

Harriet, for her part, is troubled and distracted twice over. First, there is her impending confrontation with Marion. Her indignation with her old college acquaintance—she finds the epithet *friend* sticks in her craw at this juncture—bubbles periodically to the surface: how *could* she? They had been the closest of friends at university—certainly in their final year—even if circumstances and distance had subsequently conspired to keep them apart, their friendship dwindling over the years of marriage and careers to the exchange of occasional letters and latterly merely Christmas cards. Until now she had always nursed a vague regret at letting what had been a heady and intense closeness wither, but her overriding feeling at this moment is fury at Marion's behaviour; the betrayal cuts her deeply. She has tried to rationalise Marion's actions: her youth, her undoubted terror at her predicament, perhaps panic at the thought of being shamed as girls still were in those days, no matter how much the papers trumpeted the new freedoms offered by the pill and the rise of feminism. Some sister Marion had proved to be!

Her second and more recent worry she hugs close to herself, sick with dread at both its import and the urgency of finding the best way to reveal it. Once more she tries to distract herself with her Kindle, but the words dance meaninglessly in front of her eyes, the only consolation being that she is spared the need to make conversation with either of her travelling companions.

There is another indecipherable announcement. People freeze, shushing offspring as they try to make out the words, paper cups halfway to mouths, hope flowering as it inevitably does that they misheard last time, that it is some other flight that is delayed or cancelled, that somehow, miraculously, the technical fault has been righted, the missing cabin crew have materialised and the tiny window in the crowded sky that allows one plane from thousands to depart or land has remained open just long enough—

'That's us they're calling, I think,' says Lionel in a half-whisper, as though trying not to alert the rest of the passengers bound for England. 'I'm sure she said Gatwick.' He cranes around to peer at the departures board, which is just too far away to allow him to make out which plane is now boarding. 'Shall we make a move?'

Reluctant to relinquish their seats in case he is mistaken, Hester hesitates. No point rushing anyway; in accordance with her usual thrift, she had refused to countenance paying for priority boarding. The public address system booms suddenly with another announcement, clearly mentioning their flight number and destination this time.

She nudges Harriet. 'Looks like we're in luck. Let's make a move. Lionel?'

They gather their belongings while a fair number of those standing disconsolately around them eye up their chances of securing their vacated seats and begin edging their way towards the trio as surreptitiously as they can.

By the time they reach the back of the queue, Harriet has her nose buried in her Kindle once more; either she has downloaded an exceptionally engrossing novel or she is avoiding conversation. Hester suspects the latter.

As they shuffle painfully slowly towards the departure gate, she is once more aware of an anxious Lionel at her shoulder, desperate to conduct a sotto voce conversation as the chances of their promised tête-à-tête diminish.

'Hester, my dear, I was hoping we might—'

'Let me just find my passport—'

'It's there, on top of your purse.'

'So it is! Couldn't see it for looking.'

'Hester . . . I know this isn't quite the time—'

Hester drops her boarding pass. Lionel scrambles to recover it.

'All fingers and thumbs today,' she says with a feeble laugh.

'Yes. Look, we need to talk.' He flicks a glance at Harriet, apparently oblivious, who may be distracted but whose hearing is acute. He raises his eyebrows. Mouths, 'About . . . you know . . .'

Hester nods. Jerks her head towards her sister. Mouths back, 'Sorry.' She shakes her head regretfully as though at a loss as to how to proceed.

Lionel, exasperated, takes control. Clearing his throat, he says, 'Harriet, forgive me.'

She looks up, around, as though surprised at her surroundings, regards him quizzically.

'Harriet, would you mind awfully if we swapped seats? So I can sit next to Hester on the flight?'

'Oh!' says Hester, confounded by this sudden offensive.

'Oh . . .' says Harriet with a faintly bewildered air, 'I suppose . . .'

'Jolly good,' says Lionel with unusual decisiveness, his face set with a firmness Hester has never witnessed before. 'That's most kind of you. We both appreciate it. Don't we, Hester?'

And Hester, cornered, has no option but to agree that they do.

CHAPTER 49

Chemistry had been—well, he doesn't want to sound overly cocky, but frankly it had been a piece of piss. It was like he was channelling Ralph or something. If he'd written the paper himself, he couldn't have come up with a more favourable choice of questions. Genius, all that advice to think about practical application: it all made sense. Of course, once it was over and the candidates slouched, round-shouldered, claw-handed, out of the examination hall, he'd bitched with the rest of them and moaned for England about the unfairness of the examiners and what a shit paper it had been, but he was doing cartwheels inside and couldn't wait to text his mentor. In fact, he'd do it right now . . .

'Awright?' Jez has crept up on him out of nowhere, Ben having managed to avoid him until now, sitting as far away as possible in the exam.

'Fuck off, Nairstrom.' Ben's thumbs dance over the phone. He turns his back on Jez to prevent him seeing the screen.

'You never answered my texts.'

Is that a tiny note of self-pity in Jez's voice?

'Wonder why that was, dickhead.'

'D'you read them even?'

Yes, that is most definitely a pleading tone he can hear.

'No. Why would I wanna read shit from a shitty shitface whose brain-dead brother trashes my aunts' place?'

'I said I was sorry!'

'Yeah?'

'Yeah!'

'Well, sorry is fuck-all good to me, when the house has been, like, totally wrecked and I have to work all weekend when I should be revising. Still, one good thing: I really know who my mates are now.'

'I'd've helped. Only had to ask.'

'Yeah, right.' Ben starts to move away.

Jez follows him. 'That black tart gave Hedge's goolies a right kicking. Man, has he got his pants in a wad.'

'Good. Except she's not a tart and she happens to be Louisa's sister.'

'No way! That is one mean—'

Ben swings round. 'Don't!'

'What?' Jez looks genuinely bewildered.

'Whatever you were going to say: just don't. I'm warning you. Now piss off.' And with that Ben strides away without a backward glance.

'Wanker!' calls Jez but without much conviction. He waits for Ben to turn back. Ben doesn't.

Ben looks around for Nats at the school bus stop but without success. It's only as the bus pulls into Pellington that he sees her whizz past on her bike. Of course. She cycles everywhere; that's why she's so fit. He dodges this way and that through the disembarking passengers with hurried apologies, yelling, 'Oi, Nats, wait!' and is gratified when she slows to a halt and looks back. For a moment he thinks he sees a faint smile on her lips. He jogs to catch up with her as she climbs off the saddle and starts to wheel her bike towards the lane.

'Wotcha,' he says. Even in school uniform she looks neat, braids caught in a band at the nape of her neck.

'Well?'

He knows she means the exam.

'Yeah. Good.'

'Serious?'

'Pretty fan-fucking-tastic in fact.'

This time a definite smile. 'Cool. So old Ralphie came up with the goods?'

'And some.'

They walk on for a few moments in comfortable silence, until Nats breaks it. 'Any word from Finbar?'

'Nah. Still, no mobile so . . .'

'Fingers crossed, yeah? You nervous? About the house?'

'You kidding? I'm shitting myself. They may be old but they're not batty. Or blind.'

Nats gives a theatrical groan.

That reminds him. 'This play you're in. What is it?'

'*A Doll's House*.'

He nods; he hasn't a clue. Nats regards him pityingly. 'Ibsen. About a woman who breaks out of a conventional marriage. Leaves her children. Very shocking.'

'Yeah?' Most of his friends' parents are divorced.

'At the time, dolt. Late nineteenth century. Early stirrings of feminism, Miss Rogers says.'

This doesn't surprise Ben; most of the boys have the drama teacher pegged as a weirdo, possibly lesbian. He thinks it wise not to divulge this to Nats.

'Got a big part, have you?'

Nats grins. 'Only the lead. Nora.' When Ben doesn't respond she says with exasperation, 'It's a big deal. I'm playing a Scandinavian, Ben! Guess what colour they generally were. And are.'

'Oh, right,' says Ben, flummoxed. What's she getting so wound up about?

'Colour-blind casting, Miss Rogers calls it. Can't believe my luck, having a teacher like her, giving me such an opportunity.' She looks as though she might be settling into a lengthy lecture when they round the final bend in the lane to find Daria anxiously peering out of The Laurels' sitting room window. She dashes out on to the path to meet them, brow furrowed.

'Quick! Quick!'

Nats and Ben start running.

⌣⌣⌣

'I thought there was a fire,' grumbles Ben, having assured himself The Laurels is still intact.

'Idiot boy!' cries Daria. 'Not fire. Smell!'

Nats sniffs again, screws up her nose. 'It's pretty gross, isn't it?'

'Is terrible!' wails Daria, moving a startled Milo out of reach of the rubbish bin. 'Worse than Finbar! I send Artem out to buy . . .' She waves her hand around.

'Air fresheners?'

'*Tak*. But he is saying, no, they are horrible. They will know. But this; this is . . .' She flaps her hand in front of her nose. 'And then he leaves for airport. I try boiling up borscht but still this terrible smell.'

She's right: the pungent, oily odour of varnish has permeated the entire house. Ben and Nats look at one another; the same thought strikes them simultaneously.

'Curry.'

'Look, they love curry,' insists Ben as Daria's face darkens at the perceived slight to her own cooking. 'We can say we thought you'd be, like, fed up with Italian food, pasta and that, so we've done you an international meal, Polish and Indian.'

'Belarusian,' corrects Daria sternly.

'Okay, Belarusian, whatevs. I'll nip out to the village shop, see what I can find.'

'Why don't I go?' says Nats. 'On the bike. Much quicker. You start grinding spices or whatever. Do the onions and that.' She extracts a little notebook from her backpack. 'What am I buying?'

Ben rattles off a list of ingredients that she obediently writes down. He dashes to the larder, calling over his shoulder, 'Hang on.' He emerges with a bag of sugar. 'Great. I'll do crème caramel too with caramelised orange peel. So one orange too, firm as possible.' She adds that to the list.

'Do we really need a pudding?'

'For Aunt Harriet? You bet. Plus, burnt sugar is a really strong smell. So's sugared orange peel. That plus the curry—'

'Okay,' says Nats, convinced. 'I'm off.'

'Oh God,' says Ben. 'Money. I haven't got—'

'Sorted.' She disappears.

Ben sets to with pestle and mortar, preparing the curry paste, then chops his onions. In no time at all the kitchen is filled with the tantalising aroma of exotic spices frying in oil. 'Open the door into the hall, Daria, will you?'

The smell starts to creep through the house, overlaying the varnish. When Nats returns twenty or so minutes later, laden with the groceries, she bounds in with a cry of triumph. 'Result! Smells like an Indian takeaway now. Here you go.'

Daria looks up at the kitchen clock anxiously. 'It will be ready? Before they are returning?'

'All good,' says Ben, swiftly slipping the chicken breasts into the bubbling sauce. 'Bish bosh, get this lot going and then leave it to simmer while I finish off the pud.'

Nats, in the throes of making tea, says, 'Just wish we knew where Finbar was. Did he say which train he was catching?'

'The ten o'clock,' says a welcome voice from the garden door. 'What delicious bouquet assails my senses? Do I detect a hint of garam masala?'

'Finbar!' cries Daria delightedly, only just stopping herself in time from hugging the dishevelled old man, cloaked once more in his habitual aroma. Somehow he has contrived in a few short days to undo all the improvements in his emanations that her crafty washing of his jacket had achieved.

Ben reflects that all they needed to have done was to install Finbar in the hall on the aunts' return to entirely mask the smell of varnish. Nevertheless, he's as pleased as the two girls to see the old boy safely returned and even more pleased to see him clutching a large and extremely well-wrapped parcel. He turns down the heat under the curry and continues with his preparations, listening in as Finbar, already in full flow, gently lowers his load onto the kitchen table.

'. . . extraordinary,' the old man is saying as his grimy fingernails start picking at the string. 'I had an entire block of four seats to myself. All the way to Edinburgh! I think perhaps there was something wrong with the other seats because no sooner had people sat down than they moved elsewhere. Still, I had plenty of legroom.'

The string is proving surprisingly resistant to his efforts. Ben hands Daria the kitchen scissors.

'Anyway, all went remarkably smoothly yesterday. I must say, these modern trains are a revelation! We arrived exactly on time, I alighted and set off for my destination. My new friend in the New Town— what a pleasing synergy that description has!—had given me the most precise directions, which I followed slavishly without mishap.'

Ben pops the bain-marie containing the crème caramel in the oven and joins them at the table, where Daria has started to unpeel layer upon layer of bubble wrap, until a bored Milo seizes a length of string dangling over the edge and almost pulls the precious parcel onto the floor.

Daria snatches up the figurine, Nats snatches up the foiled and frustrated baby, and with Finbar not even pausing in his narrative, they all move into the carpeted sitting room, where Daria kneels at the coffee table to continue her task in relatively greater security.

'I will confess to a little weakness on my part, however, during my Scottish sojourn. One reads the most salacious things about our northern cousins and I must admit I had always believed the fried Mars Bar to be an urban myth. Imagine my wonderment, then, on walking down Broughton Street in the gloaming to see a fish-and-chip shop advertising said delicacy. I felt it my bounden duty to try one and I can report that they are astonishingly tasty, especially if one has a sweet tooth. A very sweet tooth.

'But I digress. I reached my destination, introduced myself to the vendor and found all to be in order, although I will own to a little disappointment that he invited me no further than the hall. Nevertheless, our transaction was conducted with admirable celerity and civility and within five minutes I found myself possessed of the coveted prize and on my way back to Waverley Station. Now, it seemed to me a heinous oversight to visit Auld Reekie and not pay my respects to Sir Walter and his faithful hound Maida and, there being no further trains that night, I thought what could be a more delightful extension to my little adventure than to bed down at the feet of the great man in Princes Street Gardens?'

Daria has finally unveiled the shepherdess to assorted sighs of delight and relief.

'Ah, there she is! Home at last! Daria, my dear, whatever is the matter?'

For Daria is staring horror-struck at the figurine, standing so winsomely on the coffee table with her trademark smirk.

'What is it?' says Ben, looking from Daria to the shepherdess and back again. The figure looks just like the one that he remembers from many a visit to the aunts.

'Look . . .' she whispers, pointing. 'Look at the shoes.'

They all look. Two neat pumps with china bows.

'Two bows.' She fashions their shape in the air.

'So?' says Nats.

'Hester and Harriet, their lady, she has lost a bow. Broken. Not by me,' Daria adds swiftly.

'Shit,' says Ben, his elation evaporating.

Finbar steps back in a swirl of BO. 'We'll simply have to knock one off.'

'No!' gasps Daria.

'We might break the whole shoe off, the whole foot,' says Nats. 'The entire thing might shatter.'

All four of them chip in with suggestions involving increasing degrees of risk.

Ben checks his phone. 'They'll be here in a minute. We have to do something!'

Milo, unregarded at the feet of the agitated adults, considers the pretty lady abandoned on the coffee table. The shepherdess, all seven inches of eye-wateringly expensive bone china, represents to Milo not a valuable collector's item but an intriguing new toy, something unfamiliar to explore with his mouth or test for its percussive qualities. One eager hand strains towards her, but the alluring prize is just out of reach. He settles back on his padded bottom, momentarily thwarted.

The shepherdess simpers; Milo lusts, apparently impotent. He reaches up to find the edge of the coffee table with two chubby hands, grips tightly, steadies his vast nappy-swathed bottom, and heaves; inch by painfully slow inch, he hauls himself upright. Were the shepherdess not calling her siren song, he might well have crowed his triumph and attracted attention, but all his thoughts are focused on the lovely shepherdess, smiling at him so coyly, so invitingly. He shuffles two precarious steps and, teetering alarmingly, lets go of the coffee table with his right hand and reaches out to grab the figurine's fragile neck. And before the horrified and belatedly alerted adults can intervene, he stumbles, sending the shepherdess skittering across the table to tumble over the opposite edge.

There is a tiny terrible silence then pandemonium erupts. Milo bursts into noisy furious sobs and thumps down on the carpet, Ben scuttles around to retrieve the shepherdess and Harriet's old jalopy coughs its way to a shuddering halt outside.

'Quick,' hisses Nats, 'shove the sodding thing up at the back of the shelf!'

Daria scoops up her wailing child and hurries to the front door.

Ben, about to do Nats' bidding, stops with his hand halfway to the shelf. 'Well, fuck me. Look.'

Nats and Finbar hurry over to join him. One china bow has been neatly sheared off its shoe.

'*Mirabile visu!*' The old man beams. 'That boy will go far.'

Ben shoves the figurine into the far corner as a commotion in the hallway draws their attention. The aunts' familiar voices ring out.

'Oh, how lovely to be home!' cries Harriet.

'What is that *smell*?' demands Hester.

CHAPTER 50

'An inspired choice,' says Hester, as they all crowd around the kitchen table.

'Yeah?' Ben is trying to enjoy his curry (maybe a touch more cumin next time?), which miraculously has stretched to seven helpings (including a Tupperware serving for Finbar, who had scooted off as quickly as he could once it was dished out), but is still on tenterhooks about the house. So far the aunts appear to have noticed nothing amiss, presumably having been overwhelmed by the size of the welcoming committee. Nats had inevitably excited barely contained curiosity and Aunt Harriet is stealing sly glances at her as she eats. He notices how uncharacteristically quiet his aunt is.

'Making curry,' explains Hester, tucking in with gusto. 'God knows we've had some spectacular food over the last week—not to mention the wine—but there's absolutely nothing quite like a good old curry, is there?' She adds hurriedly, in case Daria should be offended, 'And borscht, of course. Mustn't forget the delicious borscht.'

Daria glows with pleasure. Milo, sitting on her lap gnawing on a rusk, is eyeing the last forkfuls of her chicken hopefully. 'Milo is missing you so much,' she says as Harriet offers the forefinger of her free hand to distract him.

Harriet's heart swells: how she has missed the little darling, too.

''Course,' says Ben, still slightly miffed at the promiscuity of Milo's affections, 'he's got a new favourite now.'

'Oh, really?' says Hester, with the merest hint of frost. She eyes her quasi-grandson critically.

'Oh yes!' gushes Daria. 'Natalie. Milo loves Natalie!' Oblivious to the resentment brewing in several breasts, she adds, 'And Barry, of course. He is new friend also.'

'Indeed?' The iciness is indisputable now. A week away and the child appears to have acquired a whole new set of acquaintances! 'And who, pray, is Barry?'

Too late, Daria sees the abyss yawning before her. 'Ah . . . he is . . . friend of Artem,' she stammers lamely, appealing silently to her brother for assistance.

Artem, a mouthful of spices and meat awaiting mastication, chokes slightly and, eyes watering, volunteers the intelligence that Barry is an occasional colleague.

'Indeed?' Hester is clearly unsatisfied with the response. 'In what capacity? And how did he come to meet Milo?'

'Oh . . .' Artem, unused to prevarication, flounders. 'He came in for a cup of tea. We were mending . . . yes, mending—'

'A fence, wasn't it, Artem?' Nats leaps into the fray, antennae twitching. Ben never said how forbidding the tall, skinny aunt was. The plump one seems a poppet.

'Yes! A fence. He came round to the cottage. After work. One day.'

'For a cup of tea?' Hester manages to make it sound extremely unlikely, if not unsavoury.

'And *kulduny*,' offers Daria, as though this will ameliorate the tension.

It doesn't.

So, thinks Hester, *feet under the table already, if this Barry creature is invited to sample Daria's cooking. Must be a fast mover.* She notes Daria's heightened colour and tenses. *Oho, so that's the way the wind is blowing, is it?*

357

'Had chemistry today,' Ben butts in, swiftly gathering up the plates with Nats' assistance.

'Oh, Ben! Of course,' says Harriet, emerging from her trance. 'How dreadful of us! We didn't even ask. How did it go?'

'Good, yeah.'

'Better than good, you said.' Nats grins.

What an enchanting smile, thinks Harriet. *And that extraordinary hair!*

Hester, seeing Ben duck his head sheepishly and redden slightly at the girl's intervention, thinks again, *Oho!* What on earth has been going on in their absence? First Daria and now—

'Had some help; well, quite a lot of help,' explains Ben, testing the temperature of the crème caramel dish. Ideally, he'd have refrigerated it for a couple of hours but it'll have to do.

Harriet looks questioningly over to where he stands at the counter. Hester, scenting intrigue, inspects the black girl: surely not? She looks even younger than her nephew.

'Yeah, this bloke Ralph—'

Ralph? thinks Hester testily. *How many more of them?*

'Very nice man,' interrupts Daria.

'Son of Dad's boss. He, like, tutored me. Tell you something, first time any of it's made any sense.'

'That's excellent, Ben!' says Harriet. 'What good fortune that your father has the connection.'

The atmosphere eases a fraction. Ben, with apologies for its sloppy consistency, dishes up the pudding. Everyone grabs a spoon and digs in. Everyone except Hester, who regards the creamy blob in her bowl critically. 'This needs a spell in the fridge. It's not really set, I'm afraid, Ben.'

'Hetty!' says Harriet indignantly. 'He's rushed over straight from school—after an *exam*!—to cook us a lovely welcome-home meal! Honestly! I think it's delicious, Ben dear. Thank you.' She glowers at her sister, exasperated by her ingratitude. For heaven's sake, they've only just got things back to normal after the ghastliness of the last few days, not to mention the edgy weeks that preceded their trip to Italy. She's tired, anxious about tomorrow and the horrible intelligence she is harbouring; the last thing she needs right now is Hester finding fault with everything and everyone.

'. . . good time?' Ben's voice drags her back. He's appealing to both of them, but especially Aunt Hester, who, aware that she is indisputably in the wrong, is filled with self-reproach and looking like thunder; anyone unacquainted with her temperament would assume her to be sulking. As indeed Nats, outraged on Ben's behalf, does. 'How was the Riccardi bloke? I know he can cook, but what's he like? Looks a right bastard on the telly. Really full of himself.' He glances over and mouths, 'Sorry,' to a frowning Daria.

Harriet looks at her sister. Waits. Silence. Everyone shuffles uncomfortably on their chairs. Really, she can be the most provoking woman on the planet! She doesn't even appear to have heard the question.

'I think he could be somewhat unpredictable at times, but your aunt had the most marvellous time,' Harriet says. 'Tiring, though. The course, I mean. Quite exhausting, in fact. He worked them extremely hard.' She wonders why she is always the one to make excuses for Hester. Whom, she notes, is now managing to force down the pudding she had so cavalierly condemned seconds before; a pudding of which she, Harriet, would gladly have had second helpings had there been any.

Hester, meanwhile, mechanically spooning crème caramel into her mouth, is mired in her own miserable thoughts. The excitement of getting home, the warmth and bustle of the welcome, the commotion of getting everyone seated had, for a blessed spell, distracted her from the elephant lodged firmly in the corner of her mind ever since they left the airport. In fact, ever since she and Lionel, with Harriet standing tactfully a few yards away, ostensibly out of earshot, had parted in the baggage reclaim area, where, to her intense but guilty relief, Lionel had still been waiting for his suitcase when theirs had already been disgorged onto the carousel.

'Artem will be waiting for us. We must dash.'

'But, Hester—'

'I'm sorry, Lionel, we'll speak tomorrow.'

'But, Hester—'

'Sorry about dropping off on the plane. I know you wanted to . . . We'll talk tomorrow, I promise.'

'But when, Hetty? When?'

'First thing.' His face had brightened, eyes shining with hope. 'No, sorry, evening. I'm going with Harry to see . . . you know, about Stephen. I'll . . .' *Oh God, this is horrible.* 'Yes, I'll . . . soon as we get back.' Darting forward. Clash of glasses. A maladroit kiss, just missing his lips. 'Sorry, sorry.'

'I love you, Hetty.' Forlorn, barely audible.

'Yes. Bye. Sorry.'

The elephant is wide awake now, trampling around and trumpeting loudly, demanding attention. What she really wants is to settle down and talk things through with someone she can trust, someone who will understand and help her make sense of her muddled emotions. Harriet. She wishes their guests gone, the conversation silenced, the house theirs once more; knows even as she wishes it what an ungrateful wretch she is.

'Lovely, Ben,' she says, scraping the last of the barely tasted caramel out of her bowl. 'In a day or so, I promise to tell you all about Signor Riccardi. Quite a character, believe me! And, my Lord, so talented.'

'Yeah?' says Ben eagerly, glad to have Aunt Hester back in the conversation and to be, it appears, restored to her good books. 'Did he do all that stuff with—'

'Ben, dear,' says Harriet gently, 'we're both pretty whacked. Would you mind awfully . . .'

''Course, 'course,' says Ben hurriedly, as Nats leaps up to clear the table. 'We'll just load the dishwasher and get going.'

'Sorry,' say the sisters in concert, getting up themselves.

The party breaks up instantly with universal relief; there's something out of kilter about everything, everyone on edge. The visitors swiftly tidy the kitchen despite Hester and Harriet's protestations, and within minutes everyone is trooping to the front door, Milo waving goodbye frantically over his mother's shoulder.

'House is clean,' says Daria, buckling him into his buggy. 'Sheets changed.'

'Daria, you shouldn't have!' says Harriet, revelling in anticipation of sinking into her own fresh and sweet-smelling bed.

Daria shrugs dismissively. 'Please! I like to clean.'

This is something the sisters will never understand.

'The tank is full,' says Artem, handing over the keys. 'Oh, and that knocking noise?'

Which one? thinks Harriet, but nods.

'Barry took a look and has fixed it.'

Has he indeed, thinks Hester.

'How kind!' says Harriet. 'Oh, very nice to meet you, Natalie. I never asked: are you in Ben's year?'

'The year below.'

'Well, I very much hope we'll see you again.'

Ben glows inside; at least Aunt Harriet has taken to Nats. He's not at all sure about Aunt Hester. She's been really *weird* all evening. But, weird or not, she's made no comment about the house or the smell. Maybe they've got away with it. A weight drops from his shoulders.

Nats musses Milo's hair and blows him a kiss, then retrieves her bike. She straps on her helmet.

'Walk you to the road?' says Ben.

'Sure. You getting the bus?'

'I guess.'

'God!' says Nats, once they're out of earshot of Daria and Artem, who are still making their farewells. 'Harriet's lovely but that Hester! Is she always such a grump? Talk about jealous!'

It's Ben's instinct to leap to his relative's defence, except that it's hard to find any excuse for his aunt's peevishness.

'Yeah. Know what you mean. She's like that sometimes. Worse even.'

'Worse?! She couldn't have been more rude if she'd tried.'

'Oh, trust me,' says Ben with feeling. 'She could.'

Nats flings one leg over her bike and gets ready to cycle away.

Suddenly, Ben finds himself saying, 'You fancy going out at the weekend? Movies or something?'

She takes her foot off the pedal and stands in the lane on tiptoe, steadying the bike under herself, staring straight ahead. For a moment Ben thinks she hasn't heard him, then, worse, that she's trying to find a way to say no.

There is a very long silence during which Ben, panicking, thinks: *I should have kept my stupid mouth shut. What the fuck was I thinking?* Then Nats climbs off the saddle, wheels the bike as close to him as she possibly can without actually running over his shoes and looks up at him towering over her. 'Are you asking me out?'

Ben, uncomfortably aware of his spots at such close quarters, is cornered. Thank fuck Artem and Daria will be walking the other way. He pulls back, squirming inside, and affects as nonchalant a tone as he can muster. 'S'pose. Yeah.'

Nats nods, then removes her glasses, her myopic eyes widening.

Oh Jeez . . .

'Out, as in boyfriend and girlfriend?'

He gulps. This sounds serious. 'Well, yeah . . .'

She searches his face for a few agonising seconds. 'Okay.' It comes out flat, neutral.

'Really . . .?' stammers Ben, floored. Astounded. Terrified.

Nats skewers him with her intense gaze. 'There are conditions.'

'Okay . . .' What now?

Nats inhales deeply then starts. Her voice is just the tiniest bit wobbly initially but strengthens as she gets into her stride. 'First, what happens in our relationship stays in our relationship.'

Ben goes to speak, realises there is more to come, shuts his mouth abruptly.

'Neither of us at any point, no matter what the provocation, no matter how pissed or out of it we might be—' *Pissed?* thinks Ben. *You? Seriously?*—'ever divulges anything personal about our relationship. No little quirks, no little anecdotes, nothing. It's private. Second, neither of us, either during or after we are . . .' she hesitates, selects the words carefully, 'seeing each other, ever disses or badmouths one another. We show respect and decency towards one another at all times.'

She doesn't wait for him to respond. 'Third, in the stratospherically unlikely situation that one of us ever comes into possession of an image that shows the other in a compromising, pornographic or simply less than flattering light, we will never upload it to Twitter or Facebook or Tumblr or Instagram or their successors, no matter how tempting the prospect might be.

'Fourth, should, as is more than probable, the relationship prove to be more than a passing whim, and we progress in time to intercourse, we will ensure precautions are taken and we will be respectful of each other's feelings and at no stage feel pressured into doing anything with which we are unhappy or uncomfortable.

'Fifth, and finally, when our relationship implodes, as statistically it is likely to, given our youth and inexperience, whatever the hopes we may currently entertain for it, we will terminate it in a proper manner, face to face, not by unfollowing each other on Twitter or unfriending one another on Facebook, or texting or announcing the split on any type of social media. Deal?'

Chin aloft combatively, Nats stops; Ben realises a response is at last required.

'Er . . . yeah. Wow. Deal.'

CHAPTER 51

'Gosh,' says Harriet, easing her behind into her capacious old armchair and letting her muscles relax, 'we go away for five minutes and look what happens!'

Hester grunts as she places a cup of tea beside her sister. She crosses to her own chair and sinks into it, head back, eyes closed.

'You all right?' says Harriet.

'Fine.'

'What is it?'

'What?'

'Whatever's bothering you.'

'Nothing's bothering me.'

'Oh, come on! You virtually bit poor Ben's head off over supper.'

Hester appears to ignore the criticism but in truth it cuts deep because she knows it's deserved; she gets up abruptly and disappears into the hall.

Harriet calls after her, 'And that nice little friend of his. Natalie. Barely spoke to her.'

Hester returns with a pile of post. A sizeable pile of post with a number of bulky envelopes. She starts to sort the letters and packages into two piles, one either side of the coffee table. Harriet's soon towers over Hester's, mainly thick, oversized envelopes. Her heart sinks. She'd forgotten all about them. Oh Lord . . .

'I think we need to have a chat, don't you?' says Hester over her shoulder, hurrying out of the room a second time.

Flouncing, thinks Harriet. She wills her racing heart to slow: anyone would think *she* was in the wrong.

Hester returns with half a bottle of red and two glasses; she pauses in the doorway and sniffs. She sniffs again.

'What?'

Hester wrinkles her nose. 'Can you smell something? Like nail varnish?'

'Nail varnish? No.'

Shrugging, Hester resumes her seat. 'Must be the spray polish Daria uses.' She reflects that the only time Mr Sheen is much in evidence is when Daria tries to restore order and cleanliness to The Laurels, usually when its owners are absent. Perhaps she's just forgotten how pungent it smells. She pours two generous glasses of wine, nudges one across the table, then, peering intently into her glass so as to avoid Harriet's eye, says with a nod at the envelopes, 'What's going on?' Did Harriet but know it, Hester's heart is dancing an uncomfortably lively jig too.

'Oh, Hetty . . .' says Harriet, a world of hurt and misunderstandings in those two little words.

They both swallow hard, thinking simultaneously how ridiculously hard it so often is to be brutally honest with one's nearest and dearest. Both women, to varying degrees and depending on the subject matter, will wade fearlessly into difficult and uncomfortable territory with friends and acquaintances but faced with the prospect of disclosing their inmost thoughts to one another will prevaricate, shilly-shally and tiptoe around each other's sensitivities for ages. Except that today both recognise that a decision point in their lives has been reached and on this occasion there is nowhere to hide.

'Harry,' says Hester, lowered eyes glittering, 'you know I'd never do anything to hurt you . . .' Anticipating Harriet's scepticism she adds quickly, 'Not intentionally. You know that, don't you?'

Harriet, for all that she longs to regain her old camaraderie with her sister, finds herself instantly recalling the events of the past week, not least Hester's duplicity over Stephen's letter, never mind the prickly weeks that preceded their trip to Italy. She tries valiantly to set her continuing rancour aside but it has been suppressed for too long and now it bubbles up and out. 'But you have hurt me, Hetty. A great deal. You've kept things from me. Gone behind my back. And I'm not just talking about Stephen. When were you going to tell me about Lionel? Because he's asked you to marry him, hasn't he? Or at least move in together?'

Hester, not having anticipated quite such a frontal assault, or at least not quite so soon, recoils and immediately goes on the offensive herself. 'I would have told you sooner had you not got yourself caught up in all that ghastliness with Mary. I hardly thought it was the time or place to discuss matters of the heart while you were embroiled in all that. Be reasonable!'

'Reasonable! I've been nothing but reasonable since you became besotted with a chap you'd only met five minutes earlier but whom you nevertheless confided in—'

'Besotted? I am not besotted—'

'Telling him all sorts of private details about me—'

'I was worried!'

'Not worried enough to tell me about it! Instead of which, you put poor Stephen through absolute hell—and me, come to that—leaping to assumptions and leaving me to make amends to him! God knows the last thing I want to do is go traipsing all the way to Devon tomorrow.'

'I told you I'd go with you. And I've already said sorry. What more do you want?'

Glaring at Hester's hurt face, all Harriet's pent-up grievances spill out like lava scorching down a mountainside. 'And then you have the brass neck to challenge me about looking into my options when you start making plans behind my back to set up a ménage à trois without so much as a by-your-leave. What did you expect me to do? Move into one of the garden sheds?'

Hester, who truth be told had fleetingly entertained ideas of them building an annexe in the garden—a really *luxurious* annexe, with power showers and Italian ceramic tiles—for Harriet, knowing how much she values her privacy, before dismissing it as madness, blushes furiously.

Her sister reads the reaction as anger and counters accordingly. 'Did you seriously expect me to welcome Lionel here with open arms? Into our home? Someone you've known for precisely a week?'

Ten minutes earlier, Hester would have been more than happy— would have been so relieved—to talk through her dilemma with Harriet, to explain that she likes Lionel a great deal, that she never expected to find herself in this situation (carefully avoiding any reference to her ill-judged weakness for Teddy Wilson), that everything has happened with alarming speed, and on the one hand she is terrified that she will commit herself to an uncertain future with a virtual stranger, and on the other hand that she may throw away a final chance of love before age and possible decrepitude overwhelm her. But in those intervening ten minutes Harriet has hurled accusations at her, berated her, thrown her apology—her heartfelt apology—back in her face and made the ridiculous suggestion that she would be relegated to a kennel in the garden. Hester finds herself cornered and that is never a good position for her, since the only way she knows how to respond is to come out fighting.

As she does now.

But she chooses her tactics with care. Instead of reacting with outrage and vituperation, like her sister, Hester opts for the quietly dignified approach. Calm but firm. She knows how it irritates Harriet when she refuses to engage on her terms.

'Eight days actually. Look, I can see that you're upset, Harry, and I hesitate to give further offence, but I'd really appreciate you telling me what exactly you have against Lionel.'

Harriet decodes her sister's salvo as an oblique accusation of volatility and a question disguised as genuine bewilderment designed to trick her into saying something that will ever after be used to reproach her. She has in her armoury one devastating weapon, but for the moment she chooses not to unleash it. Instead, she takes a deep breath, steadies herself and deploys the tried and tested technique of batting the question back.

'This isn't really about Lionel, Hetty, is it? It's about us.'

'Oh?' Hester can see how Harriet wants to play this, but she's damned if she'll make it easy for her. She empties the last dregs of the wine into their glasses, dividing it with scrupulous fairness.

'You know it is. Have you decided you no longer wish us to share our lives?'

She could have said 'live together'. She could have said 'share this house'. But she fancies her choice of words sounds more weighty.

'No!' cries Hester, realising even as the response leaps automatically from her lips that she means it. Very, very much. Suddenly she's on the back foot—how did that happen?—trying to reconcile two apparently diametrically opposed choices. 'Of course not! Oh, Harry, it's not a case of either or . . . it's just . . . it's just . . .'

Harriet can't ever recall seeing her sister quite so lost for words. It's her chance to be facilitative. Gracious, even.

So, more gently: 'I don't want to deny you a chance of happiness, Hetty, honestly I don't, and if I have to move out—'

'No, no!' Hester is in an agony of guilt.

'—if it comes to that, so be it.' *Please, please, don't let it*, she prays silently with a sudden lurch of fear. 'I just want to understand: what's so special about Lionel? Apart,' she adds swiftly lest that sound too critical and personal, 'from the fact that he clearly adores you.'

Hester, cantankerous, formidable Hester, softens. Then flounders. 'He's very . . . kind,' she manages after some thought, conscious of how mealy-mouthed it sounds.

Harriet pounces, but with good humour, intending to signal a shift to less confrontational ground. 'I grant you that, but so is my dentist and I wouldn't marry him.'

'There are worse things—'

'Or live with him. My dentist, that is.' Harriet smiles. The smile fades apologetically. 'Sorry. Didn't mean to be flippant. Look, Hetty, I hesitate to ask for fear of giving offence, but I must: what precisely do you have in common?'

Hester, still flustered, opts for the obvious. 'Food?' She regrets it the instant she says it.

Harriet's roll of the eyes confirms her misjudgement. 'Food? You know what they say about too many cooks. Look at the fuss you make when you have to share the kitchen with Ben.'

'I do not make a fuss!'

Harriet gives her sister a mordant look. 'If that's you not making a fuss, God help him when you do.'

Hester sniffs. 'Face it, Harriet, for whatever reason, you've taken against him. Poor man, I've no idea what he's done to deserve your disapproval. Mark you, let's not forget, you do have form in that regard.' *Oh hell*, wails Hester inside the instant the words emerge, *whatever possessed me to open that particular can of worms?*

Ice descends instantly. 'I beg your pardon?'

'Forget it. I'm sorry.'

'No, no, please.' Harriet's mouth tightens. 'I seem to recall that the last time you had a . . . let's call it a *tendresse* . . . for someone—' Teddy Wilson lours over them both '—we ended up in the most unholy mess. And plastered all over the papers.'

'I wasn't alone in being taken in,' says Hester hotly. 'Everybody in the village . . . and it was only the local papers . . .' She tails off as Harriet raises a sceptical eyebrow and Hester judges it wise to move on. But while she may change tack, her resentment remains. If anything, it increases. 'Be that as it may, I think you at least owe me the courtesy of an explanation as to why you have taken against Lionel so violently. He has been unfailingly kind and supportive through what I would be the first to accept has been a terrible and torrid time for you, but I'd love to know precisely why—aside from jealousy, which frankly is the only reason I can come up with, apart from sheer bloody-mindedness, snobbery and a dog-in-the-manger attitude—you find him as unacceptable as you clearly do.'

Harriet, stung by Hester's unjust accusations—snobbery? That's rich coming from her!—and trying to fathom whether her sister really is seriously suggesting she might want Lionel for herself—imagine!—does as she is bid. And tells her.

CHAPTER 52

Harriet half-heartedly sifts through the glossy brochures, their pages bloated with superlatives and impossible camera angles, while straining to hear the conversation in the kitchen. For once she has no compunction about eavesdropping; things have reached such a pass with Hester this evening that earwigging seems the least of it. The look on Hester's face when Harriet had imparted to her what she had gleaned while surfing the internet will long remain with her. Half of her feels she has discharged a necessary duty; the other half feels a complete heel. *Well, he shouldn't have tried to deceive her,* she thinks in self-justification. *Better she knows the worst now rather than—*

The sitting room door bursts open, startling her, as Hester enters and makes for her armchair. Harriet hurriedly covers the pile of house particulars with her paper, aware that her attempted subterfuge has not gone unnoticed. Hester, she sees with alarm, has a bottle of brandy in her hand. This does not bode well. Brandy is for crises. She waits for her sister to speak, the worm of self-reproach still squirming inside. She knows that she should not have dropped her bombshell in temper; it smacks of spite. She should have been rational, measured . . . God knows, she should have been a lot of things . . .

Hester pours two over-generous measures of brandy into their unwashed wine glasses, a solecism that almost makes Harriet cry out. She smothers her astonishment in a cough. Tentatively she reaches for her glass and imbibes a huge swig. Hester does likewise, then picks up her knitting and sets to at a cracking pace, the needles clattering like typewriter keys.

Harriet can bear it no longer. 'Well?'

'Sorry?' Hester knocks her glasses down from their nest in her hair and shoves them into position. Behind the lenses, she looks less vulnerable, more ready for a fight, despite the pretended incomprehension.

Harriet grits her teeth and presses on. 'Did you get hold of him?'

'Yes.' Hester addresses herself once more to her knitting.

Harriet, perfectly aware that Hester does not need to look at what her needles are doing, indeed is capable of knitting, watching the television and reading a book simultaneously, feels her temper beginning to fray again. No, she will not let Hester rile her, nor make her feel guilty, not this time. She perseveres, taking a casual sip of brandy. 'And what did he say?'

'He's coming down tomorrow.'

Harriet almost chokes. 'You've invited him down here. In spite of . . . after what I told you? What . . .? Why . . .? Is he denying it?'

Harriet does not deign to look at her. She says coldly, 'I haven't yet asked him. I prefer to face these sorts of . . . unpleasantnesses head on.'

You hypocrite! thinks Harriet.

'I thought I owed him at least that. It was hardly the sort of conversation to have on the phone.'

'Right.' Harriet digests the response. 'Did you give him any—'

'No.' Hester has finished her brandy and pours herself another. She waves the bottle vaguely in Harriet's direction, who holds up a hand in refusal.

'I'm driving tomorrow, remember?'

'So you are,' says Hester crisply.

Harriet, the conversation clearly at an end, returns to her crossword. Not a single clue makes the slightest sense.

The sisters sit either side of the hearth quietly seething.

〜〜〜

Hester is still in a state of shock. The grenade Harriet had lobbed into her muddied thoughts not fifteen minutes earlier has shaken her to the core. Beyond the core. She feels in turn angry, humiliated, heartsick and confused. Her first instinct had been to disbelieve Harriet, a reaction that speaks volumes about the sorry pass to which their relationship has come. She would never, ever, have accused her sister of deceit until . . . well, until this past week. Which, she reasons, can mean only one thing. Either, as Harriet is alleging, Lionel has been stringing her along from the start or, possibly worse, Harriet has descended to unspeakable depths in an attempt to wreck Hester's burgeoning romance. Neither interpretation is palatable. Both find her at the mercy of another's machinations, a situation for which a woman of her steely fibre is signally unsuited. She had managed to keep the conversation with Lionel mercifully short by pretending to be so exhausted by their travel she was en route to bed. So thrilled had he been at the prospect of seeing her the following day that he had not questioned the urgency. 'Yes, yes, of course, my dear, I'll be down as soon as I can. I can hardly wait. No, don't worry about directions. Just give me the postcode; I'll use the sat nav. And give my best to Harry, won't you? Now you get yourself off to bed, Hetty dearest. Sweet dreams.' Sick with dread, she imagines what he must be supposing: that she is about to accept his proposal.

For the first time in years, Hester drops a stitch.

⌣⌣⌣

Sitting opposite, Harriet stares blindly at the crossword. She would dearly love another brandy, if only to blunt the edges of her nagging conscience, but dare not risk it: she has a long drive tomorrow—alone now, evidently—and does not want a muzzy head to add to her troubles. But she's worried that she will be out of the house when Lionel visits. Suppose he manages to spin Hetty another pack of lies? Suppose the sudden invitation has alerted him to some potential danger? Now he has all night to concoct a convincing narrative.

For heaven's sake, stop it! she admonishes herself. *Hetty is fore-warned and she's not an idiot. She'll be on her guard. And Lionel Parchment is no Teddy Wilson.* Except he's indubitably a fast worker. She almost has to admire the speed, not to mention the skill, with which he's so comprehensively penetrated Hester's armour and invei-gled himself into her affections. A month ago, or less, she would have scoffed at the possibility of Hester being swept off her feet, would have had nothing but admiration for any man who might have the temerity to try.

Well, there's nothing more I can do now. Hetty's obviously not going to discuss it with me, not in her current mood. And in any event, I've got quite enough on my plate. The thought of her impending meeting—she had been about to say confrontation—with Marion is enough to set her stomach churning again.

⌣⌣

Hester, oblivious to her dropped stitch—a mistake that will cause intense chagrin weeks later when she finds it—knits on, reliving all the conversations she and Lionel had had at the hotel, or as many as she can recall, looking for inconsistencies, for the slightest suspicion of fabrication. If he were simply intent on making a fool of a suscep-tible woman, surely he wouldn't be so eager to see her tomorrow? Or is it a game he plays on holiday: persuading some gullible widow or spinster to fall for him, to make him feel powerful, more of a man? And if that were the case, wouldn't the embarrassment in her room the other evening have severely dented his amour-propre, making him run a mile rather than seek to continue the liaison?

None of it makes sense! she thinks bitterly, shooting a look at Harriet sitting opposite, cool as a cucumber, doing her wretched crossword. Swathed in righteous indignation, Hester thinks: *He must have the chance to explain himself at the very least* ... And fast on the heels of that thought: *I can't bear it if Harriet is right. She'll be gloating for months.* That she might be unfairly attributing her own propensities to her sister does not occur to her.

But what does is a realisation so astonishing that she blurts out unthinkingly, 'Dear God!'

Harriet drops her pencil. 'What is it?'

Hester's face is a picture of almost comical disbelief. 'I've only just realised. You went on the internet! While we were in Italy! That's how you contacted that old friend from uni! And ordered those brochures! And all that stuff about Lionel—you used a computer!'

'Yes. I did.'

'But you don't know how to! You've never used a computer in your life.'

'Well, I have now,' says Harriet tartly. 'It's hardly rocket science, after all. Alfonso showed me how to get online and left me to it.'

'And how many times have I offered to do that?' demands an exasperated Hester, recalling the hours she's spent filling in forms, ordering things online and typing to Harriet's dictation over the years.

'Well, I had you to do it for me before,' says Harriet. 'I could hardly ask you on this occasion, could I? Anyway, I think I'll take this up to bed. Goodnight.'

Hester, dumbstruck, can only stare as Harriet retrieves her pencil and, paper clutched to her bosom, marches from the room. *Flouncing*, thinks Hester.

Both sisters are painfully and privately aware that they have breached one of Mother's unbending maxims: they are without a doubt about to let the sun go down on their mutual wrath.

TUESDAY

CHAPTER 53

'You found us then!' Marion, beaming, bears down on Harriet's car, wellingtons sloshing through a large puddle in front of the back door. Voluminous trousers sag over the tops of the boots, beneath a thick sweater far too big for its wearer and a green padded gilet. Harriet levers herself out of the car, to be enveloped in an angular hug and hustled across towards the farmhouse, unfortunately straight through the muddy water, which splashes over her unsuitable court shoes. A sharp wind whistles through the yard.

'Should have warned you to wear old footwear,' says Marion heartily, with a smoker's cracked chuckle. 'It's always soggy in these parts. Rains like billyo ninety per cent of the year. Oh, and something warm. This place is like a fridge most of the time.'

Harriet, who has dressed in what she classifies as smart but casual—a corduroy skirt, linen blouse and classic navy jacket— lies quickly, 'Oh, I never feel the cold,' as she follows Marion down the chilly hall towards the kitchen, the draught swirling around her ankles.

'Take a seat,' says her hostess, lifting a huge cushion off an ancient Windsor chair, a cushion that unfurls, yowling in protest. Marion drops the cat on the floor, from where it glares at her before slinking off towards the corner nearest to the Aga, which to Harriet's relief is pumping out considerable heat.

'Don't mind cats, do you?' Marion is filling the kettle at the Belfast sink. She erupts again into a throaty laugh that instantly takes Harriet back forty-odd years. 'Hope to Christ not: we've got rather a lot of them.' She looks up and over Harriet's head and lets out a sigh. 'Oi, you two, what are you doing up there? Down you get, you little horrors.'

Harriet swivels around to see a pair of tiny heads peering at her from the top of the enormous Welsh dresser. As Marion marches towards them, the kittens skitter in opposite directions and scramble down from shelf to shelf, miraculously avoiding all of the many plates the dresser displays. Once at ground level, they regroup and hare across the flagstones to hole up under a sideboard. Harriet peers around to discover two other cats curled asleep on chairs dotted round the edges of the vast kitchen.

'Golly,' she says, disconcerted by the unblinking malevolence of the displaced cat eyeing her from the corner, 'you do have quite a few, don't you?'

'Fifty or so, give or take,' says Marion, hovering at the stove. 'At the moment. I've had to start turning them away, except then people just dump them on the doorstep in the middle of the night. But you're all right with them, are you?'

'Er . . . yes,' says Harriet, stunned. 'I mean, no, I like cats. But . . . *fifty*? Do they all live in here?'

Marion erupts, eyes crinkling. 'Are you kidding? Come and see.' She beckons Harriet to join her at the window. Harriet, dying for a coffee, notices she is still holding the kettle that hasn't quite made it onto the hob yet.

They gaze out over a landscape of cages and runs, filled to capacity, as far as Harriet can judge, with cats of all shapes, sizes, ages and breeds.

'Good grief!'

'I know,' says Marion wryly, surveying her domain with something like despair. 'It's an awful responsibility. And getting worse by the day. This is what happens when times get hard. People can't afford to get them spayed, then they can't afford to feed them, and bingo! They end up dumping them on us. Still, better they dump them here than on a motorway. Bastards.'

'Us?' says Harriet.

'Oh . . .' Marion's face clouds instantly. 'Me and Chris.' She tries a brief smile. Averts her eyes.

'Shall I do that?' says Harriet, relieving her of the kettle and swiftly placing it on the Aga. The past floods back: she'd forgotten Marion's propensity for distraction and her apparent inability to do two things at once. 'Where will I find the coffee?'

⌣⌣

A few minutes later they are both seated at the table, nursing strong black coffees. A battered biscuit tin has been retrieved from the larder containing, to Harriet's disappointment, a few rather crumbly Bourbons. 'Don't eat a lot of sweet things,' says Marion by way of apology, pushing the tin across to her guest. 'Or do much cooking these days.'

Oh dear, thinks Harriet, *what about lunch?*

Marion gives her an amused look. 'Don't panic. I went to good old M&S and stocked up yesterday. Wouldn't wish my efforts on my worst enemy.'

Phew, thinks Harriet. 'Well, I barely lift a pan myself. Leave the whole kit and caboodle to Hester. Except the eating, that is, as you can see. That I can manage, only too well. Hester's always nagging me to lose a couple of stone. Perils of ageing, alas—not that you look any different.'

Marion grunts, evidently unconvinced; she turns to look out of the window and Harriet sees that once more she's lost in thought. Or memory. Whatever it is, it's painful. Harriet recognises that flayed look. She takes the opportunity to study Marion's face covertly, searching for any shred of resemblance to Stephen. It's hard to see under the wrinkles: perhaps there's something about the eyes . . .

'So?' says Marion with a brittle smile. 'What's the big mystery? What's dragged you all this way? What is it you couldn't say in an email or on the phone, my dear old chum?'

⌣⌣⌣

'You found us then.' Hester waits at the gate as Lionel unfolds himself from his meticulously maintained pale blue Morris Traveller. In spite of everything that is preoccupying her, she cannot suppress her admiration. 'Gosh! What a beauty. I haven't seen one of these in years.'

Lionel beams his delight. 'Oh! Thanks. My pride and joy.' He pats the bonnet affectionately as he approaches.

Hester angles her face to accept a kiss on the cheek.

He steps back, disconcerted, looking over her shoulder as if expecting to see Harriet waiting behind her.

'She's out for the day.'

'Ah!' His relief is obvious. 'Of course. Gone to see . . .?'

'Marion. You know, Stephen's . . . Yes.' She gestures towards the front door. 'Please . . .'

Looking up at The Laurels' facade and sweeping a glance over the front garden, his face registers appreciation. 'What a delightful house!' He turns back to take in the lane and the fields beyond. 'Quite bucolic. And so peaceful.'

'Well, compared to Greenwich, I dare say.' She forces a laugh. 'Let's go in and I'll make us some coffee. Then we can have a proper chat.'

⌣⌣⌣

Marion is convulsed, the backs of her hands wet with the tears she has been trying unsuccessfully to stem; she lunges across to the counter to grab a roll of kitchen paper and rip off several sheets in which she buries her face, shoulders shaking. Mortified and alarmed, Harriet sits motionless the other side of the table waiting for the paroxysm to pass.

Finally, Marion manages to regain sufficient control to sit back and take some deep, calming gulps of air. Harriet senses, however, that her grasp on her emotions is tenuous in the extreme.

'I'm sorry . . .' she murmurs, wondering why the English spend so much of their lives apologising for others' transgressions. If anyone ought to be contrite—

'Liverpool?' Marion gasps again. She balls the kitchen paper and dabs ferociously at her eyes. 'For God's sake, Liverpool?!'

Harriet gapes at her. Is she *laughing*?

Marion catches her expression and howls afresh, her whole body vibrating as she seeks to staunch the flow of tears, every glance at her visitor's bewildered face seeming to prompt a fresh bout of helpless weeping. She hauls herself to her feet and blindly staggers from the kitchen. Seconds later comes the flush of a cistern.

Harriet waits.

Marion, eyes firmly on the stone floor, slowly returns. Her lips, twitching, seems to have a life of their own. Harriet waits some more. Finally, in barely above a whisper . . .

'Let me get this straight. You think that I got pregnant in my third year and, for reasons I don't fully understand, decided to have the baby in Liverpool—of all unholy places—and give them your name at the hospital? Is that about the size of it?' Marion claps her hand, still clasping the sodden paper towel, over her mouth as though trying not to let anything else out.

'Yes,' says Harriet, as stoutly as she can manage.

'My dear, dear Harriet, are you completely out of your mind?'

⌣⌣⌣

Lionel blindly clatters his cup onto its saucer and stares incredulously at Hester, sitting opposite awaiting his response, her face implacable. Shakily, he places the coffee on the table in front of him, eyes never leaving hers.

'My dear Hester . . .'

He looks a question and Hester, despite her intention to keep her silence, finds herself replying, 'Harriet.'

'Oh . . .' She watches his Adam's apple bob as he swallows. 'But how did she . . .?'

'Electoral roll.'

'Ah.' He couldn't look more guilty if he were an actor playing Man Caught Out In A Lie.

'So?' Her voice sounds grating even to her ears. 'Don't you think you owe me at the very least an explanation?'

An unsteady hand goes up to smooth his hair back as he leans towards her. 'Hester, my dear Hester, I was going to tell you—'

'Spare me the violins, Lionel, please, and just answer the question. Are you or are you not already married?'

'Married? For heaven's sake—'

'So she's just taken your name, has she? This woman you live with? Ruth Parchment?'

～～～

Over the past week Harriet has been through more than any decent woman, any reasonable, law-abiding woman, should be expected to endure, and Marion's derision proves the final straw. She is tired, distraught, angry at herself, at Hester, at the world in general and, at this precise moment, above all others, Marion. Harriet struggles to hang on to the remaining shreds of her temper. Arguments, she knows only too well from long and bitter experience, are won by measured words, by calmness, by logic. Not by losing self-control, by letting fly, by throwing— no, hurling—caution to the four winds. Despite which, she does just that.

All the pent-up fury occasioned by Hester's unjust accusations, the hurt she has unnecessarily caused Stephen, her ill-judged amour and by the unpleasant events surrounding Mary's accident comes to a head and lands squarely on Marion's.

'You think it's funny? You cavalierly abandon your child, you try however ineptly to cover your tracks, to wash your hands of all responsibility and then, when confronted with your betrayal and duplicity—you laugh! You wriggle even more! You know, I used to respect you, Marion: I always admired your uncompromising take on life, the way you spoke your mind and to hell with the consequences! Well, how wrong was I?' The contradictions in what she has just said strike her. 'Or how right!'

'Harriet—'

'Oh, no, I haven't finished!' There's an enormous, choking boulder of anger and resentment pressing on her chest. 'Don't start offering excuses! Are you going to deny saying—and to think we all laughed! *I* laughed—that you would do that very thing if you were ever in that position? Do you?'

'No, I—yes, I—it was a—'

'Shut up!' Harriet can feel her face suffusing with blood as her ire mounts to ever greater heights. 'And now, when the chickens come home to roost and that poor boy—*your son*—when he needs you—not, thank God, in any maternal sense, because that really would be beyond a joke, but because he craves reassurance—you play dumb. What kind of a fool do you take me for?' Before Marion has a chance to reply, she surges on. 'Was it jealousy? About me and Mark? Was that it? Because I used to see you watching us, don't think I didn't. Was it just a way to get back at me—God alone knows why, you were supposed to be my *friend*—because he fancied me, not you?' She has to stop now if only to draw breath.

Marion sees her opportunity and takes it. She's not laughing now.

'If I was watching you, it was nothing to do with Mark, you idiot! Harriet, you have to be the absolute limit! I wasn't watching that beefed-up God's gift of a prize prick—I was watching *you*.'

〜〜〜

'What did you say?' cries Lionel, falling back as though punched. 'Ruth . . .?'

'Yes,' snaps Hester. 'Precisely. Ruth Parchment. When were you intending to drop that particular little bombshell?'

His face shifts, its expression moving from incredulity to something she interprets as relief. It is swiftly replaced by something else: amusement. A smile edges cautiously towards his eyes.

'Ruth Parchment,' he says, almost on a laugh, 'Ruth Parchment isn't my wife.'

Hester jumps in. 'I don't give a tinker's cuss for whatever mealy-mouthed appellation you choose to use: partner, significant other—'

He's actually laughing now. How dare he? 'No, no, you don't understand.'

'You're right there—I don't! How long did you think you could keep this from me?'

He holds up a hand to stop her. She finds herself doing as bid. He looks as though he finds the whole subject matter extremely entertaining; indeed, as though a particularly droll joke has been played. On her.

'Ruth Parchment, Hester dearest, is indeed the woman with whom I live. Ruth Winifred Parchment to give her her full name. But she isn't my wife, my partner, my spouse, my life's companion, my other half or what you will. She's my mother.'

CHAPTER 54

Harriet stares at Marion, brain frantically looping through endless permutations, all of which point to only one conclusion. Confounded, her rage dissipating as suddenly as it had come, she is left shaken with shame and remorse.

'Oh God . . .' is all she can manage.

Marion regards her with an unfathomable expression. The glowering cat beside the Aga chooses that moment to launch itself onto her lap, reaching up with a surprisingly gentle paw to pat her cheek. Marion's hand drops onto its head and begins fondling its ears; it purrs ecstatically.

'I can't believe you never realised or at least suspected,' she says, shaking her head. 'Subtlety's never been my strong suit.' There's something of her old, mocking, mischievous self in her rueful smile.

Harriet is flailing about mentally, trying to make sense of Marion's revelation. Then it comes to her. 'But what about Alessandro?' Alessandro: an intense, largely silent Italian exchange student with whom Marion had conducted an on-off affair for a couple of terms, whose major contribution to their household had been the conjuring of vast bowls of delicious garlicky pasta in the small hours.

Marion gives a snort of laughter, startling the cat, who leaps off her lap, affronted. He slinks back towards his station, outraged tail aloft. 'Alessandro? Are you kidding? Do you know what a beard is?'

'Of course,' retorts Harriet with some heat. For heaven's sake, she's not a complete innocent! A thought occurs. 'But what about your husband? Chris, is it?'

A beat. Marion's smile slides away. 'Was. Christine.'

'Oh . . .!'

'Thirty years,' says Marion, struggling to maintain her composure. 'She died last year. Lung cancer.' Her hands find the cigarette packet on the table, flip it over and over. 'These buggers did for her. Will for me too, with a bit of luck.'

'Marion!'

'You lost your husband, didn't you, a while back?'

Harriet nods.

'Lonely, isn't it?' Marion gets up quickly, grabs the two mugs with a clatter of china and makes for the sink, turning the taps on full to cover the awkward silence. But Harriet is there beside her in seconds; her arms encircle her grieving friend and she pulls her hard into her embrace. For several moments, the two women stand locked in mutual loss, each taking comfort in the other's closeness, the smell and feel of another human being. 'Shh, shh . . .' murmurs Harriet into Marion's smoky hair. It's not the words that matter.

Finally, Marion pulls away, a brave smile pasted on. 'It's bleak, having no-one to hug, isn't it? I'm not talking about the other stuff— just a hand, a cheek, a squeeze. At least I have the cats. God! What a cliché I've become!' Harriet thinks of Milo, the joy his plump little body can bring snuggled close to hers. She rubs her hand up and down her friend's arm in silent affirmation.

'Christ,' says Marion, sniffing, 'getting maudlin in my dotage. Sod the coffee—I need a drink. Fancy joining me?'

Minutes later they are both nursing large glasses of burgundy. It's a little on the chilly side, having been stored at the back of a deep, unheated larder, but welcome nonetheless. They've each had a shock.

'I always thought that was why we lost touch,' says Marion, watching Harriet over the top of her glass.

'We didn't lose touch!'

'Christmas cards!' says Marian with some derision.

'Life,' says Harriet. 'I swear to God, I hadn't a clue. And anyway, even if I had, it wouldn't have . . .' She trails off, a whisper of doubt creeping into her certainty.

'Made any difference? Honestly?'

Nothing if not truthful, Harriet reflects. How would she have felt all those years back, realising she was the object of another girl's affections? She's really not at all sure. Blasé? Flattered? Appalled? She shrugs, confronted by old prejudices and the confusions of youth. Marion regards her with amusement.

'But you remember that evening?' says Harriet, eager to move on. 'The game we played?'

'Vaguely,' says Marion, the grumpy cat now reinstalled on her lap. She strokes it absent-mindedly. 'I do remember the bit about the baby. Sort of.'

Harriet is secretly relieved. There have been times over the past week when she's wondered if she dreamt the whole episode, or purloined it from some film or TV programme; it has happened before. So Marion's confirmation comes as a considerable comfort.

'We'd been drinking some filthy concoction Susie rustled up—'

'She was always rustling up filthy concoctions.' Marion laughs. 'Remember that gin and Ribena combo?'

Harriet does: it has lived long in her memory. It had occasioned the most ferocious hangover. She hasn't touched gin since. 'This one was pure alcohol—some medic she was going out with had liberated it from the lab—diluted with, God help us, lemon barley water. And not much of that, if I recall.'

Marion nods. It's starting to come back. Them all sprawled on the floor in varying states of inebriation playing an incoherent game of 'What if?'. What if you inherited a fortune? What if the world was going to end in five minutes? What if you found you were up the duff . . . And alongside those recollections, suddenly, another memory.

She tips the cat off onto the floor. 'Wait there!' She almost runs out of the kitchen. Harriet hears her hurrying up the stairs and then, directly overhead, the sound of drawers being opened and closed, footsteps across the floor.

Marion descends the stairs at speed and re-emerges, clutching a shoebox that she upends on the table. Dozens of photographs skitter across the surface, a few fluttering down onto the flags.

'If I'm right . . .' she says, starting to rummage through the piles. Harriet joins her at the table, looking down on myriad groupings of people she doesn't recognise, assorted scenery shots, various weddings, the guests stiff in their finery with bright, hopeful smiles.

'What are we looking for?' says Harriet, starting to spread out the photos nearest to her.

'Somewhere in here . . .' mutters Marion, rapidly flicking through the piles in front of her. 'Lois had a camera for her birthday, d'you remember? She was mucking about with it. Kept making us pose for her.'

'That's right!' exclaims Harriet, the memory springing into her mind, all of them giggling and pulling faces as Lois struggled with the flash. 'Was it that night, though?'

'I think so. Because hadn't Janet made a cake for her? With chocolate buttons on it?'

Harriet can see it: comically lopsided thanks to the unreliable college oven, the butter icing oozing over the sides from the heat from the gas fire, and craters where they had gouged out the buttons even before it had been cut into slices. It had tasted faintly of corn oil, Erica having run out of margarine. The image of the cake brings Hester to mind; she bats her away.

'Bingo!' says Marion, with a triumphant grin. 'Look!' She thrusts a dog-eared and grainy photo at Harriet. Six faces with grins and smiles ranging from coquettish to idiotic stare back at her across the decades. The hair! The makeup!

'Was I still going out with Mark then?' says Harriet, frowning at the solitary man at the back of the group, a blush stealing over her at the thought of her earlier faux pas. 'We split up that Christmas. Lois's birthday was in February, wasn't it? Valentine's Day—that's why I remember it. What's he doing there?'

Marion turns the photo round and peers at it. 'Trying to get back with you, as I recall. Quite an achievement having Mark McFee chasing after you, given his reputation. He really had the hots for you.'

Harriet smiles, embarrassment tinged with pride. Mark McFee had been a considerable catch—tall, good-looking, an outstanding athlete with an easy charm that drew all the girls. Unless, as Harriet had quite soon realised on closer acquaintance, you found his politics and world view anathema to your own. She had swallowed her dislike of some of his views for a couple of months, basking in the reflected glory of being his girlfriend, until one argument too many about apartheid. Even then, after what she had regarded as an irreparable rift, he had tried to persuade her they could compromise on their differences and had continued to pursue her. This photo must have captured one of his last attempts to inveigle himself back into Harriet's affections. It, like the earlier ones, had failed.

'God, I'd forgotten,' she lies. 'Who else was there that night?'

Marion sits down again and leans back in thought, glass to her lips. The cat sees its opportunity and leaps back up. 'Now you're asking. Could have been dozens of us,' she says, then starts. 'No, wait! Of course! It was that terrible night—do you remember? We were due somewhere; a JCR bop, I think—and then it snowed all day and the do was cancelled. So we all hunkered down and Susie got cracking with the booze and said we'd celebrate Lois's birthday at home instead. Except we only had the cake, and a stale loaf for toast, so we all got completely legless within minutes.'

'That's when we started playing that "What If?" game.'

'That's right! So . . .'

They look at one another.

Marion raises a quizzical eyebrow. 'Then we were six.'

'Five,' says Harriet. 'You can forget Mark.'

'True. Man of many talents as he was, even he couldn't have got preggers. Okay. Assuming it isn't just the most colossal coincidence that someone plumped for your name, it's got to be someone who was there that night.'

'Then let's consider our suspects. Lois . . . Erica . . .'

'Hang on. When was this Stephen born?'

'The third of August, 1972.' The date branded in her memory.

Marion works backwards, purses her lips, shakes her head. 'No way. No way could Lois or Erica have been pregnant and me not have known. The three of us stayed up in Cambridge working that summer, while we were waiting for our results. I saw them every day. There wasn't an ounce on either of them at the best of times.'

'So,' says Harriet, 'it wasn't them, it wasn't you. That leaves—'

'Susie.' Marion frowns. 'Never a close buddy of mine. I mean, ditzy as hell and I liked her well enough, but our paths didn't cross that much. She was more your friend, wasn't she?'

Harriet thinks: *Susie, of course!* Why hadn't she thought of her sooner?

'Could it have been her?' Marion wonders. 'I mean, is it likely?'

'It's possible,' says Harriet slowly. 'She always was a bit flaky. I remember she had a couple of scares when she'd forgotten to take her pill—or had a stomach bug or something.' She shakes her head. 'No, if she'd got pregnant, she'd have got rid of it, I'm sure.' Susie had taken life lightly, careering from one disastrous relationship to the next, yet somehow managing by dint of her sunny disposition to remain friends with all her exes. Always late, always panicking to get her essays in on time, forever pinching other people's clothes, makeup, deodorant, tampons, forgetting to pay her share before leaving the restaurant and, mortified afterwards, showering her creditors with money, flowers, chocolates and wine: 'I'm such a dimwit! Lose my head if it wasn't screwed on.' In and out of love, in and out of beds. But not a malicious bone in her body. Would she . . .?

'Would she?' asks Marion, reaching across to top up her glass;

Harriet covers it with her hand. 'Better not. I'm driving.' Marion shrugs and slops a generous measure into her own glass.

'You could stay if you like.' She laughs as Harriet hesitates. 'You'd be quite safe, hon.'

'No, no ...' stammers Harriet. It isn't that at all. She explains about Hester. About Lionel. About the confrontation her sister has engineered.

Marion is incredulous. 'Lordy, what exciting lives you lead! And here's me thinking you were vegetating in the country without a care in the world.' She starts to pull packets and cartons out of the fridge. 'Anyway, Susie. D'you think it might have been her?'

Harriet gets up to help lay out the lunch. 'I've really no idea. I'll have to ask her, won't I?'

CHAPTER 55

Hester is dumbfounded. She gropes unsteadily for her coffee, knocking her teeth with the mug as she gulps down the scalding contents.

From the other side of the coffee table, fingers steepled like a penitent, Lionel watches her warily.

Reluctantly, swallowing hard, she raises her eyes to his. 'Your *mother*?' The question is barely audible.

He says with a hint of asperity, 'I told you that first day, as I recall, that my wife had died. Why would I lie? What do you take me for?'

Hester, who has spent many hours pondering the same questions, finds herself adrift, unable to respond but aware how damning her silence must seem.

And damned Lionel certainly feels to judge by his reaction. 'Why couldn't you just ask me outright? On the phone? Instead of luring me down here with the impression that you were going to . . . After all the waiting and the nail-biting . . . I was ecstatic driving here. I can't tell you how happy I was! The pair of you must have been laughing up your sleeves! But then your sister's been difficult from the start. And after all I've done for her! And you, come to that. I couldn't have been more supportive over that Stephen business— well, could I?'

Hester, the coals of reproach raining down on her, shakes her head miserably.

Lionel gathers his indignation tighter around himself, all the barbs of the past week sharpening his anger.

'And then all that kerfuffle with Mary. I was there for you both throughout, wasn't I?' With Hester's head still bowed, he answers his own question. 'Yes, I was! Stood up to that ghastly bully Ron on her behalf—even though, if I'm perfectly frank, he frightened the pants off me. And what thanks do I get? I don't know what Harriet's problem is, I really don't. I've been nothing but polite and friendly, but I don't seem able to do anything right as far as she's concerned, which is rich given that she's managed to get herself into some pretty tight corners. But snooping around the internet, checking up on me! That takes the ruddy biscuit, it really does. And then, of course, I discover you've swallowed her spiteful, mean-minded rubbish hook, line and sinker!'

～～

Lionel, of course, has only just met Hester; indeed, he really hardly knows her. The mysterious alchemy that creates the emotion called love cannot hope to erode old loyalties and affections, the ties that bind the present to the past. Hester is nothing if not loyal. Harriet may have her faults—on a bad day Hester would describe them as legion—but it is for her to enumerate them if necessary, not some Johnny-come-lately who has only just made her sister's acquaintance. So while Hester is prepared to weather Lionel's denunciation of her own shortcomings, she is quick to defend the absent Harriet from egregious accusations of spite and mean-mindedness, faults of which she herself might sometimes be accused but of which she would the first to absolve Harriet. One of her father's expressions springs to mind: *Now, just a cotton-picking minute . . .* accompanied in the same instant by the certainty that Harriet would probably abhor its provenance and use.

'Well?' demands Lionel, glaring at her. 'Don't you think you owe me an apology, Hetty?'

Yes, thinks Hester, *I probably do,* but that is not what finds its way out of her mouth.

'My sister was merely looking out for my best interests, as she always has; I will not apologise for what she did,' she says, neatly sidestepping her own culpability. 'I am sorry you appear to think I tricked you into making the trip down here, but I felt I needed to see you face to face for this discussion. You had asked me to marry you, Lionel! It's a big step at any time, but at our age?! For heaven's sake, why wouldn't she be concerned for me?'

Disconcerted by Hester's combative riposte, a far cry from the contrition he has anticipated, Lionel visibly wilts. 'I was going to tell you about Mother, of course I was,' he says in a more placatory tone. 'But you asked me hardly anything about my life and personal circumstances.' A tinge of resentment returns to his voice. 'I would have told you had you asked.'

Hester goes to remonstrate then realises with some discomfiture that Lionel is right; too flattered by all the unaccustomed attention, she had rarely probed very much into his own history. Indeed, it had been Harriet who had been the more curious.

'Be that as it may,' she says more gently, 'what exactly are your plans for your mother? How old is she, by the way? Is she in good health?'

Lionel, sensing the conversation shifting into less troubled waters, relaxes. 'She's ninety-five.' He allows himself a proud smile. 'Fit as the proverbial. Fearfully independent. Gets about in one of those little buggies. I have trouble keeping up with her!'

'Ninety-five . . .' says Hester faintly, conjuring up an ancient crone, all gums and incontinence.

'All her own teeth,' offers Lionel as further proof of the maternal vigour, promptly confounding her.

Hester regroups, feels her way to her next question, a particularly tricky one. 'And had I . . . were we to . . .'

Lionel nods eagerly, catching her drift.

'Would you expect her to . . . live with us?'

His gaze sweeps around the room.

'Nearby—I meant nearby,' she adds swiftly. She thinks she detects the tiniest hint of disappointment before he rallies.

'No, well . . . there's still a lot to be decided,' he says gamely. 'And not just about Mother. There's Harriet, too, to consider.'

Hester bridles. She'll deal with Harry, thank you very much. Or, rather, leave Harriet to her own devices. Imagine if she were to catch a sniff of this conversation!

'But,' he continues blithely, unaware of the storm clouds gathering opposite, 'I did take the precaution of looking into options in the vicinity last night . . .'

'Options?'

Lionel, oblivious to the ice in her tone, elaborates. 'Yes, you know: sheltered housing, residential homes, that sort of thing. And I see there's a very pleasant—'

The froideur increases. 'And is this for your mother or for Harriet?'

Dimly, Lionel registers the change in temperature. He gives a hollow laugh. 'Now, Hetty! Mother, of course.' He pauses, considers. 'Although, I do believe they will take anyone over sixty . . .'

Hester, conveniently suppressing the memory of her fleeting plans for housing her sister in a garden studio, tightens her lips. It does not go unnoticed.

'Hetty, my dear, I was joking!' stammers Lionel, with a valiant attempt at a waggish smile. It falls on very stony ground.

'And what does your mother feel about being uprooted at her vast age and transplanted to a hostile environment?'

'Hardly hostile, my dear. I'm sure she'd find it most comfortable.'

'So she hasn't the first inkling about your plans?'

A slippery look flashes across Lionel's face. Suddenly he won't meet her eyes.

'I thought as much.' Hester sniffs.

Lionel, mild-mannered as he habitually is, has reached the end of his considerable tether. He has accommodated Hester's procrastinations, tolerated her impatience and losses of temper, provided comforting shoulders aplenty, soothed troubled breasts, withstood Harriet's snubs and outbursts and drunk far more wine than he thinks altogether healthy on numerous occasions over the past several cataclysmic days. And all because, for reasons he cannot entirely fathom, he happens to have fallen for the woman opposite. He decides once and for all to place all his cards—some of which he considers none too bad—on the table.

'Hester,' he says gravely, sitting straighter and looking her right in the eye, 'I think the time has come for us to be completely frank with one another.'

'Absolutely,' says Hester cautiously. She has the oddest feeling that somehow she is losing her grip on events. She inclines her head: *go on*.

'Permit me to lay out my stall. I've thought long and hard since we met. We are neither of us in the first flush of youth. We have by the greatest good fortune met and found a kinship. Well, in my case, something rather stronger than that. Our best years may be behind us, but with luck we have sufficient years ahead that we could enjoy together, bringing one another mutual support and affection, if not, dare I say it, love. My financial resources may be modest, but I have some capital in my flat and a small pension and Mother fortunately still has sufficient savings to pay for her care for several years. I know some might consider me selfish to put my immediate needs and desires above those of my aged parent, but to be brutally honest I have been a dutiful son and a reliable husband all my life and I think it not unreasonable to put my own desires first for once. I think between the two of us we could make a pretty good fist of a marriage, with perhaps, if the past week is anything to go by, some rather lively times.'

Here he hesitates, gulps, gamely continues. 'And if your reservations have anything to do with . . .' he looks down at the floor, 'that . . . unfortunate incident in your room the other night, then I understand there are steps I can take to . . . ameliorate the problem.'

Her heart goes out to him, to his bravery.

He ploughs on quickly, lest she interrupt. 'I have no desire to face the rest of my life alone and neither, I suspect, have you. I fully accept we have a number of issues to resolve—not least the futures of our nearest and dearest—and I won't lie: Mother does have her moments. But, as I say, I am unashamedly doing this for myself. And, I hope, you. I do not see why I should forgo a last chance of happiness. And I cannot believe that Harriet, despite her misgivings, would want to deprive you of the same. There it is.'

Hester is moved. Touched by his obvious sincerity, his honesty, his unexpected eloquence. Watching him now as he lets out a long sigh, like a runner exhausted after a gruelling race, she sees what this has cost him. And feels cut to the bone that what had started as a slightly offbeat flirtation under that beguiling Italian sky should have come to this. She does not deal well with difficult emotions and situations, never has; she would rather sidestep or ignore matters that threaten her carefully cultivated self-control than let her guard slip. Harriet is the emotional one: she it is who expresses her feelings without embarrassment, unafraid to let others see her vulnerabilities. But the fact Hester keeps her counsel, appears always in control—legacy, perhaps, of her firstborn status—does not mean she feels things any less keenly.

'Lionel,' she says gently, not sure at all where she is going, 'you have been an absolute rock this past week.' And she means it. A baptism by fire doesn't come close to describing the experiences to which Lionel, a virtual stranger, has been exposed thanks to his entanglement with the Ribbleswell siblings. He has negotiated the tricky terrain of sisterly disputes and rapprochements with commendable adeptness, at times taking responsibility for frictions not of his making. He deserves better than the erratic affections she has shown him. He deserves, she suspects, a better woman than she.

Unflinching self-analysis is both Hester's strength and her curse. What she evades on the surface still seethes beneath. She acknowledges to herself that she has been unfair to Lionel, glad to lean on him when the need arose but dismissive of his tenderness and attention when other more pressing issues erupted. She realises with an unpleasant jolt that with her suspicions (or, rather, Harriet's) laid to rest, she is back where she started: altogether undecided, caught between the certainties and complacencies of the past and the unpredictable possibilities of the future.

Lionel senses a change in the air. He opts for one final press of his suit.

'Hetty ... dearest,' he begins with none of his previous fluency, 'I know there's a lot to consider. It's been a bit of a whirlwind, hasn't it?' He tries a little laugh. 'Like teenagers, almost!'

Hester looks taken aback. Oh dear ...

'I mean ... eight days!'

He leaves a pause in case she wants to reply. She doesn't.

'But sometimes you just *know*, don't you?'

Except she clearly doesn't.

'I mean, all our shared interests: cooking, food ...' He scrabbles for more proof of their compatibility. Fatefully, fatally, he summons his trump card: 'And bridge, of course.'

Hester's mouth drops open before she can stop it. *Bridge?* The mortification of their one partnership at the table washes over her afresh. An image of Peggy and Cynthia comes to the fore, the pair of them waiting to pounce and exploit Lionel's inexperience, if not total ineptitude, while she sits opposite, impotent, her bids misinterpreted, her signals unread. And what of her long-time partner, so finely attuned to the vagaries and nuances of her game? What of Harriet?

CHAPTER 56

'You can't,' says Marion.

'Can't what?' says Harriet, taking a roll.

Marion slides the butter across the table. 'Ask Susie.'

Harriet's knife stops its journey through the roll. 'Why not?' A horrible thought. 'Oh God, Marion, you don't mean—'

Marion purses her lips. 'No. But good as. No, I shouldn't say that. But you won't get much change out of the poor love these days, I'm afraid.'

'Tell me,' says Harriet, appetite gone.

'She's in a home, poor darling.' Marion sniffs. 'Bloody Alzheimer's, can you believe it? Early onset. Lois told me last time we spoke.'

'Oh, Marion!' *She's younger than me*, Harriet thinks, a chill running through her. A chill not only at life's vicissitudes, but because the trail has once more run cold.

'I know. Shitty doesn't begin to describe it. Such a livewire, bless her.' Marion hands Harriet a bowl of tomatoes; she takes a couple without thinking.

'That's it, then.' She is filled with despair. Poor Susie. Poor Stephen. 'Hopeless.' *Everything's hopeless*, she thinks, fighting tears.

'You could always ask Mark.'

Harriet's heart somersaults. 'Mark McFee? Why on earth—'

'He's her cousin, remember? He might know something. Worth a shot, wouldn't you say?'

∽∽∽

'Here you go.' Marion swivels the laptop around to show Harriet some pictures. A screen full of different images of the same handsome silver-haired man in late middle age, sleek with the unmistakable patina of wealth, a suspicion of jowls developing.

'Gorgeous as ever,' says Marion. She registers Harriet's bemusement. 'What? I can't admire beauty from afar, even if I don't want to get into bed with it? He always was a bit of a looker.'

'God, yes,' agrees Harriet, remembering the hungry eyes that followed them wherever they went. She had been aware they weren't for her. 'Not that he didn't know it.'

Marion swings the laptop back to face her and starts typing.

Harriet stares out of the window, thinking, *Susan . . . lost. All that spirit, the sheer joy in life . . .*

Marion peers at the screen for a moment. 'Okay, we've got contact details for work but not a home address or telephone number. Still, I suppose the office is worth a try? Let's see.' She picks up the telephone.

It doesn't take long. No, the receptionist can't divulge Mr McFee's personal details, but she will take a message. Yes, she will pass it on immediately. No, she has no idea when Mr McFee might be able to return the call.

'Sure you won't have another drop of wine?' Marion refills her own glass as Harriet refuses. In truth, right now there is nothing she would like more than something to steady her nerves: the thought of speaking to Mark McFee after forty-odd years is ridiculously nerve-racking. They had not parted on the best of terms when she had finally managed to convince him that she had no intention, whatever blandishments he might employ, of resuming their relationship. That attractive face had then revealed the wolf behind the smile: in memory she almost fancies he had bared his teeth. It had shaken her at the time, that visceral reaction to being thwarted, the spoilt rich boy denied his heart's desire for once.

'If he decides not to ring back, I guess that's it,' she says. Despite all that's at stake, she almost hopes he won't. The past can stay buried. 'Dead end.'

'Well, we tried anyway,' says Marion robustly. 'You could write to him, I suppose, at the office. Anyway, one jolly good thing out of all this: we've met up again. Friends are always important but when you get to our age, they're a godsend.'

As are sisters, thinks Harriet, wondering how Hester is doing. Their parting this morning had been more than cool, Harriet ashamed of her intemperate revelation about Lionel; not the fact that she had told Hester—she *had* to be told—but the way in which she had done it, with, she cringes to remember, such self-righteousness. She had seen the hurt in Hester's eyes and been instantly sorry to be the cause of it. She wonders now for the hundredth time if their relationship can survive its recent turbulence; more alarmingly, wonders if she really wants it to.

'You all right?' Marion leans forward to catch Harriet's eye. 'Lot on your plate, by the sound of it. Want to talk about it?'

Harriet finds she does. Very much.

CHAPTER 57

'So. Hester.'

'Lionel.'

Unexpectedly, he leans towards her and seizes her by the upper arms, looking deep into her eyes. She is glad he is just a little taller than she is.

'You are a remarkable woman, Hester. I mean that. I shall always treasure our week together.'

'Oh, Lionel . . .' Faced with the inevitable, a resolution she has engineered, she has to stop herself uttering some banality about staying friends. But he is there ahead of her.

'We'd have made a good team, I think. Could have had a lot of fun. Still,' he manages a sad smile, 'it takes two to—'

'Tango. Yes.' She drops her gaze, unwilling, unable, to continue the scrutiny. She has rarely felt so wretched. Tilting her face up she plants a swift kiss just beside his mouth. 'Goodbye, Lionel. You've been so . . . so kind. Understanding. I hope you find what you're looking for. I really am very fond of you. And I'm—'

'Sorry? No, there's no need, my dear. I'm sure you believe you're making the right decision. It's just a shame it doesn't accord with mine.'

Lionel Parchment makes his dignified way around the front of his immaculate car, insinuates himself behind the wheel and with a final, almost regal, wave drives away down the lane and out of Hester's life.

'So. Harriet.'

'Mark.'

A moment on the doorstep, each trying to mask their surprise at the depredations of age. Harriet suspects she comes off worse from the inspection, wishes she had worn something a little more . . . well, what? Alluring? Provocative? And why? Why on earth should Mark McFee's opinion matter to her in the least? All the same, she regrets her untrimmed hair, the dowdiness of her outfit. In contrast, he looks sleek, polished, *rich*, in his expensive shirt and Italian loafers.

Mark steps back into the spacious hall with a sweeping gesture. 'Please.'

She cannot suppress a small inhalation of admiration as she takes in the exquisitely proportioned hall with its wide staircase up to a galleried landing. 'What a beautiful house!' The interior delivers on the promise of the gravelled drive between ancient oaks to the imposing entrance, where she had pulled up in her shabby car in a spit of stones.

I won't be intimidated, she vows, as Mark shows her through to an enormous lounge looking out over immaculate lawns to a large pond. *Please don't let there be a duck house*, she thinks, *I shan't be able to contain myself.* She makes her way over to the long windows, as much to compose herself as to check, to find Mark close behind her, glasses of champagne in hand.

As he passes her one, his mouth twitches. 'I got the serfs to shoot the ducks before you arrived.'

She gives a shout of appreciative laughter and as he joins in, she realises it's going to be all right. For a moment she considers refusing the drink, then decides that might be misconstrued. *I'll just sip it.*

'You've got my measure, I see,' she says with a smile, raising her glass in a silent toast.

'Oh, Harriet, I never had your measure,' he says sadly, touching his flute to hers.

They stand together in momentary silence, then, to cover the awkwardness, lift their glasses in unison.

～～～

The speed with which Mark had returned Marion's call had disconcerted her. He had sounded courteous but businesslike and, having established Harriet's whereabouts and proposed journey home, had immediately invited her to call in en route. 'Unless you'd prefer to arrange another date? Or would like us to meet somewhere neutral?'

She was surprised how accommodating he was being, thinking, *No, let's get this over with. Sooner the better.*

'Want me to come with you?' Marion had said.

'Why? Do you think I need protecting?'

'Do you?' Marion had given her a searching look.

～～～

Mark turns back from the window. 'Thank you for coming.'

Harriet pauses, glass halfway to her lips. 'You don't know why I'm here.'

'Oh, I think I do.'

Harriet cannot fathom the crooked smile. If she didn't know Mark McFee of old, she would describe his expression as almost fearful. To cover her confusion, she takes a gulp of the ice-cold champagne. It's delicious. She flicks him a look; he drops his eyes.

'I won't keep you long,' she says, unaccountably uneasy. Are they alone in this enormous house? Wanting to put a little distance between them, she makes for the fireplace and chooses an armchair in preference to the sofa. 'Let me come straight to the point. I want to talk to you about Susan. Your cousin Susan.'

'Susie? I don't think so.' His initial friendliness seems to have evaporated, his face now shadowed and unreadable.

406

Has she hit a nerve? Is Susan's illness an unmentionable topic in the family? The thought that it might be makes her bridle.

'I don't mean to upset you, Mark, but I know all about her condition. It's a terrible tragedy for the family, I'm sure, but I really need to—'

'No, no.' Mark is shaking his head vehemently. He drops down on a sofa opposite and knocks back the remainder of his drink.

Harriet forges on, embarrassment warring with indignation.

'I'm sorry, Mark, but I must insist—'

'No, Har, listen—'

No-one has ever called her Har except him. She had liked it at first then, as their relationship unravelled, had started to regard it as a clumsy way to try to appropriate her for himself. Forty years on it still grates.

'It's Harriet,' she says tightly.

'I'm sorry. Harriet. There's no point talking to Susie. I promise you. Or about her. It's me you want.'

∽∽∽

'Visitor?' says Peggy Verndale, materialising from who knows where, both dogs in tow, inquisitive noses twitching. All three of them. She has an uncanny knack of silently appearing at the most inopportune moments. Hester drags her eyes away from Lionel's car rounding the distant bend.

'Oh! Hello, Peggy.'

Peggy is still staring at the disappearing car. 'That's an old one!'

Hester frowns fiercely.

'I meant the car! Gosh, I had one of those donkey's years ago when I first learnt to drive. A friend?'

'Yes,' says Hester. As Peggy's eyes gleam with curiosity, she adds swiftly, to deflect any further probing, 'Anyway, how are you?'

'Never mind me,' says Peggy heartily, still peering up the lane. 'How about you? Glad to be back?' She glances at her watch. 'Good heavens!

That time already? Teatime and a half.' She looks up expectantly, so that Hester has no option but to invite her in.

Peggy swiftly ties the dogs to the gatepost and scurries after Hester into the hall.

In the kitchen, Hester turns from the sink where she is filling the kettle to find herself alone. 'Peggy?'

'Coming.'

Hester makes for the larder in search of biscuits, then, puzzled by silence, retraces her steps. Peggy is standing in the hall inspecting the staircase, running a finger up and down one spindle.

'Problem?' says Hester, making Peggy jump. She snatches her finger away.

'No! No, not at all. Just thought I . . .'

'Yes?'

'I . . .' She looks around desperately, then flaps her scarf. 'Caught this on the . . . thought there was a splinter.'

'A splinter?' Hester steps towards her for a closer look.

'No, look, on second thoughts,' gabbles Peggy, a glance sweeping around the sitting room, 'forget the tea. I really ought to get back. The dogs, you know . . . and Ronald . . .'

She's out of the door and down the path before Hester can gather her thoughts.

'I'll ring you. Bridge on Thursday? Great.' Peggy fumbles with the dogs' leads and in seconds is almost sprinting up the lane.

'What the hell?' murmurs Hester. Then she shouts after Peggy, 'We had a nice holiday. Thanks for asking.'

⌣⌣⌣

Harriet is on her second glass of champagne without realising it. By the time Mark interrupts his narrative to refill her flute, she's too astounded to decline.

'I can't believe it,' she stammers, fury strangling her voice. 'How could you? How bloody could you?'

Mark lowers his head in mortification. 'I know. I know. Unforgivable.'

Harriet stares at him; she doesn't need to ask the question.

'I was angry with you. All right? No, more than angry. I was furious. You dumped me! No-one had ever done that before. And you made me beg . . .'

'I didn't! I told you I don't know how many times that it was over.'

'All right! But I begged all the same. I was . . . beside myself. Enraged. And I couldn't let it go. I loved you, Harriet!'

He looks across at her, imploring her understanding. Her face is granite. He stumbles on.

'Then this girl—'

'Girl?'

'Leona. Leona Porter. First year. Biology. She worshipped me.'

'How very gratifying.'

'Harriet, believe me, I know how this is making me sound. A shit.'

A pause for her to comment. Is he expecting her to argue? She doesn't.

'So, the inevitable. She gets pregnant. I mean, we weren't even going out any more when she told me.'

'How long after we . . .?'

He gulps a mouthful. 'Week or so.' Taking in Harriet's flinty expression, he adds, 'Yes, I know. It was on the rebound!'

'A week!'

He nods miserably. 'Like I said. A shit. Anyway . . . just my luck, she's Catholic. Won't have an abortion. I thought, *Okay, then have the baby if you want, but I'm not marrying you.*'

Harriet shakes her head.

'I was twenty-two, Harriet! I didn't love her. It would have been a disaster.'

He reaches for a decanter, slops some whisky into a pair of tumblers and passes one to Harriet. She finds herself taking it unthinkingly, downing a mouthful.

'She disappears. I mean—' as Harriet's eyebrows go up '—I mean, I didn't see her around any more.'

'That must have been a relief,' says Harriet acidly.

Mark flinches but soldiers on, eyes fixed on the floor. 'Months go by and I sort of forget about it. Her. Then I get this letter. From Liverpool. God knows why, she was from Surrey. Anyway she sounds desperate, wants to see me. So I go up there. What else could I do?'

Well, thinks Harriet, *you could have ignored it.* Is glad that he didn't.

'I presumed she needed money . . . She's working in this café, no friends, hadn't dared tell her family. Thought they'd disown her: can you imagine? She tells me she's going to give the baby up. I thought, *Thank God. Few more weeks and the whole wretched business will be over.* Next thing I know, she's gone into labour and we're tearing off to the hospital. I don't know what's going on and then suddenly she grabs my hand and starts crying. She's seen someone she knows—someone she was at school with, working at the hospital. Unbelievable. This girl doesn't see her, but she's scared witless all the same. Thinks she'll bump into her, or this girl will see her name, and it'll all come out. She's pleading with me to help her, so when they admit her, I take over and I think, *What if they don't know her real name? What if—*'

'So you give them mine.'

'Yes.' Now he does look at her. 'God, Harriet, it was madness, I know. I was panicking and I had this woman waiting to fill in the form and I suddenly thought of you. That night in your flat, that stupid game we all played . . . And I thought how things might've been different . . . if you hadn't . . . if we had still been . . . well, none of this would have happened.'

Harriet is almost apoplectic with indignation.

Mark sees the pit he has dug and scrambles to extract himself. 'I'm just telling you! Being honest. I know it's ridiculous: of course it wasn't your fault, but I wasn't thinking straight! Christ! It was a moment of complete insanity. I told them I didn't know who the father was, I was just a friend. And once I'd done it—given them your name—I couldn't undo it. But I swear, Harriet, I've regretted it ever since. It was—'

'Unforgivable.'

'Yes.' He looks her in the eye, naked, humbled. 'Unforgivable.'

And then, in that moment, in that creased, lived-in face, scarred by life and time, she sees the handsome boy she'd once, well, she has to admit, she'd once, however briefly, been in love with. And somehow, like a weight lifting, the anger melts away. What does her outrage achieve? What does it matter now? What does any of it matter except finding the answers Stephen craves? She has done better than she ever hoped: found both his parents.

'Oh, Mark . . .' She shakes her head sorrowfully. Silence cloaks the room; shadows deepen in the corners. Distantly, she hears a clock strike the hour.

He clears his throat. 'Harriet, I know there's nothing I can say to undo the wrong—'

'There's nothing you can say, that's true. But there's something you can do: you can help me find Leona, so I can—' She stops as Mark shakes his head. 'Mark, you owe me that much!'

'No, you don't understand. It's too late.'

She looks at him, aghast. 'Oh no, please don't . . .'

He nods. 'Car accident. About ten years ago. I saw it in the paper.'

She sighs, head falling back against the cushions. Just when a resolution was within reach . . . 'You didn't keep in touch, then?'

He shakes his head. 'What for? As far as I'm aware, she went back to uni, finished her degree. Like me, she wanted to put it all behind her.' He sees her face harden. 'But I never forgot, Harriet, I swear. That I had a son somewhere.' He glances over to a family portrait on the piano: a strong-featured woman with glossy hair expertly coiffed, flanked by two pretty daughters, Mark standing with a hand proprietarily on his wife's shoulder. He seems lost in thought.

411

'He's not after anything, Mark. I've only met him once but I'd bet my life on it. All he wants is reassurance. About his family history. That there's nothing untoward lurking anywhere in the genes.'

He's still staring at the photo. 'Not on this side. Not as far as I know, anyway. Both my parents made their nineties. And I can tell you that Leona went on to have twins, two girls. One of them presents a children's programme on TV and the other—we can check online, I'm sure—went into medicine. Both hale and hearty, as far as I'm aware. Will you be contacting them?'

'God, no!' Harriet is appalled. 'I shall just tell Stephen what I've discovered and then it's up to him. Can you imagine? If those girls were suddenly to discover they had a half-brother and no mother around to explain?'

'Same applies to my girls,' says Mark soberly. He goes to say something, reconsiders.

'What?'

'I was just thinking: everything comes home to roost in the end, doesn't it? All the little threads in our lives, the tangles they create.'

She nods grimly, thinking of her own threads and tangles. 'Will you tell your girls? Your wife?'

'Ex. I think she'd just regard it as confirming her prejudices about me.' He gives a wry smile that fades quickly. 'The girls, though . . . I don't know.'

'If Stephen wants to meet you . . .?'

His face brightens. 'If he wants to, yes. God yes. But I realise it has to be his call.'

She looks into the depths of her whisky. 'I have to ask, Mark . . .'

He sits forward. 'Go ahead.'

'Your daughters, Stephen . . . there aren't any other offspring I should know about?'

He erupts with a full-throated laugh that blends surprise with relief. 'Christ, woman, I'm no Boris Johnson! I admit I wasn't always the most faithful of husbands but, no, I'm quite sure there are no more little McFees populating the realm.' He shakes his head ruefully. 'I see I haven't gone up in your estimation at all. Not that I blame you.' He reaches for the decanter as she empties her glass.

She shakes her head. 'Good heavens, no more for me. I've had far too much already.' She gets somewhat unsteadily to her feet. 'Could you call me a cab? And recommend somewhere to stay? I'm certainly not fit to drive tonight.'

'Cab?' Mark sounds incredulous. 'Don't be daft, woman. You'll stay the night.' He's back in control now, the businessman brooking no arguments. 'I've got more bedrooms than I know what to do with. And a fridge full of food. Besides, we've forty or more years to catch up on. Now, let me show you the rest of the house.'

CHAPTER 58

Hester looks once more at the clock. Seven fourteen pm. Still no word from Harriet. When she set off first thing this morning, there had been no discussion about what time she might return but now Hester, fretting, is itching to start preparing supper, if only for something to do. She has been wandering between sitting room and kitchen ever since Peggy fled, picking up and then discarding her knitting, flicking desultorily through the newspaper, even guiltily scanning Harriet's pile of house brochures, her gloom compounded by the sight of so many patently unsuitable dwellings her sister had felt driven to consider. Once she had even reached for the phone, thinking: *I'll call Lionel, tell him I've made a terrible mistake.* That madness had swiftly passed. It's not Lionel she wants; it's Harriet.

She thinks suddenly of Finbar. That's an idea. There's someone who's always pleased to see her. She hurries through into the kitchen and starts rummaging through the larder, noticing how denuded the shelves are. Once Harriet's back with the car, she'll make a list and they can go for a big shop tomorrow. Time she made a fresh batch of biscuits, perhaps a fruit cake. Harriet loves a Dundee.

414

'Finbar!'

The old man is scuttling up the narrow pavement towards the brow of the hill, en route for the Cask and Glass, no doubt. He turns back and waves, then starts to retrace his steps, eyes lighting up as he spies the basket.

'Hester! What an unqualified joy! I was just on my way to . . .' He trails off as he eagerly explores the basket's contents. 'Such riches. You are, dear lady, as I have had occasion to remark more times than I care to recall, a peerless creature of fathomless generosity. Dare I hope there might be some of your incomparable ginger biscuits secreted within?'

Hester apologises, explaining about her lack of provisions.

'No matter! I might say that that nephew of yours, whom as we both know is no nephew at all in the strictest sense of the word, does a fine line in biscuits himself.'

Hester bridles. 'Only because I taught him how!'

'Indeed. Unselfishly imparting your knowledge to a tyro, as a beneficent aunt should.'

Hester, remembering her churlishness over the crème caramel the night before, squirms.

'And what, pray,' continues Finbar, unaware, 'did you make of the exquisite Natalie, enchanting imp that she is? Did you not marvel at her quick wit?'

'Er . . . yes, delightful,' manages Hester, shamed afresh at her less than fulsome welcome of their guest. 'She seems very . . . nice,' she finishes lamely.

'Hester,' says Finbar sternly, pausing in the throes of stowing his improvised hamper in the depths of his trolley, 'do I detect in that faint praise a hint of . . . well, I hesitate to name it . . . prejudice?'

'Prejudice? No!' cries Hester, shaken to the core. That he should think . . . ! 'Finbar! I am cut to the quick that you should—'

'I apologise unreservedly,' he says hastily. 'I was simply disconcerted at what I read as your—forgive me, but "nice" is such a lukewarm, namby-pamby word and not one I expect to figure in your lexicon—lack of enthusiasm for our young Andromache.'

'Andromache?' echoes a bewildered Hester.

'Indeed,' says Finbar, warming to his theme, 'for does that name not mean "fighter of men"? And did not she fearlessly . . . ah!' The awful realisation of what he had almost let slip hits him.

'Fearlessly what?' Hester sniffs a secret.

'Nothing!' says Finbar airily. 'I was merely prattling on about her general sangfroid. I suspect that very little would disconcert her.' He swiftly changes tack. 'Are you intending to attend her theatrical performance? I am very much hoping for an invitation myself. It's many a long year since I saw any Ibsen.'

'Ibsen? Theatre? What are you talking about, Finbar?' Hester has a sudden horrifying vision of the smelly vagrant seated in a crowded, overheated auditorium, members of the audience collapsing like ninepins as the stench overwhelms them.

'Ask Ben,' he says, starting to edge away up the hill, trolley in tow, towards the pub. 'Forgive me, Hester, and thank you for the victuals, but my presence is required yonder for a game of backgammon. *Vale.*'

⌣⌣⌣

Hester marches smartly back to The Laurels, deep in thought. Attending this school production might be an excellent way of making amends to Ben's young friend and restoring herself to his good books. And perhaps at the same time effecting some sort of rapprochement with Harriet, although she very much hopes that can start tonight . . . Her mobile rings just as she reaches the gate. She ferrets frantically in her anorak pocket, through a mess of tissues and crumpled shopping lists.

'Harry? At last! Where are you?' She hopes Harriet has had the sense to stop the car before using her phone. Mercifully, there's no background sound of any traffic.

She listens intently as Harriet briefly imparts her news. 'Oh, Harry, that is wonderful! What a relief! So how did—no, save it until you get back. What time should I expect—? . . . Oh, I see, you're still at Marion's . . . What? You're not at Marion's? Then . . .?'

Her sister hurriedly explains.

'No, well, in that case of course you mustn't . . .' *Why did you have a drink in the first place?* she thinks, irritated. *There's so much I want to tell you!* 'Who is this chap again?'

Harriet sounds distinctly odd—a bit giggly, in fact, as though she's sharing a joke with someone.

'Someone from uni . . . I see . . . What? Lionel? No, of course he isn't! He left hours ago. What? No, I'll tell you all about it tomorrow. You'd better get off, then. Don't want to keep you. Bye.'

Well! So much for them clearing the air tonight. What on earth is Harriet doing, staying the night with some chap Hester has never heard of? That sounds most . . . she had almost been going to say *improper*, then the memory of herself and Lionel in her room in Italy comes into her mind. *Irregular*, then, she corrects herself. She wishes she'd thought to ask if Harriet has spoken to Stephen.

⌣⌣

Harriet has. He had been so excited, so grateful, as she told him what she had discovered, only to floor him with his mother's demise. But then, hot on the heels of that revelation, the news that he had a father—a father who would love to meet him, should he so wish.

'God, I never expected . . . I mean, I hoped, but . . .'

'He'd like the chance to explain everything to you in person. Apologise.'

'Yes . . .'

'You don't have to decide now, Stephen, it's a lot to take in. It's been a shock, obviously. Take your time.'

'Is he . . . is he there now? With you?'

Harriet had looked across the room to where Mark waited anxiously, following her every word and reading the kaleidoscope of emotions flitting across her face. She gave him a reassuring smile.

'Stephen, my dear, why don't you sleep on it? Talk to Emily, see what she thinks . . .'

'Yes . . . I will. Thank you. Harriet, thank you. You don't know what this means to me.'

Oh, but I think I do, she had thought, eyes still on Mark. *Your lives— yours, Emily's, Mark's—will never be the same again.*

'Ben?'

He leaps up from his bed as though bitten, scattering textbooks all over the floor. Why hadn't he checked the number before answering? He'd been certain it would be Nats. Hoped it would be.

'Aunt Hester?' he says cautiously, heart thumping, hands suddenly clammy. She's rumbled him, spotted the repairs, finally noticed the new wallpaper, clocked those sodding curtains . . .

'Sorry to interrupt your revision, my dear.'

She sounds okay, cool. Not cranky at all. His pulse slows.

'No worries.'

'Everything going well? Is it English and maths on Thursday?'

'Yeah.' It might be a trap, he realises . . . 'Yeah, just going over the Shakespeare again.' The Shakespeare that makes so much sense now he's been through it with Nats.

'Excellent. Well, the best of luck. I'm sure you'll be fine.'

Is that why she rang, just to wish him luck?

'Just two quick things.'

Oh, here we go.

'Finbar mentioned something about your little friend—Natalie, is it?—and a play?'

'What? Oh, yeah.' Phew. 'It's called *A Doll's House* and she's got the lead,' he says proudly.

'The lead?' There's no mistaking the admiration in her voice. And the surprise. 'Really? The lead? Nora?'

'Yeah. Like she's got this well weird teacher and she don't—*doesn't*—care about colour and stuff.'

'Well . . .' A moment while Hester digests this intelligence. 'I was just wondering if you might be able to procure us some tickets. You know how your aunt and I love the theatre.'

'Serious? 'Course I can. Yeah, easy. It's on in three weeks. Friday or Saturday?'

'Oh, the last night, I think.' A tiny pause and then, with a hint of devilry, 'I understand Finbar is hoping to see it as well.'

'Finbar?! In our school hall?'

It's clear he's thinking what she had thought a little earlier.

'My sentiments precisely.'

'Jeez, be even worse than on the train. Least on a train you can open a wind—' Oh fuck.

'Train? What on earth would Finbar be doing on a train?'

Ben grimaces into the phone, desperate. 'I was just, like, thinking of enclosed spaces,' he manages lamely. 'You know, what with the niff and that . . .'

'Indeed,' she says, then to his relief switches to another track. 'The other thing was to ask you a favour.'

'Me?' He's instantly on high alert, heart once more beating its painful tattoo.

Inevitably, Hester misconstrues. 'Not if it's too much trouble,' she says with a sniff.

'No, God, no, anything. Sorry, I didn't mean—' There's nothing he wouldn't do for either aunt, *ever*, if only they could remain in ignorance of the bottomless doo-doo he'd landed himself in at The Laurels on Friday night. Anything. *Anything*.

'When is it you finish your exams?'

⌣⌣⌣

Harriet can't remember when she's laughed so much. It's such a relief after the last week or so—no, longer, much longer than that; ever since the rift between herself and Hester began—to just let go. To spar with someone so diametrically opposed to most of her views as Mark, who holds his corner with sly good humour. On occasion he espouses opinions so contrary that she is convinced he is simply winding her up; then she revels in exposing the contradictions and inconsistencies in his assertions, to earn his mocking admiration. And as they banter back and forth across the huge kitchen table, littered with the remains of the scratch supper he'd thrown together, she reflects how improbably likeable she finds this mature Mark, only too aware of his own frailties and absurdities, as she likes to think she is of hers. The image of him she has carried since their brief, ill-fated liaison all those years ago fades as the evening wears on, replaced with a wry acceptance that while they will never agree on fundamentals such as politics, she can still enjoy his company. The realisation brings with it at least a partial understanding of Hester's surrender to Lionel's advances.

She has eschewed any further alcohol since the whisky, mindful of tomorrow's drive, but accepts a coffee. Getting up to make it, he offers another outrageous observation, hoping Harriet will rise to the bait. Instead, she bats it away, laughing.

'You are incorrigible.'

'One tries.' A beat. His back to her, he says with sudden sobriety, 'You really are a very forgiving woman, Har.'

She doesn't correct him this time.

'You have every right to despise me. That was a terrible thing I did.'

Harriet shakes her head, only too aware of the mutability and fragility of life. 'Oh, Mark, don't! Bitterness is such a pointless, destructive emotion.' She thinks again of Hester. Longs to expunge their mutual unkindnesses. 'We all make mistakes . . . we have to learn to forgive.'

Facing her, his customary chutzpah restored by her absolution, mirth dances in his eyes. 'You, Miss Ribbleswell, are indeed divine. I've always thought of you as the one who got away. You'd no doubt say you had a lucky escape.'

A delicious wave of pleasure at the corny compliment washes over her. 'Are you flirting with me, Mr McFee?'

He puts the coffee cup down in front of her, leans towards her and gently cradles her chin in his hand.

'Flirting, woman? I'm propositioning you.'

WEDNESDAY

CHAPTER 59

Hester hums as she potters around the kitchen waiting for the *Today* programme to start. She's been up for over an hour, having lain in bed watching the dawn light strengthening and listening to the birds squabbling noisily in the treetops. Time enough to review her actions with brutal honesty and reassure herself that she has made the right decision about Lionel. Bless him, she wishes him well, will always be grateful to him for the gift of his affection. Looking out over the garden, dew carpeting the lawn, she is filled with a sense of purpose, the future brighter than it has seemed for months.

⌣⌣⌣

Harriet hums as she bowls along deserted country lanes towards the motorway, lips crimping in a little smile from time to time. She had crept away just as dawn was breaking, leaving a scrawled note of thanks on the kitchen table for her host. Not for her an awkward breakfast exchange in the unforgiving morning light; she is confident Mark will feel the same and appreciate her delicacy. When they meet again, *if* they meet again, last night's events can be conveniently glossed over as befuddled memories, and they can greet one another as friends, nothing more.

As she fervently hopes she will be greeting her sister in a few hours. So much to tell her; so much to learn. About Stephen, Mark, Lionel.

Last evening's stilted phone conversation had spared them both detailed explanations of their respective encounters, each recognising the necessity of a proper heart to heart.

⌣⌣⌣

I'll make her some biscuits as well as a cake, thinks Hester. To hell with my nagging. In fact, I will never nag her again about her weight. It's all in the genes anyway. Just my good fortune to have got the thin ones. I should be grateful.

⌣⌣⌣

I'm starving, thinks Harriet, picking up a bitter coffee when she stops to fill the tank. She looks at the dispiriting pasties, glistening with fat in the heated display. Thinks of Hester. Opts for a banana instead.

⌣⌣⌣

Hester is just balancing the last chocolate-dipped biscuit on her improvised stand when she hears the unmistakable rattle of their old car pulling into the drive. She rinses her hands swiftly and hurries down the hallway, inexplicably and ridiculously nervous.

⌣⌣⌣

Harriet yanks on the handbrake and switches off the engine. Golly, she's stiff. She wants coffee, a shower, a change of clothes, food and her sister. Not necessarily in that order. She looks up to see Hester standing in the doorway, a hand raised in greeting.

Home. Home at last.

⌣⌣⌣

'You sure she meant me? This is Hester, the scary one?'

'Defo. And she wants to see your play.'

'No way! I thought she hated me.'

'C'mon, no-one could hate you, Nats,' says Ben before he can stop himself. He cringes: she'll think he's a right lame-arse. But he means it. Although he can see that Hedge and Brick might not share the sentiment.

'Aw,' says Nats with a wide grin. 'You are so sweet, boyfriend. You want to meet after school to go over R and J again?'

Ben wants to meet after school, all right. But poring over the finer points of *Romeo and Juliet* is not exactly what he has in mind.

⌣⌣

Hester, at the stove assembling a full English breakfast for her sister, listens with frank astonishment and mounting indignation to Harriet's account of her detective work and the unearthing of a catalogue of long-buried secrets.

'Good God, what is it with you and lesbians?! And this Mark creature! First time I've heard of him. Whatever possessed you? A hedge fund manager *and* a landed Tory? Lordy, you must have shredded him!'

'We had an exchange of . . . views,' says Harriet primly.

'I bet you did! Wiped the floor with him, I should imagine. What a total and utter bastard!'

'He was very young at the time,' says Harriet in mitigation. 'We all were.' She feels the tiniest bit disloyal to her ex-boyfriend for such a mealy-mouthed apologia.

'Stuff and nonsense. His behaviour sounds positively feudal. *Droit du seigneur* and all that.'

Harriet judiciously decides to halt her defence of Mark McFee at this juncture. Irresponsible as his conduct may have been all those years ago, she's not sure it was quite on a par with Hester's accusation. However, her sister is no fool and, should Harriet protest too much on his behalf, Hester might start asking more questions about him that Harriet would really rather not answer.

'So,' she says with some trepidation, 'your turn now. Tell me all about Lionel.' She reaches for the last slice of toast.

Hester, remembering her earlier vow just in time, bites back a comment, saying instead, 'Yes, I will. But first, I've a bone to pick with you.'

⌣⌣⌣

'Age guide?' echoes Harriet, with a sudden loss of appetite, hand suspended over the marmalade jar. 'You mean it shows . . .?'

'Yes,' says Hester grimly. 'So if you'd bothered to look, you'd have seen that Ruth Parchment was a good twenty or so years older than Lionel!'

Harriet thinks fast. 'Yes, but he could have married someone much older—'

'Except he'd already told us his wife—Connie—had died!'

'Oh God,' says Harriet miserably, automatically resuming her interrupted task and spooning a large dollop of marmalade onto her toast. 'I'm so sorry, Hetty. It was late, I was tired . . .'

How much marmalade does she need? And all that butter!

Harriet cringes. How could she have been so stupid? 'I'm such a fool. Still, in the grand scheme of things . . .'

'Yes, yes,' says Hester shortly with a sigh. 'What's done is done. And it would still have meant I was taking on two people, not one. Not,' she continues, as Harriet relaxes and lifts her toast, 'that I blame Lionel. Not at all.' She dares her sister to argue. 'Why shouldn't he look for comfort in his old age? Not everyone's as lucky as we are. We've got each other.'

Harriet is up and around the table in a trice. She grabs her sister fiercely and hugs her tight. Hester does likewise. And peace finally breaks out at The Laurels.

⌣⌣⌣

'Are we expecting visitors?' says Harriet.

They are in the kitchen. Hester, having replenished their supplies at the supermarket—where she had flown around throwing all manner of comestibles into their trolley as if she feared rationing were about to be imposed—is now restocking the larder.

Harriet knows better than to offer to help, given her sister's idiosyncratic storage system. Flicking through the calendar on the wall she finds only bridge afternoons pencilled in at regular intervals, a dentist's appointment for Hester in a week's time and *Play* written in for three weeks ahead. 'Or a siege?'

Hester stops rearranging the tinned tomatoes in date order. 'Well . . .' she says tentatively, 'I was wondering how you felt about us having a little party?'

'A party? Us?' says Harriet, nonplussed. Parties are things they generally leave to the likes of George and Isabelle, whose gatherings they attend with marked ill grace, largely on account of Isabelle's execrable cooking.

'Why not?' Hester sits at the kitchen table.

Harriet hands her a mug of coffee and joins her.

'I thought it could be a sort of celebration. For Daria. You know, getting her leave to remain.'

'What about Artem?'

'Oh, he won't begrudge his sister having a little do, will he? He's so thrilled for her. And it would be a way to thank them. For looking after the house while we were away. Plus, it gives me the chance to try out my new Italian recipes—teach them to Ben.'

'He's up to his eyes in exams at the moment.'

'Yes, but he's finished in a fortnight's time. He's very keen.'

'You've got it all worked out, haven't you?' Harriet's delighted to see Hester so enthused by her plan.

'Well,' says Hester, twisting her wedding band, 'I thought . . . well, it would be a sort of celebration for us, too. You know, after all that's . . .'

'Yes,' says Harriet, her heart full. 'Oh yes.'

⌣ ⌣ ⌣

Later, in the sitting room after one of Hester's steak and kidney pies for supper and several glasses of a fine Merlot, she hands Harriet a list. It reads:

Ben & Nats

Artem

Daria/Milo (?Barry)

Isabelle & George

Peter & Elizabeth

Peggy & Ron

Cynthia & Roland

?Finbar

'Roland? Cynthia and *Roland*?'

'Well, I thought we ought to ask her, and I know he's a bit of a dry old—'

'*Rupert*, Hetty. Her husband's Rupert. The dog's Roland. Roland and Rufus.'

They both erupt. It's a minute or so before either of them can speak again.

'And Finbar? Seriously?'

'I know,' says Hester, still bubbling with laughter, 'But I thought if it was a nice evening, he could always sit in the garden . . .'

'And if it's raining?'

Hester takes a pen and scores through Finbar's name. 'He'll get all the leftovers, anyway. He does very well out of us, the old devil.'

Harriet looks at the list again. 'Barry? This is Daria's . . .?'

'Friend,' says Hester firmly. 'A good friend, that's what Artem says. But you saw how she blushed when his name was mentioned. I just thought we should give her the option.'

'He's a carpenter, isn't he, or something? Useful contact.'

'Harry! I was thinking of Daria's love life. Although now you mention it ...' She looks around the sitting room. 'I wondered if it wasn't time for us to redecorate. The place is looking awfully shabby. That paper's been up for God knows how long: look how faded it is. And those curtains came from Mother. They must be a good forty years old. I've only just noticed they aren't really long enough.'

Harriet peers over at the offending curtains, then around at the piles of detritus that litter the room. Hetty's right: the room, indeed the entire cottage, is decidedly dingy. No wonder Peggy is always so sniffy when she visits.

'And I thought,' continues Hester enthusiastically, spurred on by Harriet's lack of objection, 'we might consider doing something different. Pale emulsion, say, instead of wallpaper, do away with the dado rail, hang all the pictures on just one wall.'

'Like the bedrooms in Italy.'

'Exactly. Replace the carpets, obviously: something neutral, oatmeal perhaps. Chuck out these old rugs. There's a brilliant website—'

'Steady on!'

'Oh, Harry! Don't be such a stick in the mud. Life's too short. Let's splash out for once. We could see if that chap Peggy uses is available. Or we could do it ourselves—why not? I'm sure Artem would gladly lend a hand. You never know, we might be able to get it done in time for the party ...'

Harriet frowns, dreading all the upheaval and thoroughly sceptical about Hester's newfound appetite for change. 'Wouldn't it make more sense to decorate after the party? In case anyone has an accident? You know, drops food or wine on the new carpet.'

'We're organising a party, not a riot! For heaven's sake, no-one's going to wreck the place. Besides, you're always saying we need to have a good sort-out. Throw out all the rubbish. I mean, look—' Hester grabs a brochure at random '—trekking in Vietnam! Can you see either of us ever doing any trekking anywhere?' She tosses it into the waste-paper basket. 'Think what a difference getting rid of most of this stuff would make. Piles of papers and books we'll never read again and all these ghastly little knickknacks that belonged to Mother: we're always moaning about what a pain they are to dust.'

'Dust?' says Harriet. 'Don't make me laugh. When was the last time you wielded a duster?'

'My point exactly. Let's chuck the lot of them, be really ruthless and start afresh. What do you say?'

'I say the day you can be persuaded to throw anything away without a fight will be a first.'

Harriet looks across at Hester, rejoices to see the excitement in her eyes, the hunger for some hard physical work to fill her days, a shared task to bind them close once more, and surrenders. Maybe it would be cathartic—even fun, once they get started—to clear out all the rubbish (really dispose of it, not just move it somewhere else), streamline their lives and start a new chapter. Hester is watching her intently.

Thank God, thinks Harriet, *I've got her back*. But she won't make it too easy. 'There's just one condition. And it's not negotiable.'

Hester thinks exultantly, *I've got her back*. She can afford to be magnanimous. 'Name it.'

Harriet points into the corner. 'The first thing to go is that god-awful shepherdess.'

ACKNOWLEDGEMENTS

As ever, love and thanks to Ann Stutz, tireless in her support and encouragement. The many friends and readers who urged me to send Hester and Harriet off on a new adventure. My agent Jane Gregory and Stephanie Glencross at Gregory & Co, Annette Barlow and Genevieve Buzo at Allen & Unwin in Australia and Clare Drysdale and Sam Brown at the London office, for their enthusiasm and wise advice. My brilliant copy editor Ali Lavau whose eagle eyes spot every infelicity and the wonderful Sarina Rowell, proofreader extraordinaire. Once again, huge thanks to Galina Caldin, Translator, Russian Translation Service, United Nations, for vetting Daria's Belarusian and Yvonne Coen QC, not only for legal advice but also for visiting every bookshop in New Zealand to check they were stocking *Hester & Harriet*. Any misinterpretations of their advice must be laid squarely at my door. Andrea Silvestri and Nicoletta Crawford-Silvestri for their advice on Italian cuisine and language. Will Hayes for putting me right on the lingo and behaviour of today's teenagers. Tony Ranzetta, my Latin teacher a hundred years ago, for bringing that language to life for me (and Finbar). Finally, my husband, not only for scrutinising the many and various wines Hester and Harriet manage to imbibe in the course of a week or so, but also for his love and support, along with that of my sons.

ABOUT THE AUTHOR

Hilary Spiers writes plays, novels and short stories. She enjoys giving a voice to ordinary women in sometimes extraordinary circumstances. Hilary's first novel, *Hester & Harriet*, published in 2015, is a delightful introduction to these two remarkable sisters.